the

LESLEY THOMSON grew up in west London. Her first novel, *A Kind of Vanishing*, won the People's Book Prize in 2010. Her second novel, *The Detective's Daughter*, was a #1 bestseller and the series has sold over 750,000 copies. Lesley divides her time between Sussex and Gloucestershire. She lives with her partner and her dog.

STELLA DARNELL runs a successful cleaning company in west London. Her father was a senior detective in the Metropolitan police. Like him, Stella roots into shadowy places and restores order.

JACK HARMON works the night shifts as a London Underground train driver. Where Stella is rational and practical, Jack is governed by intuition. Their different skills make them a successful detective partnership.

By Lesley Thomson

Seven Miles from Sydney

A Kind of Vanishing

The Detective's Daughter Series

The Detective's Daughter

Ghost Girl

The Detective's Secret

The House With No Rooms

The Dog Walker

The Death Chamber

The Playground Murders

The Runaway (A Detective's Daughter Short Story)

Lesley THOMSON

the playground murders

First published in the UK in 2019 by Head of Zeus Ltd
This paperback edition published in the UK in 2019 by Head of Zeus Ltd

9 7 5 3 1 2 4 6 8

A catalogue record for this book is available from the British Library.

ISBN (PB): 9781786697264
ISBN (E): 9781786697233

Typeset by Divaddict Publishing Solutions Ltd

Printed and bound in Great Britain by
CPI Group (UK) Ltd, Croydon CRO 4YY

Head of Zeus Ltd
First Floor East
5–8 Hardwick Street
London EC1R 4RG

WWW.HEADOFZEUS.COM

For Melanie

Prologue

May 2018

Rachel Cater parked by the war memorial. She prayed that her mother's twenty-one-year-old VW Polo would start again. Her plan depended on a swift exit.

Her mum said never make life-changing decisions in the small hours. *Everything looks better in the morning*. When Rachel had woken to the alarm, her decision was unchanged.

Rachel Cater was having an affair with her boss. Chris Philips owned an antiques shop in Cheltenham. On her first day he had promised Rachel that he'd train her to be a dealer. Over a year later, she was still his secretary. But soon they would be married. When Chris left his wife and daughter. This was Rachel's nocturnal resolution. By his own admission, Chris wasn't a finisher. She would have to finish it.

The affair had begun on a Monday (now Rachel loved Mondays, weekends were a desert without Chris). It was five months almost to the day. She'd brought him his coffee (black, two sugars). Suddenly Chris had broken down. He'd held her to him and sobbed his heart out. Rachel's dream came true.

He'd told her about his wife Penelope. That he was questioning his feelings for her. Rachel stroked his hair (as soft as she'd imagined) and listened as Chris declared his marriage was over.

She'd finished it then too. Made him pull himself together, reknotted his tie, smoothed his hair. Handed him a tissue. She'd swept into the main office and informed Ian, Chris's assistant dealer, and Carol who did the books that Chris and she were visiting a client. 'My training's started,' she'd said.

'What? Wait I've got a meeting with him.' Ian was pissed off that Rachel typed Chris's letters up before his own.

'Cancelled,' said Rachel.

'About time.' Carol was nice, but Rachel knew not to get on the wrong side of her.

Rachel had driven them to a hotel outside Cheltenham where Chris said he wouldn't be recognized. He booked a room with his personal AMEX card or Carol would have queried it. The rest, as they say…

When Rachel told her mum, Agnes Cater said she'd hang fire on the bubbly. Was Chris having his cake and eating it? '*I'm* only worried for you, pet, I don't want you hurt again.' Would this latest man of her dreams leave his wife?

Chris was all over her whenever they were alone. They went to the hotel every week. Rachel insisted on the same room: 245. Nothing special, bland furnishings and décor with those pictures of landscapes intended not to offend rather than to please. For Rachel, room 245 was their bridal suite. Chris fretted that the staff knew them; Rachel was glad. She and Chris were the perfect couple.

Almost perfect. One thing about Chris was that he was indecisive. It drove Ian and Carol mad. Rachel had been head-girl, she'd won a Duke of Edinburgh award and run the London Marathon. She *was* a finisher.

Early closing in Winchcombe. As she'd anticipated, there was no one about. Abbey Terrace was deserted. Frozen, Rachel stamped her feet. The VW's heater had packed up. When she and Chris were married, she'd have a company car. A Lexus like his wife. Ex-wife. *She won't need it!*

People – her mum's friends, the doctor – called Rachel a saint for nursing her frail mother. Rachel would shrug. 'Mum saw me into the world, it's right I make her last years comfortable.' Chris loved her for that.

Rachel didn't feel saintly. She'd tried to be civil about her rival. But, as days dragged into months, largesse was subsumed by the green-eyed monster. *Did they sleep in the same bed?* When Penelope Philips rang the office to speak to 'my husband', Rachel silently urged Chris to *tell her about us*. He said he didn't want to hurt her. *She hurt you!*

Rachel wanted Penelope wiped off the face of the earth.

Chris had advertised for another advisor, one who could hit the ground running without training. Rachel's 'training' was in room 245. Rachel was his rock.

Yesterday she lost it.

'She's the *devil*! Don't feel sorry for her. You're sitting on a gold mine. Cash it in and live your life.' Still Chris couldn't do it.

She wouldn't knock. The house would soon be hers. She'd walk in and catch Penelope unawares.

Christopher Philips' secretary kept copies of his keys. She knew his greatest secret.

Mum said you had to be cruel to be kind.

Chapter One

November 2018

Trudy Wates stopped inside Stella's porch. The front door was ajar. She had two choices. Step away and call Stella – better still the police – or venture inside and check the place herself.

Since she'd started working as Stella Darnell's PA a month ago, Trudy knew that she had a hard act to follow. Her predecessor, Jackie Makepeace, had anticipated Stella's every requirement before Stella realized what she required. Trudy had set about proving herself a match for Jackie (now running Stella's fledgling detective agency). Trudy intended to exceed expectations.

Stella would hate to be interrupted while she was deep cleaning for a client. Trudy must present Stella with a problem solved. She tipped open the door with a gloved finger.

The ground floor – living room and kitchen – appeared untouched. Easy to tell because of course Stella kept her own house as clean and tidy as she did her clients'. Trudy climbed to the half landing.

The first door was shut. A burglar could be lying in wait.

'Who's there?' Trudy had left the front door open so that she could be heard from the street. She was in her forties but went to a boot camp twice a week and walked whenever possible. She carried a penknife, an unwanted present from her husband that, since his death, she treasured. It was her talisman.

Trudy flung wide the door. No one in the bathroom. *One down. Two to go.*

She climbed the stairs to the top landing and approached the room that faced the street. If there was someone in there she would confront them.

Stella's bedroom. Her bed was neatly made without a crease. Trudy found no one inside the built-in wardrobe. A lingering whiff of Stella's perfume was distantly reassuring. She caught herself in triplicate in the three mirrored doors. She looked rigid with tension. Since becoming a widow she had aged years. She gripped the knife and went back along the landing.

Later, Trudy would tell the police (they sent Chief Superintendent Cashman, presumably because Stella was a copper's daughter) that the intruders had only been in Stella's study where they'd tried to steal Stella's computer and her printer. The monitor lay by the door, wires trailing. Paper files were strewn on the floor. Cashman said that the thieves had been interrupted, perhaps by Trudy parking up (a horrible thought). Trudy told Cashman that Stella would have to confirm what, if anything, had been stolen.

Trudy had nerved herself to make the call.

'Stella, I'm afraid I have bad news...'

Later still, Stella would praise Trudy for her swift handling of the situation.

Trudy sailed through her probation. As she often did, she talked to her dead husband. 'I will survive.'

Chapter Two

December 1980

'Is he dead?' Lee asked.

'Yeah completely. Look, there's blood.' Danielle crouched beside the body. She levered the jaws open with a stick and revealed sharp teeth. Crimson liquid pooled around the tongue.

'Yuk!' Lee edged back. 'I don't think you should do that.'

'It doesn't hurt.' Danielle splayed her hand on the body. 'He's warm. He died *just* before we found him. His neck was squashed with a brick. Like this.' Danielle did a handstand beside the dead body. She flipped onto her feet.

'How do you know?' Bile rising in his throat, Lee didn't want to find out.

'I'm a detective.' Danielle dipped the stick inside the cat's mouth. She smeared blood on the tarmac.

'Don't touch it!' Nicola squeaked.

'It can't hurt me,' Danielle reassured them. Nicola hadn't meant that.

Danielle shoved the cat's body with her stick. Blood trickled from between his lips onto the road. 'Shall I cut it up so we know how it died?' Buoyed by this idea, Danielle got over her irritation that Nicola was there. A dead body was no different from one that was alive. The cat looked the same. Asleep like Robbie.

'You just said it was with a brick,' Lee said. 'If Sarah sees it she'll have nightmares then Alan will kill me.'

'I still have to do a post-mortem. Like the police did with Robbie. They chopped him up.' Danielle had forgotten she'd told them about the brick.

'They did *not*.' Nicola put her face in her hands.

'They wouldn't do that to Robbie.' Lee put his arm around Nicola.

Leaning into him Nicola said, 'I think she was run down. Mum says cars go too fast down here. She had a go at your dad the other day, Danni. He was in a sports car. Mum said he stole it.'

'He didn't.' Danielle tipped the cat's hind leg with her stick. Her own mum had accused Eddie of nicking it for his fancy woman. 'He took me out. It's an MG.'

'Wow,' Lee breathed.

'Policemen go faster than my dad. In a panda car with a siren.'

'Nee-nah, nee-nah!' Chasing about in circles, Jason was a panda car.

As the light failed the black cat merged with the black tarmac. Danielle told Lee, 'We have to move it out of the way of cars.'

'Don't! It's got germs!' Nicola tugged Lee's arm.

'We should go. Else we'll get the blame.' Lee dug in his pocket for his lighter. He flicked it on and held it up.

'We should call the police,' Nicola said. 'If it was with a brick, that's murder. A brick wouldn't move by itself.'

'I'm the police.' Danielle hadn't considered this complication. 'It could have been a car. That's why I'm going to do the post-mortem.' The dancing flame lent an infernal aspect to the scene, the children's faces made demonic.

'What's that?' Sarah Ferris was racing Kevin Hood along Braybrook Street. As they reached the cat, the lamp-posts went on.

'Nothing, babes!' Lee stepped in front of the cat.

'Show me.' Alan Ferris's daughter was more than capable of seeing blood without flinching. Sarah gazed at the dead animal. The little girl, eyes wide with curiosity, could have no inkling that very soon her own neck would be compressed by a house brick until she could no longer breathe.

Danielle grabbed the cat's tail and dragged it into the gutter.

The group considered the furry mass. The cat was large with a collapsed tummy.

'I think it's old,' Sarah decided. 'Is it dead like Robbie's dead?'

'Yes,' Nicola snapped at her.

'Robbie didn't get runned down,' Sarah said.

'No one said he did, darlin'.' Danielle imitated her older sister Maxine being nice to Jason. 'Best you go to bed. No nightmares.' She yanked Sarah to her.

'You can't chop it up,' Jason said. 'It's not yours.'

'I'm a detective,' Danielle repeated.

'Can we play Doctors and Nurses with it?' Sarah enquired.

'It's dead so it doesn't need nursing or... doctoring.' Danielle forgot to be nice.

'Let's pretend it's alive. Like you did with Robbie,' Sarah said.

'Sarah!' Lee snatched her hand. 'We're going. And don't tell your dad about this, OK?'

'Ouch.' Sarah squirmed crossly. 'I want to stay for the chopping.'

'We should tell the owner. They'll be waiting to give it its tea,' Nicola said. 'When Spiderman didn't come back, Robbie cried. I did too. He'd got stuck in next door's shed. He was starving. Robbie was allowed to give him Whiskas with a fork.'

'Robbie's dead,' Danielle said.

'He wasn't then. Spiderman is alive,' Nicola mumbled.

'Has this cat got a collar?' Danielle wished Nicky would shove off. She folded her arms.

Kevin felt under the cat's chin. Revolted, Jason sniggered. In his doctor's voice, Kevin reported, 'She doesn't have no collar.'

'A collar. Not no collar,' Danielle barked. 'You don't know it's a lady.'

'It's had babies, that's why it's all flabby like that.' Kevin did sound like a doctor.

'I know.' Danielle tapped her front tooth. Her notion of a detective was derived mainly from *Scooby-Doo*. 'We'll call on everyone in the street and detect the owner. Kevin, you're my sergeant.'

Kevin scrambled to his feet and stood next to Danielle, hands behind his back like a policeman.

'There's *hundreds* of houses in this street,' Sarah said.

Everyone went quiet as they digested this.

'Spiderman crosses the road as soon as he comes out,' Nicola said at last. 'He goes in a straight line. If this cat does that, it lives there.' She waved a hand at the house behind them. A decorated Christmas tree sparkled in the window.

'It does live there,' Danielle stated firmly.

'How can you be sure?' Nicola asked.

'I keep saying, because I'm a detective. I'll sling it behind there and people can work it out for themselves.' Tiring of the operation, Danielle pointed at the memorial for the three dead policemen. She hauled up the cat in both hands. More blood spewed from its mouth. The children scattered like birds.

'Dead! Dead! *Dead!*' Jason did a war dance.

'We should tell the owner since you know it's them in that house,' Lee stepped in.

'I'll do it.' Nicola went up to the house where Danielle had agreed that the cat had lived.

Sarah dragged on her brother's Harrington jacket. 'Lee, I got to tell you a secret.'

'Not now,' Lee hissed.

'There's no one in,' Nicola said.

'Danielle did it.' Sarah whipped around. Danielle was behind her, cradling the dead cat in her arms. Sarah giggled although it wasn't funny. She might be six but she knew that she'd made a terrible miscalculation.

'You're getting on my nerves, Sarah.' Lee parroted the phrase his stepfather used on him.

The door juddered open as if jammed by something. A woman in a paisley apron, straggly hair pinned back and so thin that her bones seemed close to the surface of her skin, rubbed her nose with a hanky. To the children she looked impossibly old.

'I ain't giving you no bob a job so you lot can scram!'

'We came to ask—' Nicola began.

'Is this yours?' Danielle pushed Nicky and Lee aside. She thrust the cat at the woman. This was her case.

'I… I…' The woman gripped the door. 'Bingo! Where did you find her?'

'On the road. He's been run over. He's dead.' Danielle decided saying this was less trouble.

'Where Bingo's gone she can't feel pain,' Nicola soothed.

'He made noises and coughing.' Danielle was informative. 'He died from blood loss like Robbie. If we'd found him sooner he might be alive. He'd be a vegetable though.' Her imagination ran free.

'I had her tea ready for him! Salmon from the market. Bingo.' The woman wailed into her hankie.

'He's dead so he can't swallow,' Danielle explained.

'My cat Spiderman likes salmon,' Nicola told the woman.

'What is salmon?' Sarah asked Lee.

'Here you are.' Danielle pushed the cat at the apron. 'I'm a detective. I can do a post-mortem on him for you.'

'Thank you, dear.' Dumbly the woman accepted her pet.

'Is there any money?' Jason asked. 'We brought your cat back.'

'Shut up, Jason.' Danielle hauled him back to the street.

The children clustered around the memorial stone.

'She'll be so sad.' Nicola was crying.

Thinking to console her, Lee gave Nicola his Bic lighter.

'She's lost her cat at Christmas!' Nicola shook as sobs took over.

'It's not Christmas yet.' A thought occurred. 'It'll be your first Christmas without Robbie.' Danielle was pleased by the coincidence.

'I better get indoors, we're meant to be decorating the tree.' Nicola looked suddenly confused. This year they hadn't bought a tree. Had her dad forgotten to get it from the market?

'We do ours on Christmas Eve,' Danielle asserted, although the timing varied and often didn't happen at all.

'Only if Dad's gone burgling,' Jason corrected her.

'Shut up!' Danielle dragged him off down the street.

A figure flitted between light spilling onto the pavement. From one house came a fairground rendering of *Away in a Manger.*

Danielle Hindle shone her torch where she'd shown them the dead cat. She traced drops of blood to another stain in the gutter. The Christmas tree in the window of the cat's house cast coloured light onto the street. Danielle went up to the door. She was shorter than Nicola so had to reach up to ring the bell. She heard shuffling. The door opened.

'Yes?' It was the lady again.

'Please can I see your cat?' Danielle asked nicely. Really she didn't have to ask at all. It was her job.

'Bingo?'

'Yes, that one.'

'She's died, dear.' The woman might have been consoling the child. 'Wasn't it you who brought her to me?'

'It was, but I was made to by my friends. I need to see him.'

'Her. Bingo was female. I wish I'd kept one from her litters. All those kittens…'

'I need to see her. To confirm how she died.'

'My husband's buried her in our garden.' The woman looked confused.

'He shouldn't of.' Danielle was properly cross.

'Why not?' The woman put a hand to her chest, the girl's official tone had made her feel guilty.

'I need to see what's inside. Rules are rules.' Like a man in the dole office had told Joy Hindle when she'd asked for a sub. Her daughter watching closely, missing nothing.

'Now, you stop that this instant. That's rude. Do you hear?' The woman gathered her wits.

'He died from a brick being pressed on him,' the girl asserted.

'He was run over.' The woman shook her head. Who told her that?

'June, what's going on?' a man called from inside the house.

'Not with his neck all squashed. Blood spurted out. If he'd been run over by a car there'd be marks. From the tyres. He would have been in the road.'

The girl was standing on her head.

'I'll get the police on you!' June was properly frightened.

'I am the police.' Danielle put her hands in her front pockets.

'Leave us alone.' June slammed the door.

'Police,' Danielle called through the letter box. 'Open up!'

The door swung away. Danielle's knuckles were grazed as the flap dragged over them. A man burst out. He grabbed her arm. 'Get lost, kid. You upset my wife and you've upset me.'

'I'll get my dad on you!' Danielle struggled. The dad of her imagination upheld the law.

'You tell your dad to come here. I'll sort him!' The man put up a fist. He got a look at the kid. 'Holy shit! Eddie Hindle's girl!' He shoved his hands into his trouser pockets. Calmly, 'Tell Eddie, it's disgusting sending you to play jokes. And at Christmas.'

'It's not a joke.' Danielle was properly cross. 'I'm investigating the murder of your cat.'

'What the hell…' Later, Norman Barton would link Sarah Ferris's killing with the death of their beloved Bingo; the child had as good as confessed that she'd murdered her. The Bartons would have been a gift to the prosecution, enabling them to present a pattern of behaviour. They said nothing. No one told on the Hindles.

Danielle climbed the park gate. She ran up the steps to the bandstand and did a dance from *Fame* in imitation of Maxine. She finished with a handstand and continued on to the playground.

She felt thwarted. They should have let her see what the cat looked like after it was more dead. They shouldn't have put it in a garden, that was for flowers.

In the dark of the playground Danielle Hindle came to a conclusion that changed her life for ever. Murder was easy. She'd already crossed that line. Her mum's voice in her head, the girl told herself that there were *No two ways about it, you better sort out that tell-tale Sarah Ferris.*

Lee prayed that his mum and Alan were down the pub. Seven years ago was when his mum had met Alan Ferris. They never missed an anniversary.

'Robbie didn't have an accident.' Sarah pronounced each syllable.

'Yeah, he did, Sarah.' Lee was searching in the cupboard for something for supper. He took out a tin of alphabet spaghetti. It was a half tin, but he wasn't hungry.

'He went off the slide onto the floor.' Sarah watched as Lee scooped out the tin into a non-stick pan. 'I won't eat it. It's blood.'

'It's tomato.' Silently agreeing with her, Lee returned to the larder. Baked beans, tinned sausages both in tomato sauce, raspberry jam, everything was murder.

'Why did you give Nicola your cigarette lighter?'

'Don't tell that to your dad either. About me having a lighter.'

'Now you don't have it.' Sarah giggled. 'Why did you? You like it.'

The little kitchen receded as everything became clear. Lee confided in his little sister, 'It was a present. One day, me and Nicky will be married.'

'Will you have children?' Sarah settled in for a story.

'We'll have a little girl just like you.'

Chapter Three

April 2019

'In all my years in the force, this was one of the worst murders I've seen.' Chief Superintendent Martin Cashman marvelled at a section of bare floorboards. To the naked eye it was spotless. To Stella it needed a deep clean.

'What are you doing here?' Her speech was muffled through her safety mask. She pulled it off. The last person needed at a cleaning scene was the investigation's SIO. Besides, Cashman was a Met officer, he surely had no jurisdiction in Gloucestershire.

'Nice to see you too, Stella!' Cashman grinned.

When Trudy had given Stella the brief, she'd jumped at the chance to clean a crime and trauma scene outside London. It meant that Clean Slate's reputation was spreading, but what she'd really liked was that it was in Winchcombe. A village where, a few years ago, she and Jack had solved a double murder. Despite the grim circumstances, it was a good memory. A confirmed Londoner, Stella had yet grown to appreciate the peace of the countryside. Despite the association with death, Winchcombe retained for her a tranquillity more in keeping with Jane Austen than Agatha Christie. Not that – preferring cleaning manuals – Stella had read either.

Two o'clock in the afternoon. It had rained from dawn, a relentless drizzle that slicked the pavements with a sheen of water and soaked those out in it within seconds.

Donette and Shelley, two long-trusted operatives, had come in the Transit with Darren, Clean Slate's latest recruit and an experienced crime scene cleaner. Stella had followed in her Peugeot Partner. In spacewalker protective garb, they had begun unpacking equipment and lugging it into the palatial house by the war memorial. When Cashman had turned up.

The detective dashed at his forehead with a sleeve as if he'd been hefting cleaning equipment. He was used to gruesome scenarios, but still Stella noticed he seemed tense. Not that this scene was particularly gruesome. The body was gone, the blood would have had dried.

'Why are you here?' she repeated. Since Cashman's promotion, he was generally desk-bound or, as her mum reckoned, preening himself for Chief Constable in front of cameras.

'I could say the same to you. Don't you have minions for this?'

'I don't have minions for anything,' Stella snapped. Years ago, she and Cashman had had a fling, then he'd gone back to his wife. Martin had started out in the police as her dad's mentee and ended up his best friend. In his mid-fifties, it seemed to Stella he looked more and more like her dad every day. He wore the same M&S suit and had the same burly stature (unlike Terry, Martin wasn't putting on weight).

Actually, today his suit looked more upmarket. Bar plastic overshoes covering his brogues, Martin was groomed and immaculate. Lucie May had told Stella (unwanted information) that Karen Cashman, tired of his relentless hours and of him, had finished with her husband. Stella suspected that the style refresh meant Martin was up for dating. *Please not.*

'Obviously you know what happened here.' With a sweep of his hand Cashman took in the spacious hallway, curving staircase and, through a doorway, a vast lounge. 'Antiques shop owner murdered his mistress last May because she'd threatened to tell his wife and daughter about them and put all this in jeopardy.'

Stella nodded assent. Yes she did know. What she didn't know was what a murder in Gloucestershire had to do with Cashman, a Met detective.'The area of origin was on the threshold of the living room. Brutal attack. From behind. Stabbing. Victim caught unawares, back to her killer. He made a decent job of cleaning up the walls and furniture. The carpet. Shame for him, it wasn't to your standard.' He shot her a look. 'SOCO revealed a fluorescence show, spatter, clots, globules.' Cashman paused. 'Even without him finally confessing, forensics were overwhelming.' His tone implied disappointment that the solve had been easy.

Stella knew that it hadn't been easy. The murder had occupied headlines on and off over the previous Spring and then again last month. Rachel Cater, thirty-one, was a secretary at Christopher Philips' auctioneers in Cheltenham. At four-thirty on the 13th May 2018 Cater had been stabbed fifteen times in the back with a knife that the killer had taken with them. She was reported missing that evening. Philips had put up a reward for Rachel. Agnes Cater made a television appeal asking for whoever had her daughter to show her mercy and release her in time for her birthday at the end of May. Two months into the investigation, Mrs Cater told detectives that her daughter had been having an affair with Philips and the case broke open. Steeped in motive, Penelope Philips and the couple's daughter Carrie were interviewed. They had alibis. Penny Philips had been caught on CCTV in Hammersmith on the afternoon of the murder. Her twenty-six-year-old daughter was also in London being a barrister. Or barista. Stella was vague on detail.

Chris Philips had no alibi. But the police had no body. Philips was released without charge. Outside the police station in Cheltenham he told the media that he'd been stupid but he was a lucky man, his family – until then ignorant of his affair – had forgiven him. Philips appealed to Rachel to come home and put her mother out of her misery. The resulting coverage garnered Philips no sympathy. His using the word lucky was, Lucie had said, 'frigging idiotic'.

Then police got a signal from Rachel's phone. It led them to to her body in a drain shaft and Philips confessed.

Hit by staff sickness, Stella hadn't paid attention to the week-long trial at the Old Bailey last month. Although she did remember the murder. Three days ago, the brutal killing had entered into sharp focus when, after the trial, Clean Slate was hired to clean the crime scene. Once Stella's company had finished, the property would be released to the Philips family.

'There are similarities with a case in London. Turns out it means nothing.' Martin was vague.

On her last visit to the village, while using an ATM outside the Lloyds bank, Stella had noticed the house. Double-fronted, steps to the front door bracketed by ornate balustrades, tall windows facing Abbey Terrace, she'd supposed that it would be a pleasure to clean. She was about to find out.

'I got you the job.' Cashman rubbed his chin as if uttering wisdom.

'Oh. Right. Thank you.' Trudy had said it was a 'word of mouth' recommendation from the Met. Stella might have guessed that the 'mouth' was Martin Cashman. Trudy had tried to stop Stella coming. As Stella's PA she was taking a leaf out of Jackie's book and trying to steer Stella away from being hands-on. Time was better spent building the business. But when Stella realized it was in Winchcombe there was no stopping her.

'Stella, I do *not* need to emphasize to you that neither you nor your team will discuss what you see here. With anyone.' Suddenly a copper, Cashman was stilted, arms folded. 'Clean and go. That includes the Engine Driver and Lucie bloody May.'

'I wouldn't.' Stella bridled. Jack said Cashman was jealous of him. She'd put that down to Jack not liking Cashman. Tending to accept feelings at face value, Stella rarely felt emotions akin to jealousy. She operated on the binary simplicity of dirty/clean. Her approach, be they germs or crimes, was stain by stain.

'Stick to cleaning and leave detecting to me and my guys.' Cashman was referring to the cold cases – two were her father's – that Stella and Jack had solved. 'Whatever anyone might say, Chris Philips was found guilty. He's got a long sentence and I hope that, should any Home Secretary let him out, he's too gaga to make sense of freedom.'

'I'm here to clean.' Stella pulled on her mask. At her first crime and trauma scene she'd promised herself to treat it as a cleaning job. She would consider the event that had occurred there in the context of hygienic restoration. Detection shared much with cleaning – chaotic situations requiring a return to order – she would not confuse the two. Today her concern was remedial. To establish the nature of a substance to be eradicated and apply the right chemical. *Stain by stain.* 'I signed a confidentiality agreement.'

Her dad said a detective saw a scene as a collection of previous actions to be interrogated. How did that chair get there? When was it moved? By whom? Why? Her job was to eliminate evidence of those actions. She'd expanded her business to include the cleaning of crime and trauma scenes (from a trashed hotel room to the site of a murder) because as Jackie had pointed out, it was the obvious link between Clean Slate's cleaning services and Stella and Jack's detective work.

'You and I know that any contract is fish and chip paper. I'm serious, Stella.' Cashman did a serious face.

'So am I,' Stella snapped.

Actually this case – violent and brutal – had lingered in her mind. Rachel Cater had died during a terrible attack. However, the pathologist who had examined her remains hadn't been able to confirm that Rachel was dead when Philips had put her into the shaft. Stella had been shocked by the violence of Rachel's murder and the callous disposal. 'Why are you here now? Do you need us to delay?'

'No! Like I said, I was just checking on... in case we missed anything. Not that we did.' He added hastily, 'Plus I thought I'd say hi.'

Here it was. 'Unless there's anything else...' Stella moved past him to the lounge.

The room resembled a computer-generated image of a cross-section intended to show elements of a building. The floorboards had been cut away to reveal the joists. Walking gingerly along an access plank, Stella saw holes in the lath and plaster to the basement far below.

It didn't take forensic wizardry to detect blood. The woodwork was brown where blood had seeped through the carpet and dripped between the boards. Apparently confident that he'd never be suspected, Philips had cleaned only what could be seen. Her dad used to say that arrogance and carelessness were a seasoned criminal's true enemy.

Out of the window she saw that kids were coming home from school; the butcher, in a bloodstained apron, hurried along the pavement with a delivery; a young man and woman in matching yellow anoraks were taking selfies by the war memorial. Metres away from where a murder had been committed, Winchcombe was going about its business.

The room smelled fusty. Apart from the coppery odour of blood, Stella smelled decades of dust overlaid with the admixture of chemicals used by the killer. And something else. A perfume by Carolina Herrara. Trudy wore it. Disturbed by the crime Stella, usually able to pinpoint scents right to the name, hit a blank. She liked it which was lucky since it filled the office.

'I have to get on,' she told Cashman. The brief involved removing white paint (applied for privacy during the investigation) off the front windows and vacuuming up fingerprint powder. Steam cleaning and fumigation throughout. Stella's company didn't yet offer physical restoration so she'd outsourced to a carpentry firm to make good the floorboards.

No amount of deep cleaning would erase history. Already, Stella knew, the place was known as the Murder House. The home of what reporter Lucie May had called the Antiquarian Killer.

'Philips' wife is in a safe house, her daughter lives in London. She's something legal.' Cashman was back to chatty.

'Safe from who? Christopher Philips is in prison.' Stella shouldn't have asked, she wanted Cashman gone so that they could get on with the job.

'There's always vigilantes. Someone who's spent years searching and—' Cashman caught sight of himself in a fingerprint-clouded mirror and set about smoothing his hair. 'Homicide has long-term repercussions. Terry said it makes victims of everyone. Years later people still hurt. Only the killer walks free.' He moved out of the way for Darren to pass with a biohazard container; Donette and Shelley were manipulating a giant roll of plastic sheeting through the front door.

'Unless there's anything else…'

Hoisting the police tape as if it had weight, Cashman hesitated on the doorstep. 'Actually, Stell, I was wondering about a drink. For old time's…' The cliché died on his lips.

'It looks like I'll be full-on here.' Stella tried to sound regretful although the prospect of cleaning made her spirits soar.

'Another time.' Cashman ducked under the tape and strode away up the street.

'Another time.' Stella gathered up the tape. It was no longer a crime scene. It was a deep-cleaning situation.

The unremitting light revealed infinite marks and stains, abrasions and foreign matter in the garage. It banished dark corners and shadows. Not that Stella believed in ghosts. They were more Jack's thing. He chatted to phantoms, in subway tunnels, in his house and as he drove his train past disused stations. He claimed that dead people were everywhere. Flitting a duster in someone's bedroom or over keyboards in an office, Stella could dismiss this as one of Jack's many flights of fancy. But alone in the place where Rachel Cater's body had been so violently disposed of, Stella was haunted not by ghosts, but by Rachel's last moments. As she powered the steam cleaner over the garage floor, directing it over the shaft cover (the deposition site), Stella – usually determinedly rational – imagined the young woman crumpled at the bottom. Had she woken and realized her fate? Ridiculous though it was, Stella felt that by removing all trace of the murder she was complicit in the crime.

She diverted herself with Cashman. He'd been strict on confidentiality. He knew her well enough to know she didn't gossip. He had suggested coffee yet Stella wasn't convinced that he'd come all the way to Winchcombe just for that. Or had he? Jackie said that Stella never gauged her effect on men. *They fall for you hook, line and sinker.* During their fling Martin (she corrected herself to 'Cashman' which kept him at a distance) had enlisted her help on a case; he was confidential when it suited.

Why would he think she was investigating a murder that was solved? Did the police think they'd got the wrong man? Why was Cashman in Gloucestershire? Terry would never let an innocent man go to prison to keep up his solve rate. Was Cashman checking on the work of other detectives? All angles led back to the coffee. He'd been smart and tidy. He'd come to ask her out.

Returning to the house, Stella heard shouts. A woman was yelling at Donette in the hall. Stella's staff knew to keep the prying public away from a scene. Inevitably they came; posing as meter readers, Jehovah's Witnesses, even collectors for charities, intent on seeing where a crime had been committed or a person had died.

Stella's dad had taught her to appraise witnesses at speed. Late twenties. Blonde hair hairdresser-messed, black fitted leather jacket, floaty dress with orange splodges that looked like stains. The woman's high heels raised her to about five-seven, well shy of Stella's six feet, but enabling her to tower over Donette.

'I'm afraid you can't come on site without protective clothing.' Stella pushed up the visor on her helmet. 'You have no authority.'

'I have more authority than you! Site? This is my *home*,' the woman replied hotly. 'Every minute you're arguing is another minute that Daddy is languishing in jail!'

'You're Carrie.' Cashman had referred to the Philipses' daughter. *Grown up, lives away from home*. And now, it seemed, back.

'And you're Stella Victoria Darnell!' Kicking off a shoe and massaging a stockinged foot Carrie Philips uttered Stella's full name as if it was a swear word. 'I want you to sort out this mess.'

'That's what I'm in—' Stella was reeling from Carrie Philips' saying her middle name. Stella told no one.

'Don't waste your time doing poxy cleaning.'

'It's my job...' Stella didn't say that there was little more useful and rewarding.

'Don't bullshit me! It's not your proper job.' Carrie Philips flung a look of scorn at the Planet 2000 vacuum by the stairs. 'You solve murders. I want you to find the true killer of Rachel Cater and set my father free!'

Chapter Four

31st October 1980

'Get up there,' said Danielle. 'Dare you.'

'I don't feel like it.' Robbie was scared, but he wasn't going to tell Danielle.

'You're scared.' Danielle whacked one of the struts of the very high slide making the metal ring. Her slide. That would teach Robbie to call her smelly. Danielle had taken time devising Robbie's punishment. But she'd chosen the date of the punishment that afternoon in a lesson on the history of Halloween. It was All Souls Eve. The day, her teacher said, that it was once believed the dead walked. Danielle would prove it.

Robbie, three days short of his sixth birthday and ten-year-old Danielle were alone in the playground. Robbie was meeting his classmate Kevin Hood. They always went to cubs together. Danielle had followed him.

'Kevin's coming.' Robbie said stoutly. He sensed danger.

'Don't you ever cheek me again. Yeah?'

'No never.' The boy trembled.

Danielle grabbed Robbie and propelled him up the ladder in front of her.

'I can't.' Robbie wailed.

At the top everything was spinning, the park, the bandstand, the flower beds. All of the playground. Robbie just stopped himself saying that he wanted his mum.

'Don't ever. Call me. Smelly again.' Danielle jerked him to the top of the slide.

Robbie was struck by the irony that he'd shouted it to Danielle Hindle in the school corridor to get her attention, and now he had her all to himself. Despite his terror he gave a snigger.

'How dare you laugh at me.' Hindle gave the boy a push. Hardly a push. She never touched him. Not at all.

She contemplated the ground. How like a broken doll Robbie looked. He wasn't walking. He wasn't dead.

The last of the sun broke from a cloud and flooded the concrete with light.

Danielle saw a movement in the bandstand. Someone was watching. Not someone… Sarah Ferris.

Kevin Hood found Robbie sprawled in the playground. Exasperated that Robbie was playing being shot dead and wouldn't stop, Kevin went by himself. An hour and a half later, over chicken nuggets and baked beans, he mentioned it to his mum.

Robbie had been dead when the police found him. When they questioned Kevin, the little boy had remarked that he'd got fed up with Robbie being the wounded robber who got nursed by Sarah. Had Kevin Hood pushed his friend off the slide?

If timings were correct, it seemed not. Michael Sutherland, the pathologist, reported that Robert Walsh had been dead for over an hour when Kevin had found him. Joy Hindle and her girls Maxine and Danielle had seen Kevin going into the park at half past four. They were his alibi.

*

1st December

Robbie Walsh wasn't the first child to die in a British playground – since the nineteen fifties injuries and fatalities were common – but he was the first to die in 1980. His face was splashed over the *Hammersmith and Fulham Chronicle*. Paying tribute, Miss Barnes his teacher said, 'Robbie was honest, curious and helpful, he'll be so dreadfully missed.' The inquest heard that the boy was frightened of heights. He could have panicked and slipped. He hit the ground head first, fracturing his skull in three places. The coroner ruled accidental death. A child safety group told Lucie May, the *Chronicle*'s chief reporter, that the 'height of the tower slide was equivalent to a first-storey window' and that most playgrounds were death traps. The iron equipment (Ocean Wave 'witch's hat', roundabout and rocking boat) had crushed the limbs and shortened the lives of Britain's children for decades. Wartime bombsites had been safer.

To quote Lucie May, 'Little Robbie's untimely death has left a hole in the community, neighbours adored the mischievous lad who put a smile on everyone's face.' May went on, 'According to Parks and Recreation Committee Minutes, a move "to update the equipment and replace the concrete with softer material is pending." What new tragedy must strike our kids before "pending" becomes "action"?'

A second funeral was Danielle Hindle's brainwave. Two months on and Robbie's death was making his sister Nicola annoying. A funeral was for crying, Danielle said. Nicola hadn't been allowed to go to Robbie's. If they had one Nicola would stop her snivelling and cheer up. By inadvertently offering a child the chance to grieve a loved one, Danielle was ahead of her time. Once she'd got over the idea that it was naughty, Nicola appreciated attention focused on her little brother who, as if he'd never been born, was never mentioned at home.

'We should do it where I found Robbie being dead,' said Kevin Hood.

'You don't do funerals where people die, they happen in churches where they burn bodies. This roundabout is the *catafouck*. My dad said it's called that.' Danielle did a handstand because ages ago Lee had said she was good at them.

'The what?' Lee flexed his shoulders. He was too grown-up for this stuff.

'Catapult!' Jason crowed. As Danielle's brother he granted himself authority in the impending ceremony. He was quickly disabused of this.

'Kev, you carry the coffin.' Danielle held up a shoebox. She led them to a bench by the railings. 'This is the church.'

The children – Nicky and Lee who were ten like Danielle, and six-year-olds Jason and Kevin with Sarah, Lee's half-sister – crowded around Danielle. It was properly dark. The group paid no heed to the park's closing time. Danielle produced the torch her father had stolen from Woolworths from her hand-me-down coat and illuminated an inscription on the bench.

For Robert (Robbie) Walsh 1974–1980

He will always play here

The children were puzzled by the forever nature of death. The last line encouraged Kevin to look for Robbie whenever he came to the playground. Even Danielle, puzzled by little, harboured expectations that Robbie would return.

'Why should Kevin carry it?' Nicola wondered out loud.

'Kevin and Robbie were best mates,' Danielle reminded her.

'I'm his sister.' Nicola unwrapped a stick of chewing gum and fed it between her lips. She chucked the wrapping away into the darkness.

'You are *my* best sister!' Sarah let go of her brother and snatched Nicola's hand.

'That's not a coffin. It's for stupid shoes.' Lee shoved his hands in the back pockets of his camouflage trousers. The children contemplated the image of strappy sandals with block heels on the box. £6.99. Eddie Hindle hadn't parted with money, he'd filched them from Dolcis in Kings Street.

'It is a coffin.' Danielle was haughty. 'Maxine said Robbie's coffin went behind curtains and got set on fire.'

'That's a lie.' Nicola choked back a sob.

'It's OK, Nick.' Lee kicked at the asphalt with his cherry-red DMs, new from Shepherd's Bush Market. 'We won't do that. It's not real.'

'It *is* real!' Forgetting that the purpose of the ceremony was to make Lee want to be her boyfriend, Danielle blazed, 'It's all right for you, Lee. Your sister hasn't been murdered. Nick hasn't got Robbie and we have to stop her crying.'

'It's not working so far.' Lee flicked his hair back.

'Will this make Robbie come and play?' Kevin risked the burning question.

'No.' Danielle grabbed Kevin into a hug then catching herself, pushed him off. 'Robbie is already here. In a minute he'll be at peace.'

'Oh.' Kevin pondered on 'peas', which were like sick.

'There's no curtains here, so you'll have to go without.' Danielle wielded her mother's stricture. Aiming the torch into the playground, she yelled, 'Jason, stop mucking about and get over here.'

Her brother was scattering grit at the bottom of the slide for when someone landed.

'Kevin and Jason, carry Robbie. Nicky, you're Best Mourner, you lead the way.' This was generous. Danielle longed to go first. 'When I say "Go" you come towards us. Me and Lee will sit very close in the front row of the church. We're his mum and dad.' She swept onto the bench and bashing the wood with a fist, indicated for Lee to join her. He mooched over.

'Can I be a bridesmaid?' Sarah ventured.

‘You walk with me. Robbie loved you.’ Nicky swung Sarah’s hand.

‘That’s nice,’ Lee let slip.

‘No! It’s wrong,’ Danielle fumed. Later she would see that this was when it all went wrong. Nicola being nice to his sister turned Lee’s head.

The four children, the boys carrying the shoebox reverentially as if their friend’s remains were inside, the girls in front, processed around the swings to the roundabout.

‘Put the coffin on the rounda… cataf… stick it on there.’ Danielle was tiring of the whole thing.

Kevin and Jason plonked the box on the roundabout. Danielle and Lee came over.

Danielle gave Nicky a sprig of privet (in lieu of the single red rose reportedly on Robbie’s coffin) and unfolding a scrap of paper intoned, ‘We’re here to say farewell to Nick’s brother Robbie. Fare. Well. Robbie.’ The others mumbled a response. Danielle shone the torch at Nicola. ‘Say something to him.’

‘Like what?’ Nicky looked petrified.

‘What’s in there?’ Jason piped.

‘Robbie’s ashes.’ Danielle batted her brother.

‘They’re in a pot by the fire. Did you steal them?’ Nicky was aghast.

‘It’s earth,’ Danielle admitted. ‘From the park. With one of Jason’s soldiers on top.’ Then unknowingly philosophical, ‘It’s all the same in the end.’

‘Which soldier?’ Jason demanded. ‘If it’s Buck Rogers I’ll kill you!’

‘Sssh!’ The solemnity of the occasion allowed Danielle to avoid admitting that Buck Rogers lay on damp loam scooped from a pansy bed. Borrowing from her nan when Danielle’s granddad died, she instructed Nicola, ‘Talk to Robbie, see him on his way.’

‘I don’t know what to say.’

'Say about Robbie stealing your pocket money.' Jason was inspired.

'He never.' Nicola was fighting tears.

'We got Bazooka gum!' Jason strutted about the roundabout. 'The sweetshop lady sold us two cigarettes.'

'That lady's dead now,' Danielle said as if one was a consequence of the other. 'Robbie won't do it again. Nicky, think of a nice thing.'

Everyone went quiet.

Quavering, Nicola stammered, 'Robbie, you was my brother… and I… I'll love him. *You*. To the end of time and always kiss you goodnight.' She hurled the privet onto the roundabout, missing the shoebox.

'It's time to let go of Robbie and get better.' Holding Nicola's arm in a vice-like grip, Danielle made Lee set the roundabout in motion.

The shoebox-casket glided into the darkness.

Chapter Five

9th December 1980

'Can Nicky come out?' Danielle balanced on her hands outside the Walshes' house on Braybrook Street.

'It's a bit late, love. It's nearly dark.' Gill Walsh, her hands moving about as if swishing water, appeared not to notice that the girl was standing on her head. Gill was glammed up and dressed to the nines, not for a night down the Palais, but because she never knew when she'd open her door and be on the news. She regarded Danielle, a skinny thing in jeans and a skimpy top, shivering on her step, with doubt. Since her son's death Gill's senses were dulled. Everything came from far away. Before her life had changed for ever, Gill minded that her two went round with the Hindles. Dreaming of a housing estate in Morden with a garage, she'd fretted that Nicky and Robbie's accents would get common. Then after Robbie's death, Joy Hindle shooed off a reporter. *F*** off, pushy bitch!* Not how Gill would have put it, but she'd been obscurely grateful when the man went. Recalling this, Gill relented, what was the harm? In the dusk Danielle didn't look scary. Her pinched face was beseeching, her teeth chattered against the bitter night.

'I'll give her a call.'

Danielle twirled and skipped on the path. She'd had a fight with Jason. He'd said he was going to tell their dad that she'd stamped on his Action Man gun. For once Maxine hadn't sided with Jason: 'Shut your neck!' Cheered by this, Danielle had come to call for Nicola. She'd be nice if Nicky cried.

'She's in the toilet, best you wait in the lounge, it's freezing out here.' Gill Walsh was back.

The children always met in the playground. Danielle had never been inside the Walshes' house which Nicky said they owned so they didn't need a rent book. A silver Christmas tree twisted with tinsel and white lights was in a bucket crudely wrapped in Christmas paper. A veneer cabinet housed a television showing *Top of the Pops*. Schoolgirls sang about loving Grandma. Danielle hated the song although she'd like to be on television.

Until the police took it away (her dad had nicked it), her own telly had been much bigger than the Walshes'. They took her dad away too. He was in Wormwood Scrubs prison for making a man go into a coma (like sleep, but longer). Danielle's mum got a Christmas tree from one of her men friends. It was leaning against the wall where the television had been. As she admired greetings cards pegged along a tinselled string across the room, Danielle was wistful. Her house didn't have decorations.

Danielle was alarmed by a huge photograph of Robbie above the gas fire. It was like an advert in a street. He had on a white shirt and a bow tie and a red waistcoat. She almost expected the larger-than-life boy to speak. She said, 'I'm sorry he's dead.'

'That's nice, love. Isn't it, Bob, what Danielle said? About Robbie. She paid her condolences.' Gill Walsh's sentences were plucked from a jumble of incoherent thoughts.

At thirty-nine, Bob Walsh was ten years older than his wife. Until a few weeks ago, he'd considered himself the luckiest man in the world. Gorgeous wife, two lovely kids, a thriving market stall. Then on 31st October it all went wrong. Bolt upright on the settee, he was apparently deep in the *Evening Standard*. In reality, Bob read the words to find a reason for his living nightmare. 'Yes.'

'Is that Robbie in his coffin?' Danielle asked.

'It's at my sister's wedding.' Gill started at the question. 'Robert looked a picture that day.' She pulled a face as if screaming without sound. Danielle promised herself to try it later. Pleased at herself for being nice, she dredged up a hazarded gathered notion. 'Robbie will return like Jesus. He'll rise up.'

The gas fire hissed. The room was stifling. The smell of liver and onions that, earlier, the depleted family had picked at, lingered.

'What you on about?' Bob Walsh flung down the paper.

'Nicky doesn't mind about Robbie. We had his funeral. She's not sad now,' Danielle enthused. 'I wish I could have seen him dead. And not just Buck Rogers.'

'She means well, Bob. She's too young to understand...' Gill flapped over the newspaper and bundled it onto her husband's lap.

'She understands, all right. She's a troublemaker, that one!' Bob Walsh clawed at eczema on his forearm. 'That whole family should be locked up!'

'Danielle's being nice.' Her hair glossy, cheeks rosy, a flowery blouse tucked into ironed jeans, Nicola was the antithesis of her wraithlike parents. Only her eyes, flicking to and fro between them, betrayed a child that was haunted.

'Yes.' Losing one child had robbed Gill of maternal skills. Her daughter confused her.

'What funeral? I said you was too young to go!' Bob worked on a time lapse.

None of the children had been allowed to go to Robbie's funeral. Although Kevin Hood had seen 'the box with Robbie lying still as a stick inside' come out of the Walshes' house. Nicola's parents, shot with grief, had sent her to the Hindles where, alone in the house, Danielle and Nicky spent the time parading in her big sister's dresses, daubing on Maxine's make-up to Abba's LP *Voulez-Vous* on Maxine's Barbie record player.

'We had a funeral in the playground.' Danielle ignored Nicola's warning look. Since Robbie's accident no one was meant to go to the playground.

'You played a game.' Bob Walsh's nails rasped on his skin.

'It was real!' Danielle protested. 'To make Nicky better.'

'Where do you think you're going? You are not going out!' Bob Walsh took refuge in prohibition.

'Let them go, Bob.' Before he could argue, Gill scooted the children out to the street. Returning to the overheated lounge – since Robbie, she was always cold – she relaxed. Without Nicola, she could pretend that she and Bob were just starting out. With no kids to break their hearts.

At 5.35 p.m. the park gates were locked. Traffic hummed on the West Way. Wind rippled the water in the ornamental pond, rattled the clump of ornamental grasses and set up an eerie howl in the bandstand. Gill Walsh had been generous in saying it was nearly dark, it was dark. Lamplight accentuated shadows and a sense that the park was far from London's rush-hour streets. Above, smudged clouds curdling against the mauve sky provided perspective for passing painters.

Anyone looking downwards might have seen Danielle and Nicola scale the railings and race across the lawns to the playground. Kevin Hood and Jason Hindle were playing tag with a torch, flitting like spirits between the play equipment that in the crazy light might be slumbering dinosaurs. Sarah Ferris huddled up to her big brother on the roundabout. She was crying.

'They should be in bed.' Danielle was livid. If she'd known Lee would be there she wouldn't have called for Nicola. The funeral hadn't worked. Nicky still cried for nothing. Danielle was running out of ways to put Lee off Nicky who by rights should be dead too.

'I had to bring Sarah, my mum's at the pictures with Alan.' Lee pulled a face of embarrassment rather than annoyance. He hated his stepfather, but he loved his half-sister.

'You could have left her.' Losing her own sibling made Nicola untypically grudging.

'She's not allowed to be alone. Danielle brought Jason.'

'He brought himself,' Danielle corrected Lee. 'Jason's thick. He can be left alone.'

'Sarah's lost her charm bracelet, we've been looking for it.' Lee ran a hand over his new buzz cut. Which no one had mentioned.

'Did you find it?' Nicola was concerned.

'Those things are stupid,' Danielle said.

'Alan gave it to her. I gave her a charm. Best Sister. It cost all my money.' Lee beat a rhythm with his fingers on the roundabout at this memory.

'You *all* have to find it!' Sarah scuttled over to Jason and Kevin who were testing the limits of the rocking boat.

'I've looked everywhere.' Lee stopped drumming. In a fatalistic tone he said, 'Alan'll kill me.'

'It's not your fault.' Nicola sat beside him. Lee shuffled closer to her. 'Sarah should have been careful. I'm not allowed to wear jewellery out.'

'Your dad will blame you.' Danielle agreed with Lee. She wandered over to the swings.

'He's *not* my dad!' Lee took out a cigarette, stolen from his stepfather, then put it back in his Harrington.

'Maybe it's at home,' Nicola said.

'She had it when we left, she was going on about it. She likes my charm most.' Lee looked briefly happier.

'Who's that?' A yell.

Nicola and Lee looked to where Kevin was pointing. A face, pale as the moon, was suspended. It rose and fell. A chain creaked. *Up. Down. Up.*

'I'm a murder-er!' The voice was like a sigh.

'It's Robbie!' Jason screamed. 'He's *back*.'

'Stop it!' Lee strode to the swings. He grabbed the torch and thrust it at the apparition.

'Scared you!' Danielle's wild laughter clattered around the playground. In the glare, the pinch-faced ten-year-old, hair straggling around her neck, did resemble the dead returned.

'You scared Sarah,' Nicola said gently.

'Yeah. You did.' Lee flashed the torch at the small children, smiling sheepishly, none of them looked scared. 'I'll get it in the neck from Alan if she has nightmares.'

'What's a murderer?' Sarah asked.

'See?' Lee, his buzz cut making him look tougher than he dared to be, patted the girl. 'Danielle's mucking about, babe, don't listen.'

'I saw the man from Abba by the off-licence. He's coming.' Danielle's eyes were wild. '*He's* a murderer.'

The group closed ranks.

But Nicola stayed. They all knew that Danielle decided when they went.

'You've never seen a murderer,' Jason told his sister.

'You don't know *anything*,' Danielle grated. 'Shut up!'

'I have seen one,' Sarah confided to Lee in a stage whisper.

'No. You haven't,' said Danielle. The person in the bandstand on the night when Robbie had died (Danielle didn't call it murder) had been Sarah. Tell-tale. That girl needed teaching a lesson.

'Don't talk like that, Sarah!' Lee knew that if Sarah came out with that at home, his stepfather would string him up. 'No one's seen one.'

'If someone makes someone dead they are a murd-rah.' Sarah felt her way towards comprehension then announced, 'I know one.'

Nicola let out a blood-curdling scream and clutched Lee's arm in fright.

In the dying light, a man in a duffel coat, a pocket torn loose, the other bulging with a can of pale ale, shambled past the witch's hat towards them. Every child knew who he was.

The man from Abba.

'Come on!' Lee shouted.

The children ran for their lives.

A boy in love, drugged by the exquisite sensation of Nicola holding onto him, Lee forgot about his baby sister. By the time he came to his senses, it was too late.

Chapter Six

1980

Hooking his jacket off his chair, Detective Inspector Terry Darnell headed out. He'd be home early for once. Not that Suzie would call twenty past seven early. Or that he called it home since Suzie no longer lived there. She'd left him seven years ago, taking Stella with her. The house was a bolt-hole where he microwaved shop-bought shepherd's pie and fell into bed. Mostly alone. Terry kept the place spick and span for when his family returned. 'The Twelfth of Never, Popsicle,' Lucie, his erstwhile sleeping partner said. 'Get real, Tezza, they're gone for good.'

Terry never told Lucie that he couldn't give up hope. Going by Lucie's waspish remarks about his family, she knew.

A hand caressing the brass handrail, Terry hurried down the stairs. For the middle-aged detective, the art deco police station with wood-panelled corridors and marble floors – a homage to a past civic pride – was his true home.

He'd reached the stables when his pager buzzed. Back in the call room, he found a spare phone and punched in CID. 'Darnell.'

'Guv, we've got a body.' Martin Cashman always sounded out of breath. Not because he was unfit, but because keeping fit, he moved fast.

Terry's mood lifted. Suzie used to accuse him of caring more about victims than his family. Yes, all right, he wanted justice for the crime, but she had no idea how much he cared for her and for their daughter. Right now though, a body meant not going back to his empty house. A body meant the day wasn't over.

Siren blaring, Cashman gunned the Ford along Shepherd's Bush Road. Absorbing the details, Terry felt dread. Not this. *Never this.* They'd caught the case that no detective, however crap their private life is or dedicated they are, ever wants.

In the eighteen fifties the West London Line railway cut Wormwood Scrubs Common in two. The larger tract of land of bushes and trees was a hint of rural freedom within sight of the prison. The 'offcut' beyond the tracks, the property of the Metropolitan Board of Works, was named Little Wormwood Scrubs and by the twentieth century was a park. Bandstand, café, annually planted beds and an ornamental pond fed by Counters Creek, a river which ran underground through Hammersmith and Kensington to appear as a green-slimed trickle into the Thames at Chelsea.

There had been a playground in the park since the Second World War when children, scrambling over rubble and girders on the bombsites, inspired a vision of a space in which they could learn and play.

A boy in the nineteen fifties, Terry was in the vanguard of this lucky generation. Growing up near the prison, Little Wormwood Scrubs had been his battleground. He'd flung himself down the slide, driven the iron rocking horse hard and sent the juggernaut-heavy roundabout into what passed for a spin. With other boys, he was a robber, cowboy and the cop he was to become. Blood – real and imaginary – was spilt. Their games were serious, harsh rehearsals for life.

No game that Terry had played was as serious as the death of a child.

In the glare of arc lamps the playground could be a bombsite, the swings gutted ironwork, the witch's hat a house mangled by the Luftwaffe's payload. White-suited forensics picked over the concrete and hunched around the slide.

A woman constable guarded the scene. As Terry made his way between flower beds that, dug for winter, might be fresh graves, a fine rain dampened his face and blurred the kids crowding around the gate, their high-pitched voices like geese: *'Who's dead, miss? Is there a body? Let us have a look? Miss! Miss…'*

Three decades became yesterday, the boys and girls could be Terry's mates. The kid in the baseball cap was Ray Chilton reincarnated. Ray, who had stolen a jar of gobstoppers while the owner was out back getting Terry's copy of the *Beano*. So implicating Terry in his crime. A gum-chewing girl recalled Evelyn Roper who'd rammed her hand down Terry's shorts behind the drinking fountain and claimed he'd got her 'up the duff'. The girl was eyeballing Janet the WPC as if contemplating her next meal. Terry felt the ghost of his ice-cold fear when, hazy on the facts of life, he'd submitted to blackmail and handed Roper his weekly pocket money. Nowadays, Terry dealt with the facts of death.

Five kids. Turning up his collar against the insidious drizzle, Terry brooded on how in the blink of an eye he'd be scanning their adult rap sheets. Shepherd's Bush and Acton was a brick's throw from the avenues of Kensington. Ray Chilton was behind the high walls of the Scrubs now. Aggravated burglary and resisting arrest, Terry had a scar to prove it. When this lot were too old for kiss chase, their career choice was real cops or real robbers.

'Sir, sir. What's gone on?' Gum-chewing girl shouted when Janet opened the gate for Terry. It was a school night, for Christ's sake. Didn't their parents care what they were up to? He had no idea of Stella's whereabouts. She decided whether to see him on access weekends. Twice she'd opted out. Stella was fourteen, so legally Terry had the right to keep an eye on her. In practice that was a joke.

The tent was behind the witch's hat. Terry knew this was the second fatality involving a child in weeks. He recalled pictures of the boy in a QPR strip – Robert something – who'd fallen off the slide and smashed in his skull. The boy had died on Halloween. All Souls' Eve. The night when (a bid to keep him indoors out of mischief) Terry's mum would remind him that the dead walked. Not murder, so CID had bowed out, but Terry had read Lucie's thing in the paper. When Stella was little and his mum lived nearby, he'd brought Stella here. She'd been fearless on the same slide and demanded Terry push her on the swings. *Higher. Higher!* Now a teenager (the word scared him), Stella was too old to come to harm in a playground. The ways in which she could be hurt increased daily.

The odour of faeces hit him when he flapped open the tent. The child's bowels had evacuated. His first body had been a road traffic accident. He'd gulped in air to avoid throwing up. Ten years on, in his mid-thirties, Terry could wolf down a full English before a violent crime scene.

Nothing prepared you for this.

The girl lay face up on the concrete. Her skirt was rucked at the back revealing white frilly knickers, otherwise she looked arranged. Hair coiled around her neck, white socks pulled up to her knees, a Fair Isle cardigan buttoned up. Her hands, dusted with dirt, were folded together on her lap. Like a stone saint in a church. The neatness stopped his heart. Her killer had a signature.

Terry put the little girl's age at five, perhaps six. A graze on her knee was raw pink where she'd picked at the scab. Worn soles and scuffed uppers told him she'd chased about and taken risks, no doubt in this playground. Like his Stella, this girl hadn't been afraid of getting hurt. *She should have been afraid.* The wound on her knee would never heal.

A police photographer moved around the tent, taking pictures from every angle. Each flashbulb pop made the girl appear to shift as if this was a game and she would spring into life.

'This is a rotten business, Detective Inspector Darnell.' Replacing a thermometer in its leather case, Michael Sutherland the pathologist spoke softly as if not to wake the girl. 'Death was between two and four hours ago. I'll know better back at base.' The bow tie, brogues and trilby suggested that Sutherland had been called away from a gentlemen's club circa 1932. In fact he was a Shepherd's Bush lad who'd been in Terry's class at Old Oak Primary. Where Terry could chat with strangers gleaning clues from laconic conversation, Sutherland, always a shy boy, had kept his nose in a book. Bodies were a medical phenomenon to be cut open, the organs weighed, tested and bottled. As if sharing a private language, a corpse would yield to Michael the manner of their death and the life they'd led. Chalk and cheese, Terry and Mike had been friends at school and, over the odd pint, they still were.

'Any thoughts on cause of death, Mike?'

'Judging by bruising on her nose and beneath her chin and petechial dotting in her eyes, the killer pinched her nostrils shut and suffocated her. Then for good measure crushed her neck with a crude object – a brick or stone. See those rough abrasions? The attacker applied considerable strength, the hyoid is crushed.' He indicated dark bruising and ripped skin on the girl's neck.

'Are you sure?' Terry grimaced.

'Not until I'm back.' Sutherland never speculated. Like Terry, he knew not to fall foul of counsels' searing interrogation. He confined himself to incontrovertible facts.

'Death would not have been quick.' Sutherland contemplated the girl. 'All the same, no sign of a struggle, no skin lodged in her fingernails, but look at the size of her. Sarah would have been no match for the slightest attacker.'

'Sarah?'

'There's a name tag.' Sutherland pulled a face as if to say he was smart, but not that smart. He lifted her shoulder and tipped the collar of her cardigan.

Squatting beside Sutherland, Terry read a sewn-in label. Sarah Ferris. A lock of the girl's hair flicked his hand. Soft as a cat's. He caught a whiff of shampoo. Terry could identify all kinds of smells, flowers, cleaning fluids, bodily fluids, drains and perfume. The shampoo was Boots Apple Blossom. Sarah's mum used Persil's Non-Biological. Clean clothes, clean hair. Sarah Ferris may have been out past her bedtime, but she was cared for. The reassuring smells of daily living were cut with the particulate odour of body fluids.

'I'll start tonight, if you want to be there.' Sutherland snapped shut his bag.

'I do.' He didn't.

Martin Cashman, Terry's young DC, opened the tent flap. Heftily built with stubble that defied a morning shave, the bloke had much to learn, but all the same, Terry trusted him with his life. Cashman stood aside for Sutherland to leave then gingerly entered. Cool as a cucumber with a high-rise suicide or bicycle fatality involving a lorry, he fumbled to shut the tent. No copper took a dead child in their stride.

'I've got the names and addresses for those kids.' Cashman took refuge in his notebook. 'Lee Marshall says he can't find his sister. We've had to stop him barging over here. He says she's hiding in the playground. Won't take no.' He let himself look at Sarah Ferris. Her lifeless eyes were fixed on the canvas roof as if for a dare. Cashman puffed out a sigh. *I'll blow your house down.* 'Looks like we've found her, sir.'

'What is his sister's name?' Terry wanted Lee Marshall's sister to be alive and hiding in bushes. Stupid, since Sarah belonged somewhere and in the next hour several lives would be shattered for ever.

Cashman read from his notes. 'Lee's ten. Lives with a sister aged six, his mum and a man he called Alan. In a flat on Braybrook Street.'

'And his sister's name?'

'I didn't ask.' Cashman frowned.

'What's the bet Lee's stepfather is Alan Ferris?' Terry contemplated Sarah as infinite sadness threatened to overwhelm. If Stella died, he'd kill himself, no question.

While they'd been talking, life had truly become extinct. Sarah's body was shrunken and waxy, bruised shadows shaded hollows in the cheekbones.

'A girl called Danielle Hindle claims they were chased by, listen to this boss, "The man from Abba."' Cashman tapped his pencil on the paper. 'A proper little attention-seeker... kept doing handstands while I was talking to her.'

'Kids seek attention for a reason. Did you ask Hindle what she meant?'

'I thought it was a lie...' Cashman blustered.

'I'll talk to them.' Terry gave the lad a break. This was tough even for seasoned blokes like himself. Cashman had the makings of an excellent detective.

'This Danielle said that Lee went off with a girl called Nicola. Actually Nicola was there, but she didn't confirm or deny. Like she was struck dumb. Hindle said it was Nicola's brother Robert Walsh who died in that accident on the slide there, remember?'

Terry nodded.

'...so this Danielle reckons Sarah got upset because she'd lost a bracelet. A present from this Alan. Danielle said Alan would kill Lee for not minding her. Danielle's words.' Cashman stopped.

'It's a turn of phrase. Keep it in mind. Stepfathers have a lot to answer for.' Terry lived in fear that Suzie would meet someone else who would become a dad to Stella.

'Lee thinks Sarah stayed looking for it and we've scared her.' Cashman pulled a face. 'They weren't keen on the police.'

'We live in hope of winning the hearts of babes.' Terry was wry. Musing, he added, 'Likely she's a relation of Eddie Hindle. Career burglar. He's due out of the Scrubs any time soon so lock your doors.'

The photographer's flash caused a glint on the child's wrist. Peeping out from the cuff of the cardigan was a silver dog. Terry said, 'Sarah found her charm bracelet.'

Cashman's radio crackled. After an interchange with the station, he said, 'Sarah Ferris has the same address as Lee Marshall.'

'Let's go.'

At the park gate, Terry heard his name called.

'A girl's been murdered, DI Darnell, care to confirm?' Lucie was always first on a scene. The intrepid reporter's MO was to fish for facts by uttering falsities to be affirmed or denied. Regardless of either, she'd file a story.

'Throw this cordon wider! Get this lot backed up to the bridge,' Terry hissed at Cashman. He was thankful that the rain had stopped. Forensics needed the weather on their side. A full-blown thunderstorm wouldn't have deterred Lucie May.

'Give me a statement, Inspector Terence!' Lucie beseeched as if harmless.

'I have to get my sister.' The boy in the baseball cap.

'Lee, is it?' Terry turned his back on Lucie.

'Can I go in the playground? She'll think she's in trouble. I won't go near there.' The boy jerked a thumb at the tent. The other children crowded around him.

'Not right now, Lee.' Terry took in the little gang. 'Have you been playing here this afternoon?'

'Only after school.' The gum-chewer who, Terry guessed, was Danielle Hindle, hung on Lee's arm. With her other hand she yanked on the gum between her teeth, pulled it to a string, spun it around her finger and biting it off resumed chewing. A seamless exercise. He met penetrating green eyes.

'Danielle Hindle?'

The girl offered a 'what's it to you?' shrug.

'I'm not interested in whether you lot were bunking off. Where were you this afternoon?' Terry smiled. He was surprised when Danielle smiled back.

'We *were* at school. We come after,' Danielle asserted.

'Can I get my sister?' Lee pleaded.

'What's your sister's name, son?' Terry loathed the tightrope between truth and concealment.

'Sarah.'

'Sarah…?'

'Sarah Ferris.'

'She isn't called the same as Lee cos his Mum had a baby with another man.' Danielle made this sound rude.

'Janet's got the car, guv.' Despite the Arctic temperature, there was a sheen of perspiration on Cashman's forehead. Lucie had given him a hard time.

'Sir, I need to—' Lee started.

Danielle yanked his arm. 'You can't, Lee, all right? Sarah is fine, the policeman said!'

The policeman hadn't said, but Terry wasn't about to contradict her.

'What about the man?' One of the small boys, his crew cut and crumpled shirt untucked, hung upside down from the railings. Danielle dragged him off. Terry saw a family likeness, ski-jump nose, freckles, but the brother hadn't been blessed with eyes like a tiger.

A stillness descended on the group.

'The man from Abba that you told the constable about?' Terry prompted.

'Jase, tell him!' Taking her hand off Lee Marshall's arm Danielle gave her brother a shove. 'Don't lie!'

'He was in the playground.' The boy reached for the railing. Danielle slapped him off.

'Can you describe him to me, Jason?' They needed a photofit and fast. Terry didn't agree with Cashman that Danielle had lied about the man. In his experience kids rarely lied about important stuff. Attention seekers were a copper's friend.

'He's got long slimy hair and a beard with bits,' Danielle said. 'Like Benny in Abba. Like him.' She fixed on Cashman.

Cashman's face was a picture, at another time it would have been funny that he'd been compared to the Swedish pop star on a very bad day. Tonight nothing was funny.

'He's got on a dirty blue duffel coat and jeans.' Danielle was disapproving.

'You saw him here this afternoon?' Cashman coaxed.

'Jason did. He's my brother,' Danielle said. 'We ran.'

'He killed Robbie!' Jason said.

'Shut up, Jason!' Danielle punched the boy.

'Robbie?' Terry knew who Robbie was, but he wanted to hear it from them.

'Robbie is Nicky's brother. Last week we had a funeral in the playground.' Danielle was a gift.

'And blood!' Jason was suspended from the railings.

'Blood?' Cashman homed in.

'He's lying. My dad's the only one who listens to him.' Danielle pulled Jason off the railings again and held him in a police officer's disarming grip. Terry resisted stopping her, he wanted Danielle Hindle on his side.

'Danielle says he's lonely.' This from the other girl.

'That's Nicola.' Danielle was at his elbow.

Sister of the dead boy. Terry was struck by the girl's detached air as if she didn't care, as if life was incidental. 'He's a child molester.'

'How do you know that, Nicola?' Terry was sharp. The investigation was gaining traction.

'Danielle says he murdered my brother.' Nicola reacted with surprise at her own words.

'Because it's true.' Danielle was wrapping her gum in silver paper. She was no litterbug.

'Has he mol— hurt any of you?' Terry was looking at Nicola, but she'd resumed her silence.

'Not yet, but he will.' Danielle slipped the gum in her pocket. 'Where's Sarah? If she's hiding, she'd be here by now.'

'I want you all to work with me, OK? That means going home now. We've got your addresses, I'll be visiting each of you.' Danielle had the same intense expression as Stella when – if Suzie was nowhere near – Terry used to tell her case stories. When Stella had wanted to be a detective like him.

'Is it true that a little girl has been murdered?'

Shit.

Silently Terry cursed Martin Cashman for not cuffing Lucie and bundling her into a van.

'There'll be a briefing later!' he informed the reporters. He didn't need the likes of Lucie fire-breathing down his neck. Ex-Beatle John Lennon had been murdered in New York the night before. In the UK it was today's news and Terry hoped Lennon's death might draw the heat from this case.

'I'm not going nowhere without my sister!' A proper little bovver boy, Lee looked ready to punch Terry.

'Have you lost your sister?' Lucie thrust forward her Dictaphone. 'What's her name, what's *your* name, darling?'

'Sarah…' Lee told her.

'Leave!' Terry instructed Lucie, who in turn fixed on his flies. 'Lee, the best thing you can do is leave Sarah to us. Come on, lad, I'll give you a lift home. You did your best. We'll handle it from here.' He had a brainwave. 'Danielle, please would you get your friends to go home? Be my assistant?'

'Right, go or I'll arrest you all,' Danielle Hindle told her crew. Even Lucie baulked. Linking arms with Nicola Walsh, Danielle tugged at the sleeve of Lee's Harrington jacket. 'Come on, Lee, I'll take you home.'

'Lee's going to show me where he lives,' Terry said.

In the car, Terry switched off the police radio in case anything about Sarah came over. Staring at his lap, Lee looked too blitzed to take in anything.

Every police officer dreaded informing people of the fatality of a loved one. Top of that list was breaking the news to parents that their child was dead. Robert Walsh's death had been an accident so Terry wasn't involved. But murder put him at ground zero. As senior investigating officer, Terry could delegate the task, but he knew that a victim's family was key to an investigation. He needed to meet those who had mattered to Sarah. He wanted to see her home and learn about her everyday life. He must discover what and who she'd liked. Who hadn't liked her. Few murders are committed by a stranger. While they discovered if the man from Abba stalked the minds of kids or was a flesh-and-blood suspect, Terry was on the alert for the slightest sign that someone in Sarah Ferris's family already knew that she was dead.

Braybrook Street was a row of houses by Wormwood Scrubs Common. By day the Scrubs was a place to kick a ball and walk the dog. At night it was a yawning void wrought with dread possibility.

Fourteen years ago, on the day that Stella was born, three police officers were murdered by an armed gang near where Cashman parked up. Terry had been going to Hammersmith Hospital to see baby Stella when he was recalled to duty. He had joined a fingertip search on the common. His mum had kept a newspaper photo of a line of shirt-sleeved constables, Terry nearest the lens, crawling over summer-parched grass. Sick at heart – as he was now – Terry had known that he'd find nothing to bring the dead officers – dads like himself – back to life. Suzie never forgave him for not seeing their child. Terry reckoned that along with the three officers, his marriage died on 12 August 1966.

'We live upstairs.' Lee let them into a pebble-dashed house with a trim front garden. A man's racing bike, the front wheel removed, was chained to a drainpipe by the door.

The hallway, lined with creased woodchip wallpaper, reeked of congealed fat. In Terry's childhood house around the corner, the equivalent door had led into the lounge with a kitchen beyond. Lee's family lived in the upstairs flat which, Terry supposed, must be a squeeze for four. *No longer four.* They waited while Lee unlocked a door on the landing.

Terry sniffed. Shepherd's pie. His favourite when his mum had cooked it. Nowadays he made do with shop-bought. No one in this flat would be eating supper tonight. He imagined whisking the boy down the stairs, across the park to the playground where they'd find Sarah Ferris perched on a swing wearing her charm bracelet. *Safe and sound.* So much for lucky charms.

'Take us to your mum and dad, Lee,' he said.

'Alan's not my dad. My dad's dead,' Lee retorted.

Inside, Terry heard the theme tune for *Dallas* from a television.

'Say I didn't mean to do it.' Lee barred their way.

'Do what, Lee?' Terry kept his eyes on the boy. 'What didn't you mean to do?'

'Nothing. Say I did *nothing*!'

'Did you do nothing?' Kids killed their siblings. Had the girl got on her big brother's nerves? The unwanted half sister. Had Lee Marshall been anxious to get into the playground to find his sister as a ruse to look innocent? Terry's gut told him no.

'Nicky was scared so…' Eyes brimming. Lee clenched his lip between his teeth. 'It's my fault.'

Terry let himself breathe. 'Lee, why don't you go up to your bedroom while we have a word with your mum and... and Alan.'

'He'll kill me.' Lee was factual.

'We're the police, lad. Your stepfather can't hurt you.' Terry hoped that was true. Lee refused to move.

In the kitchen there was barely room for a table and chairs. Blinking in the strip light, Terry kicked something. He'd upset a cat's dish of milk. The liquid absorbed into the sheet of newspaper beneath. When he lifted his shoe, the paper stuck to it. The *Sun*. Page three. He ripped it away and, scrunching it up, saw nowhere to throw it. He placed it on the table.

Lee had a cloth and was wiping up the milk. Terry wondered what else the boy was used to mopping up.

'You're late, Lee, love.' In spray-on jeans and a pink cotton shirt knotted at the waist, Farrah Fawcett-Majors banged a plate of shepherd's pie and cauliflower onto the table. She whipped away the tea towel, sending the plate to the edge. Lee caught it. Terry glimpsed a packet of Yeoman's instant mash on the counter. His mum had used real potatoes.

'Who are you?' Lee's mother whisked the tea towel.

'Jesus, Cathy, d'you have to ask! They're police.' A pouty Elvis, a black cowlick over his forehead, wandered in from an adjoining room where Terry could now hear Lennon's 'Imagine'. 'What's Laughing Boy done now?'

Terry's mum had been Scottish. Since her death it meant that he warmed to anyone with the accent. Not this time.

'Is there somewhere we could go, Cathy, Alan?' Terry would rather not talk in a room in which there were knives.

'What's he done?' Elvis went serious.

'This way.' As she passed, Terry caught Cathy Ferris's perfume. Avon's Sweet Honesty. When he'd been shopping for Stella's thirteenth birthday last summer, the woman in Boots had suggested it. Perfect for the new teenager. Stella had seemed pleased, but Suzie called it 'fuddy-duddy'. Thinking of Suzie, Terry realized that it wasn't Farrah Fawcett-Majors who Cathy Ferris reminded him of, it was his ex-wife.

'Lee, go up to your room,' Terry murmured to the boy.

'He can stay and hear it for himself!' Alan Ferris frogmarched his stepson to a black leather couch (Alan's dowry, Terry guessed) and, prodding Lee's chest, propelled him backwards. Lee clasped at the arm as if anchoring himself on a stormy sea. Alan took the matching armchair and topped up a tankard from a bottle of Double Diamond, taking a slug.

The television was showing the assassinated Beatle's distraught fans at a candle-lit vigil outside his apartment block. Terry was more of an early Beatles man, he'd danced to 'Twist and Shout' down the Hammersmith Palais. Right now, it wasn't easy to imagine anything at all.

Cashman found the remote and muted the bit about imagining there was no heaven.

'If he's been shoplifting, throw the book at him.' Alan Ferris caught his wife's expression. 'He has to learn. You spoil him.'

'If anyone spoils anyone, it's you giving Sarah expensive jewellery.' Cathy Ferris sounded weary of a well-worn interchange.

At the mention of Sarah there was a beat.

'Where is Sarah?' Alan tipped the bottle at Lee.

'Actually, I'm really sorry to—' Terry spoke to Cathy Ferris.

'*Where* is she?' Alan lunged at his stepson. Cashman manoeuvred Ferris back into his chair. So far, apart from Benny in Abba, Terry's money was on the loving father.

'I'm sorry to tell you that the body of a little girl fitting Sarah's description has been found in Little Wormwood Scrubs Park. The child is wearing a skirt. A label with the name "Sarah Ferris" is sewn into the child's cardigan...'

Ferris was up out of his chair. He swung a fist at the wall, punching so hard that his knuckles split. His hand ran with blood.

Cashman and Terry wrestled him back into his chair. There was an animal sound, long and high. Cathy Ferris bent double as if in agony.

Lee fluttered about her. 'Don't, Mum. Don't. It's all right. It's OK.'

'I told her to keep off that slide. I told you, Lee.' The words were a dreadful keening.

'I'm sure she listened,' Terry said.

Abruptly, Cathy wiped at her eyes. 'It's a mistake! Lee brought Sarah home. She's asleep upstairs.'

Keeping an eye on Alan Ferris, Terry nodded at Cashman to go and see. He'd ride a stripping down from his boss if Sarah was curled up in bed. Kids swapped clothes. He wanted to be wrong. Ferris was nursing his fist. Terry gave him his handkerchief. As he took it from him, their eyes met. The man knew his daughter wasn't in her bedroom. Was that parental instinct or something darker?

Cashman was back, Janet with him. Their faces said it.

'See, she's all tucked up. Now go away and leave us alone. *Out!*' Cathy hugged herself.

'Cathy, Sarah is not there.' Terry kept his voice even.

'They've got her in the playground.' Lee shook violently. Janet guided his mother to the couch. From somewhere she'd found blankets which she draped over Cathy and Lee's shoulders. From the kitchen, Terry heard the kettle.

'Alan, I'm sorry but we need you to provide identification. Janet will stay with Cathy and Lee.'

'I'll get Danielle.' Lee flung off the blanket and was out of the door before anyone could stop him.

'Sarah is good at sports,' Cathy Ferris said. 'Long jump like her brother, and catching. Her teacher says she is the…' The past tense came down like night. Defeated, Cathy was stranded in a life that had cut loose from its moorings.

'How?' Alan Ferris bound Terry's hanky around his fingers.

At last the question. Terry braced himself. Ferris's dramatics could be a ruse to deflect suspicion. A fractured hand was nothing compared to life meaning life. He didn't sugar the pill. In some concession, he let three seconds pass then, 'Sarah was murdered.'

Chapter Seven

2019

'Did your dad dying make you follow his footsteps and become a detective?' In a tight pink skirt suit, blouse revealing a fan of creases converging to her cleavage, Lucie May was, as she'd declared when she'd breezed into Stella's office in knee-high spiky boots that added to her six feet, 'dressed to *kill*!'

'It wasn't a decision. I solved a murder case that my dad had stored in his attic. It went from there.' A bus drifted past the window. Stella caught the eye of a bald man with glasses on the top deck. She looked away first.

Lucie May scribbled shorthand in her journalist's notebook. There was already writing. Stella wouldn't put it past Lucie to have written Stella's replies on the way to the office. For the umpteenth time that morning, Stella regretted agreeing to the interview for the *Daily Mirror*. Carrie Philips would arrive in an hour. Philips and Lucie must not meet.

It was three years since Clean Slate had increased staff and office space to accommodate the detective service, specifically cold case murders. However, recently there'd been a dearth of deaths (Jack's joke) so they'd relied on bread and butter work: witness statements, tracing heirs and loved ones and background checks for employers. Loath to fan the flames of domestic turmoil, Stella stopped at divorce surveillance. The interview had been intended to drum up business, but yesterday Stella had met Carrie Philips. She should have put Lucie off. Plus Stella was tired of the father's footsteps hook. Terry Darnell died seven years ago, was she still following him?

The door opened and Beverly poked her head in. 'They've delivered the dry ice to here! I tried to redirect them to the warehouse, but they'll only go to what's on the docket.'

'It's fine, Bev.' Stella was happier discussing cleaning products. 'I asked them to send the nine millilitre pellets here. For emergencies. We'll store them in the freezer outside the conference room.'

'Copy that.' Beverly's head vanished.

'You never know when you need dry ice!' Lucie cackled. 'I can see you rising out of the clouds to "Rule Britannia" on a Wurlitzer!'

'It's for cryogenic cleaning.' Stella hastened to stop Lucie running with the image. 'Instead of chemicals.'

'Back to murder!' Rapping her retractable pencil on the pad, Lucie rolled her eyes. 'C'mon, dude, give me spice and grit! Daddy was your hero then ker-plonk, he toppled off his pedestal! Before he died he tried to call you, but you'd changed your number without telling him so you never said goodbye. Milk it, bubs! Get readers sobbing into Kleenexes, not checking if it's time for *EastEnders*!'

'The idea is to attract cold case clients. Not make them cry.' Stella couldn't bear to be reminded that for the last months of Terry's life, she'd hardly spoken to him.

'Emotion is the driver.' Lucie was pencil ready. 'Trot on, ducks!'

'When I was eighteen Dad sent me a police application form and a postal order to buy something nice,' Stella obliged.

'What did you buy?'

'A set of cleaning equipment. Mum tore up the form.' Stella had said this in another interview she'd done for the local paper. It was old news. 'The next day I got my first job.' She'd wanted to be a Met detective until she was seven when her parents divorced. She didn't tell Lucie that her mum warned that Stella would be on her own for life if she joined the force. Her mum and Lucie May were best enemies (as opposed to friends). Jack put this down to being in love with the same man.

'You wanted to be a detective when you were a kid. You dumped the ambition when your mum dumped Terry.' Lucie was writing as if to dictation. 'Did he share teccy tips with you?'

'When I was four, we got a cadaver dog. An Alsatian. I got sent to the headteacher for telling kids that the dog found corpses.' Stella had sat cross-legged on cold lino in the head's office writing out the times-table on a length of bus ticket roll that Miss Swan made a thing of cadging off conductors. She'd wondered why she was in trouble for telling the truth.

'Way to go!' Lucie May's pencil was a blur on the paper.

'Don't put that!' Stella's mother crashed into the room as if on a police raid. When Clean Slate was a start-up operating from Stella's bedroom, Suzie Darnell had handled admin while Stella cleaned. Nowadays Suzie ran the customer database and offered caustic opinions without waiting to be asked.

'Did Terry show you a dead body?' Lucie paid Suzie no attention and when Stella shook her head was businesslike: 'We'll say he did.'

'He would have if the opportunity had arisen,' Suzie said. And then as if referring to pocket money or Easter eggs, 'Terry robbed Stella of her childhood.'

'Yesss!' Lucie had struck gold.

'That's fake news!' Stella was appalled. Suzie described her marriage to Terry as a wrong turning. Jack said that Terry was the love of Suzie's life. In Lucie's hearing Suzie would never concede anything positive about Terry. Keeping to safer ground, Stella embarked on a sales spiel. 'I promise a rapid response to "death and chaos" situations. I sanitize drug dens, mortuaries and scenes of long-term death and suicide. I've got certificates in crime scene clean-up and hypodermic needle collection, deodorizing and the removal of contaminated flooring. I can't turn the clock back, but I can restore order.'

'You can't turn the clock back, but you can keep it ticking. Coo-ell!' Lucie crowed. 'Wait. What did I say? You'll drive the *Mirror*'s readers to suicide or have them fleeing to a drug den if I write this. They hate swearing and nasty subjects.'

'...my passions are deep cleaning, dog walking and dinner with friends.' Stella had learnt that filibustering kept Lucie at bay.

'Less of the "I".' Suzie waggled a finger at her daughter. 'You and Jack are a team!'

'Jack prefers to be anonymous.' Stella was patient. Her mother adored Jack.

'Don't encourage that! With those looks and charm, he's your poster boy!' Lucie shrieked.

Suzie Darnell slapped the door jamb. 'Stell, I'll see you Sunday. Will Jack bring the kiddies?'

'No.' A constant question, although her mum knew that Jack's ex had forbidden him to let Stella see his twins. Milly and Justin would be three in June. That fact would give Lucie grit and spice.

'How's it going as the wicked stepmother?' Lucie enquired sweetly.

'Stella, sorry to bother you.' It was Trudy Wates, her PA.

'"The Disinfecting Detective!"' Lucie chirped merrily. 'Tell me about your most recent cleaning scene. Was it a good old-fashioned murder?'

'No.' Stella would be in serious trouble with Cashman if she discussed her trip to Winchcombe. She smiled at Trudy. 'Yes?'

'Carrie Philips is in reception. She's early.'

'The daughter of the murderer?' Lucie's pencil was a dart ready to aim.

'No.' Stella only lied on special occasions.

Chapter Eight

2019

At last the barcode took and an image of a Bourbon biscuit packet popped up on the screen. Jack preferred a real assistant, but the queue to the till stretched to the back of the shop and he was determined to keep pace with technological change. One day there would be no people and if he couldn't self-checkout he'd have no biscuits.

On a charm offensive with Stella's PA, Jack was bringing biscuits for the meeting. The Sainsbury's Local used to be the minimart owned by Dariusz Adomek, Clean Slate's friend. Dariusz sold it last year and had returned to his native Poland. Jack was pleased that Dariusz had profited by the sale, but missed their chats. Unlike this machine, Dariusz had a heart and didn't beep.

Stella's office was fronted by a black door (Lucie May called it Downing Street) set between the Sainsbury's and a dry cleaner's. Jack had to say his name twice before Trudy buzzed him in. She didn't like him. Stella said he was imagining it. Jackie said Trudy was protective of Stella's time. Trudy was nothing if not efficient. It was this that Jack disliked. Efficiency left no room for spontaneity which was where, Jack believed, real life was found. He was disgruntled at how things had turned out because it was him who'd suggested Stella free up Jackie to manage the detective business and get a new PA. No one questioned why Stella should need protecting from Jack. Stella would say he was over sensitive. (Actually, non-judgemental, she'd never say that, but still Jack made Stella his conscience.) Trudy had been at Clean Slate since last autumn and was, as Beverly put it, 'magic'. Heigh ho.

The fragrance of a lavender plug-in caught his nostrils on the stairs. Since Stella had taken over the building, she'd had the hall and staircase decorated rosy white. Gone was the threadbare lino in favour of a carpet that didn't show stains. Not that stains had a chance to show themselves before Stella eradicated them.

On the landing outside reception, Jack prepared a smile. He'd rather head on up to the meeting, but it wouldn't do to bypass Trudy. Maybe she did like him and it was him that wasn't keen on her.

'How's it fadging?' Beaming, Jack took loping strides into the office, smacking his hands as if cold. Realizing this might imply criticism of the temperature – Trudy's remit – he unbuttoned his coat. 'It's lovely and warm in here!'

'The heating's been off. I've just mended the thermostat.' Pounding at top speed on her keyboard, Trudy didn't pause. Jack saw she wore a big woolly scarf.

'Well done! Brrr!' Tied in a knot of his own making, he knew he'd done nothing to make Trudy comfortable around him.

'They're upstairs.' Trudy looked up with a sudden smile, her eyes inscrutable behind reactive lensed glasses. She fixed her gaze on his chest. Jack attributed avoidance of eye contact to shyness, but Trudy had got the job because she was a no-nonsense woman, deft at defusing difficult customers and judging excellent cleaning operatives. Short, mid-forties, her pale translucent complexion suggested oxygen starvation although she worked long hours and had seemingly boundless energy.

'I brought biscuits!' Jack cried.

'Beverly got them.' Trudy cracked open a stapler and extracted a bar of staples from a tray in her desk, slotting them in as if loading a gun.

'You can't have too many biscuits.' He remained hearty.

'You cannot,' Trudy agreed.

Jack thought that Trudy could do with the whole packet. Thin as a rail, he suspected she had an eating disorder. On the team night out, she'd had no more than a starter portion of Caesar salad. Given to off-the-wall deductions, Beverly had put it down to Trudy being left-handed. Bev had said that like her brother, no one would have taught Trudy to hold a fork. Whatever the truth of this, right now Trudy was jotting something down with her right hand so that blew Bev's theory from the water.

'Carrie Philips is here.' Trudy resumed typing. 'You just missed that reporter.'

'Oh! Right.' Jack had thought he was early – he punched the air, the gesture of a man totally on top of things – and fled upstairs. He was sorry not to see Lucie, then annoyed with himself for thinking that she'd have protected him from Trudy. Ludicrous.

Clean Slate's top floor was above the old mini-mart and the dry cleaner's. A laminated notice on a door read 'Murder Incident Room'.

'Carrie is in the loo.' Beverly patted the chair next to her. Just thirty and recently married, she was perpetually optimistic. Initially a byword in scatterbrained inefficiency, over the years under Jackie's tutelage, she had become sharp as a knife. Beverly covered all bases and missed nothing.

'Sorry I'm late, I was chatting with Trudy.' That hardly described their cool exchange.

'Good.' Stella wanted him to like Trudy. 'You're not late, Carrie was early.'

On an oval table were jugs of water in which floated slices of lemon (Trudy's touch), glasses, a plate of Bourbon biscuits, a flask of coffee and Clean Slate branded mugs. In the centre, like a miniature spaceship, was a conference call telephone. Stella sat at one end with Beverly at her right. Two bulging files at the other end and a steaming mug of some kind of fruit tea (another Trudy innovation) signalled Carrie Philips' place. A fan of appropriate stationery, Stella had one of Terry's unused police notebooks.

'Twins OK?' Stella asked Jack. 'Trudy said Justin was off colour.'

Jack felt a frisson of shame. One, Trudy had remembered his son had missed a day of nursery. Two, even though she'd only seen them once as babies, Stella always enquired after the twins. He inwardly tsked for his own ungenerous thoughts.

'Fine!' He put his biscuits beside the latest Clean Slate cleaning brochure displayed on a shelf unit by the door and sat next to Beverly. Immediately he sprang to his feet as the door opened and Stella introduced him to Carrie Philips.

Nodding at him, Carrie ignored his outstretched hand. Jack saw strain and grief in the lines around her mouth and creasing her forehead. She looked older than mid-twenties, her father's imprisonment for murder had piled on years. Jack didn't think her rude. She looked windswept as if her father's life sentence had tumbleweeded her far beyond the prosaic business of niceties.

'Daddy didn't do it.' Blowing on her tea, Carrie sent up a puff of fragrant steam. 'You're all thinking, "Yeah, she would say that" – that's what the police think.' She flourished a yellow legal pad and scribbled a heading at the top.

'We keep an open mind,' Stella said. 'Please tell us your take on what happened.'

'Dad left his shop and drove home.' Carrie's plodding delivery suggested she'd related her story many times. 'Where you were yesterday.' She scowled at Stella as if Stella had trespassed. 'He found that woman's body in the sitting room. She'd been stabbed with a knife. The police called it frenzied. Daddy had to get rid of the body.' Carrie drank some tea. Jack saw her hand tremble when she replaced the mug on the table. Carrie was left-handed. She too was thin as a pin. He glanced at Beverly. But her theories flapped in the wind and doubtless she'd abandoned her view that feeding yourself was easier with the right hand. For himself Jack noted that Carrie's pen had green ink which he associated with mental instability.

'Why didn't he call the police?' A detective's daughter, Stella would say that. Preferring to exist under the legal radar, the police had never been Jack's first resort.

'He panicked. They'd think he did it. He was right because they did think that! He had to wrap her in plastic sheeting to stop blood getting everywhere. The only place he could dump her was that drain. He had a huge amount of cleaning up to do.' Outrage flitted across her face as if by leaving a body behind, the murderer had caused untold inconvenience. 'And he had to move her car. She left it by the war memorial.'

It seemed that Rachel Cater had thoroughly inconvenienced her father.

'Did your father know the victim?' Stella swished to a fresh page. Jack had no trouble picturing Stella as a high-ranking Met officer like her dad.

'I knew nothing until the police found the body.' Carrie took a biscuit but didn't eat it.

'Did your father know the victim?' Stella asked the question as if for the first time.

It wouldn't be out of the question for the client to be the murderer. For now, Jack shelved this option. Stella said he complicated things.

'You know he did!'

'I want to hear it from you.' Stella was sexy when she was stern.

'She was his PA at the auctioneer's.' Carrie Philips fiddled with a fearsome lime green pendant shaped like a rugby ball that hung around her neck like a penance. 'She was sleeping with him.'

'How long for?' Mini Stella, Beverly, was also using a police notebook.

'A month maybe. My mum called her a man-eater.' She pursed her lips as if this wrapped it up. An untruth which Carrie Philips would know they could confirm. According to the trial reports, her father had been seeing Rachel Cater for over six months.

'Christopher Philips confessed.' Stella faced her.

'He didn't do it.' Carrie smouldered. 'The police lied.'

'How did the police lie?' Stella would take on a case that detectives – her dad – had not solved. Jack knew she'd draw the line at any suggestion of a police cover-up.

'That Cater woman was going to tell my mum that Daddy was leaving her. The cow!' Carrie was like a fizzing fuse wire.

'How did the police lie?' Stella persisted.

'They're only interested in targets.' Carrie took another biscuit although she hadn't eaten the first one.

'Why couldn't your father tell your mother he was leaving?' Logical and unassuming, Stella believed that what will be, will be. When Cashman had dumped her to return to his wife Stella had accepted it. Yet Jack suspected she'd minded. He felt for Rachel Cater that Philips had dragged his heels ending his marriage. Feeling powerless, she'd taken matters into her own hands and gone to tell his wife. A decision that proved fatal. Jack had many times imagined telling Cashman where to go. *Get a grip*. Stella hadn't seen the man for months. As if she could read his thoughts, he caught Stella looking at him. Their gaze locked. Jack felt a stir of desire and grabbed a biscuit. When he looked again Stella was frowning at her notebook, a faint flush reddening her cheeks. Sometimes they were entirely in accord.

'He'd never leave my mother. Daddy wanted to end it with Cater. She went nuts, he had to fight her off and he stabbed her in self-defence. The police didn't believe him.'

'Are you saying that he did kill Rachel Cater?'

'I'm not *saying* anything.' Carrie tipped back in her chair, a sulky teenager. Perhaps catching what she had said, 'He didn't murder her. He's not like that.'

'You're saying that Rachel Cater came armed with the knife?' Terry had taught Stella to interject. *Don't let a subject tell a story their way. Surprise them into admission.*

'Where else did she get it?' Cater shrugged.

'Did she plan to kill your mother?' Jack thought that one thing you could find in most houses was a knife.

'Yes, of course. Obviously.'

'Why obviously?' asked Jack.

'It just is.' The sulky teen again.

'Your mother was seen on CCTV in London. How did Rachel Cater gain entry to the house?' Mindful of safety, Stella would be nervous of the chair-tipping. If it gave way Carrie would whack her head on the window sill.

'She'll have gone through Daddy's private possessions, found his key and sneaked in to confront my mother. Then the real killer called. Cater opened the door. She pretended she was Mrs Philips and got herself murdered.' Carrie flew forward on the chair. 'Aren't you listening, the point is my father *wasn't there*!'

'Rachel Cater was your father's secretary – she had a legitimate reason to have his key.' Stella continued writing in her notebook. 'My PA has mine. Isn't it an incredible coincidence that your father's mistress was there at the same time as the murderer?'

'Call it what you like.' Carrie told the conference phone as if there were unseen listeners. The police didn't care that *she* seduced *him*!'

'It's not an offence to have a relationship with a colleague.' Jack tried not to look at Stella. 'Painful if there are others involved, of course.'

'They were taking a risk. Clients, and other staff could think it unprofessional,' Stella said. 'But sometimes it's unavoidable.'

Stella didn't catch his eye this time, but he felt her awareness of him as if her fingers were brushing his skin, unzipping him...

Jack's reverie broke. Did Stella think their own relationship was unprofessional? Was six months a cooling-off point? Was she dropping him a hint that they should cool it?

'Dad would never have left me.' Carrie stated fact.

'Leave you?' Jack barked. 'It was your mother who was betrayed.'

'None of this is the point. Which is,' Carrie banged the table, 'Daddy wasn't there!'

'Why did he say he was there?' Stella didn't try to temper the woman's temper.

'Just find out who killed Cater and get my dad out of prison.' Carrie shook her head as if they were all idiots and she was wasting her time.

Jack felt a wash of disappointment. He loved working with Stella, he wanted this case to be 'real' so that they could be a team in more ways than one. When Stella had told him about her encounter with Carrie Philips at the crime scene clean-up, he'd hoped that it wasn't simply that the woman couldn't accept that her father had committed the worst of crimes. He wanted it to be a miscarriage of justice. Fair enough to believe your father incapable of murder. Stella would have trouble thinking Terry could murder. Jack, on the other hand, had spent several years convinced that his father had killed his mother, so couldn't empathize. He swallowed hard. At nearly three, Milly was gifted with rapier perception, would she ever doubt him as he had doubted his father?

'He disposed of the body. Why go to lengths to cover up a murder that he didn't do? Was he protecting someone? Your mother, for instance?' Stella trod where angels feared to go.

'Why would he?' Carrie snarled. 'No. Lucky for her – she's always had luck – she has an alibi.'

'Did anyone see Rachel arrive at the house? Did she come there alone or with your father perhaps?' Stella didn't kowtow to clients.

'There were no witnesses. Cater's prints were on the finger plate, meaning she let herself in.'

'When did they find the body?' Jack wanted to hear how Carrie told it.

'Some three months later. Rachel Cater's watch smashed against the wall of the shaft. It gave the date and time of the murder. The thirteenth of May at four-thirty.' She murmured, 'Daddy was careful not to hurt her.'

Bully for Daddy, Jack thought.

'Did anyone know Cater and your father were involved?' he asked.

'No. She put fake meetings in his diary. Dentist, a visit to assess an antique. Bitch!' Carrie exclaimed as if this was news to her. 'Cater told Carol and Ian – they work there and are really nice – that Dad was training her up. Liar! She was after him from the start.'

'How do you know?' Stella probed.

'It's obvious. She was on the shelf, desperate to have babies. It came out in court. Daddy was a sitting duck!'

'The police said that your father forgot to take out the phone battery. It was how they found the body,' Beverly said.

'Isn't that proof?' Carrie was triumphant. 'If he'd wanted to murder her, he'd have made sure they didn't find her.'

No one pointed out that Chris Philips had gone to enormous lengths to hide Rachel Cater's body. But for one slip it was likely that Rachel Cater would never have been found.

'She bought disposable phones – burners, criminals call them – so that they could call each other. How sick is that?'

'Are you sure that your mother didn't know about Rachel Cater?' Stella asked the question forming in Jack's mind.

'Neither of us knew until she told us. It was a blinking bombshell!'

Belatedly – Jack had been pondering on when he'd last heard the word 'blinking' – he queried, '"She"? You mean "he", your father?'

'No, my mother… yes, *he* that's what I meant.' She tutted as if cross with herself. 'Cater accidentally on purpose rang her cousin on the secret phone. She said that it was a friend's phone, but her cousin had taken down the number. When she remembered this, she gave it to the police. They traced it to where it was when in powered down. In our garage.'

Carrie didn't look pleased by this. She appeared oblivious to the fact that Rachel Cater had been brutally murdered by someone, if not Christopher Philips. While it would be shocking to discover that her father had betrayed her mother and had quite possibly killed his mistress, still Carrie might have had some compassion for the victim. Had Carrie murdered Rachel Cater in blind jealousy? Had Christopher accidentally put himself in pole position as prime suspect? Why court discovery by hiring Clean Slate? If Carrie depended on them failing, she hadn't bargained on Jack's photographic memory and Stella's bloodhound nose.

'When they found the corpse, the police arrested my parents.'

'Why was your mother arrested? Unless the pathologist was wrong about the time of death, she had an alibi,' Beverly chipped in.

'Alibis can be faked.' Carrie didn't expand.

'Miss Philips, would you like more tea?' Beverly nodded at the empty mug.

'No thanks.' Carrie smiled. The smile didn't reach her eyes, yet Jack judged it genuine. She looked wary, as if of danger. Carrie was at the end of her tether. Whatever she was hiding – Jack was convinced there was something – Clean Slate was her last resort. He leaned forward, intending to indicate that Carrie's last resort was a good one.

'What I've said is what Dad said at his trial. But I think this is what happened.' Carrie took a third Bourbon, this time holding it like a conch that gave her the floor. 'Dad found Cater dead and yes, he was protecting someone. My mother! He thinks that prison would kill Mum. He perjured himself.' She nibbled the biscuit, not chewing, but seeming to compress it against the roof of her mouth with her tongue. 'My mother hasn't visited Dad since he was put in there. She's got police protection, would you believe? Dad is innocent!' She chomped the rest of the Bourbon and smacked off crumbs. Job done.

'Your father hid a murder victim and hampered the police search. That's not legal.' Stella spoke without judgement.

The wary look again.

Jack asked, 'Could someone at the auctioneer's have discovered their relationship? Perhaps Carol or Ian were jealous of Rachel for being your father's favourite?'

'It wasn't a relationship. He planned to end it. He doesn't have favourites. Only me.' Carrie took another biscuit, hoarding it with the other two. A sign that she lacked love? 'Officer Cashman told me that no one else had motive. Once the Gloucestershire police found her in the shaft they stopped looking.'

'Cashman!' Jack uttered in a spray of biscuit crumbs. 'Why was he involved?'

'Because of my... it was nothing to do with him.' Carrie Philips subsided with a huff.

Jack stared at his cooling coffee. If they took the case Stella would see Cashman. Lucie May had warned Jack that 'Cashback's wife had dumped him.' (Lucie had names for everyone.) 'Be on your toes, Jackanory, he'll want to warm his cockles at Stella's fire.'

'Why do you think your mother killed Rachel Cater?' Stella didn't pick up the mention of Cashman. Why not?

'She was in London.' Beverly pressed the point home.

'My mother is the jealous type. Never get on the wrong side of her. Chief Superintendent Cashman knows perfectly well that she did it.' Carrie didn't answer the question.

'He doesn't know.' Stella laid down her pen.

Jack drank cold coffee. There was only one way Stella knew what Cashman thought. She had talked to him.

Chapter Nine

1980

'I didn't do nothing. I love those kids.'

'You love them so much you were skulking in their playground after dark. Why were you there, Derek?' Cashman asked.

'This is a mistake,' said Derek Parsley. 'It's not fair.'

'We've got witnesses say you were there, Derek,' Cashman said.

'It's not fair.' Parsley, who Terry and Cashman did think looked like Benny from Abba, if he'd lost all his money and was homeless, pulled at the paper one-piece they'd given him after taking away his bloodstained clothes for analysis. A waft of sweat hit Terry's nostrils. No one had put the man through a shower.

'What's not fair, Derek? That the kids wouldn't play your games?' Terry rubbed clammy palms on his thighs. This was his first big case. A game changer. A child was dead. If he messed up he'd be back in uniform. The press, with Lucie first at the trough, would devour him.

It was two days since the murder. Last night, they'd picked up Parsley (the nursery rhyme surname was a sick joke), wandering in the park in blood-soaked clothes. He had nothing to change into. Terry saw the case snapping shut. But then Parsley went silent on them. At least now, along with the dawn chorus, he was talking. Whining.

'I wouldn't hurt them.' Parsley dashed at his eyes. 'They're my friends.'

Cashman exploded. 'Friends? They're babies. You're a thirty-four-year-old tosser who waves his todger at shop windows! Now it seems you've cranked up your act.'

Bull's eye. Parsley clocked that they knew about the Leeds indecent exposure charge. Calmly, because with Cashman going off on one, he'd better be the good cop, Terry said, 'Derek, tell us why you killed little Sarah.'

'What are you, some kind of weirdo freak?' Cashman lunged at Parsley.

Terry grabbed the back of Cashman's belt and hauled him down into his chair. If Parsley clammed up again, he could walk. Parsley hadn't wanted a solicitor even though Terry had urged him to get one. They hadn't got the blood results back, but Parsley and Ferris shared the common group 'O' so despite the blood on his shirt and trousers, the chain of evidence was flimsy. A wily defence barrister could cross off the blood as his client getting messy while he tried to revive the girl. Some detectives might go with it, but Terry wanted a confession.

'I tried to help her,' Parsley said.

'Help her? What with?' Terry nudged.

'I found her bracelet. I put it back on for her. It's not fair.' Parsley lapsed into his mantra.

'You mean you nicked it off of her?' Cashman had got control of himself.

'Where was the bracelet, Derek?' Terry cajoled.

'By the swing. I put it back on her.' He shook. 'She didn't ever know, did she?'

'You found Sarah alone in the playground. She was upset because she'd lost the bracelet her daddy gave her and she knew that he'd be cross. You expected a reward, didn't you? Naturally you did.' Terry craned closer, ignoring the stink. 'Sarah was six, Derek. Thing is, she was too young to know about evil. She thought you were nice, didn't she?'

'Yes,' Parsley agreed. 'She was nice too.'

'Yes. She was. Her family thought so. Her mum's heartbroken. Her dad blames her big brother.' Propped on elbows, chin on his fists, Terry did regretful, eyebrows up, mouth turned down. 'You finding her bracelet turned you into Father Christmas come early, especially for Sarah. She made you feel ten feet tall! Then she announces she's going home to show her daddy and it all goes pear-shaped.'

'Let's be real, Derek, why would that little angel want a smelly old bloke for a friend?' Cashman clenched his jaw. His wife Karen had just had a baby girl, he was fit to kill Parsley. 'Sarah had Jason and Kevin lapping up her every word. A brother looking out for her and a daddy she loved best in the world. She didn't need you. Did you unzip yourself and scare her?'

Parsley squirmed. Terry followed through, 'Sarah spoilt the game. It wasn't fair, like you say. After what you'd done she chucked your kindness in your face. You taught her a lesson.'

'No.' Derek Parsley waved a hand in front of himself as if clearing a cobweb.

'You crushed her neck with a brick. Then to be on the *safe side*, you strangled her.' Terry batted his coffee beaker. It was by accident, but he let it roll off the end of the table, sending a trail of coffee over the worn wood and splashing over the lino.

'I didn't do *nothing*,' Parsley protested. 'Sarah was my friend. I hid the brick so she couldn't be hurt any more.'

'Sarah's blood was on your shirt,' Terry said.

'She wasn't your friend,' Cashman said. 'You hid the brick so that it wouldn't be linked to you. You pressed it down on her neck. Hard. Like this.' He mimed the action. 'She never stood a chance. Sarah trusted you and you killed her in cold blood.'

'No!' Parsley clutched at his paper overalls, his eyes darting, tongue licking his lips. It seemed to Terry that the blokes who did stuff to kids were always hopeless scrawny specimens. Terry couldn't help feeling sympathy for this man who deserved no sympathy at all.

'Why a brick, Derek? Did you hate her that much?' Terry caught himself clutching at his own shirt like Parsley. He too could do with a wash. 'You put all your weight into it. She never had a chance.'

'She was all upset that her bracelet was stolen.' Parsley scratched his head in apparent bewilderment. 'I never saw no brick.'

Parsley was signing himself into prison.

If it was possible, it was the brick that had got to Terry the most. A knife was more personal than a gun, but still a stabbing involved minimal contact with the victim. Strangling was intimate. The brick spelled intimacy and hatred. Pure and unadulterated. The killer had straddled Sarah. Pressed down on her throat, crushing her. Terry flicked his head as he heard cartilage snap and crunch.

The door opened. Sian from reception.

'Not now!'

Sian blanched. Terry was known for his permanent good mood. Parsley was getting to him too.

'Derek, you're not a kid, you know right from wrong. Have a think about what happened. When we come back, we want the truth, OK?' He paused the interview. Terry had a feel for interviews, Parsley was talking, they'd crack it before close of play.

'Sorry,' he told Sian when they were in the corridor. 'That was totally uncalled for.'

'Already forgotten, sir.' Sian wasn't alone in being prepared to forgive Terry Darnell anything. 'There's a girl asking for you.'

'A girl?' Terry's heart leapt. Stella never came to his work. 'It's my daughter.'

'It's not Stella, sir.' Most staff in the station had seen Stella grow up. They'd minded and fussed her, given her pens and paper to draw pictures if Terry was out on a job. He'd find her hunched over a desk in the back office. She only used one corner of the sheet. Terry had kept all Stella's artistic efforts.

'...she says you're her assistant.' Sian was straight-faced.

'My assistant?'

'She'll only talk to you. I tried telling her you're busy.' Sian tutted. 'A right stroppy little madam. She should be at school!'

Despite everything, Terry smiled. Danielle Hindle. When he and Cashman had visited the Hindle household Terry had been unsurprised by the chaos presided over by Maxine, the older sister who was a little younger than Stella. Unlike Stella, Maxine was smothered in make-up and had no respect for the police.

Danielle Hindle, her skirt tucked into her knickers, was doing a handstand by the noticeboard in the foyer. 'Not at school?' He did mock stern. He needed a laugh.

'Yeah, well, you said to come if I could help.' Danielle walked two paces on her hands then toppled. Catching herself like an acrobat, she landed upright. 'You said I was a detective.'

'I did.' Terry was glad the super wasn't around to hear him recruiting kids into the force. He had no memory of saying Danielle could be a detective, but since they'd found Sarah Ferris's body he'd barely slept so he probably had. He sat on the bench in the foyer. 'What have you found?'

She came and sat next to him. She was chewing gum. He opted not to tell her it was dangerous to do gymnastics with something in your mouth.

'Lee's my boyfriend now. Nicola cries still. Even after our funeral.' She did the spinning gum thing on her finger. Terry said nothing about that either. He felt disproportionate disappointment. He'd dared hope that the girl had a lead. Something that boxed off Parsley. Instead she'd come to tell him she was going out – did kids go out this young? – with Lee

Marshall. 'That's nice. Lee needs someone supporting him at this difficult time. Now, Danielle, if you'll excuse me, I have to—'

'He put her bracelet on.'

'Lee?'

'The man from Abba.' The girl glanced at the door as if afraid of someone.

'Did you see him?' Terry kept calm.

'I went back to the playground. He was in the dark. He goes, "Run away or I'll murder you too. He was sticking it on her."' Danielle's green eyes were saucer round like a cat's. 'I swear on my life.'

Terry guessed that Danielle Hindle was seldom taken seriously. He'd hesitate too if it weren't that he knew she was telling the truth. They had kept back two pieces of information. Sarah's bracelet had been restored to her wrist, and that the murder weapon was a brick. Apart from the team, two people knew this. The killer and victim. And a witness. Parsley had been seen fastening the charm bracelet onto Sarah's wrist. The case was closing before his eyes.

'I believe you. Go on.'

'I hid in the bandstand and saw him do it.' Danielle Hindle was precise and unflappable. Terry's mind was racing. She'd convince any jury. Even without a confession, the judge would send Derek Parsley down.

'So, am I a detective?'

'Yes,' Terry agreed absently. He'd get justice for little Sarah. He'd make Stella proud.

Chapter Ten

2019

Stella tugged Stanley's lead as he tried to lift his leg against the marble 'headstone' on Wormwood Scrubs Common.

'Your father didn't see you for weeks.' Suzie Darnell nodded at the memorial.

Although mother and daughter knew the names off by heart, they paused to reread the gold lettering inscribed within an oval frame below the London Metropolitan Police Crest.

HERE FELL

PS

CHRISTOPHER HEAD

PC

GEOFFREY FOX

PC

DAVID WOMBWELL

12th AUGUST 1966

'It was only two days, Mum.' This was an old chestnut. 'Dad had no choice.'

Years after Terry's death in 2011 – Stella's parents had separated in 1973 – Suzie Darnell groused that Terry had put the force before his family.

'We all have choices.' Suzie continued along Braybrook Street. A long road of terraced houses facing the common. 'Those men will never be grandfathers.'

'Some of them are.' Stella regretted suggesting the Scrubs for their Sunday afternoon walk. It was going to spark contentious memories. The air was cold, the grey sky threatened rain although Stella's weather app had said that there would only be a shower at nightfall. If they'd gone to Richmond Park they could have sheltered under a tree.

'If Terry'd been in that patrol car, you'd have had no father.'

Jack reckoned that the slaying of the officers on the day that Suzie became a mother had shocked her more than she could admit. The terrible event brought home to her that her husband did a dangerous job. Suzie had loved Terry and she still did.

'You know what I mean, those three officers are not here to appreciate them.' Suzie's furious pace forced Stella into a trot to keep up. 'Like me.'

'Like you?' Some years ago, her mum had got Stella and Jack combing through her rubbish bins for long-lost items. Stella had suspected that Suzie was getting dementia. Thankfully a false alarm. With no work to use her skills, Suzie had got depressed. Stella asked her mum to build and maintain the customer database and Suzie became her old self again. If she was depressed now, Stella would be stumped for a solution. In the early days, her mum had run Stella's 'bedroom-office', but first Jackie and now Trudy did that and anyway, Suzie as her PA was a recipe for disaster, they'd constantly be at loggerheads. A deep clean was Stella's cure for ills, but Suzie loathed embarking on so much as a polish.

'I don't have grandchildren.' Suzie flew onto the common (resembling a giant bird in her Driza-Bone coat), Stanley – off his lead – galloped at her heel.

'Yes you do! Dale has Kerry and Brian.'

'Byron.' Suzie snatched off her maroon beret (a new look), gave it a flap and crammed it back on her head. 'Dale lives in Sydney. I've seen his kids a handful of times. I mean nothing to them. They stay at the meal table under duress. Robyn's mother is Super Gran, knitting, babysitting, school runs and heaping them with sweets. "Lollies", they call them. A daughter is for life, a son is yours until he gets a wife.'

'Dale's divorced.' Confounded by the phrase 'daughter for life' Stella battled for the facts. 'Mum, they're teenagers. They don't need babysitters. At their age I didn't speak at supper time. I hated people's mouths moving with food inside them.' She shuddered at the memory. Still a reality…

'Your grandparents were dead by the time you were four. Byron and Kerry call her "Nan-ma"! For Heaven's sake, they're nearly old enough to drive.' Adroit at changing tack, Suzie had abandoned the babysitting/knitting argument. She grabbed a gap in the traffic and swept across Scrubs Lane.

'What do they call you?' Stella scanned for a change of subject but could think of nothing remarkable about the villas facing the park. Clean Slate had four clients in Dalgarno Gardens but, intimate with the database, her mum would know. Waiting while Stanley sniffed a lamp-post, she read graffiti daubed on the railway bridge.

'Fancy climbing up there just to write "Nerd"!' she said. 'Jack says those tags are on Street View in 2012. The bridge is rarely cleaned.'

'That Bella woman had babies at fifty so it's possible.' Beret askew, Suzie sailed into Little Wormwood Scrubs Park. Suzie always called her 'that Bella woman'. Jackie said it was Suzie sticking up for Stella. Her mum wasn't Switzerland when it came to taking sides.

'Heterosexual women often stop contraception around that age because they're not menstruating and sometimes they get pregnant.' Stella wasn't prone to jealousy, but preferred not to dwell on how Bella had conceived.

'Clean Slate has four clients on Dalgarno Gardens!'

'I know,' her mum said.

In the park, they cut through the Sunday afternoon crowds braving unseasonal wintry weather for April. Families, children on scooters, elderly couples, an old man, head bowed, inching along aided by a walker. Two women ambled gloved hand in gloved hand across the lawn. This made Stella think of Beverly, Jackie's assistant and their trainee detective who had married her long-term girlfriend. Bev had finally come out although Jackie said she'd always known. Little got past Jackie.

The Darnell women, mother and daughter, were women of action for whom leisurely perambulation was anathema. At a brisk rate they rounded the bandstand and arrived at the playground.

There were no children. Stella thought this strange for three o'clock on a Sunday afternoon.

Her nana (not so different to Nan-ma) had brought her to the playground when she was a toddler. Stella pictured Nana as always laughing which, for a woman widowed in her forties, couldn't have been true. She'd pushed Stella on the swings and perching her on the roundabout, walked it around and around. Nana had pushed Terry on the same equipment when he was little. A symmetry that Stella would be unwise to share with her mum right now.

There was little recognizable in the present-day playground from Stella's – or Terry's – day. Primary-coloured plastic shapes on a rubberized surface could be modern art. Gone was the witch's hat beneath which Stella had caught her sandal. And the rocking boat onto which children piled, sending it plummeting and soaring over pretend high seas. The custard yellow chute looked safer than the skyscraping slide that Nana had forbidden Stella (a courageous and curious child) to climb. A jungle climbing frame offered only soft landings. Bars boxed in the swings, preventing children tumbling out like Mickey Beech in Stella's class who'd knocked out half his milk teeth.

'What's that woman doing?' Suzie stopped at the gate. A notice warned that no dogs or ball games were allowed.

'Sitting.' Stella had forgotten that Jack planned to take his kids to this very playground that afternoon. It was his access weekend. Bella had said that Stella wasn't allowed to meet the twins, they'd suffered disruption in their infancy six months in. Stella might only be passing through Jack's life. Bella didn't want them getting attached. Jackie, who was allowed to babysit them, thought this absurd – Stella and Jack had basically been counting for years – and Jack shouldn't stand for it. Stella was sorry to know them only through photographs, but respectful of the rule. She wouldn't have wanted to meet her father's new girlfriend, although as far as she knew there was only Lucie and Stella who had met her. Stella didn't want to bump into Jack with his twins now. Bella would think it was planned. She nodded at the woman on the bench. 'She's got no coat, she must be cold.'

'Adults shouldn't hang around playgrounds without children. If she was a man, we'd be worried.' Suzie could heap on disapproval at the drop of a hat.

'Maybe she used to play here. Like Dad did.' If they'd gone to Richmond Park they could have looked at the deer.

'Maybe she's wishing that someone would make her a grandmother.' Suzie harrumphed.

'Mum, I'm not getting pregnant!' Slow to spot the heaviest of hints, Stella got this one.

'You're not too old. You've got a man. You know he's fertile and he'd make a great dad.'

'He's already making a great dad. I'm fifty-three! I *am* too old.'

'You're not fifty-three until August, I should know.'

The maternal gene had passed Stella by. Children were noisy, messy and unpredictable. While she'd like to meet Jack's twins there'd be time enough when they were adults and had learnt to clean.

'...you'd be a marvellous mum,' Suzie rhapsodized. 'You're lovely with kids. What about that client who sent flowers because you had her son laughing after he'd broken his arm?'

'Mum, please! I barely have enough time for Stanley!' Stella clipped on the poodle's lead. He sat in anticipation of a liver treat.

As if she hadn't heard, Suzie said, 'Two kids were murdered in this playground. Terry solved the case.'

'I'd forgotten.' If this chilling information didn't change Stella's mind about motherhood, it got her attention.

'Nineteen eighty. You were fourteen, thankfully too old for playgrounds. A boy and a girl were found dead.' Suzie pursed her lips. 'Oh. How did Creepy Lady leave without us seeing?'

''Spect she walked.' Stella eyed the empty bench. Never mind being a mother, when she was with her mum, she became a crabby adolescent. Her phone rang.

'Bev, it's Sunday, why are you working?'

'Carrie has come through with a time to see her mother,' Beverly said. 'Tomorrow afternoon. I know you're free, I checked your online diary. Can you ask Jack?'

'Jack?' He was with his twins. Stella decided, 'I'll go anyway.'

'Why not ring Jack and see if he's free?' Suzie missed nothing. 'I hope you two haven't fallen out. Your biological clock is ticking. You haven't time to start again with another man.'

*

After she'd dropped Suzie at her flat in Baron's Court, Stella drove home along the Great West Road. Beverly had texted that Jack could make the meeting. Bev could talk to Jack when he was on an access weekend. Actually, he'd never forbidden Stella to call him. It was her own rule. Stella felt excited. A case meant researching background information, interviewing witnesses, visiting a crime scene in search of missed clues. She and Jack would be a team again.

Passing over Hammersmith flyover, Stella woke Stanley as she exclaimed, 'Where in my life do I have the time for children?'

Chapter Eleven

2019

Two thirty p.m. Little Wormwood Scrubs Park. A woman sat on a bench in the playground. The prison dominated the skyline, a black fortress against the grey. Leaves rustled as a breeze carried them across the rubberized ground. The sun had gone in. The woman observed to herself that there was a nip in the air.

A tall man in a black coat cavorted with two children. A boy and a girl aged about three. He had the same liquid brown eyes as the girl and fine features as the boy so, the woman presumed, he was their father. The boy had the sort of blond hair that would darken with time.

Despite the equipment – a chute, swings, jungle climbing frame – they kicked a football about. They could have gone into the park for that, she noted with irritation. The man had an accurate back-heel pass that sent his daughter into a fury because her brother got to the ball first. Her own style was to kick wildly then rush after the ball, her flapping Batman cape making her demonic.

Glancing up, the woman noted with satisfaction that a camera fixed to a pole by the gate had been smashed by kids. It captured nothing.

The temperature dropped further. The woman, in her mid-forties, her face wrapped in a scarf, decided that the dad had the look of Liam Gallagher. Or the other brother. So far Liam hadn't whipped out his phone to snap his kids' every move. Nor was his head buried in Facebook, like most mums.

Jack had seen the woman. Unreasonably he'd wanted the playground to themselves. Someone on their own – no children – made him wary. A man on his own would have put Jack on high alert. He told himself to relax.

Milly was particularly excitable today. Into everything, bellowing for Jack and Justin to 'watch me!', she hurtled down the chute or demanded Jack push her on the swings. ('Do more up!') Justin wasn't watching. Clasping Portus Teddy who went everywhere with him (Jack dreaded Portus going missing on his watch), he'd straggled off to the railings and would be examining insects. Justin was a budding naturalist. Bella said he'd be a botanical illustrator like her. Jack was reminded of himself at that age, studying the intricate engineering of spider's webs.

Lucie said children were a menace. 'So much for caring for you when you're old. They'll have you in a nursing home the first time you forget what day it is.'

Aware that Justin's insipient independence tended to mean he got less adult attention, Jack went over to his little boy. His heart flipped when Justin showed him a woodlouse on its way to the shops.

'That's not yours,' the woman on the bench told Milly. The nosy girl had found a discarded sweatshirt draped over the bench.

'Is it yours?' Milly asked.

'It's far too small for me.' The woman looked away. 'Some kid has left it.'

'It is mine as I do have it.' Milly twisted her shoulders in a fashion no doubt intended to charm.

'It's wrong to steal.'

'It's not stealing. I did finded it.'

'Found. It's rude to answer back.' The woman was tiring of the interchange.

'You said things to me so I answered back at you.' Milly spoke with elaborate care. She examined the sweatshirt and pulled a face. 'It's dirty.'

'Don't touch it then.'

'Milly!' Jack had only taken his eyes off Milly for a second.

With a shrug Milly pranced across the playground to her father.

The woman folded her arms and looked the other way. Some children could really get on your nerves.

Jack watched his daughter fly along the pavement, cape billowing. She leapt and swerved to avoid the cracks as he did. Justin, more contemplative, paused then did a jump or stopped altogether to watch the progress of a beetle. Milly had Jack's rampant curiosity. 'What's this?' 'Why?' It had driven his father to distraction. Justin, like Jack, saw the minutiae of other worlds. Nearly three years of being a parent hadn't dulled Jack's amazement that two small people shared his characteristics yet had independent personalities.

Jack was happy to delay getting to Bella's flat in Dalgarno Gardens. He hated saying goodbye to Justin and Milly. Usually he had them to stay for a night in the week, but he was doing extra driving shifts for London Underground. A wave of sickness had drastically depopulated the rota. Jack wouldn't see his children for ages.

Milly was at the entrance to Bella's flats. When he caught her up, Jack was astonished to see her reach the buzzer. They were growing up so fast.

'Hello?' Although they were a minute early for the appointed handover time and the intercom system had a camera, Bella always answered as if she wasn't expecting them. Motherhood hadn't come naturally to her.

'Hi, Mummy, it's us all back!' Milly sounded equally astonished to hear Bella. But for Milly life was one big wonderful surprise.

The door clicked open. Milly tore up the stairs raucously lah-lahing a tuneless tune. Unlike Jack – or Bella – she was only quiet when asleep. He felt a woolly grip of his fingers. Justin's mittened hand had sought his. In the boy's expression, Jack read his own dread of parting.

Bella was in the hall, a glass of red wine in her hand, her mass of curly black hair tumbling from its pins. Her eyes – Justin's eyes – were outlined with kohl and eyeshadow. Distantly Jack registered that it was unusual for Bella to wear make-up unless she was working in the artists' room at the Kew Gardens Herbarium. Milly had disappeared into the flat without kissing him goodbye.

'Mills says you went to the *Wormwood Scrubs* playground.' Bella looked at him over the rim of the glass. Her emphasis suggested the prison. Jack disliked that Bella drank in charge of the children. He was of the mind that imbibing alcohol, like drink-driving, clouded judgement and rapid response. He'd once made the mistake of saying this and Bella had retaliated with a list of 'don'ts', all of which he did. Her key rule was that the children could not *ever* meet Stella Darnell. That one he had not contravened. Bella had never forgiven Jack for loving Stella more than her. A fact that Bella had known before he did.

'They loved it,' Jack said without considering if they had. He had loved it.

'Who's this stranger Milly spoke to?' Bella took a sip.

'No one. Someone on a bench.' Jack felt Justin's grip tighten. The boy guessed that Milly had inadvertently got Jack in trouble. He didn't want his children to be mindful of keeping the peace between their parents, a childhood burden Stella had carried which, he suspected, had his mother lived, would have been his too. He beamed reassuringly at his son. 'Milly and Justin know not to talk to strangers, we've discussed it.'

'Don't *discuss* it! Don't let them. Kids were murdered there in 1980, did you know that?'

'No I didn't. But 1980 is nearly forty years ago. Kids are murdered everywhere.' Jack saw Bella's appalled expression. *Shit*. 'Not anywhere. Not *here*. Look, we all had a good time, didn't we!' He swung Justin's hand as if it were a lever that would work a response.

'Yes, we did,' Justin said on cue.

'Milly needs to go to the toilet and wants you to do it.' A man came into the hall and encircled Bella with an arm. Short, stocky, thin frameless glasses, cropped grey hair, a green V-neck jumper over a white T-shirt. The black jeans were tight for any man. Certainly one in his fifties.

'Jack. Harry.' Bella nestled up to the six pack showing through two layers of fabric.

Harry.

'And you are?' Jack heard himself sounding like his own father. Cold and unrelenting. *Get away from my children.*

Harry and Bella answered in unison.

'I'm Bella's bloke.'

'Someone I work with.'

'What was that you said about not talking to strangers?'

'Harry's not a stranger. The kids love him.' Bella didn't sound sure of the last bit. *Shit.*

'Can Daddy come for tea so he can know Harry?' Justin piped.

'Well…' Bella had a rictus smile.

'Cool idea, little man!' Harry flashed a big grin at Jack.

'I was going to say that I decided…' Bella looked shifty, 'well, actually, Emily said… and it's OK… that Stella Darnell can see the kids. Seeing as you're still together. But…'

'Generous of you.' Lovely Emily, Bella's best friend right back to their school days, frequently tempered Bella's strictures. Bella had named Milly after her. Jack let Bella struggle with the unveiling of her hypocrisy. She'd let their kids meet Harry while Stella was still persona non grata.

'They must *not* talk to strangers. Will you make Stella Darnell understand that?'

'Stella would understand. Her father was a police officer.' A stranger was in his children's home. A stranger got to see Justin and Milly eat and play. Go to the lavatory. The stranger shared a bed with their mother. Children were murdered by their stepfathers.

His phone beeped. Beverly. 'I have to go.' Jack crouched down and held Justin. Jack kissed him. The boy didn't move. Jack recognized himself with his father for a new term at boarding school. He was both the boy and the man. Thickly, he managed, 'I love you, Justy. Tell Milly too.'

Jack took the stairs three at a go, coat flying like his daughter's cape. Stella could meet his twins. He should feel on top of the world. But all he saw was six-pack Harry having tea with his children.

After his mother's death, Jack believed that he could never know a worse pain than her wrenching absence. When he became a father he discovered that he was only on the foothills of the pain it was possible to feel.

Chapter Twelve

2019

Stella picked up her rucksack and came out into reception. Trudy was at her desk. Stella had an idea that she'd already said goodnight to Trudy, but immersed in the Cater case, had lost track of time. Jackie wanted her to speak to Trudy about her long hours. Stella – who also did long hours – kept forgetting. Now was her chance.

'Get off home, Trudy. It's past seven.'

'I like a clean slate for the morning!' Trudy punned. She punched holes in a sheet of paper and clipped it in a lever arch file.

'It could wait until tomorrow.' Stella never left anything until the next day, often working through the night. She did not expect it from her team. Tonight she was leaving 'early' because Jack was coming to supper.

'I won't tell Jackie if you won't!' Trudy winked.

Stella accidentally winked back. She'd drifted into a tacit conspiracy with Trudy. Where Jackie encouraged Stella to eat fresh food, Trudy brought her ready meals, usually shepherd's pie, Stella's favourite. Jackie tried to encourage Stella to cultivate interests outside Clean Slate. Trudy encouraged Stella to stay late and arrive early by what Jack said was 'presenteeism'. Stella disliked secrets, especially ones from Jackie. She colluded with Trudy because it suited her.

Trudy was good at secrecy. Beyond glowing references (she'd been a 'first-rate medical secretary, our loss is your gain!'), and despite Beverly's oblique probing ('Trudy, help! I have to make a stew for five, bet you're a fabby cook...'), they knew little about Trudy's life beyond that she was a widow. From comments she'd made Beverly had decided Trudy was estranged from a child. On team bowling nights, Trudy always got a clutch of strikes, but, never a gossip, offered no chit-chat. She never accepted invitations to Jackie and Graham's Friday night family supper. A refusal that was extraordinary to Jack who never missed one. Stella said that people's lives were their business and that all that mattered was that Trudy was as good a PA as Jackie had been. Stella liked that Trudy drew a line between work and social.

'I'll finish this and get going,' Trudy reassured her now.

Stella caught a glimpse of Trudy's screen. Before she could stop herself, she read out, '"My mother is a murderer." What's that?'

'The report from this morning's meeting.'

'What report?' Stella was dismayed. What happened in the Murder Investigation Room stayed there.

'Bev gave me her notes and a photocopy of your notebook. I'm creating one document that you can all refer to.' Trudy whipped her hands off the keyboard as if burnt. 'Was I wrong? God, sorry, Stella! Don't blame Beverly, it was my idea.'

'It's a great idea. Just it's more work for you. Detective work is outside your remit. I always do my own typing for that.' Stella tugged her collar out from her jacket.

'Your job is to solve the crime. Mine is to make that possible. Actually,' Trudy swivelled to face Stella, 'if you don't mind me saying, Stella, this is a tough one. Daughter trying to prove Daddy didn't do it. She would say that, wouldn't she? Early days, but do you have thoughts about who did it, a gut feeling?'

Stella didn't generally hold with gut feelings. Like her dad she followed the evidence. But even Terry had had hunches. In fact she did have preliminary thoughts and saw no harm in sharing them with Trudy.

'Christopher Philips confessed to the murder. Even Carrie admits that he disposed of the body. If he didn't do it then he's protecting someone. Carrie thinks it's his wife, her mother, so this isn't about a woman unable to face that her parent is a murderer.'

'Penelope Philips certainly had motive, she wouldn't be the first partner to kill her husband's lover. Even if Christopher Philips didn't kill Cater, he betrayed Penelope. Maybe he confessed because he feels guilty for betraying her,' said Trudy.

'A big price to pay for guilt. After all adultery isn't equivalent to murder.' Stella wondered vaguely if the late husband had been unfaithful. Or if, an adulterer, he was as good as dead to Trudy. Whatever, as Clean Slate offered its customers, Trudy had come to them as a fresh start.

'Some might disagree.' Trudy pulled the typed notes off the printer. 'That said, if Christopher jumped to the conclusion that his wife murdered his mistress he'd have revised it. You and Bev put that Penelope Philips was seen on CCTV in London. She's in the clear.'

'She could have paid a contract killer.' Stella played devil's advocate.

'She was stabbed multiple times. Wouldn't a hired killer get it right first time?' Trudy stapled the report. 'You have this, I'll email it to the team.'

Stella knew little about contract killings, but agreed that a professional would do a 'clean' kill. The police had said the frenzied attack signified high emotion, suggesting it was personal, but they should rule out nothing.

'Whoever did it wanted someone dead.' Trudy turned off the printer with a hollow laugh. 'Those types wouldn't come cheap. Chris Philips might have skimped and hired an amateur. His house is mortgaged to the hilt and the lease on his antiques shop is about to run out. I'm guessing that his mistress was bleeding him dry. That's motive.' She sighed. 'What a terrible thing to happen in a such sweet little place in the country.'

'I've been there.' Had they not gone to stay in the Cotswolds Stella doubted she'd be with Jack now. She glanced out of the window. 'It's going to rain, you should get going.'

'There was something about Carrie that I don't trust.'

'What?' Stella had felt something similar, but put it down to Carrie's accosting her at the crime scene clean-up.

'Hard to say. Reading your very thorough notes, Stella, I feel there's something she's not saying.' Trudy fitted the dust cover over her machine, one of her many innovations that Stella liked. 'It may be nothing. I'll sleep on it.'

At the door, Stella flourished the report. 'Thank you, Trudy, this will be helpful.'

'It's what I'm here for.'

Trudy would never be Jackie, but she was close.

Out in the street, Stella cogitated on Trudy's observation. Beverly hadn't noticed anything. Jack had had to rush off to drive a train, he'd have told her if he had suspected Carrie of withholding information. It was all too common for a client to give an incomplete brief. Some people wanted crimes solved to suit rather than uncomfortable truths uncovered. They were unwilling to give up secrets that cast them or a loved one in an unflattering light.

Mulling on the case, Stella dodged idling traffic on the green and, attracted by appetizing smells, headed to stalls erected in the centre. Unlike her dad, not being in CID, Stella didn't have jurisdiction to work on current crimes. She stuck to cold cases. Any murder investigation was clouded by the passage of time, the scene of crime became layered by other events, clues vanished. She never had the golden twenty-four hours in which a murderer stood the most chance of being caught. She had no access to police files. Or did she? Maybe she should have that coffee with Martin Cashman. *Bad move.* Martin would discourage her – forbid her – to re-examine any murder.

Stella stopped by a stall selling Italian street food. She got out the report and in the light of her phone scanned Trudy's perfectly laid out text. Carrie had said, *'Chief Superintendent Cashman knows perfectly well that she did it.'* Stella had contradicted this. At the crime scene, Cashman had told her that the police had got the right killer. Her contradiction wasn't in the notes because no one, including herself, had written it down.

Lured by a garlic aroma Stella did an untypical thing and bought a slice of pizza from the stall. Clutching the warm paper, she looked across the green to Clean Slate's offices, easy to spot above Sainsbury's orange sign. The top windows were dark. A light burned in the outer office. Trudy always turned everything off. A break-in.

Ever since Trudy had foiled a burglary at Stella's house a year ago, Stella had become hyper-concerned about security. She had believed her house – once Terry's – impregnable. She was heading back to the road when she guessed the truth. Trudy hadn't yet left. Whatever Stella said to her, Trudy would not leave until her in-tray was empty.

Her mind returning to the burglary attempt last November, Stella bit into the succulent slice. She had to gasp in cold air to mitigate burning. Terry's computer had a bios password (it was several years old) no serious thief would bother with because they'd never crack the code. Stella couldn't lose the suspicion that the intruder had been after something else.

Stella considered going up to the office and shooing Trudy home. Except if Trudy had no one waiting for her there it was unfair to make her leave before she was ready.

Munching on the pizza, Stella felt cheered by her chat with Trudy. She'd tell Jack about Trudy's suspicion that Carrie Philips was keeping something back. Rachel Cater's horrendous murder would mean that she and Jack must return to Winchcombe. The village where Jack reckoned that their relationship had begun.

Chapter Thirteen

1980

'This what you're looking for?'

Sarah expected to see the Man from Abba. Danielle Hindle was by the gap in the fence. She held up something. The charm bracelet.

'Yes,' Sarah cried. She had known that her brother would be the one in trouble if she'd lost it.

'Come and get it.' Danielle slipped through the fence into thick bushes.

Sarah was unsure who frightened her more. The man from Abba or Danielle Hindle. She remembered Robbie's cry. A lump landing like a sack. Then the quiet like hiding. She had run to the side of the bandstand. She wasn't invisible like in games at school. The movement gave her away. Danielle was on the top of the slide. Staring at her.

'Come here.'

Sarah wanted her bracelet so she did as she was told.

Danielle was in the bushes. Putting the bracelet to her lips she bit on it. Sarah gasped as, with her teeth, Danielle pulled off a charm.

Best Sister.

'Don't do that.' Fear was drowned in fury. Sarah flung herself at the older girl.

Danielle hit her. Distantly Sarah wondered at the hardness of Danielle's fist. Like stone. Then everything disappeared.

Clouds raced across the darkening sky. From the park came the sound of an ice-cream van still plying a steady trade in the run-up to Christmas. The prison loomed on the horizon, the flint towers issuing a dire warning to miscreants. It was trying to snow, random flakes fluttering, but never settling.

Despite the cold, while it was still light the playground had teemed with children, tearing across the concrete enacting variants of games going back centuries which generally involved an odd one out (Puss in the Corner, Bad Penny, Piggy in the Middle, You're It). Kids had lurched the rocking boat forwards and upwards, bulleted down the slide and launched skyward on the swings.

The gates closed at dusk. Now it was quiet and seemingly empty. The two children on the roundabout might be tricks of the dark.

'Nice Doc Ms.' Lee pushed until the lumbering roundabout gathered speed and leapt on.

'Thanks.' Danielle kicked the heels of her new boots against the wood slats as Lee often did. Blackness whizzed by. When she was married to Lee they'd dance at the Palais, skate down the Bayswater rink and snog in the Regal like her mum and dad had. There would be no housework like Nicky had to do. Debating whether to tell Lee this so he'd want to marry her, instead she mined his unexpected compliment. 'Why do you like them? My boots.'

Lee played his torch over his own cherry red Doctor Martens. 'They're the same as mine.'

'Are they?' Danielle was overjoyed that he'd noticed. It made up for him not crying for Sarah like Nicky did about Robbie. She'd hoped to snog Lee to make him forget about Sarah.

'They're for boys,' Lee decided.

'They're not!'

'Where's Nicky?' Lee hung off the running board like a water skier, his bottom inches from the concrete.

'She's indoors.' Sarah being murdered had made Nicola cry more. That morning Nicola lost her writing pencil. Although Owen Jones offered his Zippy pencil (from TV's *Rainbow*) she'd gone on crying. She'd stopped when Lee gave her his chewed school pencil.

'Since that mad funeral-thing and... and everything, she's stayed in.' Lee flashed the torch about, briefly revealing the witch's hat, the swings like waiting enemies.

'We could do a funeral for Sarah like we did for Robbie, if you like.' Danielle should have thought of it sooner. She'd been busy being a detective for Inspector Darnell. This reminded Danielle about the man from Abba. She announced, 'I'm scared.'

'What of?' Lee aimed the torch into the darkness, lighting up the slide ten feet away.

'The murderer who murdered Robbie and Sarah.' Danielle gave an exaggerated shudder.

'Robbie wasn't murdered,' Lee said. 'He fell off the slide and hit his head.'

'Do you like ice skating?' Danielle shuffled closer to Lee.

'My dad's more scary than Abba man. He gave me a thrashing with Sarah's bicycle pump.' Lee fired the torch at a bluish tinge on his forearm.

'Poor you!' Danielle cooed. 'Why did he do that?'

'I told Sarah off for messing with the single I bought, Spandau's latest.' Lee rolled down his sleeve and did up his cuff, patting it smooth.

'But Sarah's dead.'

'Before. Alan remembered last night. He went mad.' Lee warmed his palm with pretend heat from the torchlight. He couldn't dwell on his sister's death for long. Blindly he'd gone over that night trying to find the moment when he'd made the biggest mistake of his life.

Danielle burst out with the chorus of 'To Cut a Long Story Short'. She stopped when Lee didn't join in. With a Nicola sigh, 'You look like Martin Kemp.'

'No I don't.' Nevertheless Lee blushed.

'You're exactly like him.' Danielle saw she'd hit the jackpot. 'Is your record all right? I'd kill Jason if he did that to mine.'

'You don't have any records. Maxine said.' Lee recalled an argument between the Hindle sisters that had happened when he still had a sister.

'I do,' Danielle said.

'It sticks at the start.' Lee braked the roundabout with a foot and got off. His hands in his Levi pockets, he mooched about being Martin Kemp.

Danielle knew that Lee had a paper round so could buy nice clothes and records of his own. No one would employ the Hindle girls in a shop, their father's reputation had seen to that. Jumping off the roundabout, she flung herself into a handstand. It had impressed Lee in the past and with her boots… 'Your dad should have punished Sarah, not you.' She was clear-eyed about injustice.

'He ain't my dad. Sarah's his real kid so he sticks up for her.' Lee was bewildered. Sarah being dead hadn't stopped Alan giving her special treatment.

'Sarah's spoilt.' Danielle spoke his forming thought. 'Not any more. Not now she's dead.'

'She's not.'

'Not dead?' Danielle fell out of her handstand and jarred her back against the roundabout's running board. It hadn't hurt, but for Lee's sake, 'Ouch.'

'Not spoilt. Sarah can't help what Alan gives her.' Lee was unaware of Danielle struggling to her feet.

'It's because she's the youngest. Jason's like that.' Danielle clambered onto the roundabout and stood on it, feet apart to keep her balance as it slowed. 'I was youngest till Jason. I never got spoilt. Dad likes him best too.'

'Alan's not my dad.' Lee stamped on a freeze-thaw crack in the concrete. 'I hate him.'

'You could kill him.' Danielle wished Lee could see her on the roundabout.

Suddenly his torch went the other way.

'I called on you, but Maxine said you'd gone here without me!' Nicola wore her new coat trimmed with fur. Nicola's dad sold clothes in the market and gave her the best ones.

'I said to come here.' Danielle was quick. Lee must not know that she'd lied to Nicky.

'You told me Nicky wasn't coming.' Now Lee did point the torch at Danielle.

Nicola's expression hardened. 'You've got on boy's boots.'

'Lee likes them.' Danielle leapt off the roundabout and landed badly, grazing her knee. She pulled out a packet of Juicy Fruit from her dress and offered it to Lee.

'Not on girls I don't,' Lee hurried to clarify.

'Girls can wear what they like.' Danielle fiddled with her laces.

'They look nice.' Nicola never ganged up on people.

'Thanks.' Danielle chewed laconically.

'Are you missing Sarah?' Nicky asked Lee.

Danielle should have said that. It sounded nice.

'A bit. Yes. I made a thing in the bedroom with her dolls.' Lee was sheepish, thankful that in the dark the girls couldn't see his face.

'My sister says your dad used to make you mind her so he can do sex with your mum!' Danielle said.

'He's *not* my dad,' Lee fumed. 'They don't do that anyway!'

'Nor do mine.' Nicola's lip wobbled. 'I wish I'd been nicer to Robbie.'

'You are nice.' Lee flashed the torch on and off like Morse code. He went over to Nicola.

'Were, not are.' Miss Blythe, Danielle's teacher, had said Danielle had a very high IQ. In English lessons, she understood the difference between then and now. 'Sarah can't be nice to Robbie now because he's dead and gone. And so is she.'

'Maxine said you got to go indoors,' Nicola told her.

'She can stuff it.' Danielle jutted out her chin. 'Anyway dead people walk, Miss Blythe said so.'

'She said your dad's back from prison.'

'It wasn't prison. He goes off selling clothes. He makes loads. More than your dad.' Danielle stamped her boots.

All the local children knew that Eddie Hindle's business trips were at Her Majesty's Pleasure.

'I might go now,' Danielle said as if the idea had just occurred.

'You the last one?' The keeper was locking the park gate when she reached it.

About to lie on principle, Danielle pictured Lee kissing Nicky on the swings. 'There's two in the playground. They wouldn't come even though I told them to.'

'Where you been?' Eddie Hindle was sprawled on the couch, a cigarette burning on his lower lip. A second-time-around Mod in suit and tipped back trilby, Hindle was trim and dashing.

'Out.'

'Got you a present.' He sucked on his cigarette.

Danielle knew that his presents were nicked. A doll, a bracelet that Maxine hated, perfume for her mum. He'd given Danielle the boots because they didn't fit Jason. This time it seemed Jason had got a gun. He was playing with it by the telly (rented because her mum was sick of it being carted off).

Jason rat-a-tatted at her with the gun. Danielle pictured him flying off the slide like Robbie who her dad had said, 'cracked his head open like an egg.' Lee would be nice when she cried. Jason would never grow into the Doc Martens.

'How long are you here?' Danielle asked Eddie the question she always asked.

'For good, darlin'!' Eddie always replied.

Chapter Fourteen

2019

'Did you ask Trudy to do this?' Jack was reading the notes that Trudy had typed from the Philips case meeting.

'No, I haven't involved Trudy in detective stuff. She did it off her own bat.'

'That was nice.' Habitually suspicious of good deeds, Jack tried for a positive response. 'Another brain. Although perhaps too many cooks.'

After supper, Jack had suggested going upstairs and discussing the case *after*. He'd expected Stella to argue, but she'd begun unbuttoning his shirt before they got to the bedroom. Two hours later they'd been startled awake by Stanley barking. Stella was in time to see a cat high-tailing over the back wall.

At five past two, Jack in T-shirt and boxers, Stella in her dad's dressing gown, sat in the kitchen drinking tea and reading the file Carrie had brought.

'Can there be too many cooks?' Stella rarely cooked. Supper had been microwaved shepherd's pies with frozen peas in deference to Jackie's 'eat more vegetables' campaign. Jack had brought a bottle of Merlot. She tapped her police notebook. 'Trudy missed a bit.'

'Where?'

'Bev pointed out that Penelope Philips had an alibi so why did Carrie still believe that Penelope killed Rachel? Carrie said, quote, "My mother is the jealous type. Never get on the wrong side of her."' Stella drew a biro line between paragraphs in Trudy's report where the text should have been.

Jack vaguely remembered the comment, but it had been blown to kingdom-come when Carrie had mentioned Cashman. After that he'd been unable to concentrate. 'Penelope Philips could have got home, found Cater there and realized about the affair. She totally lost it. I'd want to kill Cashman if I found him in your spare bedroom.' Jack was instantly furious for revealing that, just after they'd had the best sex ever, he'd let slip that he considered Cashman a threat. Jackie said that Cashman was in their relationship because Jack put him there. Stella rarely experienced jealousy, she wouldn't get it. And nor did he want her to get it. If Stella thought he was jealous of her, she'd flee to the hills.

'You couldn't kill anyone.' Rifling through the papers, Stella sounded like she was convincing herself. 'Here's the CCTV image of Penelope Philips in London. Oh.'

'What?' Did Stella ever compare Cashman to him? Jack blotted out the image of Cashman and Stella in the very same bed upstairs. Jackie had to remind Jack that he had children with another woman. Jack knew he needed to shape up.

'Look at the street name.' Stella was examining the CCTV picture.

'Dalgarno Gardens. That's near the playground where I take the twins. Bella lives round the corner.' Jack felt himself redden. 'Actually, Bella said—'

'I've got four clients in that street. When Carrie told us her mum went shopping in London, I presumed she meant Oxford Street not Shepherd's Bush.'

'There's Westfield Shopping Centre.' Although technology moved fast, Jack had expected a grainy black and white still, or like Street View which rendered pedestrians faceless phantoms. The shot of Philips walking along the pavement was sharp and in colour. 'She's not carrying any shopping bags.'

'Perhaps she hadn't been yet.' Stella laid out the double-page spread from the *Daily Mail*. Beneath the heading, 'Dead Woman Dumped in Drain' was a shot of 'the murder house where killer Philips cavorted with his mistress'. A circle marked the garage where the body was found. Rachel Cater, aged thirty-one, had lived with her elderly mother in a rented flat in Cheltenham. A photo of a woman with frizzed hair, glasses and a snaggle-toothed smile was captioned 'the victim'. Jack berated himself for the surprise that Rachel wasn't conventionally attractive. Penelope Philips, on the other hand, was stunning even in a street lens. Narrow determined features betrayed intelligence. Inset was 'Chris and Penny' on their wedding day in 1989 captioned, 'betrayed Penny not ashamed of six-month bump!' In another photo blurred by falling snow, heads down Carrie and her mother hastened to a 'waiting police car'. In this story no one was innocent.

'I don't have a spare bedroom,' Stella said.

'What?'

'You said you'd kill Martin if you found him in my spare bedroom.' Stella studied the article. 'Unless you count my office which used to be my bedroom.'

'It was an example.' Jack drank from his empty mug in a bid to erase the stupid comment.

'An example of what?' Stella could be like Stanley with a captured sock, she wouldn't let go.

'Of how jealousy leads to murder. Not me, obviously.' Obviously. Bella had called him a creature of the night because he walked London streets in search of murderers, looking for a person with a mind like his own. 'Carrie believes her mother killed Rachel out of jealousy.'

'That would hardly help.' Stella fanned out cuttings on the table. Several showed Carrie Philips outside the court after her father was found guilty of the 'heinous crime'. A fist in the air, 'Daddy didn't do it' (the *Mail*). 'Daughter insists father is innocent' (the *Guardian*). No sign of Penelope.

'Christopher Philips cleaned up after the murder. Still the police found bloodstains. Philips must not have expected to be caught.' Stella paused. 'Cashman was there.'

Jack felt his insides drop. 'You didn't say.'

'I don't talk about clean-up scenes, you know that.'

'You sometimes do,' Jack objected. 'There was that one in Mill Hill last month.'

'That's because you were meant to be doing it with us, but you had to babysit.' Stella was looking at a picture of a younger Rachel in a graduation gown clutching her degree. An older woman in matching skirt and jacket, a handbag dangling from one hand, stood beside her. *Proud mum with tragic Rachel.* 'Cashman said to say nothing, especially to you. This was before I met Carrie. That put the case on a need-to-know basis. You *need* to know.'

'Why was he there? He's in the Met.' Jack gripped the table. How many times had Stella met Cashman?

'He never said.' Stella found an article with an aerial view of the house. The lawn stretched to the river that ran through the village. 'Martin suggested coffee, but I said I was working.'

Martin.

'He came to Winchcombe to ask you out.' Jack heard his voice as if from underwater. Stella needn't have told him about the coffee. *He needed to know.*

'No.' Stella wasn't duplicitous, yet Jack felt she wasn't telling him everything. 'Christopher Philips told police he tried to end it with Rachel Cater and she'd threatened to tell his wife and that's why she was at his house.'

'So Philips finds Rachel there and knowing she's going to wreck his marriage has no choice but to kill her.'

'There's always a choice,' Stella said.

'He chose to have an affair with her. Rachel looks nice, that smile is warm and friendly. Her poor mum.' Jack examined a picture of a flat in a block with wraparound balconies imitating streets. The ghostly image of a woman stared out over the rail. Jack felt a pang. The elderly woman looked scared. The photographer had got her to pose – grieving mum alone in the world – and Agnes Cater obliged. The media were heartless. Jack felt complicit.

'Who apart from the Philips family had access to the house?' Stella wondered.

'They probably had a cleaner.'

'Why would a cleaner kill their client?' The idea would be beyond Stella's comprehension. She emptied all the papers onto the table. Jack divided newspaper cuttings from a batch of interview transcripts. A DVD was labelled 'Cater TV coverage'. Carrie was planning to appeal her father's sentence. Clean Slate's work was to be the linchpin. If they found irrefutable evidence that Christopher Philips was guilty, Jack expected that Carrie wouldn't pay their bill.

The murder house was a large Georgian affair. Perfect for Stella and him, with Milly and Justin. A devil whispered hotly into his ear that it was also perfect for Stella and Cashman. 'Did you pick up any clues while you were cleaning the scene?'

'I got a sense of the layout. Rachel was killed in the lounge and carried out to the garage. All fifteen wounds were in her back. That suggested she trusted her attacker. Carrie believes that her mother didn't know about Cater.' Stella restacked papers. 'What if Penelope Philips had guessed? Jackie once said Graham couldn't hide that he was having an affair.'

'Has Graham had an affair?' Jack depended on Jackie and Graham, his surrogate parents, being happy. Jackie was in Manchester for a fortnight staying with her eldest whose partner had had a baby. She'd abandoned him for a 'real' son. Jack banished the thought. He was morphing into a green-eyed monster.

'Of course not. Just that Penelope Philips' family might be wrong in thinking that Penelope knew about Rachel.'

'We see what we want to see.' Jack saw too much.

'You can't fake CCTV. Penelope Philips was in London,' Stella said. 'However, she has motive and it's too soon to rule her out. The time of death might be wrong.'

'What if Rachel Cater had enemies.' Jack contemplated the graduation picture. 'Somehow I doubt it.'

'Trudy is on it.' Stella nodded.

'Why not Bev?' Jack was wistful for when it was just him and Stella on a case. Yet he'd pushed Stella to take solving crimes seriously and to expand her team.

'With Jackie away, they're divvying tasks.' Stella scanned the court transcript. A giant spiral-bound document. 'Rachel had one enemy or she'd be alive. There are positive statements from her colleagues: "Helpful in a crisis", "thoughtful", "unselfish", "generous", "always bubbly".'

'Not that they'd be likely to say she'd nicked a stapler or taken all the milk without buying more,' Jack said.

'Stealing a stapler isn't a reason to kill.' Stella was jotting down points from the transcript.

'Want to bet? Offices are hotbeds of personal space protection. You know that from cleaning them.'

'It says here that a Kevin Hood saw Rachel parking outside Philips' house. He was walking his mother-in-law's dog. He noticed that her brake light was broken. He called out, but she didn't hear. It was just after two thirty because he heard the church bells chime.'

Jack leaned over Stella, sniffing her hair. Rousing himself, he read Hood's evidence aloud: '...I'd left my car for a valet at the garage and spent the afternoon at my mum-in-law's on Back Lane. I got a list of jobs! I mended a pane in her greenhouse, put up a shelf in the lounge. She made scones. I collected my Audi from the garage. The purple VW was still on Abbey Terrace as I drove past. I nearly left a note about the light, but my wife says I'm a busybody. The six o'clock news came on the radio as I left Winchcombe.' Jack sat back in his chair. 'So this Kevin Hood has provided two time frames. Rachel arrived at the house at two thirty and she hadn't left by six. Presumably because she was dead.'

'I forgot to say.' Stella twirled her dressing gown cord. 'Trudy reckoned Carrie wasn't telling us something. She found a gap in her story that didn't add up. I kind of agree. Why is Carrie so convinced that her mother killed Rachel? She has an alibi, after all.'

'Ironic, since in Trudy's report she missed out what Carrie actually did say.' Jack was mealy-mouthed. 'People's impressions are not always useful.'

'Trudy wants to help.' Stella flapped back his fringe.

'Maybe she's fed up being a boring old PA. Solving murders is sexier than typing cleaning estimates.'

'Do you think so?' Stella looked genuinely interested by what she would never for a minute have entertained.

'Ignore me. I agree with Trudy. Let's be cautious about Carrie. She's too close to the murder to be objective. That could be a problem.' Jack began washing their mugs at the sink.

'We'll check out all angles,' Stella agreed. 'Start big and home in, Terry said.'

'Bella's got a boyfriend.' Jack rammed the scourer into a mug.

'That's good.' Despite Bella's embargo on Stella seeing their children, Stella was consistently nice about Bella. 'What's he called? Have you met him?'

'Harry!' Jack scrubbed at the mug as if crushing the breath out of Harry. 'I could kill him!'

'Why?' Stella's lack of possessiveness was no measure of her love, but Jack wished she'd mind even a teensy bit about Bella. It made his own vengeful feelings darker still.

'I don't want him near my children.'

'They're not just yours. You've said Bella would be happier if she found someone who loved her.' Stella tapped the DVD of news items against her palm.

'I don't want him in the house with my children. Bella hardly knows him. He could be a murderer.' Jack's stomach fizzed at the vision of his twins scampering into Bella's bedroom in the mornings and snuggling up with Harry. Fists balled, he leaned against the counter. 'He could be a paedophile.'

'Maybe she has checked? You're good at recognizing murderers, what did you think?'

Stella was well aware that years of searching for his mother's killer had given Jack the ability to spot a murderer. However, this wasn't fear that his children were sharing their home with a murderer, Jack disliked the fact of Harry. He wanted him eviscerated.

'Plenty of biological fathers kill their children. There was that man who jumped off Beachy Head with his daughters.' Stella wasn't helping. 'If those children had been with their mother and her new husband they'd be alive.'

'That's because he saw them as an extension of himself. Children are separate beings, parents have to be prepared to let them go.' Jack wished he could take his own advice. They lapsed into silence and read through the file. Stella had started a new notebook. Jack's photographic memory saved him the trouble of writing stuff down.

Around them the house settled into the night, floorboards eased, against the intermittent shudder of the fridge came Stanley's rhythmic snores from his basket.

At last Stella put down her pen, yawned and stretched. 'Agnes Cater confirmed in a statement that her daughter expected to "wed Mr Philips".'

'Philips called his wife "blameless".' Jack scanned an article from *The Times*.

'Mrs Cater said that Philips wanted Rachel's children. That could have been a mother's wishful thinking. Mum wants me to, oh never mind.' Stella restacked the papers. 'Perhaps Christopher Philips saw it as a fling and mention of marriage and children scared him off.'

Jack was hit by the horrible thought that Bella's ban on Stella seeing the twins suited Stella. She never complained that she couldn't meet them.

'Bed!' Stella gave him a kiss. 'We've got a long drive in the morning.'

'Where are we going?'

'Winchcombe.' Stella was halfway up the stairs. 'If Penelope Philips is a murderer, you will spot it right away.'

Chapter Fifteen

1980

'Let's have a funeral for Sarah, like we did for Robbie,' Danielle said.

'There's no point.' Lee hung motionless on the swing.

Sarah's body had not yet been released to family. The police had finished an examination of the playground. The white tent had long gone. Only a snatch of police tape snagged in a tree beyond the railings snapped in the breeze. The news had reported that a man was being questioned about Sarah's murder. He was rumoured to be the tramp who had been hanging around. Although a suspect was in custody, few parents let their child play there. The diminished gang had the playground to themselves.

A pall of melancholy had enveloped the children. All but Nicola (forbidden the playground) were by the swings. Crouching, Jason scraped a twig over the concrete, watched beadily by Kevin as if the operation was critical. At six years old and with little grasp on the meaning of death, the small boys had privately agreed that Sarah would get bored of being the patient (especially a dead one) and come skipping back. Nicola and Lee had taken refuge in each other. Neither discussed their lost sibling.

Only Danielle faced reality. She was infuriated that Sarah was still being dead yet Danielle wasn't allowed to see what happened to her next. She applied herself to her other task. When Danielle had informed Inspector Darnell that she was going out with Lee, she'd expressed her intention. Since she couldn't see Sarah's body, she'd get on with marrying Lee. This was more realistic than might have been thought because a girl in their class had started issuing licences. Only really stupidly they only worked if the boy asked the girl.

'A funeral would mean we could have Sarah dead,' Danielle said. A funeral meant that she and Lee could be the mum and dad.

'I don't want to.' Lee's stepdad had threatened to make him sit up all night with Sarah's body. *So you know exactly what you did.* Lee said to himself, 'It is bad.'

'Sarah being dead wasn't your fault.' Danielle took his hand. Lee snatched it away.

'She went looking for her bracelet.' Lee hung on the swing chains. 'You said she was in front.'

'Nicky dragged you off or you'd have seen Sarah wasn't there.' Danielle could be reasonable.

'It's not her fault,' Lee said. Yet doubt crept in. Had Nicola made him leave Sarah? The evening when he'd last seen his sister was a confusion. A white tent, the police car and his stepfather punching the wall as if it was Lee.

'Don't blame yourself, love.' Danielle echoed her mum comforting Cathy Ferris. Personally, Danielle thought that Lee's mum should be in trouble. If she got sent to prison Lee could come and live with the Hindles. Danielle held fast to the fact that when Lee found out that Sarah was dead it was her he'd run to, not Nicky. Conveniently she'd blanked out that Maxine had stopped Lee in the street and brought him to theirs. She considered whether to tell Lee that next All Hallows' Eve Sarah would walk.

'There she is!' Lee got off the swing.

'Sarah?' Danielle got a shock. It was too early.

'Nicky.' Lee acted like Danielle was stupid. 'Who's that lady with her?'

'It's a teacher.' Permanently in trouble, Jason scrambled into the shadows.

Nicola Walsh was unlatching the gate. Beside her was a woman who looked to the children about ten feet tall, her high heels like stilts. She wore a raincoat with padded shoulders and a smart bag on her shoulder.

'This is Miss May,' Nicola announced.

'I knew that,' Danielle said although she hadn't.

'Lucie to you lot! I'm not a bloody teacher.' Lucie May dropped in a swear word to get the kids on her side. 'My teachers couldn't wait to see the back of me! I was always sagging school. Bunking off, to you! Do we hate school?'

'Yes,' they chorused obediently. All except Danielle who came top in reading.

'Miss... wants to talk about Sarah because Robbie is being dug up.' Nicola clamped a hand over her mouth as if she too had sworn.

'Exhume, not digging up.' Danielle sidled up to Lee.

'You're a proper detective!' Lucie winked at Danielle. 'What's your name, hun?'

'Danielle Hindle. I'm with Lee. Sarah and Robbie played with my brother Jason. It's sad what happened. Lee's dad says it's his fault. He was lured off by Nicky so didn't hear Sarah screaming. I don't blame Lee.'

'He's not my dad. I didn't hear nothing,' Lee mumbled.

'Anything,' Danielle whispered a correction.

'Sarah screamed?' Lucie did a sad face. 'I'm a reporter. I'll make sure your story is told properly. So, take it from the top, what exactly happened?'

Lucie May was the Pied Piper as she trooped the children over to the roundabout. Perching between the hold bars, she patted it for them to join her. Danielle sat next to her.

'As I said to Nicky, it's my job to capture baddies and make them pay for their crimes. I can't do it alone. You're on the ground, you know the players and their tricks. You have ears and brains. Working together we'll lock up the murderer so no more children die.' Lucie passed round a bag of Merry Maid toffees.

Danielle unwrapped a sweet and gave it to Kevin. Putting an arm around him she said, 'You don't have a big sister to save you, so if you behave, I'll make sure you don't die too.'

Kevin was aware that their older siblings had not saved Robbie or Sarah, but beaming, he accepted the toffee and Danielle's unexpected attention.

'I'm taping your clever ideas. OK with you, Danielle?' Lucie May had divined the ring leader. She took a small black object from her bag.

'Are you police?' Schooled by her father, Danielle gave nothing away for free. 'We're only meant to talk to Inspector Darnell.'

'The police would be nowhere without you and me.' May shook the bag for Danielle to take another toffee.

The police detective had said to stay away from reporters, but now Danielle recalled him talking to Miss May. Anyway, Danielle wanted to be on a tape recorder.

'Who hates stupid grown-ups telling them what to do?' Lucie May held out her recorder.

'Me!' they shouted.

'Who wants to start?'

Danielle put up her hand. 'The man in the playground was going to kill us.'

'No he wasn't,' Nicola objected.

'You weren't there.' Danielle dipped her head to Lucie's recorder. 'Lee and Sarah didn't see him. I came back by myself to the playground. He said he was going to do a murder. So I ran.'

'That was a different day. You told Lee that Sarah had gone.' Nicola rarely argued with Danielle, but the recorder had made her brave.

'I never did!'

'It's easy to make a mistake when you're scared,' Lucie trilled. 'Where was Sarah?'

'She lost her charm bracelet. She was looking for it when the man murdered her,' Danielle said.

'How do you know if you left first?' Lucie's eyes twinkled like a friend.

'I found the bracelet.' Danielle was unruffled.

'So you were with Sarah.' Lucie May jerked the recorder closer to the girl. This was new information. In one of his mealy-mouthed press conferences Terry had not mentioned this.

'I came back for Sarah even though he might kill me too.' Excited by the interview, Danielle lost control of her facts. 'Did you want to talk just to Lee and me?' The lady would write in the newspaper that Lee was her boyfriend. 'Lee came to my house when Sarah was dead and cried.'

'I never.' Lee was puce.

'Nothing wrong with a few tears, big man. Your sister was dead.' Lucie thrust the toffee bag at Lee. 'Tell me all about Sarah. What was she like?'

'She was funny!' Kevin snuffled into a hand. 'She said rude words.'

'She did *not*.' Lee shoved Kevin, making him choke on his toffee. Regarding him as a pet, Danielle pulled Kevin to her.

'Good for her!' Lucie did Lovely Aunty for her niece and nephew on high days and holidays and in pursuit of a scoop. However, even as a child she'd been wary of children. Unpredictable and self-serving, they emitted secretions and broke things. 'We hate goody-two-shoes, don't we?'

'Yes!' The group were in unison.

'My mum used to say, "No one's an angel except an angel."' Bloody silly. Lucie wondered again what her mum had meant.

'Sarah wasn't an angel, she was a tell-tale.' Danielle felt emboldened to tell the truth.

'She was not,' Lee stormed.

'She told your dad you'd let her go on the slide when he said not to in case she cracked her head open like Robbie and she did.' Danielle heaved for breath. 'And she made you buy her a charm with your paper round money.'

'I didn't mind.' Lee got off the roundabout.

'Keep it real, Lee.' Lucie eased off a shoe and massaged a developing bunion. 'My sister nicked my make-up, stole my fags but boy, was she was as innocent as the day is born if I was stupid enough to tell my mum. Angels are no fun.'

'She did once tell on you, Lee. For letting her go on the slide,' Nicola said. 'And your dad hit you, I stopped your nose bleeding, remember?'

'He's not my dad.' Lee rubbed his nose as he recalled the incident.

'He liked Sarah best, but now she's gone he'll like you better,' Danielle said.

'He wants me to die,' Lee said. 'Sarah knew how to get her way with Alan. She'd ask for chocolate and he'd give it to her. And a Barbie.' He looked across the concrete to where the tent covering Sarah's body had been as if it was still there and his sister might emerge from it brushing herself down and saying how she'd fooled him.

'Who gave her the charm bracelet?' An item of jewellery, riddled with symbol and portent, the bracelet was a gift to a tabloid reporter.

'Alan. She had a heart, a Mickey Mouse, a dog and letters spelling her name. And a telephone. I got her the angel saying "Best Sister". The man from Abba stole the bracelet.' Lee put a hand to his mouth as if this had just occurred.

Lucie thrust the recorder at Lee. 'Do you mean Derek Parsley took it?' Lucie was sure that a tramp called Derek Parsley would be charged with Sarah's murder. She'd file the story after she'd finished with this lot. She was always ahead of the facts. Terry was no help.

'Sarah found it.' Danielle tossed a sweet wrapper away. Kevin retrieved it for putting in a bin later.

'She didn't or she'd have come home.' Lee ran the zip on his Harrington jacket up and down. He was obliquely aware that talking to the reporter was wrong.

'Sarah had on the bracelet when she was dead.' Danielle spoke into the recording machine.

'How do you know Sarah was wearing the charm bracelet, darling?' Lucie ogled Danielle encouragingly.

'Inspector Darnell told me,' Danielle insisted. 'With the Best Sister charm missing.'

'Do you mean Sarah had the bracelet, but the lovely generous gift that Lee bought for his beloved baby sister wasn't on the chain?' Lucie often tried out phrases that later would flow so naturally from her keyboard.

'Yes.' Danielle was patient. Of course that was what she meant.

'Fancy.' Lucie lit a cigarette, juggling her lighter with the Dictaphone. Out of the mouths of babes.

'Charms are expensive. They cost two pounds fifty.' The sweets were eaten and Danielle was tiring. 'The man from Abba murdered Sarah and he murdered Robbie.'

'Are you two going out?' Lucie aimed the recorder at Lee and Nicola. Her tactic was to embarrass the kids, put the cat among the pigeons and see what feathers flew.

'No. They're not!' Danielle scoffed.

'A bit.' Lee reddened.

Nicola stood primly to attention.

'Once, long ago, when I was your age I snogged my boyfriend in this very playground. My sister fell in that pond.' Lucie waved towards the park. 'Not my fault. My mum and dad should have been minding her, not me.'

Nicola perked up. 'Lee wasn't to blame for Sarah.'

'Lee, tell you what, Mr Man. Give us your phone number and your mum's man and me can have a little chat, how's that?'

'We're not on the phone,' Danielle said. 'Dad didn't pay the bill.'

'Lee is on the phone.' Nicola was proud by proxy. Then a moment of her old maternal self, 'We have to go. Kev, your mum doesn't know you're here, she'll be going spare. I'm not meant to be here either.'

'I'll come too,' Lee said.

The three children headed for the gate.

'It's shit being dumped,' Lucie said to Danielle as they watched Jason's kamikaze launches off the slide.

'I haven't been dumped!' Danielle retorted. 'I dumped *him*.' She stared at her boys' boots.

'Lee is a rescuer. He only feels sorry for Nicola. Who wants pity? The world's divided between persecutors, rescuers and victims. And leaders like you, kiddo.' Lucie emitted a ball of smoke. 'Sarah was a tell-tale, was she?'

'She got people into trouble.'

'Who?' Lucie tossed her stub away. It glowed in the dusk.

'Sarah told her dad about Jason pissing on the swing. Alan hit Jason. My mum said she'd get my dad on Alan. But she didn't because everyone's scared of him and Dad was in prison.' Danielle added, 'Dad would have killed him dead.'

'It must have made you cross, your little brother hurt and nothing done,' Lucie crooned. 'Did Sarah get you into trouble too?'

'I'm not stupid.' Danielle shouted at Jason that they were going. 'He crushed her with a brick.'

'Who crushed who, gorgeous?' Lucie yawned, patting at her mouth as if bored.

'Mr Parsley. The Abba Maniac.' Danielle recalled a word from the newspapers.

'You're one smart cookie, Danielle.' Lucie May produced a card. 'If anything occurs here's what you do, luvvy. Call me. From a phone box. Reverse the charges. Keep this to ourselves. No point worrying Inspector Darnell. He only wants facts.' Lucie clicked off the recorder.

'Will what I've said be on television?' Danielle flicked the card over her fingers.

'You'll be famous.' Lucie May lit another cigarette. She handed Danielle the bag of toffees. 'Danielle Hindle, this is your life!'

Chapter Sixteen

2019

The rain had stopped by the time Stella pulled off the M40 onto a winding country lane. She passed a signpost for Winchcombe. Jack sat up when they reached the high street. Having offered to drive, he'd fallen asleep as soon as they hit the motorway.

On her trip to clean the crime scene, Stella hadn't paid attention to her surroundings. Now she spotted changes. A building society had taken over the Lloyds bank and the post office was now a shop selling gems. There were two new clothes shops and a hairdresser's instead of one of the butcher's. The beauty parlour had gone. Thankfully, the Winchcombe deli was as busy as ever because she and Jack had planned on lunch there after interviewing Penelope Philips.

'What if she won't talk?' Stella slotted the van by the war memorial where Rachel Cater had parked on that fateful day.

'She's returning to her old home to see us so she'll hardly go "no comment" on us.' Jack ran a comb through his hair.

They were both startled by a shriek like a tortured child.

'Stanley's awake.' Jack peered over the rim of a box-shaped bed lined with fur – attached to the seat – a gift from Lucie May for 'the small poodle with a lion's personality'. Hitherto having only seen the dog as a means of leaving poo on her carpet and demanding attention, Lucie's generosity was a volte-face. Jack reckoned she wanted something and indeed Lucie had kept ringing since the day she'd overheard that Carrie Philips was coming to the office.

'I hope Penelope Philips doesn't mind dogs.' Stella wasn't looking forward to meeting a woman whose daughter believed she was a violent killer. There was no nice way to mention that.

'Her husband's lover bled all over her front room, I don't imagine she'll be overly worried about pawmarks,' Jack said. 'Stella, I can meet Lady Penelope on my own if you're worried.'

'I'm fine.' As ever, Jack had read her mind.

Jack and Stella were early so they went for a stroll along the main street. In the distance came the hoot of the steam train. The classic railway, run by volunteers, added to the impression that Winchcombe belonged in a bygone age.

'We're in *The Railway Children*.' Jack sighed happily. Stanley drank from a water bowl outside the Emporium gift shop which was displaying some thirties' style posters, adding to the impression.

'Is that your favourite film?' Last week Bev had made them do a quiz from one of her magazines on how well you knew your partner. Jackie got full marks on Graham. Beverly filled in what her wife should like despite Jackie's warning about trying to change her. Trudy and Stella hadn't joined in. If Bev had intended the quiz as a means of probing into Trudy's private life it had failed. Stella's refusal was because, a gatherer of facts, she knew that Jack's mother had been murdered when he was little. Aged seven he'd been sent to a boarding school in Kent. His father – prime suspect for the murder – died in Scarborough District General when Jack was in his twenties and while he'd left the bedside to get a coffee. The media reported that the 'orphaned son of the murdered woman' had gone to Australia, but once, when they'd been talking about Stella's brother who lived in Sydney, Jack had commented that he'd never been 'down under'. These snippets won Stella no points in the magazine quiz.

'Yes, it is my favourite film. That bit on the platform where the father emerges through the steam.' Jack's eyes misted up as if the memory was his own.

'Do you imagine you're getting off your train to meet your children?'

'Maybe.' Jack scooped Stanley up as a lorry mounted the kerb at the awkward turn into North Street. 'Thanks, Stell!'

'For what?'

'For knowing how I tick!' Jack gave her a lingering kiss.

Stella doubted that actually she had any idea how Jack – or anyone else – 'ticked'. Taking Jack's hand she led him back to 'the Murder House'.

When her home became a crime scene the police had moved Penelope Philips to a safe house in Broadway, a nearby village. Stella and Jack knew it from their previous visit to Gloucestershire. Although her husband had been in prison for months – on remand and then when he was found guilty – Penelope had not moved back to Winchcombe. Stella would make it her business to find out why.

At the scene clean, Stella had been surprised that, given the house was in the middle of the village, a brutal murder had gone unnoticed. Now Jack reminded her that it had happened in the afternoon on a day when Winchcombe – unlike Hammersmith – still had early closing.

'OK, so we're agreed.' Stella paused outside the old Lloyds bank. 'You give a sign if you reckon she's a murderer.' When Stella had first known Jack, his reliance on portents and instincts had alarmed her. She was unconvinced by Jack's claim that he could tell a psychopath (he called them True Hosts) just by following them down a street. She didn't relish the idea that Jack followed anyone. But stalking came with detective territory so she'd reluctantly accepted it. Over the years they'd solved several cold cases, and Stella had seen that Jack saw what others missed. What she missed.

'I'll fiddle with my coat, like this.' Jack brushed one of his lapels as if at a stain on the fabric.

The latch buzzed open as soon as Jack pressed the bell. Stella checked the street again. Carrie had warned them about reporters. Stella expected Lucie May. A man taking cash from the ATM looked authentic, but so would a person intending to look authentic.

Stella considered that, murderer or not, she'd feel safer with Lucie than Penelope Philips. As she stepped into the dark hallway, her heart missed a beat.

Although the curtains and blinds were closed, Stella could see how clean the place looked. This somewhat allayed her nerves.

A shaft of sunlight slanted across the carpeted floor. Stella faltered. She saw a body there. Face down in pooling blood. Spatters covered the walls and the lounge door.

'Do come in.' As if they were on a social call.

Stella looked at the carpet again and saw only the slant of sunlight.

In brown cords, angora jumper draped with a silk scarf that Stella recognized from the Emporium's window, Penelope Philips was every inch a respectable Cotswold Woman. Perfume, the scent uncompromising, hit Stella's nostrils. Her hyposensitive olfactory sense identified Molecule One, the perfume that Bev's wife Cheryl had got for her. If anyone was changing anyone, Cheryl was affecting Bev. In a good way, for Bev was happier. Distantly Stella noticed that Molecule One wasn't the scent she'd caught on her last visit to the house. Good Girl, that was the name. She gathered herself. Terry said don't get bogged down with irrelevancies. He also said not to ignore trivial detail.

With a chilly smile, Penny Philips raised a hand signalling for them to go into the lounge. Stella disliked that they were as good as trapped in the house with Philips. Even if she wasn't a murderer, she wasn't exactly friendly.

The floorboards had been replaced. A new carpet laid. Stella caught a whiff of gloss paint and saw that the skirting boards gleamed. Two floral-patterned sofas and a coffee table on which was the beginnings of a jigsaw faced a huge television that was on the way to being a cinema. Everything was spotless. Stella relaxed. A scrupulous cleaner, Philips would not be a violent murderer. They could relax. Perching on one of the sofas, Stella tried to catch Jack's eye.

But looking down, Jack was brushing at the lapel of his coat.

Chapter Seventeen

1980

'If you find the murder weapon you're home and dry.' Lucie sat up in the bed and lit a cigarette. In a shirt of Terry's that she'd commandeered and wearing a beige-coloured BA eye mask from a recent trip to the States pushed up onto her forehead, she looked alarming, as if she'd been kidnapped.

'We don't need it. We have a confession.' No point in keeping that back, Lucie told him she'd found out as soon as she arrived. And no point in wondering who in his team had leaked the information. It was him.

'A confession is so much confetti, here today, mashed in a puddle tomorrow.'

'We'll find what he used to crush her neck.' Terry found the manner of the little girl's death as upsetting as the fact of it. A strong man had used his might to mash the life out of Sarah. Michael Sutherland had suggested that defining lines either side of a wide area of deep abrasions on the skin were achieved with a weapon such as a brick.

'If he's got any sense he's got rid of it.'

'It must be somewhere on the common.' Terry blinked at the smoke. He wished that Lucie wouldn't light up after sex. It was his fault that she was there. Lucie had found him in the pub with the team, on a high that they had a confession. Frustrated that he couldn't share the news with Suzie and Stella, he'd cracked quicker than Derek Parsley. And here they were with Lucie puffing on a post-coital fag. Despite her relentless chase of a story, Terry trusted Lucie. He owed her this one. 'Danielle Hindle will do well in court. She's an incomparable witness.'

'Please tell me that you're not relying on that little madam!' Lucie's mask gave her the look of a fly with more than one pair of eyes. Which sometimes he thought she must have. She missed nothing. 'And what's a friggin' incom-bloody-parable witness?' She sucked in a long drag, holding in the smoke as if it was dope. Terry wished Lucie would give up, one day it would kill her.

'It's what a judge once called Bernard Spilsbury, the godfather of pathology, before, and during the Second World War.' Terry was reading Spilsbury's biography. Suzie would grumble that he was never off the job. At least crime was something that he and Lucie shared. And good sex. *Not as good as Suzie.* Terry banished the thought. 'Reading' was an overstatement. The last few nights, he'd reread the same page before falling asleep with the light on. Suzie used to lean over and take the book out of his hand. Lucie – in her portable darkness – never noticed.

'Danielle Hindle is a ten-year-old kid. She's got you round her little finger. Like Stella, she canters rings around you.' Lucie contemplated her cigarette. Even she knew when she'd overstepped the mark.

'If Danielle Hindle's dad was a banker or a lawyer and not an incompetent burglar, Danielle would be looking at university. As it is she wants to join the police. Sometimes rehabilitation comes out in the new generation. Her writing's good, she's clever, she can express herself. OK, so her spelling's bit off, but better that than being stuck for the right word. That's what I tell Stella.'

'How do you know?' Lucie blew smoke at the ceiling.

'From her letters.'

'Who to?' Lucie pressed home.

'Me. OK. Forget I said that!' *Bloody idiot.*

'She writes you letters?' Lucie ground out her cigarette in the ashtray that Suzie had bought for his mum while they were all on a holiday in Dorset when Stella was a baby. When his mum had died of lung cancer three years later and he was clearing out her house to return it to the council, Terry had kept the ashtray and, reluctantly, let Lucie use it.

'Her teachers say she's a bright kid if only she'd concentrate. With her home life, it's no wonder. Where could she do her schoolwork?' Terry recalled the chaos in the Hindle house when they'd gone there to talk to Danielle. A teacher had told him Danielle was good at art but wouldn't take any painting home: 'It'll get thrown away. Eddie Hindle is a nasty piece of work. When he's out of prison, Danielle and her brother as good as live in that playground. For different reasons, those kids prefer it to their home.'

Lucie snuffled down in the pit of his arm. 'Sweet that she writes to you, Tel. Let's see.' She moved her hand down his stomach. One thing about Lucie, she was blatant. Terry nudged her away.

'It's against the law to bring evidence home. It would be inadmissible in court. You know that.' He pinched his nose. He had a full-blown headache.

'That girl's got you by the short and curlies.' Lucie illustrated this with a tug beneath the duvet.

'Ouch!' He'd scooted the letters under the bed seconds before Lucie had come out of the bathroom. Had he anticipated that he'd be stupid enough to invite her back, Terry would have properly concealed them. 'Anyway, like I say, no smart-arsed barrister will get one over on Danielle Hindle.'

There was a click and a flare. Lucie lit another cigarette. She leaned over the bed and dropped her lighter into her handbag. She kept it close should she need to jot down some fished-for nugget in her pad. Like him, Lucie was never off the clock. Unlike him, she never took her eye off the ball.

'Danielle Hindle told me she wanted to be a reporter.' She yawned.

'Have you talked to her?' Terry jumped out of bed. Grabbing his trousers he hopped and staggered into them. 'You had no right to go near her! Not without her parents' consent. Not even then. Lucie, I'm warning you. Do. *Not.* Print. Anything!' He fumbled with his zip.

A smoke ring hovered over Lucie's head like the mockery of a halo.

'I don't tell you how to do your job. Don't stop me doing mine. Those kids were happy to chatter like like my darling budgie.' Her mouth a pencil stroke, eyes blindfolded. Lucie was scary.

'She's a kid. What'd you promise, a never-ending supply of bubble gum?' He scrubbed at his hair. Being able to see did not give him an advantage.

'A minute ago you were comparing her to some ancient pathologist.' Lucie did her corncrake laugh. 'Believe me, Danielle Hindle's an incomparable liar!'

'She pointed us towards Derek Parsley. When he was picked up he was covered in blood. He's got previous. She saw him in the playground. All of that's true. Now he's confessed.' Terry pictured the man sobbing into his hands. It had been several hard days' nights.

'Until today, my geld was on Sarah's daddy. Alan Ferris is a psycho.' Despite her blackout mask, Lucie placed her cigarette in the ashtray and in her Marilyn Monroe voice breathed, 'Why sure, honey, the kid will be a damn fine witness.'

'Meaning?' Terry caught his triple reflection in the mirrored doors of his built-in wardrobe. Midnight shadow, bloodshot eyes, an arrest mugshot looked better. He couldn't remember why he'd put on his trousers. Suzie had wanted the mirrors.

His bedside phone rang.

'Guv, it's Derek Parsley!' Cashman was shouting.

'Has he told you where to find the... weapon?' Terry shouldn't grudge Martin his moment in the sun, but he did. He *really* did. He'd nearly mentioned the brick in front of Lucie May.

'He's hung himself.'

'Hung himself?' The words were foreign.

'He's dead, guv.'

'Dead?' Lucie ripped off her mask. 'Tel, come *on*.' She whipped clean knickers from her handbag and dressed with the speed of Harry Houdini in reverse.

Fixed on the tail lights of Lucie's MG, Terry mercy-dashed through the dark empty streets in his police-issue Rover. Lucie had got her scoop.

Chapter Eighteen

2019

'Carrie's Daddy's girl.' Philips was doing a jigsaw. From the picture on the box, Jack recognized Salvador Dali's *The Persistence of Memory*. Penelope had completed a clock face draped over a rock. The profusion of curves and expanse of dark colour would be difficult.

'This is a challenge, Mrs Philips,' he exclaimed cheerily. A soothing accompaniment to murder. They must leave.

'Pass me that piece, please, Jack. And for God's sake call me Penny. All my friends do.'

It was rare for True Hosts to have friends. The woman hadn't spoken with conviction. He didn't believe that she had friends. He handed Penny a jigsaw piece of entirely interlocking sides. He'd assumed she'd randomly chosen it but Penny fitted it into the dark section. A True Host would do that.

'Thank you for meeting us.' Stella must have forgotten their agreed sign. Jack was practically thumping his lapel, but Stella was fixed on the jigsaw as if she might have to join in. She was chewing spearmint gum. She hadn't chewed gum since he'd met her. A sign of nerves? Stella was rarely nervous.

'I'm guessing Carrie thinks that I killed that whore.' Penny snapped in another piece and followed it swiftly with another one. Now the sky – lurid yellow and blue – was forming.

'No,' Stella said. *Never lie to a True Host.*

'Yes,' Jack said.

'Of course.' She flashed Jack a grateful smile and indicated for him to pass her another piece. She completed another clock. This was creeping him out. A True Host, she was of course unfazed that her daughter thought her capable of murder. The second clock slimed over a table on which was another clock crawling with ants. In the centre of the picture – not yet in the puzzle – was a figure: Dali asleep, Jack vaguely recalled.

The puzzle was a perfectly executed performance. Philips was playing a game with them.

'Welcome to Ground Zero!' Penny got up. She had completed the sky. 'I expect you were promised a tour?'

Jack saw Stella start. So Carrie hadn't told her mother that Stella had cleaned the crime scene and therefore hardly needed a tour. Useful. Except they needed to leave and take stock, as Stella would say. Stella hadn't moved. Jack knew that fixed smile. She'd seen his sign after all. She was weighing up her next move. Leave. He willed her to look at him. But suddenly Stella sprang to life.

'Yes, we were promised a tour,' she said.

'The Cater bitch drove me from my home.' Her tone brittle, Penny regarded Stanley who was preening his paws. 'That's where she was. Bleeding like a stuck pig.'

The carpet was the same tough loop weave that Bella had got for the twins' bedroom. Jack worried that it hurt their knees when they played. When he'd told Stella, she'd said that it was hard-wearing.

'This was my forever house.' Penny Philips might have been showing the place to potential buyers. Again, Jack imagined himself and Stella living there. Stella was too rational to mind that a woman had been murdered in the hall and she'd cleaned up so would be confident there'd be no bacteria. So far Jack had no sense of Cater's ghost. He wished he did. He felt a pang of sorrow for Rachel. She'd had the misfortune to fall in love with her boss.

'With Chris gone I've got my dogs out of storage.' Penny indicated the ornaments crowding the surfaces.

'Do you have a dog?' Stella asked.

'Christ no!' She completed two more pieces of the puzzle, then commanded, 'Come.'

Stella went out of the room first. Jack couldn't attract her attention without Penny seeing. He could feign illness, but knowing Stella she would suggest he wait in the van for her. Stella was rarely afraid. Jack lingered in the room and flipping over a piece saw no number on the back. Penny Philips had not been cheating. His blood froze.

Upstairs in what had been Penny and Chris's bedroom were more china dogs, a golden retriever in a running pose, a spaniel begging. A mausoleum of a four-poster was stacked with rows of cushions, each diminishing in size down the counterpane. A style that Jack found disquieting. Where did the cushions go at night?

'Very nice.' Out of character, Stella never remarked on clients' décor.

'He fucked her right there.' Penny ignored the compliment.

'According to what we've read Rachel had never been to your house until that day.' Stella stuck to facts.

'Chris is a born liar.' Jack thought he detected hesitation. Did Christopher Philips tell lies or had his betrayal poisoned Penny's view of him? 'Carrie shouldn't have contacted you. What does she know? It was me on Terry's team. Me he trusts. He knows I'm innocent. It's in our letters.' Penny's use of the present tense was downright creepy.

'Terry?' Stella flashed a shocked look at Jack. Jack offered a shrug.

Jack mouthed, 'What letters?' Cashman was apparently concerned with Rachel's murder, but Terry had been dead seven years.

'Your father. We corresponded until the day he died.' Penny had a True Host's perception. She continued the tour. More dogs, more cushions. With her husband out of the way, Penny Philips' taste had free rein. Was she making the best of a catastrophe or had her plan worked? Kill the mistress. Frame the husband. *The modus operandi of a True Host.*

'Carrie's room.' Penny Philips straightened the duvet on a single bed and tucked a chair under a school desk. Textbooks were on shelves along with a microscope. There were also books on true crime, the Moors Murders, Ted Bundy in the States, Rachel Nickell. The seeds of Carrie's determination to be a criminal barrister? Or instruction manuals for the murder that she would one day commit? Jack wondered if Stella was thinking the same thing.

Carrie had said that she'd moved out with no intention of coming back. Did her mother hope that Carrie would return? Rachel Cater's ghost didn't haunt the house, but the presence of a girl doing her homework hunched over the desk was palpable.

'My daughter isn't talking to me. My husband won't let me visit him in prison.' Penny Philips looked fleetingly sad. Jack wasn't fooled. True Hosts imitated emotions to a T. 'Carrie says I killed that tart in revenge. Had she confronted me like they say she was going to, I'd have locked myself in the toilet and cried my heart out. I did that anyway. Me and Chris had the perfect life. Now I'll have to start again. New house. New name.'

Was doing a jigsaw a metaphor? Jack liked patterns. Penny would have to reconstruct her life. In her mid-forties there was time, but it was a big thing. If Penny Philips was a True Host then it would be business as usual. Something jarred. True Hosts were in charge of their lives. It was they who decided the fate of others. For her all apparent distress, by mentioning Terry, Penny had wanted to wrongfoot Stella. Seeing Stella clutching Stanley and staring off out of the window, Philips had succeeded. Jack longed to hold her. Penny ushered him out of the room.

'Where's your girlfriend?' She stopped at the bottom of the stairs. Stella wasn't behind them.

They found her still by the window.

'What are you looking at?' Penny was sharp.

'It's a lovely view.' Stella nodded at the hills beyond the town. The contours were outlined in Spring sunshine. Seemingly idyllic.

Frowning, Penny signalled for Stella to leave, keeping them in sight as they returned downstairs.

Jack made a silent resolution. They must get out of the house.

'...there's me thinking Chris was different to other men. Stupid! People say my girl inherited my brains – as you know she's got a very high IQ like me – except Carrie thinks the police got it wrong so she's not so smart.'

Jack hadn't read anything about Carrie's IQ. Personally he didn't hold much store by that kind of thing. It was only one way of looking at a person and missed out the best bits like ghosts and happiness.

The kitchen was unexpectedly homely. Kenwood Chef, bread-maker, jars of pulses, spices, rice, quinoa, copper pans and utensils hung from butcher's hooks. It suggested that eating was integral to the household. The knife block was empty.

Penny unlocked a door by a bright yellow plastic dustbin and marched them past a terrace scattered with tables and chairs to an old building that was bigger than most houses.

'This was the stables, but we don't ride so it's the garage. There's room for three cars.' Scooting them inside, Penny was back in show-home mode. The air was tainted by petrol, Jack guessed from a sit-on mower and a quad bike by one wall. There were no cars. There was an array of tools, hammers, screwdrivers, saws, shears, secateurs, a hedge cutter, a billhook... *What was that for?*

Penny stamped a foot on a metal cover in the middle of the space.

The drainage shaft.

Jack knew that forensics had excavated from the side of the shaft to retrieve Rachel's body without destroying evidence. As well as the screed floor, they'd fitted a new cover. A clumsy job with lumps and dips in the surrounding concrete.

'This is the longest I've lived anywhere. Chris wanted to put down roots,' Penny Philips said. 'I can leave now.'

'Isn't this your dream home?' Jack reminded her. A tease. He knew – and Penny Philips would know that he knew – that True Hosts didn't have dream homes.

'There's been a murder here. It's forever tainted.' Penny grabbed a tyre iron from the wall. Jack grabbed at Stella, but Penny was already levering up the drain cover.

A stench of blood and putrefying flesh drifted up from the shaft that, had she never been found, would have been Rachel Cater's grave.

Stanley began to whimper as if he too could detect the murdered woman, her broken body crumpled far below at the bottom of the shaft. Jack saw brown smears of dried blood where the corpse had bumped against the sides as Christopher Philips chucked Rachel in like so much rubbish. Even if the auctioneer hadn't killed her, the act was callous. Had he chosen the deposition site in panic or was it a calculated choice?

The stains and smell were in Jack's – and Stanley's – imagination. Rachel's body had been wrapped in plastic and besides Stella had cleaned the shaft. It would more hygienic than most people's dinner tables.

'Chris never told me this was here. It's defunct. Carrie could ask herself why I didn't know. The police say Chris planned the murder.' Smacking the tyre iron on her palm Penny might be a plumber discussing the pros and cons of the sewer system. 'Are we done?'

'Done? Yes!' Jack wanted them outside and driving away. Not teetering on the brink of a gaping pit with a psychopath.

'Not quite.' Stella cleared her throat. 'Why is Carrie convinced that you murdered Rachel Cater?'

'You're joking me!' Penny's laugh was a snarl. 'Wait. She didn't tell you? I thought that's what this was all about.'

'Tell us what?' Stella asked.

'How d'you think I knew Terry? My girl couldn't get to Terry because he's dead. So what does she do? She only goes and cosies up to his daughter! She knows what buttons to press.'

The huntin' shootin' accent had made way for far-from-posh West London. Doing voices was another True Host trait. They were chameleons. There was a sharp rise in tension; Jack had a clear run to the exit. Stella did not.

'Carrie read an interview with Stella in some freebie rag.'

Jack often worried that publicity would expose Stella to cranks and stalkers. And murderers. A reason he liked to go unseen and unsung. Trudy had observed of Carrie: *There's something she's not saying.*

'Come out and say it.' Penny Philips slammed a hand on a green button above the quad bike and a shutter rose.

'Say what?' Stella was peering down the shaft, Stanley wide-eyed on her shoulder.

Come on! Jack stopped himself from dragging her away.

Penny spoke above screeching metal as slowly – too slowly – the shutter lifted.

'I'm the girl they call the Playground Killer.'

Chapter Nineteen

1980

> *'I will be on the news like you. I no you sed not to speack to the reporter so I did not say ~~nothing~~ anything. Lee and Nicola told her lots, but the reporter liked me best. Miss May started on about the charms. You should arest her and lock her into prison with Derick Parsley then she cant write stupid stuff. Meet me in the Play ground arfter school. She said I will be famus.*
>
> *From Constable Danielle Hindle aged ten. (My new name.)*

Seated on a swing in the deserted playground, Terry reread Danielle's letter. As he'd told Lucie, Danielle's spelling wasn't great. Actually it was terrible, worse than Stella's at ten. The teachers had said she was smart. He supposed she could express herself which was half the battle. As for Stella, by that age she was living with Suzie and her only letters were Christmas and birthday thank-yous. On Basildon Bond paper. He'd kept them. Some months ago, going through them, Terry had noted how often Stella had put, 'I was pleased to receive your thoughtful gift' and it dawned on him that Suzie had made Stella write. She'd stood over Stella dictating the banal phrase. Stella hadn't written especially to him. Suzie always said his presents were wrong. When Stella got flu and missed an access weekend, he'd come to see her. Squatting down to kiss her in bed Terry had spotted the Tiny Tears doll still in its box under the bed.

If Stella had been living at home – this house was her real home – early on Christmas morning she'd have been tearing into his and Suzie's bedroom pleading to open her presents like she had the year before Suzie left him. Stella had liked the Sherlock Holmes set. Blanching at her carefully inscribed sentences, the politeness of a stranger, Terry had chucked out Stella's letters.

Lucie had said Terry let Danielle – and Stella – get the better of him. He did have a soft spot for Danielle Hindle. The girl wanted to be a detective. Like Stella. Then Suzie told him that Stella had 'grown out of the silly idea'. Pulling back on the swing, Terry slipped the letter inside his jacket pocket. He lifted his feet off the concrete and swung forward. Without kids racing about playing games the playground was bleak, just concrete and iron. A place of murder.

It would make his life easier if, like Danielle Hindle had suggested, the press were penned up during an investigation. Crazy slip telling Lucie about the letters. And she'd got to the kids. Terry scooted the swing higher. Lucie was only loyal to her story. Parsley's suicide had given her bigger fish to fry. She might forget the letters.

Late afternoon. The light was fading. The park would be closing. He had escaped the circus at the police station. End of investigation drinks, Christmas drinks. Terry didn't feel like celebrating either. Lennon's 'War is Over', all over the radio since his fatal shooting, kept playing in Terry's head. He thought of Sean Lennon, the little boy aged five had lost his dad. Lucie had planted a niggle in his mind. Sutherland, the pathologist, reported that Sarah Ferris hadn't died where she was found. SOCO discovered drops of blood in a gap in laurel bushes outside the fence. The drops suggested that Parsley moved her. Why? It was like he'd wanted to be caught.

Terry leaned into the swing, legs outstretched, building momentum. People compared solving an investigation to a jigsaw. An actual jigsaw was a futile pastime. The assembly of the picture depicted on the puzzle box only to dismantle it on completion. At the start of a case Terry had no idea what it would look like. Had he made the wrong pieces fit the wrong picture?

Derek Parsley had been sprawled in his cell, cut down from the window bars by the duty officer. Terry had stormed in and been stopped from doing mouth to mouth.

'No!'

Terry thrust his legs upwards as the swing flew down. The shout was an echo from his boyhood. Mr Greenwood had taken the sixteen-year-old out of the technical class. Terry was wanted at home. *'Son, your dad's dead. He's had a heart attack.'*

'Not my dad!'

Terry had stood in his parents' front garden and shouted at the sky where God was supposed to be.

He flew up and up. As a boy he'd swung until he was nearly upside down. Speed defying gravity. Terry braked with the heel of his shoe. He'd been so intent on a confession that he'd failed to protect Parsley from himself. He'd practically walked that confession out of the man. *'Come on, Derek, you'll feel better if you tell us what you did. We know, but we want to hear it from you.'* Parsley had confessed. But now no one had felt better. Terry had failed himself too.

Baying mobs had stopped traffic on Hammersmith Broadway, screaming and pelting eggs and soft fruit at the police station. *Child-Killer Skips Justice.* Lucie's front page demanded to know why Parsley wasn't on suicide watch. She left out the bit about the SIO getting his end away (Terry punished himself with crude tabloid speak) while the prime suspect was knotting bedsheets for his noose. People had wanted Derek Parsley hanged, but at their behest not his.

Terry had robbed the Walsh and Ferris families of an explanation in court. Not that you could explain the unexplainable. He rested a cheek on one of the swing chains. Parsley had been like a frightened kid, out of his depth. If he'd been found fit to plead, likely he'd have been deemed not guilty by reason of insanity. There was no good outcome for murder except to turn the clock back.

Terry got off the swing. You didn't come back from a cock-up like this.

The moving swing ghosted his presence. If only he could turn the clock back. To when his dad was alive. To when little Robbie and Sarah had played carefree games in the playground. To undo every mistake he'd ever made.

The only way to keep children safe was to never let them out of your sight.

Suzie let Stella hang about with friends after school, share Kentucky Fried Chicken buckets and see X-rated films at the Regal. Who were these friends? When they were a family, Terry used to know. He'd met one girl from her secondary school. Liz was her name. He'd liked her. Danielle Hindle's curiosity and excitement about his work took Terry back to when he was Stella's hero and Stella had wanted to be a detective.

'Did you get my report, guv?' Danielle had got 'guv' from Cashman. Hair in unruly locks, in her baggy handed-down dress secured around the waist with rope like a monk's habit, Danielle was the proverbial urchin. There it was. The look of trust and expectation that Stella once gave him.

'Report?' He kicked a stone sending it bouncing towards the slide.

'I 'specially took it to the station. So you'd see it when you woke up.' Danielle's spelling might be haphazard, but she had the reading age of an adult. She'd followed the Playground Murders (Lucie's coinage) in the papers. She had read that most nights Terry stayed at the station. *Detective vows 'I won't sleep until Sarah's killer found.'*

'I did get it. Thanks, Danielle.' He played along. *Make-believe.*

'The man Parsley hung himself by the neck.' Danielle adjusted her monk's rope.

'Yes.' Terry felt uneasy. The girl missed nothing.

'I bet you made him say he did it.' She was earnest.

'It's Christmas Eve, Danni. You should get home. Your mum and dad will be worrying.'

'My mum's watching telly. Dad's out robbing. Let's arrest him. Teach him a lesson.' Danielle's eyes gleamed.

'He's your dad, Danielle.' Terry didn't know why he said this. Eddie Hindle should be locked up. He'd only come out and go on stealing, but it would make Terry feel that his job had a point. He wondered when Eddie Hindle had stopped being a 'hero-dad'. 'It's not safe to be here, it's nearly dark.'

'The murderer is dead.' Hands on hips, Danielle spoke as if she'd dispatched Derek Parsley herself.

'He's not the only criminal.' Shivering, Terry pinched together the lapels of his jacket. He shouldn't frighten her. She didn't look frightened. 'Your letter said you talked to that reporter, Miss May?'

'She made me.' Quick as a flash.

'You're not in trouble.' Terry smiled, hating himself when the girl's face lit up. Cashman had it right when he'd said the kid craved attention.

'I shouldn't of. Have.' Danielle scowled. 'I said I'm sorry.' Actually she hadn't.

'That's OK. No harm.' *No harm.* Danielle Hindle had told Lucie the very thing the hard-nosed reporter had just got out of him. How Sarah Ferris was murdered. *Jesus Christ.* No wonder Lucie had scoffed at his calling Danielle an incomparable witness. Danielle had handed Lucie key information. Never mind Danielle and her gymnastics Lucie must have done handstands as the girl handed her a scoop on a plate. Handstands. Terry felt a cold rush through his brain as if a hole had been drilled into his skull.

'Danielle, how did you know about the brick?'

*

Danielle skipped along Braybrook Street. They reached the Hindle house as, on cue, Martin Cashman and WPC Janet Piper drew up in the car.

'Tell them we don't need them,' Danielle said. 'The murderer is dead.'

'Janet and Martin are on our team, Danielle.' Terry was getting good at games.

Eddie and Joy were on the settee kissing like teenagers. Terry rubbed the back of his neck. He'd never do that in front of Stella. Not because he was prudish – he was – but because it was plain rude. What kind of home was this for kids? Plenty of children had crap lives, it didn't make them… He wiped a hand down his mouth. This case was killing him.

Maxine Hindle was slumped in an armchair flipping through *Jackie* magazine. Jason lay on his tummy by the unlit gas fire fiddling with odds and ends of Lego. Terry doubted that Father Christmas would be battling his way down the chimney in the Hindle household.

Treading over sweet wrappers, Adidas trainers, a child's bunched pair of jeans, and a baseball jacket for the Red Sox – no doubt one of Eddie's liberations – Terry lowered the volume. Janet remained at the door. To avoid it looking like a raid, Cashman stayed in the hall.

Danielle supposed that Terry was going to tell her parents – when they detached themselves from each other – about Danielle joining the police. He hadn't disabused her. Terry wondered if the Hindles might be more upset by a daughter in the force than the actual reason. 'Mr and Mrs Hindle, Joy, Eddie, this is Janet, she's going to mind Jason and Maxine.'

'I don't need minding,' Maxine said from behind the magazine. 'My dad's innocent, he ain't done nothing!' Word perfect, Terry thought.

'Anything,' Danielle said. 'He hasn't done *anything*. That's not why they've come. I'm being in the police.'

'Wash your mouth out,' Maxine warned.

'You going to arrest them?' Danielle whispered to Terry.

'Listen, Mr Policeman. I'm enjoying time with my family so unless you've got evidence, leave my house.' Eddie grinned at Terry over his wife's shoulder.

'Eddie, it's not you I need to… Can we talk?'

'You talk if you want, mate, I'm busy.' Eddie nibbled his wife's ear lobe. 'You can't turn this place over without a warrant.'

The guilty knew the law better than the innocent.

'We would like Danielle to come with us to the station. We need you both there.' Terry picked up a crisp packet by his shoe but with nowhere to put it, dropped it again. Maxine saw him.

'Why?' Joy Hindle pushed her husband away and struggling up on the sofa snatched a lighter and cigarettes from the muddle at her feet. 'What's she done now?'

'He's trying it on. Leave my kid alone!' Eddie was indignant.

Terry was distantly gratified to see Eddie Hindle's faith in Danielle. She'd need that.

'I'm helping.' Danielle rocked on the heels of her Dr Martens. 'I caught the murderer.'

'What's she done?' About to strike a match, Joy Hindle paused.

'I'd like to ask Danielle about the murders of Robert Walsh and Sarah Ferris.' No easier than telling Cathy and Alan Ferris that their little girl was dead.

Before Terry could stop him Eddie had hold of Danielle and yelled, 'What'd I tell you about playing after dark?'

There was a lull as the Hindle children, their dad seldom there, struggled to recall what he'd said. Joy lit her cigarette.

'Please let go of your daughter, sir!' Janet was reasonable. Cashman hovered in the doorway.

During the interview Terry had fought his revulsion of Parsley. Now he felt nothing. A child. A girl. It was like an earthquake when all points of reference are buried.

'That creep's topped himself.' Eddie took a drag of Joy's cigarette. 'I blame you lot. If you'd got him sooner, those kiddies would be alive! It could have been Jason!' He pummelled a fist.

Terry was ten years younger than Eddie, yet he didn't fancy the prison-fit muscles straining Eddie's Bruce Springsteen rolled T-shirt sleeves.

'You're *so* thick!' Joy Hindle snatched back the cigarette and flicked ash into a Watney's ashtray. 'They've come for Danielle. She killed them kids!'

Chapter Twenty

2019

'John Lennon was shot dead in America on the 8th December 1980.' Stella stuffed salad garnish into her brie and cranberry ciabatta. 'It was news in the UK the next day. That afternoon Sarah Ferris was murdered. I remember Terry saying it stole the headlines.'

'I wouldn't let the twins out if there was a killer on the loose.' Jack nibbled at his quiche, his appetite had dwindled. A child being hurt was too much to bear.

'There's always a killer on the loose. Besides, your kids are too young to go out by themselves.'

It was two o'clock in the afternoon. Jack and Stella sat at the corner table in the Winchcombe deli, their 'office' when they had last visited the village. They could see who came in and the table was out of earshot of other customers.

'Tell that to Milly.' Jack laid down his fork. How much say would he have about what Milly and Justin did when they were teenagers? 'Harry Six Pack won't care where they go.'

'If he likes Bella he might like them too.' Stella's brand of logic wasn't helpful.

'He's only interested in himself.'

'Then Bella will leave him.' Stella bit into her ciabatta. 'When Dad was on that case, I was fourteen, too old for playgrounds, but when I stayed with him, I'd get a grilling. Where was I going? What time would I be back? Only go out with friends. Who were my friends? Mum had a word, but she'd be cross which made Dad stricter. It wasn't like Mum was any less strict.'

They had scoured the internet for information on the child-killer Danielle Hindle. Now Penelope Philips. Stella had ordered a couple of books. One by a male journalist who wrote for the *Sun*, the other an academic treatise by a child psychotherapist on children who kill which, Jack suggested, might provide pointers to why.

Danielle Hindle had never admitted to killing the two children. Penny Philips saying that she was 'the girl they call the Playground Killer' was not an admission of guilt. There was no shortage of material on the deaths of six-year-olds Robert Walsh and Sarah Ferris. The red-tops had called Danielle Hindle 'a freak of humanity', 'Nature's Mistake', 'Devil Child'. It was Lucie May who coined 'The Playground Killer'. Given this, Stella expected Lucie to have written a book. Lucie often claimed to be working on a book, but had not yet finished one.

Stella wiped her mouth with her napkin. 'Trudy was right about Carrie Philips not telling us everything. No wonder she thinks her mum killed Rachel Cater. When she was Danielle Hindle she murdered two of her friends.'

'Do you think so?'

'Do I think she murdered them? There was no doubt at the time.'

'But does that make Danielle Hindle prime suspect for this murder?' Dwelling on Bella's new man, Jack had actually meant Stella's comment about Bella dumping Harry.

'"A killer could kill again."' Stella repeated his own words about True Hosts. Jack felt a spark of delight that Stella took True Hosts seriously. Perhaps she'd take on ghosts next. She was swiping at her phone screen.

'Wikipedia says that Dad arrested a homeless man a week after the discovery of the child's body. Kids in my class said Dad was a brilliant detective, they wanted to meet him. I quite liked that. Except, being busy, he never came to the school. Sarah Ferris was strangled and stabbed and, it says here, her neck was crushed with a brick.' Stella gave a shudder. 'Her murder prompted Dad to revisit Robert Walsh's death a few weeks earlier. It was originally assumed that he'd accidentally fallen from the slide. Says here that the pathologist was Michael Sutherland. He was at school with Dad. He came to Dad's funeral. Dead now too. He died in a car crash.' Stella paused as she digested her words. 'He's quoted, "The balance of probability does not exclude defence wounds." Dad said Michael never committed himself to a position. He was faithful to the body. In court the defence struggled to discredit Sutherland's evidence. Dad had charged Derek Parsley with Sarah's murder. Parsley confessed then hanged himself in his cell.' Talking about Terry had brought colour to Stella's cheeks.

'Why did Terry suspect Parsley?' Nerve-racked and saddened by talk of the dead children and of Terry, Jack abandoned the quiche. Although the deli was warm and cosy, he shivered.

'Some kids in the playground called Parsley "the man from Abba".' Stella chewed on the last of her ciabatta, apparently not having heard Jack's question.

'I like Abba,' Jack said inconsequentially.

'"The man from Abba" sounds unsettling.'

'It's the juxtapositioning of a light, happy concept with death. Fairy tales are sinister and frightening. Derek Parsley sounds like a character in a children's book.' Jack felt properly cold. Behind him the radiator pumped out heat.

'After Dad charged Danielle Hindle with the murder of Sarah Ferris, he went to Mum's. I was round my friend Liz's and when I got back the next morning he was there. It's impossible to think he spent the night there, but I think he did.' Stella nibbled on a stray stem of rocket. 'I hoped that they were getting back together.'

Stella hadn't been in touch for weeks when Terry died. Mourning was harder if the relationship left much to regret.

'They should never have split up.' Jack slid a hand over hers. To his surprise – Stella wasn't hot on public shows of affection – she held it tight.

'Parsley did look a bit like Benny.' Letting go of his hand Stella held up her phone.

Derek Parsley had long lank brown hair and a straggling beard. His timid expression squeezed at Jack's heart. Parsley was one of a line of men – Colin Stagg, Barry George, Christopher Jefferies – who, failing to fit society's expectation of normal, were charged and sometimes found guilty of a murder that they hadn't committed.

Stella read from Wikipedia: 'The police found Parsley staggering across Wormwood Scrubs park, his coat and shirt still saturated with blood. The murder was two years before the widespread use of DNA. Forensics could only match Parsley's blood group to the dead girl. Martin told me…' Stella breathed in as if for a running jump, '…that after they found Parsley dead, Dad cried in the toilet. Martin respected him. He said most of the blokes were hard as nails.'

'Penny Philips talked like she was in love with Terry.' Jack swerved from the mention of Cashman. He would show Stella she could mention the man without Jack looking mental.

'One thing, Terry definitely didn't keep her letters. I doubt there even were any,' Stella said.

Jack thought this a shame. With Hindle/Philips a suspect in the Cater killing, they could do with any material that offered a clue to her personality. He believed that Stella was right. Penelope Philips was a True Host and, as he knew, True Hosts did not leave a paper trail.

'Danielle Hindle was considered an inveterate liar. Maybe Penny still tells lies,' Stella said.

'Psychopaths don't change.' Jack poked his fork at the cooling quiche.

'Do you think she murdered Rachel Cater?'

'Philips seemed less upset that Cater was murdered than that she'd have to begin her life afresh. She positively boasted about being the Playground Killer. I'll say this for Carrie, whatever she feels about her mother, she never divulged her new identity. Loyalty runs deep.'

'If Penny Philips did kill Rachel Cater she won't want us finding out. Look, this was Danielle Hindle then.' Stella passed him her phone. Rarely scared, Stella looked rattled now.

The first thing that struck Jack was how knowing the girl looked. Her smile triumphant, cocky even, she eyed the police camera as if taking it on. How many murder suspects smiled in their arrest mugshot? 'She looks intelligent. I can see why Terry took her seriously.' Exploring the website, Jack found the *Hammersmith and Fulham Chronicle*. '"While most kids are playing kiss chase, Danielle Hindle was planning murder." Lor lummy, Lucie was all over this.' He passed the phone back.

'She and Dad had started seeing each other. Mum behaved as if Dad had two-timed her although she had left him. Do *not* tell Lucie May!' Stella shot him a look. 'She's gagging to get involved in the Cater murder.'

'No way!' Jack expostulated although he'd done it before. 'Wasn't Lucie in the office the day Carrie Philips came?'

'I convinced Lucie that Carrie was there for a cleaning job.'

Jack and Stella considered that very little convinced Lucie.

'Lucie would love to break Hindle's new ID.' Jack imagined telling Lucie. He had no wish to protect a child-killer.

'Martin was a rookie when Carrie's mother was arrested. He must have come to Winchcombe after the murder to protect Penny's new identity.' Stella enlarged Hindle's photograph on her screen. 'Philips's eyes are brown. In this picture they're green. She must wear tinted contacts.'

'Good idea, because those eyes are unforgettable,' Jack breathed. 'The eyes of a killer.'

'She was a child when she murdered those children. I suppose we shouldn't jump to the conclusion that she killed Rachel Cater. Anyway, Penny has a watertight alibi.' Stella opened her notebook at the suspect list. All three of the Philips family, including Carrie, were on it. She pondered, 'Should Penny even have been in Dalgarno Gardens. Surely she was barred from returning to the vicinity of her crime.'

'Maybe Cashman waived the transgression; he wouldn't have wanted the press to get wind of it.' Knowing he was being unfair, Jack wouldn't put it past Cashman to be in cahoots with the tabloids.

'Perhaps a relative of one of the dead children found Hindle. They went to the house to kill her but murdered Rachel Cater instead. It could be a case of mistaken identity,' Stella said.

'Rachel had shoulder-length black hair. As an adult Danielle Hindle's is short and blonde.'

'But when she was ten it was like Rachel's. We shouldn't call Penny Danielle in case we do it in front of someone.'

'We've never signed an agreement, we can tell who we like. Lucie would make mincemeat of her.'

Stella was stern. 'Penny Philips has done her time, we have no right to ruin her life.'

'Hindle ruined lots of lives.' If someone murdered Justin or Milly Jack wouldn't rest until he'd found them. And then, his own life essentially being over, he'd kill them. Was Stella able to handle this case because she had no children and wasn't interested in his?

'The attack was described as frenzied. Cater had multiple stab wounds, all from behind. The killer may not have realized he'd got the wrong person until it was reported in the media,' Stella said.

'Meaning they could try again,' Jack said. 'Hindle didn't seem worried about meeting us at the house.'

'Perhaps they haven't had an opportunity. Penny's been in a safe house. If they're keeping watch, they'll know she has returned.' Stella ruffled her hair back from her face. 'By asking her to meet us there, we could have put her in danger.'

'If she's the killer, she's not in danger.' Jack rather hoped that they had done just that. 'As I said, Hindle didn't seem upset about Cater.'

'Philips,' Stella corrected him automatically. 'You often say that because a person doesn't seem upset it doesn't mean they're not. That said, she was more upset that her husband had been unfaithful. Let's add the relatives of Robert Walsh and Sarah Ferris to our suspect list.' She fired up her tablet and, locating names from Wikipedia, set about creating a spreadsheet.

Name	Role	Age 1980	Age 2019	Dead / Alive
Robert Walsh	Victim One	6	-	D
Sarah Ferris	Victim Two	6	-	D
Nicola Walsh	Sister of V1	10	49	?
Robert Walsh Snr	Father of V1	?	?	?
Gill Walsh	Mother of V1	?	?	?
Lee Ferris	Brother of V2	10	49	?
Cathy Ferris (Marshall)	Mother of V2	?	?	?
Alan Ferris	Father of V2	?	?	?
Penelope Philips (Hindle)	Killer: V1 and V2	10	49	A
Christopher Philips	Husband: Killer (V1 &V2)	N/A	55	A
Carrie Philips	Daughter: Killer (V1 &V2)		26	A
Joy Hindle	Mother: Killer (V1 & V2)	?	?	?

Name	Role	Age 1980	Age 2019	Dead / Alive
Eddie Hindle	Father: Killer (V1 & V2)	?	?	?
Maxine Hindle	Older sister: Killer (V1 & V2)	13	52	?
Jason Hindle	Younger Bro: Killer (V1 & V2)	6	45	?
Kevin Hood	Childhood friend: (V1 & V2)	6	45	

'Fourteen suspects.' Stella seemed unfazed.

'They must all have alibis.'

'We'll do a root and branch review,' Stella said. 'To give this a fair chance we need to undermine the police evidence against Christopher Philips. That means that no one's alibi counts.'

'Some of the suspects might be dead. It was over thirty years ago.'

'Glass half full, Jack,' said Stella. 'We'll start with Cater as the intended victim until there's reason to abandon it. Let's talk to Rachel's colleagues.' She packed away her tablet and stopped. 'I forgot to say, I found this.'

She put a silver object on the table next to Jack's plate. He picked it up between finger and thumb.

'I probably should have given it to Penelope,' Stella said, 'except as she hasn't been living there I thought it might belong to Donette or Shelley or maybe the decorators. I was going to ask.'

Stella never lied so why didn't he believe her?

'It's a charm off a bracelet,' Jack said after a moment. 'It's been engraved. "Best Sister." Did Danielle Hindle have siblings?'

'Two, a brother and a sister.'

'Can't see either of them giving her a charm that said that. She would have ruined their lives along with the relatives of the children she killed.' Jack turned the charm around in his hand. It was of an angel, wings folded back. 'It's not real silver.'

'It's the thought that counts,' Stella said.

'Why did you take it?'

'I just said.'

'Really why did you?' Jack fixed her with a look.

'I don't know. Is it stealing?' Unstintingly honest, Stella went pink.

'Ask your guys and chase up the decorators. If you get a negative then it might belong to Hindle or maybe to Carrie? Oh, except she's an only child,' he reminded himself. 'You did the right thing, Stella. While Hindle's a suspect we shouldn't trust her with anything. Where did you find it?'

'In the guest bedroom. That's why I was still there when Penny called me. It was on the floor beneath the sill.'

'Like the cast of this case, we shouldn't discount it until we have good reason.' While reassuring Stella, privately Jack marvelled at her temerity. Stella had come a long way with truth-bending since they'd met seven years ago. *Go, Stella!*

Watching Stella pay at the counter, Jack realized he couldn't bear to work on the case. Stella had said that Hindle had paid for her crimes. She hadn't paid for Robert Walsh's murder, Hindle was only tried for Sarah Ferris. A ten-year-old who had murdered her friends. Aged three, his children knew right from wrong. She was his prime suspect. Used to the proximity of True Hosts, Jack didn't ever want to be in the same room as Danielle Hindle again.

Stella had left her phone on the table. He looked at the picture of Hindle as a girl. *A freak of nature.* Once a person crossed the murder line, it was easy to cross it again. Once a killer, always a killer. Yet Stella had a point, it didn't mean that Hindle had murdered Rachel Cater. Jack's mind was slammed shut. He *wanted* Hindle to be guilty. He wanted her sent back to prison. This time life would mean life.

In this frame of mind Jack grabbed Stella's phone and Googled Agnes Cater. To his surprise she wasn't ex-directory. From then, silver-tongued as he could be, the rest was plain sailing.

'You look chirpy,' Stella said when she returned.

'We're having tea with Rachel Cater's mother.'

'Where?' Not the question that Jack had expected.

'Lower Slaughter.' Jack tried not to bat an eye.

Lower Slaughter was a village forty minutes from Winchcombe. More convenient than Cheltenham where Agnes Cater lived, because it was on the way back to London. Agnes Cater had suggested it because the café there did lovely cakes.

They were journalists doing a profile piece on Rachel, Jack had told Mrs Cater. It would cover her achievements, dreams and desires.

The village was teeming with tourists, sitting on the grassy banks by a stream, fingering leather goods in the shop as they ate ice creams.

They found Agnes Cater in the café's garden. Small as a sparrow, sharp eyes flitting, she beckoned them to a table away from customers. She had parked a walker behind her. Jack marvelled that she'd negotiated the steps and narrow path to get there. He took a breath. Stella had said that the interview would be one of the hardest they had done.

When a young woman came for their order, Agnes Cater was still deciding and suggested they go first. Not hungry, good manners propelled Stella to opt for a slice of lemon drizzle. After not eating the quiche at the Winchcombe deli, Jack was ready for a cream tea. Agnes Cater asked for cup of tea.

'I'll be mother.' She poured them each a cup.

Jack didn't dare look at Stella.

'Tell us about Rachel.' Stella unfolded a napkin.

'I'm recording this. I've learnt the hard way not to trust even the nicest of people.' Agnes Cater dabbed at an iPhone in front of her. 'You'd expect me to say so, but Rachel was a wonderful daughter. She was clever, sailed through her exams with a first in Art and English. It was Rach and me from when she was five.

We were close. Too close. I tried not to hold her back.' She spoke with a Gloucestershire burr.

'I lived with my mum from the age of seven, when my parents separated.' Stella offered something of herself. 'We had a dog. A spaniel named Hector.'

'You'll know then.' Mrs Cater drank her tea with her little finger raised.

Jack believed that Stella had loved Hector. He had stayed with Terry when Stella moved to Baron's Court. No pets were allowed in the flat.

'I warned her about Christopher. "He's a married man, Rach, will he leave his wife? Do you really want him to?" Rach was in love, she wouldn't listen. We don't, do we. I'm not judgemental. Rachel's dad was divorced when we met. He wasn't young, bless him, we didn't have him long.' Mrs Cater rested her cup on the saucer with particular care and contemplated the view.

'Did you meet Christopher Philips?' Jack said.

'You don't have to meet a person to know them. Rachel was biased towards him, yet she painted a figure I knew not to trust. I was so worried for her. At the start he was going to train her in antiques. After six months Rachel was still typing. He had her buying his presents for his family. Perfume for his daughter. Rach had to send his wife flowers on her birthday. *It must have been torture, but she never complained.* Once that hotel business started, there was no more talk of training. I knew he wasn't going to give up his life for her.'

'Did you say that to her?' Stella embarked on the cake.

'You have to let children learn from their mistakes.'

There are some mistakes from which there is no return. Jack piled cream and jam on a fruit scone. Everyone looked at the view.

'Did she tell you how it started?' Stella said at last.

'As she put it, "We fell into each other's arms."' Agnes Cater laughed without a trace of humour. 'Rachel came home that day full of how it was love at first sight and he felt the same. I'd suspected she'd liked him when he gave her the job. I hoped his marriage was rock solid. Rachel wasn't a marriage wrecker, but cooped up in that shop…' She sighed. 'Rachel was hurt too many times. When she said he'd told her he loved her, I tried to hope it would be different with him.'

'So nothing specific happened to make him say that?' Jack asked. Did Mrs Cater know about Penelope Philips' past?

'Not that Rachel said. She was a romantic. No harm in that.' Mrs Cater topped up their teas. 'I suspected he'd had a row with his wife. Or maybe he couldn't hold off any longer.' She offered a shrug. 'If it had been love at first sight, why didn't he tell her earlier?'

Jack slid Stella's plate across and set to on her cake. Stella shot him a glance of thanks that would melt glaciers. He longed to tell Mrs Cater how he'd loved Stella from the moment he'd met her, but hadn't had the courage to do anything about it for years.

'I wonder if Rachel wasn't searching for her dad. I'd made him out to be perfect. For her sake. I wanted him to shine in her memory. He wasn't perfect. No man is. I should have said so.'

As he finished the cake, Jack considered that Rachel had been hurt again, except this time she never recovered. Stella interrupted his thoughts.

'…had enough bother from the press. We won't add to it with another article.' Stella rose to go. Jack saw why. She found their deception unbearable.

'That's a shame, dear. I'd have liked a happy story about Rachel in the papers. I've brought pictures. I've got her exam certificates. Jack said that Rachel should be remembered for more than the way she died.' No acrimony, no recrimination. Mrs Cater was a woman who accepted things as they were.

The food was a lump in his stomach. Heavy as his conscience. Agnes Cater had given life to Rachel and she had outlived her. They had offered a chance to restore a semblance of Rachel, to breathe life into her memory. Now they were taking it away.

'…I do understand. Good news isn't much of a story.'

'Yes. Yes. It is a story!' Stella sat down again. 'We will run it. We'll do Rachel justice. I promise.'

'And how are we going to do that?' Jack asked Stella as they stood by the stream watching Mrs Cater's VW Polo drive away.

'Lucie May will do it.' Stella was steely. 'Even if I have to stand over her as she types.'

Chapter Twenty-One

1980

'There's someone in there.'

'As I explained, Danielle, we're recording this.' Terry was amazed that the girl had spotted that the mirror was two-way. Cashman was watching from behind the glass, sulking because Janet was sitting in with Terry. He hadn't bought that two hulking blokes wasn't fair to the girl. With more to learn, the young man didn't want to be fair to Danielle Hindle.

'You're a bloody fish in a tank, babes!' Eddie appeared delighted that his daughter had spotted it.

Terry was before his time in believing that a child should have an adult advocate, but Eddie wasn't a good fit. Joy Hindle had said, 'I've washed my hands of her' and ignored Danielle's 'See you soon, Mum.' Joy had known that her daughter wasn't coming back.

An hour into the interview Danielle was sticking to her story. In comparison, Parsley had been a pushover.

'What did you do on Tuesday afternoon last week, Danni?' Terry had adopted the girl's shortened name.

'I went to the playground. The one in the park where me and

you looked for clues about Sarah. School's stupid.' Bobbing about on her chair, Danielle was curiously excited.

Danielle had told him she liked school. She'd be sucking up to Eddie who doubtless went through school without touching the sides.

'What time did you get to the playground?' Terry was keeping it simple and friendly. No accusations, no tripping up, just fact-finding.

'Ten minutes to two o'clock. After dinner time when I had chips and stew.' Sitting on her hands, Danielle thrust forward happily. 'I like that best. Do you?'

'Do you, Constable Darnell?' Smirking, Eddie tried to goad Terry with the lower rank.

'Yes, I do.' It was stew for lunch the day his dad died. 'Who was with you?'

'Lee came with Sarah and Jason. Nicola wasn't meant be there.' Danielle bounced on her chair. 'I said we weren't there, but she never does what I want.'

'You lied?' Terry introduced the concept.

'You have to do that or she follows Lee about.' As if explaining to an idiot. Not wrong, Danielle's IQ dwarfed his own. 'She split me and Lee up.'

'How did she do that?' Nicola Walsh had struck him as off with the fairies, incapable of caring who went out with who. Danielle hadn't grasped the enormity of her situation. Losing Lee Marshall would be nothing to the nightmare of what lay ahead. She appeared enthused by the whole experience. Terry felt a tremor of doubt. If he'd got this wrong, that was his career down the toilet.

'She got scared of the man from Abba and Lee had to go help her. I was minding Jason. We went home.' Butter wouldn't melt.

'What about Sarah, where was she?'

'Looking for her bracelet, most likely. We all did.' Danielle heaved an exaggerated sigh and wriggled on the seat.

'Keep still.' Eddie was getting restless.

The children's statements all said that they had searched for Sarah Ferris's charm bracelet.

'Did you see that Sarah was still there when you left the playground?'

'No. Because she wasn't.'

'Where was she?'

'How should I know?' She wriggled on her hands and shot a grin at her father. Lounging in his chair, Eddie looked bored. 'Sarah was hiding from the man.'

'Do you mean Mr Parsley?' Janet asked nicely.

'Mr *Parsley*.' Eddie guffawed. He caught Janet's expression and sweeping back a hank of hair did a naughty boy face.

'That man was the one who murdered her,' Danielle said.

'Where was Sarah when Mr Parsley murdered her?' Terry noticed that Eddie was alert. He was cottoning on. Murder was way out of his league.

'I said. In the playground. She hid in the bushes to get away from… he found her because she doesn't know when to keep her mouth shut.'

'Who was she hiding from, Danni?'

'How should I know?' Her first mistake.

'Was it you?' He was careful not to lead her.

'I expect she was looking for her bracelet.' The girl didn't hesitate.

'You told Lucille May, the reporter, that Derek Parsley attacked Sarah. But you weren't there. Why did you say that?' Terry smoothed his tie. Nothing at police college had prepared him for this.

'She said I'd be on telly.' Arms folded, hard stare. 'I saw you and her.'

'Getting his leg over! What'll your boss say about that?' Eddie pounced. Terry felt sick. Had she seen Lucie in his house? Did Danielle Hindle know where he lived?

'You can't keep my little girl here, it's illegal.' As protective parent, Eddie was unconvincing. While knowing the mirror was two-way, Eddie couldn't help but check his hair.

'Danielle can stay all night answering our questions, you know that, Eddie,' Terry told him. 'Danielle, do you remember telling me you want to be a detective?'

'Yes,' she piped. 'I'm on your team.'

Eddie Hindle grimaced. His daughter crossing to the dark side and joining the force was worse than murder.

'To be clear, Danielle, did you run home without Sarah when you saw the man?' Janet was offering her a wrong way out.

'She said so, didn't she? That creep did it. Now, thanks to you, he's dead. Why are we here?' Visibly nervous, Eddie Hindle had got why they were there.

'Unless you want a perjury charge, you'll shut up!' Terry told him.

'Sarah could have come too. She wouldn't.'

'You asked her, did you?' Janet's trap sprung.

'I'm not sorry that man's dead!' Ignoring Janet, Danielle eyed Terry over the can of Coke he'd got her from the machine. 'I never touched him.'

'We know that, Danielle.' She knew they knew. She was spinning out time. She too had all night. Terry pictured Danielle at school, dominating, contrary, answering back, her popularity in proportion to her ability to scare. In the next days Danielle Hindle would become the most hated girl in the land.

'Lee was going to buy one for me.' She picked a graze on her arm and pinched the skin so that it bled. Janet gave her a tissue. The look that Danielle gave Janet could have killed.

'Danni, talk us through what you know.' Janet was a confidential friend.

'She got hit,' Danielle told Terry.

'Where was she hit?' Janet echoed the passive phrasing.

'On the neck.' Perched on a cushion to raise her, Danielle sipped the Coke ruminatively. 'With a brick. Like this.' Danielle jumped up and did a handstand. 'It was crunchy, the man said. Sarah stopped breathing.'

'Where was this?' Janet took a while with the follow-up as the truth sank in.

'He told me by the railway bridge.' A trap avoided. She was bloody smart.

'Don't tell them nothing.' Eddie tried to head them off. 'And get up right now. Stop your bloody showing off.'

'The attacker applied considerable strength, the neck is crushed.' Terry cleared his throat as he recalled Mike Sutherland's report.

'Did you do a handstand on the brick. On Sarah's neck?'

'That's what the man from Abba did. I saw it from the bandstand.'

'It's not possible to see the bushes from the bandstand.' Janet was kindly.

'You lot should shut up!' Danielle lost her temper.

'When exactly did Parsley tell you this?' Terry gave an encouraging smile. 'Or did you see him?'

'It's you that needs to be quiet.' Eddie gripped her arm.

'The day after. When he had blood on him. I said go to the police or you're in for it.'

Lucie was right. Danielle had run rings around him. Concentric bloody circles. Yet still, Terry longed to be convinced that everything she said was true. She was just a little girl who'd seen a terrible thing. She was in shock. Parsley had been their man.

'We arrested Derek Parsley the night that Sarah was attacked.' Janet adopted a puzzled air. 'You couldn't have seen him the day after, Danielle.'

'Mind your fucking nose!' Terry was almost reassured that Danielle could be a straightforward stroppy kid. 'I already told the reporter about the crunchy sound of the brick on her neck. I was going to be on the news, but she lied.'

'*Shut up!*' her father shouted. 'They can't do nothing if you zip your bloody mouth.'

'Anything.' Danielle lost her temper. Eyes were cold and unblinking. 'It's *anything*. If I do nothing I do nothing. If I can't do nothing what does that mean? It means I do some-*thing*!' No one was better at grammar than Danielle. She always sat in the front row at school.

'Don't come the fucking posh with me. You're not top of the class now. Even I know what they're after.' Eddie jumped up, kicking back his chair. It fell back with a crash. 'We are going.'

'Stay there.' Terry strode around the table, righted the chair and pointed at it. Hindle, suddenly meek, returned to it and sat down, hands clasped behind his neck.

For a moment no one spoke or moved.

'Danielle Hindle, I'm arresting you for murder…' Terry recited the words.

'Dad, tell him to stop. Say I'm a detective!' Danielle suddenly clung to her father.

'…do not have to say anything…'

Tears coursing down his cheeks, Eddie Hindle couldn't reply.

Chapter Twenty-Two

2019

Earl's Court. 1.05 a.m. Jack must reach that lamp-post before another vehicle passed him. Avoiding cracks in the paving he was walking home after his shift on the London Underground. Lucie said that he made life hard for himself (*'Just avoid dog shit, that is bad luck'*). Stella said that the cracks were freeze-thaw effect and nothing else. Jack knew they were signs. However obscure his gods, he must appease them.

He scrutinized pedestrians, tourists, clubbers and shift workers, alert for the impassive stare of a True Host. No one held his gaze as they skirted the homeless bundled under duvet mounds in doorways and on pavements.

Jack cut into a residential street. He was struggling with a dilemma. He desperately wanted to bail out of the case, but couldn't bear to let Stella down.

Jackie said that children must be allowed to fly free to be themselves. He agreed. Then thinking of Justin and Milly waking up in a house with *Harry* made his stomach clench and blackness descend.

To catch a murderer you must have the mind of a murderer.

Jack had that mind. Stella needed his mind. They had solved

cases because his left-field methods complemented her law-abiding ones. Stella was too honest a personality to get into the mind of a murderer. He could go to Gloucestershire and watch Hindle. Learn her habits. Eventually Hindle would reveal herself and he'd discover if she had killed Rachel Cater. Honesty didn't pay with the likes of Hindle. She'd run rings around them.

He could say he was ill and didn't want to pass it on. He'd played down the level of danger when Stella brought it up. He knew that there was a dangerous killer out there. And he knew who it was. Penny Philips (Danielle Hindle to him) had been angry that Carrie had involved Clean Slate. A True Host, Hindle would think nothing of removing someone in her way. Only Jack could stop her.

Jack trod on a crack in the paving. His gods were angry. He'd planned to lie to Stella. Hoping that his gods would allow him to trade right for wrong, Jack resolved to play it Stella's way for now.

Stella had no idea how long she'd been sitting at her desk staring at the attic hatch. Stanley, expecting eventual action, sat pert by the shredder, a proprietary paw on his faithful Mr Ratty.

If Terry had received letters from Penny Philips, they'd be in the attic where he'd stored files of unsolved cases. Since his death, Stella rarely ventured up there. A devotee of deep cleaning – behind bath panels and skirting boards – she avoided the one place that, if her dad's ghost did haunt his house, was where he'd be. There were no letters. She'd told Jack that it was against the law for an SIO to write to a murderer. Terry never broke the law.

When they returned from Winchcombe, Stella had dropped Jack at Earls Court station to pick up the District line train he'd be driving. They'd had no chance to discuss the case in the van because, in preparation for his dead late shift, Jack had slept all the way.

The afternoon's visit to the antiques shop had provided clarification. Ian and Carol had not guessed that their boss was having an affair with Rachel. Carol expressed frustration that Rachel had lied because 'her secret would have been safe with me'. Carol and Ian were engaged and keen to tell Jack and Stella their wedding plans. They were sorry that Rachel had died such a horrible death. They'd been going to ask her to make their cake, 'she was so good we kept saying she should be on *Bake Off*.' Their boss being in prison meant that the shop was closing. Christopher had been a good employer.

When Jack had asked if they thought him guilty they'd fallen over themselves to say yes they were sure that he was.

'Flipping odd,' Jack remarked as they drove out of the town. 'Your staff think you're great and I'm sure they'd think you innocent if you were done for murder. Even if you were caught holding a dripping knife.'

'The evidence appears overwhelming, why should they doubt it?' Stella supposed that only Jack would think her innocent. Terry had said to follow the evidence. Emotions clouded facts.

'They don't gain from his death. They're going to be out of work just when they have a wedding to pay for,' Jack had said.

In her study, Stella crossed off Ian and Carol's names in her spreadsheet. Rachel Cater had been liked. She cooked cakes for people. She had had a mother who loved her. There were no enemies. This was a concept that Stella found hard to grasp. Apart from politicians, who did have enemies? What was an enemy?

The attic was above what had been Stella's bedroom until she was seven and moved out with her mum. Returning for access weekends, the bedroom had never felt like hers. In panic lest the court found him an unsuitable father (chats about cadaver dogs, corpse decomposition and how to arrest a miscreant), Terry painted the room pink and overpopulated it with dolls. He filled the bookcase with stories about girls on horses in boarding schools that only baffled the girl who'd wanted to be a detective and solve murders.

When he retired from the force, Terry boxed up the dolls and books and replaced them with copies of *The Job*, the Met's in-house magazine, police manuals and well-thumbed volumes of the 'Police and Criminal Evidence Act'. At Lucie May's instigation, he got a computer. The bookcase was crammed with true crime and biographies of renowned detectives and pathologists. Stella's poster of John Travolta in *Saturday Night Fever* was swapped for a street map of London stuck with what her mum (Stella didn't know when Suzie had gone there) called 'Murder Pins'. When she inherited Terry's house, Stella made no changes (the pins had gone before Terry died).

After he arrested Hindle, it was weeks before Stella saw Terry. Usually critical of him, Suzie had been nice. She'd explained to Stella that her dad was ill. He'd see Stella as soon as he was better. Stella took to waiting in the entrance of Hammersmith Library after school to watch Terry entering and leaving the police station across the road. He was sick, why was he working? Gradually she saw that her mum was right, the force was her dad's family. Terry had no time for her.

It was good that Jack wasn't there. If she found any letters – she would not – she wanted to read them alone.

Stella stood up. Stanley grabbed Mr Ratty. Afraid of little, as she eased down the ladder, Stella was keyed up. Stanley whimpered. The little dog was by way of Stella's canary in a coalmine. If something was wrong, Stanley knew first.

The top of her head tingled when she poked it through the hatchway, eyes at floor level. If an attacker was waiting with an axe, this was the end. Jackie's family had a rule only to go into the loft with someone in the house in case of an accident. Stella had imported this into her staff manual. Jack said there was a ruthless killer out there. What if the killer was a step ahead and waiting in the attic? Stella went as cold as ice.

She forced herself to go up and stepped onto the boarded floor. Raising a hand, Stella confirmed that the shadow on the rafters was her own. The attic was spacious and, she quickly saw, with nowhere to hide. Aside from the boxes of dolls there was the chrome shelf unit that, too big for the hatch, Terry must have assembled on site.

She sniffed. Beneath the smell of dust and papers was something else. Gillette Cool Wave aftershave. *Terry's aftershave.* Stella clung to a rafter. The familiar tang recalled her dad as if she'd seen him minutes ago. *She did not believe in ghosts.*

Jack talked about olfactory associations. Had her expectation of meeting Terry been so strong that she'd conjured up his smell? Stella felt disappointment. It was almost as if she'd hoped to find her dad there.

The first time she'd gone into the attic, she'd discovered two cold cases on the shelf unit. One was the Rokesmith Case. When she and Jack solved it, Lucie May dubbed Stella the Clean-Up Detective. *The girl who sweeps up after her dad.* Loath to reinforce any impression that Terry was a rubbish detective, Stella decided to find her own investigations. The other case in the attic had stayed sealed. One day...

She switched on the light, a bulb furred with dirt dangling from a rafter, and read writing on the first box: '...murder.' The word was illegible. Other boxes were numbered one to four.

At the trial in 1981, Danielle Hindle was described as 'manipulative'. Jack said Penny was a True Host, a psychopath. He'd said they didn't change. The court called her a fantasist. Penny had lied about corresponding with Terry. In the playground that had been her killing field the girl must have led a parallel life. A normal chatty ten-year-old. And a ruthless killer.

Stella looked at the boxes. There wasn't, in fact, a number three. Peering closer, she made out pencil scribble: 'DH 1980 to...'

Nineteen eighty was the year of the two murders. Terry died in 2011. *DH.*

Fingers clumsy, Stella prised out the box and placing it on the floor, raised the lid. A fierce clamp gripped a batch of pale blue envelopes. The top one was addressed to the police station. 'Detective Inspector Darrnell.' Terry's rank at the time of the murders. Stella's clients often made the same spelling error. It was written by a child.

Stella recognized the stationery. Basildon Bond. Suzie had made her pen thank yous to Terry and to his sister who lived abroad for the Christmas and birthday presents. She'd made Stella spend some of her money on a pad and matching envelopes in the post office. Nervous of making a mistake (and starting again), Stella had pressed so hard that writing had indented on the page beneath, providing a template for the next letter.

I was so pleased to receive…

Stella had written Terry other letters. Private ones. She told him about her day, promised to show him the 'pot garden on my bedroom window sill' and 'Please could we go to the river on my axes weekend so you arrest that man who told me off for wriding my bike?' Fearing that her dad would find them boring after being a busy detective, Stella had thrown them away. Now Stella wondered, had she posted them to Terry, would he have kept them in a box in the attic?

She prised open the clamp and removed the bundle. There were no replies. Terry was scrupulous, he would have kept photocopies of his letters to Hindle. Yet with no encouragement, Danielle Hindle continued writing. Three notes dating from before Danielle's arrest were scribbled on scraps of paper, one on the back of a betting slip. Danielle had delivered them to the station.

Some of the stamped envelopes had been addressed to Terry's house. *This house.* All were dated after the trial when Hindle, too young for prison, had been sent to a special school in Buckinghamshire. She couldn't leave the grounds so how had she posted them? Obvious suspects were sympathetic staff. Stella had read that, despite her heinous crimes (a favourite media adjective), adults had warmed to Danielle. A bright, attractive child, they felt sorry for her, some didn't believe her guilty. Someone had translated sympathy into deed.

Most were dated after Hindle turned eighteen and been moved to Holloway Prison. Letters would be censored, but any system could be circumvented. Perhaps she'd given a letter to a visitor. Although Stella had read that Danielle Hindle had had few visitors. She also knew that there were stalkers who continued to terrorize their victims in letters smuggled out of prison. Somehow Danielle Hindle, as a girl and a young woman, had got letters to the police officer who had put her away. Stella shivered. Letters were one thing; if Danielle Hindle had tried to murder Terry, she would have succeeded.

One letter was postmarked Brighton. The cream paper weighted at 120 grams was what Stella used for client contracts. Danielle Hindle had become Penny Philips and lived in Winchcombe. Perhaps she'd come to Brighton for a seaside holiday. The next letter had been posted in Hastings along the coast. Three p.m., 12 August. The twelfth of August was Stella's birthday. Not relevant. There was one from Shepherd's Bush. Philips was not allowed to enter West London. The CCTV image captured on the afternoon of Rachel's murder wasn't the first time Penny had flouted the ban.

Eddie Hindle had visited his daughter (before he returned to prison for breaking into a warehouse and stealing a van load of prescription drugs). Staff would have kept a watch on him in case he tried to sneak out – or sneak in – contraband for Danielle. Although, a professional criminal, Eddie Hindle surely hadn't encouraged his daughter to make a penfriend of a police detective. Stella would ask Philips how she'd achieved it. At this thought, the beginnings of a headache went up a notch. It dawned on Stella that she never wanted to see the child-killer again.

She heard whimpers. She peered through the hatchway. Stanley was circling the foot of the ladder. Although Stella had first come across him up a tree – throwing caution aside he'd chased a cat – he couldn't manage a ladder. She gathered up the box and went down to him.

Of the questions buzzing like hornets in her mind one was, *Why had Terry risked his career for Danielle Hindle?*

Head throbbing, Stella settled on the carpet tiles and spread out the letters. With Stanley a warm bundle on her lap, she began to read.

In an early note, Danielle wrote as if she was on Terry's team. She had made a list of suspects – *Nicola, Mr Ferris hits Lee, Lee might of done it he hated Sarah, sack that lady policeman and have me.* Stella guessed that was Janet. Another of Terry's friends, Janet had organized his funeral. Scribbled on the betting slip – Stella knew that Danielle's father was a gambler – was, *The murdrer is the man from Abba... I will arest him and you can keep hold of him with hand cufs.* Stella imagined that, while Terry had supposed Derek Parsley the killer, this proposal must have worried him. The last thing he'd want was a child risking her life. Another letter caught her eye.

> *Dear Detective Inspector Terry, The girls here have not seen a real life murderer. They took my autograph for being on the telee. I dident see you at tea time visiting. My dad came. My mum is a bitch so is that Nicola I never want to see them. Mum can't take me to Madame Toosods like she promised. Some girls go outside so it's not fair. When you visit bring sweets, space ships and bazooka. I told the girls Im a detective. They don't believe me. If you come they wood. Its stupid Im here as Sarah was nasty and Lee hated her so thats alright now. Nicky will be on seventh heaven. Please will you fech me away? From Consterble Danielle Hindle. Ps. Please bring chocolate, Cadberrys with purple paper is best.*

Danielle had never admitted to Sarah's murder. She could only have known details that she gave the police if she'd been present. Her descriptions – a first-person account including 'the crunchy sound of brick on her neck' – had been a giveaway. Jason Hindle admitted that his sister hadn't taken him home. Only six, he couldn't estimate how much later Danielle had been. His garbled account established that he'd seen (and made no sense of) that night's episode of *Crossroads*. Danielle had returned in time for a quiz programme called *Gambit*. A discrepancy in the timeline in her statement of forty minutes.

But it was her handstands that had been the clincher.

The CPS didn't charge Danielle Hindle with the murder of Robbie Walsh. There was insufficient evidence. Robbie's injuries could have been sustained from falling, as much as from being pushed off the slide.

After Hindle's release in 1994 – she served fourteen years in three prisons – there were no letters for a year. At the special school, Hindle had got five O-levels, three A-levels. In Holloway she gained a first in Law from the Open University. She was better qualified than Stella with an 'A' in Maths 'A' level and a scraped English pass.

I'm top of the class, but then no one else can read! You wait, I'll be back at the Bailey sending those scumbags down. That'll show all of them, won't it!

When Hindle graduated the *Sun* had run a splash: 'Brainbox Killer to be QC.' Stella knew that a convicted murderer could not be a barrister. So, presumably, did the *Sun*, but it would sell copies. Danielle Hindle wasn't allowed to work with people so her choice of job was limited. Alan Ferris was quoted as 'shocked and horrified' that 'the evil monster gets chances she denied my baby girl'. The problem with murder was that no amount of punishment fitted the crime.

A later letter caused Stella to exclaim out loud. Stanley jumped. Scratching his ears, she read,

My new name is Penelope Walters. I sound like a real Surrey housewife, don't I! That explains the signature! I hope you're OK. Well done you on your promotion. You deserve it! I still dream of being your 'right hand man' one of these days!

I'm stretching my intellectual limits assembling Hi-Fi cabinets in a sweatshop outside Guildford. There's a few ex-cons who are OK in a dim as furniture way, but most of them (no men) are idiots. I'm the only one with a degree. All they talk about is EastEnders *and dieting. No one tells you it's hard on the outside. And so untidy! I catch myself missing my cell. Home Sweet Home. At least there I could read and not listen to rubbish. It's not fair.*

Stella scoured the text for proof that Terry had replied. How did Penelope Philips know that he'd been promoted? The information was easy to obtain if you knew where to look. But had Terry told her?

Knowledge of Danielle Hindle's new identity would be on a 'need to know' basis. Terry had no need. Nothing legislated for a person revealing their own identity. She read on.

...Prince Charming walked into my life two months ago! Chris Philips is an antiques dealer. We met in a coffee shop. He says it was love at first sight. I was too busy guzzling a latte to notice him! When he asked me out I went because he's the first decent man I've met. He wasn't just interested in you know what.

Now for the news! I'm having a baby. We're getting married. Please come. Here's the address.... Mum would have a fit if

she knew I was going to have a child. So would the media. Shall I invite Hello*??!!! Chris is a true gentleman. I've moved into his house. The scan says it's a girl like you've got. Any advice welcomed! Get ready for another new name – It's like* Stars in Your Eyes, *'Tonight I'm being Mrs Penny Philips!'*

Stella did the maths. If Penny Philips had Carrie in 1994, Carrie was twenty-five. Stella had placed Carrie in her early thirties. Doubtless discovering one parent was a child-killer and that your dad had murdered his mistress added on years.

Stella's headache was excruciating, but she was too wired to sleep. She carried Stanley over to her desk and sat down, opening a new spreadsheet. Over the next two hours she compiled an index of the letters. Sent date and a key piece of information, e.g.: new ID, married, pregnant, Carrie's birth, Carrie's exam results. There were fifty-eight letters. By the time she'd finished, the screen appeared to shimmer and her head was ready to split open. For the first time in her life, Stella went to bed without undressing.

By seven o'clock, the morning rush hour outside Clean Slate was in full swing. Headlights strobing through the blinds striped the walls. The woman at a desk in a pool of angle-poised light compounded the film noir effect. Stella was reading the final letter that Danielle Hindle had sent to Terry.

Someone was in the doorway. Stella had the presence of mind to aim the lamp and dazzle the intruder. She reached for her phone to call the police.

'Stella, it's me!' Trudy came into the room.

'Oh!' Stella slipped Danielle's letter under her keyboard.

'Who else would it have been?' Trudy laughed lightly.

'It's early.' Stupid. It was no earlier than the time they were usually there.

'Are you working on the case?' Trudy flicked the light switch in the main office. Vaguely, Stella noted she hadn't done so sooner. Like herself, Trudy assumed an intruder.

'Yes.'

'Would you like another tea? That one looks cold.' Trudy came over.

'I'll come and make it.' Stella enjoyed her morning chats with Trudy. 'You were right. Carrie Philips was keeping something back. Her mother was Danielle Hindle. The child-killer.' Too late Stella knew she had made a mistake. They should not share the information with anyone. She reminded herself that she trusted Trudy. Except Jack said secrets escaped when you told the person you trusted who in turn told the person *they* trusted. Yet the team would have to be told or they were working in the dark. Trudy was as good as on the team. All the same, the slip was one that Terry would not have made.

'Do you think Penny Philips murdered Rachel Cater?' Trudy said. 'Didn't the police discount her?'

'She has an alibi. But she has motive. She was very angry about her husband betraying her.' Stella couldn't bear to remember Penelope Philips. Not a great way to start a case. She must toughen up.

'Who would be?' Trudy pulled a face. 'What's next?'

'Follow the evidence.' Stella gave a grim smile. 'We need to find the relatives.'

'What do you mean?' Trudy remained outside the circle of light.

'Never once during the trial did Danielle Hindle admit to her crimes. She writes as if the murders were nothing to do with her. She wanted to be a detective like my father. I suppose that's why…' She had not meant to mention the letters.

'Maybe your dad was the father they never had.' Trudy hadn't picked up on what was much more than a slip.

'Her father went to prison and when he came out he didn't get in touch. Joy Hindle disowned Danielle when she found out what she'd done.' Stella recalled a photograph of Eddie Hindle working on a motorbike, shirt tucked into eighties-style trousers. Aquiline features, fine hair combed back from his face. The papers had described him as a charmer. Jack was charming but he was also a good dad.

'The parents sound beyond dysfunctional. By all accounts your dad was a hero, no wonder this kid wanted his attention.' Trudy switched on the photocopier and whipped the cover off her computer.

Terry was a lovely dad. Stella had seen that too late. Although Terry had never received Stella's letter asking that he deal with the nasty man at the river, Terry had arrested him. Stella was still learning how much her dad had loved her.

Beverly arrived. Stella made her tea. When Jack got there they'd have a meeting. Beverly had set up an appointment for Jack and Stella with Kevin Hood, the man who had seen Rachel Cater go into the Philipses' house. A mortgage broker, he'd been easy to find.

As Stella mashed the teabag inside Beverly's mug, she replayed Trudy's remark about Terry. Observant and hot on detail, Trudy didn't miss a thing. No PA could be as good as Jackie but Trudy came a close second.

Chapter Twenty-Three

1981

'Today, justice was done. My team worked hard to find the killer of Sarah Ferris. It gives us satisfaction to have achieved a conviction. But where there is murder, no one is a winner. This was a terrible crime, the like of which I never want to see again. The Metropolitan Police offer our condolences to Sarah's family. We hope that this verdict can bring them some peace of mind. That's all, thanks.'

Terry pushed through reporters down the court steps to the car.

'That's not the speech I signed off.' The man stared ahead, his face, pitted with acne, shielded from lenses crowding the window by a rolled copy of the *Daily Mail*. 'You left out that the Hindle girl's a freak of nature who we're happy to have locked up.'

'I couldn't say it, sir.' Sliding onto the back seat next to DCS Lockwood, Terry had expected this.

'I'm sorry?' Chief Superintendent Lockwood's eyes were narrow slits in pudgy cheeks. 'Detective Inspector, you need to get used to this lot or they'll eat you alive!'

'I mean Danielle Hindle's not a freak of nature. She's a very disturbed kid who no one likes. She latched onto me.'

'I'll pretend I didn't hear any of that, or you won't even be back on the beat wearing out shoe leather.' Lockwood surveyed the good and bad of London as the car sped towards Shepherd's Bush. Terry Darnell – Top Cat – was one of his best officers. He'd just wrapped up a highly sensitive investigation. Lockwood had put him forward for a commendation. Darnell was police to the core. But his failing was that bloody heart on his sleeve. Lockwood used his paper to swat a fly that stood for every do-gooder who made policing harder. 'The last thing I need is you having a soft spot for that girl, she's a bad seed. She should be in Holloway. A special school? Gets her own shrink, all mod cons, she'll be cossetted like Shirley Temple!'

'Yes, sir.' Terry pictured Danielle Hindle's expression when the foreman had said 'Guilty'. Perched in the dock – on a platform built so that the court could see her – unlike most of the adults in Court No 7, she'd never fidgeted. She took in everything.

Lockwood was wrong about Terry. Although he did care about those he served, whether criminal or not, he had not got a soft spot for Danielle Hindle. He was shocked that a child so young could do something so terrible as take a life. Most likely two lives. She had shown no remorse. He could not get her out of his head. What kind of child was she? He'd been taught to interrogate a crime. Where did it happen? Why did it happen? Get to know the victim and find something – anything – that might lead to their killer. Was it an ex, a sibling, a chance acquaintance, a colleague? Never had he suspected a playground friend.

Danielle was, as Terry had said to Lucie, an incomparable witness. The shuffling and coughing in the court stopped when she spoke. You could have heard a pin drop. Terry watched the girl listen to the counsel's questions and then, a smile playing over her lips, she tailored her replies to fit evidence that she'd absorbed during the trial. *Incomparable.* Danielle Hindle was beyond him. Battling to make sense of her, Terry couldn't rid his mind of her. None of this could he tell his boss.

They passed Buckingham Palace. Danielle had wanted to meet the Queen. *'Tell her I found a murderer. She will give me a medal.'* Unless Her Majesty kept to the racing pages, she'd be well aware of Danielle Hindle now. Young Kevin had said in his statement that Sarah confessed that she'd seen a terrible thing, but not said what it was. Terry had said the police were satisfied with the verdict. Not true. He was haunted by unanswered questions. Had Sarah watched Danielle push Robbie off the slide? Did Danielle find out and kill Sarah? Had Danielle stolen Sarah's 'Best Sister' charm, missing off the bracelet? They'd failed to find it in the Hindle house. Derek Parsley must have discovered Sarah in the bushes. Unable to save her he carried her into the playground where she'd be found. That explained the blood on his clothes. Terry and Cashman had as good as coerced a confession out of him. It had been perfectly legal, but Terry didn't feel good about it. The man's death was on his hands. Terry had mistaken Parsley's shaking as fear of being found guilty of murder. Parsley had been afraid of a ten-year-old child.

Broadsheet op-eds had expressed concern that the trial – a plethora of wigs, gowns, legalese and the media scrum – was crazy theatre to the little girl from Shepherd's Bush. An *Observer* pundit wrote that when Danielle stood to hear her sentence, she'd looked like the grinning Cheshire Cat. Terry had thought of his Stella. He found himself willing Danielle back in that chaotic household in Braybrook Street. Eddie Hindle, a common or garden criminal, was normal. Eddie's daughter had tipped Terry's world upside down. That she was off the streets and out of the playground gave him no satisfaction. She would always be in his head.

As the driver parked around the back of Hammersmith police station, Terry reflected that Danielle's life would never again be normal. He'd never forget the look she had given him as she was led down to the cells. *Betrayal.*

'You know the drill, Terry,' Lockwood said to him outside

CID. 'Do not think of selling your story. You're a good detective, don't chuck that away. No sympathy for the devil!'

'Yes, sir.' Terry smarted at the suggestion that he'd talk to the press. *Although he already had.*

Terry stayed so long in the lift when it reached Suzie's landing that it got called and he had to travel back down to the lobby. As it juddered past each floor he fretted about the mechanism. Suzie had complained to the management company about the shoddy cleaning and peeling wallpaper in her mansion block. When was the lift last serviced? Terry would tell Stella and Suzie to use the stairs until it got sorted.

An elderly man, coat collar up against the bitter night, wispy hair smeared over a bald pate, waited as Terry dragged aside the grille. Terry touched his forehead as if he'd forgotten something and drew the gate shut. The man got off at the next floor.

Even before he pressed her bell, Suzie flung her door open.

'Terry, what are you doing here?' She feigned surprise but Terry's heart lifted. She'd known that he would come. A cooking aroma drifted out. 'I saw you on the news. Awful about that girl. That's her life over. What *was* she thinking? How are *you*?'

Often Terry had imagined coming to the Barons Court flat and begging his wife and daughter to come home. After a few pints of Fuller's London Pride down the Ram, the fantasy gained credence, only to clarify as absurd as he unlocked his empty house.

Tonight, he was sober. He'd parked outside intending to sit there. He'd craned up and seen lights in Suzie's living room. Then he was going up in the lift.

Nor had Terry planned that when Suzie invited him in that he'd burst into tears and fall into her arms.

Chapter Twenty-Four

2019

Kevin Hood's mortgage brokerage was above a fish and chip shop on the Uxbridge Road.

'Story is, you're buying a house and starting a family,' Beverly had crowed. 'Trudy's done income and expenditure scenarios that prove you're solvent. We didn't fib about your occupations: cleaner and train driver is way cool.'

Walking past Uxbridge police station where Terry's career had begun, Stella and Jack decided that Stella would be what Jack called the awkward squad and Jack the loving partner, keen to settle the loan on their first home together. Stella's 'bad cop' would be circumspect about a loan. That took no pretence. Stella would quiz Hood's financial qualifications. Jack would be charming. He'd bond with Hood, find out about his family, any children or pets. Stuff he did with strangers anyway.

Stella wasn't keen on going undercover. Even less keen to pose as new clients for Hood, raising his hopes of new business. It frustrated Jackie that Stella wouldn't mystery-shop Clean Slate's major cleaning competitor.

The staircase reeked of stale cooking oil. Despite her suspicious mind, Stella didn't hold frayed and sticky lino against Hood.

Shabby common parts didn't always signify a dodgy outfit. Until she'd taken over Clean Slate's building, her landlord had refused to replace similar worn flooring.

Jack knocked on a door labelled 'Hood and Son make your dreams come true!'

A voice called, 'Come in, come in. *Come in.*' With increasing enthusiasm.

They squeezed into an office filled with a desk, a once white computer with a boxy monitor and two visitors' chairs. Stella spotted *Mortgages for Dummies (3rd edition)* amongst a stack of magazines and books. She hoped Kevin wasn't the dummy, then reminded herself they didn't actually need a loan. Jack said a 'good liar believes their own lies'. She didn't want to be good at lying. No sign of the 'son', unless he was Kevin.

Jack and Stella squeezed into the chairs. If anyone tried to enter, the door would hit Stella in the back. Something told her that no one would try.

The contrast between Hood and his down-at-heel office was startling. He might have stepped from *Vogue*. Under the desk, Stella glimpsed Oxford brogues. His short hair was Scandinavian blond, mussed and teased with studied negligence. His skinny 'window-pane' check sage-green suit flattered a trim figure. Stella sniffed Creed's Aventus, an aftershave worn by one of her city clients. Unfortunately, the 'top notes' of bergamot and apple were drowned by the crashing bass of the chip shop below. Either Hood sank his profit into his wardrobe or there was no profit. He wore a thick gold band on his wedding finger. Stella got the situation. Hood was soaring by the seat of his skinny-fit trousers. Her guilt at wasting his time went up a notch. On the other hand, if Kevin Hood had murdered Rachel Cater then she had no compunction about wasting his time pretending to bring work.

Hood picked up his phone and pressed a button. 'I'm busy for the next hour, Shirley. Two seconds.' He asked if they'd like drinks. His hand cupped over the mouthpiece was a giveaway, their reply could hardly be confidential. There was no Shirley. Jack must have guessed too, because like Stella he saved Hood the pantomime of pursuing the fiction and shook his head.

'We want a mortgage, Mr Hood. We're going to live together, tie the knot. Settle down!' Jack grabbed Stella's hand and gave it a courtly kiss. 'Live happily ever after!'

Yes, all right. Stella rolled her eyes at Jack.

'Call me Kevin. *Kev.* Congratulations! I can't recommend wedded bliss enough.' Kevin waggled his ring finger. So, Stella decided, he too was play-acting.

'Yes, we're moving out of London *finally*,' Jack chattered. 'To the country. Clean air, peace and quiet, birdsong, fields, cows, sheep…' A city boy, Jack ground to silence.

'We're looking to borrow no more than three hundred thousand pounds.' Stella got to business. 'We want a house. Three bedrooms. Off-street parking.'

Beverly had advised they say four hundred, but ever careful and believing her own lie, Stella had forgotten.

'Doable definitely. One hundred per cent. Let's get this party started.' Realigning objects on his desk – stapler, a tube of hand cream and an iPhone 5 – Hood opened a wallet in which was a yellow lined legal pad and a gold fountain pen. He swung the monitor to part face them and scooting the mouse, brought up a blank record screen. 'Your dream awaits!'

'How long have you been a broker?' Stella fired her first dart.

'Since school. Too many years ago to say!' Kevin must have guessed from Stella's expression what he was expected to say. 'Started at sixteen. I'm forty-five so nearly thirty years! I know the pitfalls and crevices. I'll slalom you through the rapids.' Even Stella, not given to flowery language, spotted the mixed metaphors.

'Is Hood and Sons you?' She looked about as if a father or son Hood could be concealed somewhere in the cramped room.

'I'm the son. My old man passed a couple of years ago. Bless him.' Kevin looked genuinely upset then repainted his chirpy grin. 'Where are you moving to, if I may ask?'

Stella knew from a sales course she'd attended in the early days of Clean Slate that Hood was 'warming up the customer'. She'd never got 'hook, convert, sell'. People wanted cleaning or they didn't. Lucie warned that cuts in the police meant fewer detectives, soaring crime rates and more private investigators. Clean Slate Detective Services must be competitive.

'Winchcombe.' Jack beamed.

'Lovely!' Rocking in his chair, his desperation ill-concealed, Hood jumped straight to convert. 'It's a beautiful place.'

'Do you know it?' Stella tensed. They'd hit what Lucie called pay-dirt sooner than expected.

'My wife comes from there. My mum-in-law still lives in the village.' He swapped the stapler with his phone on the desk. Nervous.

'Does your wife miss it? Quite a contrast to London.' Jack piled in, all warm and fluffy. Stella did a granite stare.

'She longed for the bright lights of London Town. Me, I'd give anything to do what you're doing. Winchcombe's heaven on earth.'

'Where did you grow up?' Elbow on the chair arm, Jack rested his chin on a hand.

'West London, Braybrook Street. You may have heard of it?'

'Is it famous?' Jack did a puzzled face. Both of them tensed.

At that moment Stella got a text.

'I have to get this,' she apologized.

Trudy told us about PP. Stop. Kevin Hood was friend of DH in the eighties. Stop. Bev. Stop

Unlike Stella, Beverly's texts were not prey to dictation software expressing punctuation in words Bev longed for the era of telegrams and trilby hatted PIs.

Stella absorbed the meaning. Kevin Hood was the last person to see Rachel Cater alive. He had also been a friend of Danielle Hindle.

'For the wrong reason. Three coppers were killed there in the sixties. Scars a place, something like that. You never forget.'

'Isn't that near where that girl lived who killed those children?' Jack sat up. 'Doris… um?'

'Danielle.' Hood's face clouded. 'Danielle Hindle. I was friends with her brother.'

'You need to see this.' Stella showed Jack the phone.

'Oh, shame she can't come. We'll find another date.' Jack was quick. He rubbed his hands. 'So, Kevin, how does this work? We tell you our salaries and you work out what we can borrow?'

'Sorry, I got sidetracked down memory lane there for a minute.' Kevin appeared ruffled.

Stella wanted to hook out more information on Hood's knowledge of Danielle Hindle, but supposed Jack was playing it carefully.

For the next quarter of an hour Hood plugged their earnings and outgoings into his computer. Finally he printed up their mortgage estimate. Beverly had inflated their income to avoid hitting obstacles that would divert from the real objective. All the same, Stella was impressed when Kevin advised them to stay under budget to allow for contingencies. If she were applying for a mortgage, she might choose him. Or maybe not. Hood had known Danielle Hindle when they were kids. He visited the village where Hindle lived now. Circumstantial, but Stella had shot him to the top of the suspect list.

Second dart: 'How well did you know Danielle Hindle?'

'Not so much. We moved to the street when I was three. I met her brother Jason at nursery school. And Robbie Walsh and Sarah Ferris.' Hood turned his wedding ring. 'The murdered children. Robbie was my best mate.' He appeared to scrutinize the screen showing their mortgage details. 'I envied Jason his two older sisters, I'm an only child. Danielle was kind.'

'Kind?' Stella didn't need to fake incredulity.

'Sounds crazy. Danielle had your back. She'd duff up anyone who picked on you.' He nodded at the loan figure. 'You've got a healthy deposit and with Jack being a tad younger, you can easily service the loan. You're good to go and get a house!'

'Have you seen Danielle Hindle recently?' Jack flapped the papers in excitement. Stella almost wished that she believed him. Not that she wanted to live with Jack in Winchcombe. She was a confirmed Londoner.

'I haven't seen Danielle since she got taken away.' Hood depressed the stapler. Closed staples sprinkled onto his pad.

'How long have you been married?' Jack asked. 'Looking for tips here, mate!'

Oh please.

'I met Theresa ten years ago. I'd seen a client in Blackfriars. I was on a bench by the bridge grabbing a sandwich. She joined me, we got talking. Love at first sight!' Was he reciting a script? Or perhaps after a decade Hood had the story down pat.

'Romantic!' Jack marvelled.

'What about you guys?' Kevin Hood corralled the staples on the paper.

'What about us?' Stella barked.

'Ah well.' Jack crossed his legs and intertwined his fingers on a knee. 'We also met by the Thames, upstream from you. I recited from my favourite Dickens novel. It was love at first sight too.'

'It was dark.' And it was a crime scene. Jack's voice coming out of nowhere had given Stella the creeps. It was love at a hundred and fiftieth sight. 'Have you seen Danielle Hindle since her release?'

'You're asking a lot of questions.' Kevin Hood stopped smiling.

'Just interested,' Jack bounded in. 'It's not often you meet someone with a claim to fame.'

'Danni changed her name. It said in the papers.' Hood uncapped his fountain pen. Stella half expected a stiletto. She was debating how quick a getaway they could achieve in the tiny room when Hood said, 'She's married with a kid. Unless that's fake news. I hope not. Everyone deserves to live their dream.'

'That's a bit rich.' Perhaps Jack had forgotten he was Mr Nice. 'She killed your friends.'

'Yes.' His expression closed. He teased the staplers with his pen. 'You're too interested. Do you really want a mortgage?'

'God yes!' Jack hooted. 'It's just I've got kids living near that playground. Makes you think, doesn't it?'

Silence. Stella, for one, pondered what it made you think.

'I get media people fixing mortgage appointments. Offering me big notes to spill my story on Danielle. Blood money.' Hood was angry. 'Real clients find out I knew her and don't return.' He chucked down his pen. A spray of green ink shot over his pad like a blood spatter test. Hood appeared oblivious.

'We must go.' Stella flapped the loan details. Jack said she was slow to get nuance. He also said green ink signified something bad. She couldn't remember what. Her mind went into overdrive. Had Hood helped Danielle Hindle kill their little friends? Had he helped her kill Cater?

'We'll be in touch.' Jack held out his hand. 'As soon as we've found our perfect home.'

'Don't wait till then. Vendors like it if you've got a loan lined up.' Eyes on Stella, Hood shook Jack's hand. He'd read her mind. They wouldn't get a mortgage through Hood and Son. She and Jack would not live in Winchcombe. They had played him.

Stella was by the door but Jack had to leave first or she'd trap him with Hood.

Glancing back, she saw Kevin Hood arranging the staples in a circle. A line trailed up to a shape like a balloon. Or a noose.

Chapter Twenty-Five

1980

Terry gathered the letter and newspaper off the door mat, distantly surprised that there wasn't more post – he felt he'd been away for weeks. It was twenty-four hours.

'Stella hasn't slept in her bed,' he had called from the doorway of Stella's bedroom. Unlike the room in his house, this one had living evidence of Stella. Books and papers were heaped on the desk where Stella did her homework, a sweatshirt was slung over her chair.

'You shouldn't have gone in there. It's private,' Suzie had said when he returned to the living room. She'd put a mug of coffee for him in the kitchen hatchway. He drank it while he tucked in his shirt and did up his tie. The coffee was hot and milky the way Suzie knew he liked it. Making love with her, Terry had felt a delicious mix of familiarity spiced with their first time in the back of his Triumph Herald fifteen years ago. He'd let himself believe that they could start again.

'I only looked in.' Stupid to admit that he'd gone right in and, with a detective's eye, raked the room for clues about his daughter. All he'd learnt was that Stella was doing photosynthesis in biology. He'd ask her about it.

Now, Terry returned to the doorstep and lifted the two pints of milk out of the carrier. Taking them through to the kitchen, he pinpointed when it had gone horribly wrong.

Numb, he'd sat on Stella's bed. Next minute he jammed her pillow to his face. Fresh cotton, it gave nothing away. *Yes it did.* It told him that Stella hadn't come home last night.

'Where is she?' He'd pulled his tie taut between his fists then swished it around his shirt collar.

'Probably at Liz's. She practically lives there.' Suzie had yawned. 'Liz's mum makes fantastic shepherd's pie *apparently*. Just how hard is it to cook up mince and mash a few spuds? The way Stella goes on you'd think it was cordon bleu!'

'You mean you don't know?' An alert had gone off in Terry's head.

'I'm not her keeper.'

'Actually, you are. For crying out loud, Suze, she's *fourteen*.' He strode out to the hall and snatched at the phone.

'What are you doing?' Suzie clamped a hand over the dial.

'I'm putting out a call. Stella's been missing over twelve hours!'

'She's not *missing*! You're not "putting out a bloody call"! Suddenly this is *The Sweeney*?' Suzie snatched the receiver off him and slammed it down on the cradle. 'I told you, she's with Liz.'

'You said "probably" and who says it's Liz?' He'd pictured the girls he'd once seen with Stella outside the Regal. Milling about like streetwalkers, eyes black with kohl, lips glossed bright red.

'Liz is Stella's best friend. A bit dull for my liking, but believe me when your kid's a martyr to hormones, dull is good. The last thing Stella needs is the Met steaming round there guns blazing.'

They had replayed an argument that was itself a replay of sundry others.

Terry shoved the milk into the fridge. There were three full bottles there already. He ordered as if Stella still sat at the table with her cornflakes every morning and drank chocolate Nesquik every night. A smell of sour milk wafted out as he shut the fridge.

'You're letting her run wild! She saw an X film the other night, did you know that? The girl I saw her with wasn't super-dull Liz. She looked like a tart!' *Suzie didn't know.* Cloaked in a red mist, Terry had unleashed the darkness of a world that he'd tried to keep from his family.

'Where was Stella last night? For all you know she's lying in a gutter choked on vomit. Or some man has stolen her virginity!' Stolen her virginity. Where had he got that from?

Terry and Suzie Darnell saw that they were not alone. Stella was in the living room doorway, keys in her hand. Staring at her parents as if they were strangers.

It was the second time in twenty-four hours that a girl had looked at him like that. *Betrayal.* He'd promised Stella not to tell Suzie about the film. He'd apologized for embarrassing her in front of her mates.

He'd promised Danielle she could be a detective.

Now Terry reached for the chair that was Stella's when she visited. He tossed the letter and newspaper onto the table.

'Stell, you're OK, I was so worried...'

Stella had pivoted on her heel and gone into her bedroom.

'Perfect father!' Suzie had slow hand-clapped.

'Stell, let me in.' Terry had tapped on the door. It was all he could do not to rest his forehead on the wood and plead.

Now, he rested his head on folded arms on the kitchen table.

'She won't come out for the rest of the day,' Suzie hissed. 'Thanks a bunch.'

'She's got to eat.' Terry had found his jacket and briefcase on the sofa where – in what seemed like a different life – he'd flung them. When Suzanne had held him, listened to his anguish that he'd imprisoned a girl younger than their daughter. It wasn't why he'd joined the police. Had she kissed him first? They'd barely made it to the bedroom.

'You think so? That girl could go on hunger strike for England.'

'I was looking out for her,' Terry told the kitchen table as if his wife was in the room with him.

'By saying her best friend's a tart! What happened to your advice about trusting Stella, she knows what she's doing?' Banging the heel of her palm on the lift button she'd snarled, 'Terry, go and arrest someone, it's what you do best.'

'I'll call you,' he'd said.

'Call me what?' Suzie flung shut the concertina gate.

'We need to talk.' Last night, in bed, she'd hinted at a reconciliation. Or he'd thought she had.

'You've done that.' Suzie closed her front door. The two women he loved best in the world were behind closed doors.

As the lift had begun its shaky descent, he had realized he'd forgotten to advise Suzie and Stella never to use it.

Now, his head in his arms, Terry screwed up his eyes until he saw stars.

'Anyone home?'

Stella! He raised his head from the table, bleary-eyed. Lucie May held a lit cigarillo in one hand, a key in the other.

'Where've you been?' She exhaled shots of smoke from her nostrils.

'Nowhere.' Inwardly groaning, Terry saw Lucie was dressed to the nines in what he called her 'killer-kit': short skirt, heels and red lipstick.

'Crap!'

'What is?' Terry rubbed at his face. He needed a shower and a shave.

'You weren't here last night. I called round.' Holding her cigarillo aloft, Lucie was neutral. 'Aqua Manda. You've been with *her*.'

Last Christmas he'd bought Suzie Rive Gauche believing it was what she'd worn. From her expression he'd known he'd got it wrong. He'd meant to ask Stella what her mum wore. Lucie had pricked a memory. Aqua Manda, of course. He couldn't write it down in front of her.

'Well?'

'I popped in.' He went on the offensive: 'What's the problem?

You wanted no strings. I wish you wouldn't smoke in the house, it gets in the furnishings.'

'Furnishings! Get you. Easy to see who's been yanking your strings.' Lucie eyed him through curling smoke. 'You're a patsy, Terry. She'll never have you back.'

'I know.' He didn't know.

'Who's that from?' Lucie stabbed her cigarillo at the letter. Terry had forgotten about it. He made to get it, but Lucie got there first.

'How should I know? Give it here.' *She was in prison. The letters would stop.*

Lucie grabbed a knife from the drainer and slit open the envelope. Terry listened to the tick of the wall clock. A time bomb.

'Jesus wept! It's *her*. The Hindle girl is still writing to you.'

'Lucie!' His shout shocked them both. Lucie only briefly. The length of ash increased on her cigarillo as she read out the letter in an approximation of a child's voice.

'"Dear DI Darnell, I am at my new school. There are not many kids here but me. All the girls are older and want to do my hair and make me go around with them like a cat. I saw you in the court but you never came for me. I am learning to knit for my baby. Except the girls say I can't have one. I'll show them. I said I was a detective with you and they told me the police are bad. The headmaster is alright. Not as nice as you. He says I can have books to read and got me *Anne of Green Gables* which is stupid so far. I hope you are well. Love Danielle. Xxxxx Five kisses because the girls say you have to have a lucky number. Mine is five like my family though that is not lucky."'

'Give it to me, Lucie.' Wearily, Terry put out his hand.

'Don't tell me you're visiting Danielle Hindle.'

'Of course not.' He kept his hand out.

'Yeah, like you didn't spend last night with your ex-wife! Terry, she's a child-killer! My lot will have your guts. *I* could have your guts. This is mental.' Lucie spoke slowly as if he wasn't right in the head.

'Suzie's not my ex-wife,' Terry said pointlessly. 'I have *not* seen Danielle. This was here when I got back this morning.'

There was a beat as they both took in the slip.

Lucie switched into gear. Her true love was her job. This was a story. 'This is hand delivered. She knows where you live.'

Terry flicked on the kettle. 'She sent the others to the station.'

'She's written often?' The ash on Lucie's cigarillo was perilously long. There was a needle in it. Lucie did it to distract interviewees. And him apparently.

'Forget I said that.' Terry smelled sweat. He disgusted himself. 'I had to develop a relationship with her to get her to talk. I want nothing more to do with her. If you breathe a word, you and me we're finished.' He lifted mugs from the mug tree.

'Having just shagged your wife, you're not in the position to bargain, Terry. I don't take hand-me-downs!' Lucie didn't look as tough as her words. Terry felt a flash of tenderness and wished he had more to offer her, she deserved it. He dropped teabags into the mugs and added boiling water.

Lucie was rereading the letter. 'Nothing about murdering those kiddies. You'd think she was writing home from a holiday camp. The kid's whacko.' She ground her cigarillo out in the sink. He never knew what she did with the needle. She sluiced the ash down the plughole and dropped the stub into the pedal bin. If Suzie was living here she'd have had a fit. If Suzie was here, Lucie would not be here.

'...she's never owned up to murder, either of them. Get real. That girl's a psychopath!' Lucie lit another cigarillo. 'No tea for me, I've got to head off.'

'I am real about her.' Terry returned to the table with the teas. 'She doesn't care about her friends. She fancied Lee Marshall but she killed his sister. She probably killed Robbie, but unless she 'fesses up, we'll never know. Perhaps in her warped world her actions make sense. I discounted her as a murderer because she's a kid. I messed up. You saw it before me.' How could a child kill another child? Terry slumped onto a chair.

'You think the best of people, I think the worst.' Lucie moved towards him. He pictured Suzie naked. He'd messed up more than the case. 'You wanted Stella to join the police. Her ma drummed it out of her. It touched your heart when Danielle said what you'd hope Stella would say. That kid used us both. She wanted to be a detective and she wanted to be famous. She's certainly famous! *Cop has Child-Killer Penfriend!*' Lucie cackled. 'The difference between you and me is I used her back.'

'Don't print this, Lucie.' He flicked at the letter which she'd dropped back on the table.

Lucie narrowed her eyes. 'What's it worth, Top Cat?'

Chapter Twenty-Six

2019

Jack and Stella knew St Mark's Church in Chiswick. They'd crept amidst moonlit shadows of ivy-clad mausoleums and crumbling angels in pursuit of clues to murder.

Today, bright Spring sunshine lent a sentimental aspect to the graves and statuary. A woman pushed a buggy cut through from Chiswick Mall. A blackbird's song won out over the scrawl of traffic on the Great West Road.

After leaving Kevin Hood, Jack and Stella decided to visit the grave of Sarah Ferris which, according to Wikipedia, was in the cemetery. Stella had expected Jack to find it quickly. At home with phantoms, he roamed cemeteries the way most people mingled at parties. But an hour in they were giving up when Stanley bolted after a squirrel. He gave chase into a corner that they'd missed. There they had found not Sarah's grave, but a headstone for Lee Marshall, her brother.

BRIAN MARSHALL 1ST MAY 1945–22ND JULY 1975

MUCH LOVED HUSBAND AND SON.

Taken from us too soon.

Lee Marshall 1970–2017

A good son and husband.

'We can take Lee off the suspect list. He couldn't have murdered Rachel.' Jack spoke first. 'He died two years ago.'

'He was forty-seven.' Stella noted that the stone needed a clean.

'I haven't been here for a while,' Jack said as if he'd neglected friends. 'Why isn't Sarah buried here too, I wonder?'

All the nearby graves dated from the nineteen seventies.

'Marshall senior gets a more fulsome epitaph than his son.' Jack read the stone. 'There's nothing about Lee being "taken too soon" although he was.'

'He wasn't taken. He killed himself.' Stella was consulting her phone. 'Lee Marshall jumped in front of a train.' Stella knew that Jack dreaded another 'one under'. 'Northern line. Tooting Bec.'

One of Jack's colleagues had developed a stutter after a suicide in front of his train. Another woman never took a shift on the anniversary of the day it happened to her. Stella was letting Jack know that it was unlikely any of his fellow drivers was involved. Jack drove the District line.

'I wonder what made him do it,' Jack said eventually.

'Suicide leaves a mess for loved ones.' When Stella was little, Terry had told her that '...once upon a time, suicides and executed criminals could not be buried in church grounds.'

'People aren't thinking straight. It's an illness.' Jack paced around the grave.

'I suppose.' Stella found it hard to sympathize with those who chose Jack's 'office' as the place to end their lives. A suicide affected other lives too.

'Lee Marshall failed to save his sister from being murdered. I imagine that haunted him.'

'It says here that Lee was with his wife when he jumped. That's particularly cruel.' Stella cupped a hand over her phone to shield it from sunlight. 'They had no children.'

'Stella!'

Stella felt a shove on her shoulder. Her rucksack was dragged off. Wheeling around to her assailant she just stopped herself punching an elderly woman.

'Get away!' Grey permed hair, watery eyes, lips crumpled by false teeth. The woman shoved a fist under Stella's nose. 'Go away or I'll get the police on you.'

'We are here to grieve.' Jack was at the foot of the grave, eyes shut head bowed.

'Grieve? My eye! You lot put my boy in there, now you can leave him in peace.'

'You're Lee's mother!' Stella shot Jack a look. They should go. *Now*.

'Lee talked about you *so* often, I feel I know you!' Jack glided around the grave. In black coats with pale skin, at a glance, they might be mother and son. 'Mrs Marshall. I'm so pleased to meet you. I'm Jonathan. Lee and I were buddies!' Jack was going undercover before her eyes.

'It's Ferris!'

'Lee never mentioned you.' Thankfully, Mrs Ferris hadn't heard. 'I knew my Lee's friends. Including that Hindle devil.'

'Everyone calls me Jack. We didn't go back that far. I'd have liked to have known Lee when we were boys. We had lots in common. We loved our mums, for one thing.' Jack was wistful.

Stella was vertiginous with horror. If this went wrong it would go very wrong. It *was* wrong. Cleaners didn't have to lie. She fought the urge to get going on the headstone.

'Lee'd be gutted to know she's sold all his things. Lock stock and barrel.' Mrs Ferris whispered as if Lee might overhear, 'Blood money.'

'She?' Jack dipped his head. Stella noticed that Mrs Ferris had used the same term as Kevin Hood.

'Once Joanne buried my Lee, she was off.'

'She saw it happen.'

'Ah, Jo. *Poor* Jo!' Jack looked stricken.

Jo must be Lee Marshall's partner, Stella supposed.

'Poor *nothing*. Witch!'

'Witch. Yes!' Jack agreed. 'Witch.'

'She never loved Lee. How could she say those things?' Mrs Ferris's energy abruptly sapped, she rested a hand on the headstone as if felled. Stella supposed if Lee was in his forties that made Mrs Ferris about seventy. Grief had scored her face with lines.

'What did she say?' Mirroring Mrs Ferris, Jack put his hand on the stone. Adept at reading body language, he'd be trying to win the woman's confidence.

'Jo only goes and tells Lee he ruined her life! Lee should have wed that Nicky Walsh, a lovely girl. I was that upset when she married. She used to come and see us. I heard she's a grandmother now. Joanne couldn't fall pregnant. What does she do?'

'What does she do?' Jack enquired of the headstone.

'He had the pick of girls. I told her, "count yourself lucky!"' Cathy gazed at her son's grave.

Stanley was nosing around the stone. Stella had fancied training him as a cadaver dog, but didn't want him starting now.

'...try managing on your own with a little boy and a dog. Alan hates dogs. Boys too.' Mrs Ferris picked at moss on the granite. She murmured, 'Joanne and me never saw eye to eye.'

'Why was that?' Jack looked sad. Stella suspected it was real. Jack wanted families to be perfect. Jackie said it was because, until Stella and his children, he'd never had a proper family. Not that they were a family.

'She was out for what she could get from my Lee. Nice home, life of Riley.' She yanked at groundsel growing behind the stone.

‘Where has Lee’s wife gone?’ Stella asked. Was Jo Marshall dead too? Given resources it would help if the suspect list was short. But not too short.

‘There.’ Mrs Ferris pointed at the grass.

‘Hell?’ Jack was tentative.

‘Australia.’

‘Do you have an address for her? I ought to send my condolences.’ Jack was talking like an undertaker.

Mrs Ferris confronted Stella. ‘I didn’t see you at the funeral?’

‘No, I…’ Beginning to believe Jack’s scenario, Stella felt guilty.

‘We’ve been abroad. We didn’t know that Lee had… passed,’ Jack explained.

They heard beeping. For a ghastly moment Stella supposed it came from the grave.

‘Alan? What’s the matter, luvvy?… See my note.’ Mrs Ferris was on the phone.

Stella heard yelling on the other end. Alan Ferris. Father of Sarah. Suspect.

‘I’ve gone to the grave. What? Sarah’s. No, not Lee! I’m leaving but I’ll have a wait for the bus. Back no later than three o’clock. It’s on the note.’ Cathy Ferris thrust the phone back in her handbag. ‘That was Alan, my husband. He’s got dementia. I can’t leave him long.’ She walked away.

‘We’ll give you a lift.’ Jack caught her up.

‘Jack…’ Stella stopped. They were detectives, they must capitalize on the turn of events. Were they cleaners, offering to drive the frail woman was only right. She’d get cold queuing for a bus.

Chapter Twenty-Seven

2019

The first thing Jack saw when Cathy Ferris showed them into the sitting room of her house on Braybrook Street was a shrine to Sarah – candles, cards, photos – nearly forty years on, Sarah was far from forgotten.

Pigtails. Pearly white teeth. She grinned as if responding to a joke. There was no getting away from the terrible fact. Cathy and Alan Ferris had lost a child to murder. Sarah Ferris looked like the kind of child who was always busy. *Keep still, Sarah love, and smile for the nice photographer.* Were Sarah alive, she'd be in her forties, kids of her own.

'Are they the bailiffs?' In a chair by the gas fire, Alan Ferris, a big man, fixed Jack and Stella with a glare in which Jack detected a glint of malice.

'No, Al. We don't need the bailiffs. They're friends of… they're *my* friends. You read your paper. We're going in the kitchen so as not to bother you.'

'Where've you been? You've been out all day.'

'I told you, I was visiting Sarah's grave. I took her lovely flowers from us. I've not been long.' Mechanical patience. Jack had seen no flowers.

‘Who are they?’ Alan Ferris bundled up his newspaper and tossed it on the carpet.

‘Nice people.’ She retrieved the paper, refolded it and returned it to him. ‘Listen, Al. Remember Ron’s coming to take you to the library. That’ll be grand, won’t it?’

Jack had seen homes of people whose relatives had died suddenly, through illness, accident and murder. Stella brought him in to clean for those poleaxed by loss. Some had decorated away reminders of the loved one. Others, like the Ferrises, were dominated by the dead.

The room was shabby, the old carpet stained, and there was a dent in the plaster of the wall above Alan’s chair. The shrine was the focus of the room. Sarah had been incorporated into her parents’ lives. Always young and full of promise.

‘Alan smashed his fist into the wall when the police told us about Sarah.’ Cathy Ferris had seen Jack notice the dent. ‘He broke a finger.’

The act of a distraught father or a clever murderer? Jack wondered.

‘Terrible.’ Alan Ferris still possessed rage. If he lost his temper, Jack wouldn’t like to be on the end of it.

‘What’s terrible?’ Alan Ferris poked a finger at the space above his nose as if adjusting the spectacles that lay on a table beside him. When Jack passed them over, Ferris took them without acknowledgement.

‘The weather. We’ll make sure you’re wrapped up for when Ron comes.’ Cathy Ferris was adroit at fending off her husband. She beckoned Jack and Stella out of the room.

The kitchen was a surprise. Modern Shaker-style cupboards, a vinyl flooring patterned like terracotta tiles, it was bright and cheery. Pots of red geraniums lined the window sill. Two ready meals from a catering company which Jack knew was for older people defrosted on a tea towel by the microwave.

‘Tea?’ Cathy Ferris grabbed the kettle.

'No thank you.' Stella wouldn't want to give Cathy extra work.

'Yes please. Milk no sugar.' Jack knew that Cathy must keep busy. Stella would be annoyed that he'd claimed to be Lee's friend. Yet Jack felt close to the man who, little older than himself, had been unable to manage life. Jack could forgive Lee's method of suicide. He'd change his mind if it transpired that Lee had killed his sister and couldn't live with the guilt any longer. Why had that idea come into his mind? Was it something that Kevin Hood had said? The man was surely one of very few who had remained loyal to Danielle Hindle.

The layout of the flat was identical to the upstairs of Stella's house. They were in what was her study, once her bedroom. A family of four (then three) occupied a space half the size of the house in which Terry lived alone once Suzie took Stella. A different kind of loss that Jack suspected had broken the detective's heart and shortened his life.

'I'll get Joanne's address,' Cathy said. 'If Alan comes in, he'll have forgotten you. Say you're friends or he'll think you're here to steal off of us.' Steadying herself on the counter, Cathy Ferris feathered her way out of a door. She could have brought them into the kitchen without bothering Alan. She had wanted them to see him.

'Lee looks like Sarah.' Stella was studying photographs stuck to the side of a combi boiler. Out of the eyeline, it was a secret shrine. Every picture was of Lee. A baby in a high chair, head gleefully tipped back, spoon clutched in a chubby fist. Jack had taken a similar picture of Milly. Lee subverting a school photo with a loose tie and cool stare. The toddler Lee 'reading' *Woman's Own* in a playpen. Lee tearing towards the camera on a trike. Aged about ten, natty in jeans jacket lounging on a patio chair with Sarah hugging up to him. Lackadaisical brother, adoring sister. The date on the print, 25 November 1980. In a couple of weeks Sarah would be dead. Lee, handsome and tall. Arm in arm with a woman in a bridal gown outside a church. Someone had scrubbed out Joanne's face with black felt tip.

'She must hate her daughter-in-law,' he said.

'There were no pictures of Lee in the front room.'

'Cathy Ferris lied to her husband about visiting Sarah's grave.'

'Maybe she did visit it then came to Lee's.'

'Why not say?' Jack said.

'Because Alan would kill me.' Cathy Ferris was back. 'He hates Lee. He wanted a virgin bride, but got me and Lee. When Sarah was taken from us Alan blamed Lee. I should never have gone with him.'

'Did *you* blame Lee?' Stella didn't beat around any bushes.

'It was my fault. I shouldn't have remarried. I just kept hoping that Alan would accept Lee. Especially when he had his own child. But after Sarah came along he was worse. As soon as he could get out, Lee went into the army. He met Joanne in Germany. Her father was a colonel stationed in Berlin. Right from the off, Joanne acted like she was better than us. Well, I suppose in a way she was. She took Lee away.' She flapped a postcard at Jack. 'This is where she lives. If you write to her, say I'm keeping up Lee's grave, that'll teach her!'

The sorrowful tone didn't match the vindictive words.

Jack took the card. 'Come Down Under!' was emblazoned across emblems of Australia: a koala, a kangaroo, shots of Uluru and the Sydney Opera House. On the back in green pen, 'It's hot! When you visit, we'll go to the beach.' Beneath was a series of characters. The card was signed 'Jo', with a kiss inside the 'o' and a heart around it. 'This is a Skype tag. Do you have a postal address for her?'

'She said she'd send it when she's settled. She never did. She's living the high life on his money.' Cathy spoke dreamily. One stage of grief was anger but, Jack wondered, was Cathy Ferris through this and now exhausted, incapable of any emotion?

'Have you talked to Joanne on Skype?' Stella said.

'I don't have a computer. It's not natural to be watched on the phone.' Cathy poked at one of the ready meals and pulled a face. 'Lee tried to get me interested in that sort of thing. He said you can find school friends. I hated school! So did Lee.'

An understatement, Jack thought, considering that Lee's school friend killed his sister.

'You don't know where in Australia his widow lives?' Stella persisted. The postmark was too smudged to read.

'She's gone. Good riddance.' In a weary monotone.

Joanne Marshall had given her mother-in-law a method of contact that doubtless she knew Cathy would never use. Perhaps the antipathy was mutual.

'Do you know where Danielle Hindle is now?' Stella popped in the question.

'No idea.' Seemingly unfazed by the sudden change of subject, Cathy answered and changed it back. 'They sent convicts to Australia. Wouldn't surprise me if Jo was from that stock.'

'She's Australian? I thought her father was in the British army?' Stella asked.

'Her grandfather was from there. His son immigrated to Britain.'

'Does the name Rachel Cater mean anything?' Jack was sailing close to the wind asking this on the heels of mention of Danielle Hindle.

'Was she a friend of Lee's?' Cathy Ferris perked up.

'No.' Jack felt shame. Lee's mother was hungry for contact with anyone who'd known her dead son. Her husband wouldn't let her talk about Lee. Joanne Marshall had gone to Australia to escape her past. There was no one to help Cathy keep the flame alive except two would-be detectives posing as Lee's friends. Stella was right, being undercover stank.

'Do you and Alan get out at all?' Stella wasn't asking as a detective, she'd be concerned for Cathy as the primary carer.

'Alan went out with the church. It gave me a break. It stopped when he took against that woman vicar. He can't help it, he thinks everyone's trying to con us. He's not wrong. Some are.' She shot an anxious glance at the front room.

'Who is out to get you?' Stella was gentle.

'Police, the newspapers, neighbours. When your child is murdered it doesn't stop there. The police treated us like criminals. They took this place apart. Inspector Darnell had his sights on Alan. He was on at Lee to give Alan up. If Alan had done it, Lee would have said so in a blink. He was a good lad. We heard who did it from a lady reporter who came knocking.' She sucked on her teeth. 'Your baby is murdered. You don't matter.'

'The police have to cover all bases. Did you have FLOs… family liaison officers?' asked the daughter of a police officer.

'Sharon and Mick were sent to spy on us. The L stands for Listening.' She fussed the geraniums, repositioning the pots. 'Neighbours said how lovely Sarah was, but it was only to get their faces on the television. They came round with stew. Alan sent them packing. We weren't charity cases. Those ones meant well. Some did a procession down our street, for bringing back hanging. They've gone into their hutches now the cameras have left. I heard that one family bought their council house on Sarah. They gave the *News of the World* a pack of lies. Most round here cross the road when they see me coming.' Cathy spoke without ire. She plucked a dead leaf from a geranium. 'I don't blame them. Bad luck's catching. What with Alan…'

'Alan?' Stella prompted.

'The dementia takes you different ways. He was angry anyway. Jealous. Hated me looking at another man. Not that I did.' Cathy looked at Jack as if she'd detected the Alan in him. As if he knew that Jack wanted to stuff Bella's bloke Harry in a box. 'Before Sarah, Alan followed me to see who I was with.' Cathy watered the geraniums with a little can, splashing the sill, pausing to prod the soil with a finger. 'Nowadays he forgets what I say. I write it out, he forgets to read it or forgets he *has* read it. If we do get out he shouts at people in the street.'

'That must be difficult,' Stella said.

'Listen, lovey, when your baby is crushed with a brick in the playground and your son goes in front of a train, nothing is difficult.' Cathy Ferris put down the watering can. 'Last week, down the market, Alan goes and drags a tiny kiddie off of her mum. Yelling she was Sarah. I stopped him getting arrested. He used to know she's dead. Now he gets muddled.' She grabbed a fork and stabbed the plastic, then shoved the containers into the microwave and set it going. 'Alan called Lee selfish for hurting me. Lee never hurt me. He was the best son. Alan never went to his funeral.'

'Is Alan the type to take revenge?' Stella wiped up pooling water on the sill with a cloth from her emergency cleaning kit and Jack recalled why he loved her. He loved Stella too much. Like Alan Ferris, he'd been tempted to follow Stella to check she wasn't with Cashman. *He had a black heart.*

'If Alan found Danielle Hindle, he'd smash her with a brick and stab her in the back with a knife.'

The microwaved pinged.

'All right, Cathy?' A woman stopped on the pavement as Jack and Stella were leaving. 'How's Al doing? Heard about that ruck down the market.'

Cathy pulled a face. 'Glad we seen you, Joy. These are friends of Lee's asking about Danielle.'

'I didn't know Lee. Or Danielle,' Stella hastened to say. Joy Hindle had retained the style of make-up and clothes from photographs of her from thirty-nine years ago.

'Why's that?' A shadow passed across Hindle's face. Then she smiled, 'Come in. You too, Cath?'

'Better not. He's in a strop because I went to Lee's grave. That's where I found…' Cathy was talking more to herself as she wandered back inside.

Stella was surprised that the women, one the mother of the murder victim, the other the mother of the murderer, were on speaking terms.

'We'd love to!' Jack spoke into Stella's silence.

Mrs Hindle showed them into a living room reeking of stale smoke. Unlike the Ferrises's upstairs flat, the Hindles occupied the entire house. The place was piled with newspapers and magazines, an open Amazon box lay at their feet, plastic bubble packing seemingly everywhere. Two plastic garden chairs faced the television. On a couch a man in his forties watched boxing on a tablet that, Stella guessed, had been in the box.

'Jason, manners. Guests,' Joy Hindle shouted although her son was two feet away. Jason glared at them, upper lip curled.

'What are you? Christians?' Jason asked Jack.

Don't say yes, Stella silently urged Jack. She knew that yes would be the wrong answer.

'They told Cathy Marshall they was friends of Lee's.' Joy Hindle whipped the cellophane off a packet of cigarettes.

'He's dead.' Jason went back to the boxing. 'Topped himself, stupid sod!'

Nothing in the thickset man with product-moulded hair, muscles bunching under a QPR shirt, evoked the curly blond cherub, angel to his sister's devil from the eighties' press cuttings.

Stella planned interviews, arranging questions into information-gathering and suspect-probing. This morning they'd been ambushed twice. She rarely operated on instinct, but her gut said leave. She reached for Jack's hand too late to stop him cosying up to Jason on the couch.

'They've never met Lee.' Joy lit a cigarette and leaning over him slammed shut Jason's tablet. Her son looked about to protest, but stopped himself.

'What do you mean?' Stella breathed in smoke and suppressed a cough.

'You're that cleaner who goes after murderers.' Gimlet-eyed, cigarette smouldering between her lips, Joy tossed the packet between her hands like a grenade. 'Listen, lady! Alan Ferris is a first-class bastard to Cath, but you piss about with either of them, you got me to face. Leave her alone. No point proving Danni didn't murder those babbies, she's guilty as sin.' Joy jerked her head at Jason. 'Get tea and open them biscuits.'

Stella had assumed that, however outrageous Jack's stories, people believed him. Joy Hindle had not. She grappled for a way to refuse tea and biscuits and flee.

'Your daughter was guilty. We're writing a book on *why* she killed Robbie and Sarah. To understand and stop it happening to other little children.' Jack was nodding wisely as if he agreed with himself.

She *loved* Jack. Stella's limbs went to water and she collapsed in one of the garden chairs.

'Who better to ask than her family?' Jack furrowed his brow. 'We really hoped we could meet you.'

'You're talking bollocks, mate.' Jason returned with four mugs of tea in one hand and a plate of pink wafers in the other. 'That won't work with my mum.'

As she took one of the mugs off Jason, Stella smelled the soap that Jack used. Absurdly, this made her warm towards him. She heard Terry, *Never let a prejudice, towards or against, skew your judgement.* No, OK.

'The point is, why did she do it?' Stella fixed on Jason.

'Jason, tell us what you think. You two hung out in the playground.' Jack was being man to man.

There was a report. Then another. *A gun.*

Stella gripped her tea. She should have trusted her instinct and got them out of there.

Jason had trodden on the bubble packing. 'Simples. She wanted a go on the slide. Robbie was in the way.'

'It was an accident?' Jack sounded disbelieving.

'No way. More like she wanted to see what happened when he splattered all over the ground.' Jason laid the plate of biscuits between him and Jack and took a handful. 'Know what? If Danielle's getting paid for a book, that's blood money.' That phrase again. 'It belongs to her victims. That's us.'

'We're not victims,' his mother snapped.

'Yeah. We are. We didn't do nothing. She don't get any name calling. We didn't change our names.' Slopping tea on his jeans, Jason slapped at the denim. 'We deserve compensation.'

'He's right for once.' A woman, metallic-coloured hair stiff with spray fanning out at an angle over her puffa jacket, an apricot poodle in her arms, filled the doorway.

Stanley had escaped from the van.

Stella started forward then spotted a pink collar around the dog's neck. Not Stanley.

'That's Maxine, my eldest.' Joy fired smoke at the ceiling. 'Max, these are doing some book on Danni.' She pointed her cigarette lighter at Stella. 'She's the daughter of that policeman who was sweet as pie then arrested Danni.'

'Police. How come you let them in?' Maxine Hindle demanded. The dog looked more outraged. Stella knew that look from Stanley.

'They're not police. She's a cleaner. He drives trains.' Joy knew more about them than they did about her. Stella, who never felt afraid, felt afraid.

'Danielle came from a good solid family, we can see that. You guys didn't murder anyone, so why did she?' Jack said. Stella thought that the Hindles might find 'good solid family' a stretch.

Joy slurped her tea and grimaced. 'Jase, this milk's gone.'

Maxine burst out, 'Everything's about her. She just wants attention. Want my opinion, there's too much understanding and not enough hanging. Danielle was an evil cow!'

'She killed a cat. That's the first sign,' Jason said. 'She'd crush Tom Fluff given half a chance.'

'You never told me that.' Joy snatched up a black cat curled asleep in Jason's corner of the couch that Stella had taken for a cushion.

'She only went and gave the dead cat to the owner,' Jason said through a mouthful of biscuit. 'Danni squashed insects. She crushed the cat's neck. Ask me, that was practice for Sarah. I was scared to go to sleep or she'd crush me. Danni made me wet the bed.' Gone was the iron-man image. Jason seemed eager to talk.

'You wet it anyway.' Maxine shielded the poodle from Tom Fluff's haughty stare.

'What do you mean, she crushed a cat?' Stella recalled that Sarah Ferris's neck had been crushed by a brick. Police never found the brick.

'She pressed on its head with a brick.' Jason put down a half-eaten biscuit. 'Don't say nothing, Danni said she'd kill me.'

'She better not hear you dobbed her in with two book writers.' Maxine had gone pale. Stella felt uneasy with the Hindles – though none of them provoked the chill she got even thinking about Penelope Philips – but she was surprised that Hindle's family were frightened of her.

'That's how she killed Sarah,' Jack breathed. He too was pale. Stella remembered that when Jack was little he'd had a cat called Brunel, named after the engineer. She could answer that in a quiz about her partner if someone asked.

'Have you seen Danielle since she left prison?' Jack wiped a hand down his face.

'She'd be dead if she tried coming here.' Maxine Hindle rocked her dog like a baby. Stella wished she'd stop, the poodle looked set to bite.

'I'd knife her.' Jason began testing his biceps, perhaps to distract from the business of bed-wetting.

'You'd get banged up like your sister and Eddie, *God rest his stupid bloody soul!*' Perched on the other garden chair, Joy danced Tom Fluff on her lap, white-booted paws dangling.

'It's good of you to give us time. We'll leave you in peace.' Stella got up.

At the door, Stella skidded on a copy of *Autocar* lying on the mat. Maxine steadied her with a vicelike grip. Cradling the poodle, she accompanied them out to the street.

'One more thing. Did you know Lee Marshall?' Stella did the detective exit ploy.

'Only when we were kids. Alan Ferris said Lee killed Sarah, but he doted on her. He got the blame. I heard what happened to him. His wife must have been in bits. Meanwhile, Danni gets all the luck, murdering's made her rich. Big house and car. She gets away with murder.' The pun appeared unintentional.

A souped-up Ford Fiesta, throbbing with a hip-hop beat, did fifty down Braybrook Street.

'How do you know?' Stella asked.

'I know my sister.' Maxine presented her dog with a twig from the path. The poodle seized it between sharp teeth. 'Every day's a clean slate. Those kids were then, this is now.'

'Have you seen Pen— Danielle?' Stella was thrown by her cleaning company's name although it was a common term.

'Danni will never be sorry.'

Chapter Twenty-Eight

1994

Terry was forty-five today. Later he'd have drinks down the Ram with the team. They'd sent him a card. A picture of a vinyl disc, 'Young Free and Single.' Ha ha. Terry wasn't single. He was married. It might be nearly twenty years since Suzie left, but he kept faith that his family would come home. Not that at twenty-eight Stella would live in his house. Their house.

It was summer, but it didn't feel like it. The weather was cold and windy. It had rained in the night. Terry was relieved to find the playground empty. He sat on the bench by the gate, put there in memory of Robbie Walsh. *Who will always play here.* Wet Wet Wet's 'Love Is All Around' had been on the radio as he'd eaten his cornflakes. Terry had imagined dancing to it with Suzie at Stella's wedding one day. He shifted on the bench. Now was definitely not the time to have a love song on replay in his brain.

Stella had said she'd pop into the pub and give him his present. She'd cancelled. She had a boyfriend and he had tickets to *Four Weddings and a Funeral*. Not that she'd told him any of this. Suzie put him in the picture. He'd seen Stella hand in hand with some boy – he wouldn't say man – on King Street last week. He'd been driving with nowhere to pull in. He should have beeped his horn.

He was risking everything coming to the playground.

When Terry got the letter – the first for a year – he'd thrown it away. Then chucking a tea bag in the bin, he'd seen it and had to read it. He'd considered moving except she'd find him. She would always find him.

He would tell her to stop writing. OK, so she'd done her time, but she'd never shown remorse. He was a policeman. It was his job to catch the bad people. That should be enough. It was not.

He'd know Danielle Hindle anywhere. Arms like a robot, fast walking like she had stuff to do. Girl on a mission. Not a girl now. Her body language might be the same, but the well-to-do woman in a wool coat and Russian-style fur hat laden with West End shopping bags was miles from the bubble-gum touting kid in bovver boots who'd paid such close attention to the sonorous declamations of bewigged adults. This escapee from a shopping spree at Harrods with gelled nails, her hair tinted a tasteful auburn, carrying the air of entitlement of a smart denizen of South Ken or Gloucester Road, was born again. A far cry from the kid on Braybrook Street.

Terry needed to hear Hindle express remorse. Some crimes haunted him because he'd never solved them. He'd solved this one. The killer was walking towards him. Like a drug fix he needed her to say she was sorry for the murders (he was in no doubt that she'd pushed Robbie off the slide). Hindle had to acknowledge that she'd ruined lives. Then he could forget her.

Hindle joined him on the bench. *She was pregnant.*

'I have to go.' He'd been a bloody idiot.

'I just got here!' She looked stricken. Terry felt sickened, as when he let Stella down. She wasn't Stella.

'Danielle, if someone sees us you'll go back to prison. I'll lose my job.'

'No one will see us.' She laid protective hands on her stomach, wanting him to see. Lucie used to say that Hindle ran rings around him. The girl, described in court as cool and manipulative, complained in her letters how life was unfair. As if life was a game at which you could cheat.

'It's Penelope. Think *Thunderbirds*!' She flashed a smile of even white teeth. 'I'm having a baby. I was keen to tell you face to face. Before the police inform the papers.'

'The police don't do that.' Terry knew there were bad apples who leaked stuff to the media. Christ, he'd accidentally done it himself. Lucie held secrets that could get him disciplined. Now it gradually sank in. Hindle was still manipulating him. She'd suggested she would talk about her crimes. She only wanted to tell him she was going to be a mother. She'd duped him. And of course he knew her new identity. Not via the police, Hindle had told him in a letter. He cleared his throat. 'Are you allowed to keep it? The baby?'

'What kind of question is that?' She flared up. 'What, you think I don't have the right to kids? I changed Jason's nappies enough. I've got a law degree!'

'You told me.' Terry knew all Danielle's achievements. He read her letters. He read the papers. Lucie May told him. Murderers getting top marks in exams sold copies. 'Is the father sticking by you?'

'Sticking by me? Like I'm damaged goods? Chris thinks he's lucky to have me. He's an antiques dealer. With his own business and a big house.' She flourished her Mulberry handbag.

'How did you meet him?' Terry's mind was on Stella's new man. Whippersnapper in posh strides. 'Did he write to you in prison?' Hindle wouldn't have been allowed letters from strangers, but rules got broken. Some women felt sorry for men in for murder, even married them. Fewer men. It was sick to be attracted to a child-killer.

'I went for a secretarial job in his shop. I'm a fast typist. It was love at first sight. Don't look like that, it happens.' She nudged his arm. 'When the kid's old enough I'm going to train as a dealer. He promised.'

'I'm not looking like anything.' Terry shrank from her. He did know you could fall in love right there and then. He'd loved Suzie from the moment he'd pulled her over for driving without due care and attention. He hadn't booked her. *Bad apple*. But the girl he'd put in prison was not capable of love. 'Can you trust this man to keep your secret?'

'What secret?'

'Who you are? Your past.'

She touched her hat as it needed adjusting. 'Chris knows me *now*, that's what counts.'

'You haven't told him.'

'Don't start. You got any idea of the prejudice against ex-cons? The law helps the rich get richer. My dad couldn't get a job because he'd been inside.' Her upmarket accent slipped to Shepherd's Bush. 'He sold my story.'

Eddie Hindle had died in an RTI earlier that year after a night celebrating a bank raid. Terry had known it would end badly for Hindle. The ever-longer sentences as his crimes escalated. He hadn't anticipated the banal ending. Hindle had tripped in a gutter and fallen under a twenty-seven bus on Hammersmith Broadway.

'We're going to be a proper family.'

'Hasn't your probationary officer advised you to be honest?'

'I should never of listened to you. You lied to me.' Her eyes bored into him.

'You lied to me.' He had lied to her.

They sat in silence. Across the playground two crows were squabbling over a hamburger bun. No kids about, it was too cold. Terry found himself scanning for childhood ghosts, those boys now men. Delving deeper into time, he saw his mum pushing him on the roundabout. Unlike the other mums who walked it around, she'd have one high-heeled shoe on the running board and scoot it up to speed.

'Like I wrote in my letter, it's a girl.' Penelope spoke as if their previous interchange hadn't happened. 'She'll love me. Chris isn't God's gift, but it's not about looks. She's called Carrie like Carrie Fisher in *Star Wars*. I saw the film after I went away.'

Went away. Much of police work was running up a down escalator. Stupid to expect that Hindle regretted anything. Terry got up again. She didn't notice.

'I haven't got a dad.' She was staring at the spot where Sarah Ferris had been found. 'I'm twenty-four. If I was your daughter, it would have been different. Thinking about it, Stella could be my sister. If this was a boy I'd have named him Terry. Carrie sounds a bit like it, doesn't it?'

'How do you know about Stella?' His head reeled; he'd never replied to the letters. He'd told her nothing about his life.

'I'd love to bring Carrie here to play.' She was pettish. 'If I told Mum, can you see her face? I'd have come in Chris's Jag 'cept it's at the garage. That'd put the wind up Jason! He told the papers I tried to kill him when we were kids. God knows what they paid him for that. He's still at home having his socks darned. I saw him through the window. Little gobshite!'

'If you're seen here the baby will be taken away. You're breaching the terms of your licence.' Stupid to be the police officer now. He took a step away from the bench. He couldn't leave, he had to hear her say it...

'I'm sorry that I killed them. I did a terrible thing. Robbie was getting on my nerves. I pushed him. I was horrified by what I'd done. I'm sorry. Sarah said she'd tell. I was top of the class, my life ahead. It was wrong. I am so sorry...'

He heard only the cawing of the crows picking and tearing at the mouldy bun.

She got heavily to her feet. 'Don't worry, Terry, I won't let on I saw you. They'll believe me, people do.' Her smile chilled him.

For a dreadful moment, Terry thought she was going to kiss him. But she went on ahead out of the playground. At the gate, she called back, 'I'll write when Carrie's born.'

'Don't…' But she was out of earshot. It was cold, yet Terry was sweating. Watching her stalk past the bandstand, the bags swinging, Terry saw the girl, hands swishing the air. He'd forgotten to tell Penelope to stop writing.

'That looked cosy, darling!'

'Lucie! What are you doing here?' *Shit.*

Safari jacket, cargo pants, camera slung around her neck.

'My job.' Lucie bared her teeth in a wolfish grin. 'What's your excuse?'

Chapter Twenty-Nine

2019

'Maxine propelled herself pole position for prime suspect.' Jack put down the ginger beers and dropped a scattering of tomato ketchup and vinegar sachets beside the glasses. He took two bags of crisps from his coat. Jack's appetite was insatiable. Lucie said he had hollow legs.

'If Maxine has seen Penelope, she's unlikely to have mistaken Cater for her.'

'What if Maxine intended to frame Danielle?' Jack said.

'Good point, although it didn't work,' Stella agreed. 'I still go for mistaken identity. We also have Jason and Joy Hindle, plus all the playground gang. Nicola Walsh and Kevin Hood. Let's keep Cathy and Alan Ferris.' Stella was scribbling the names in her notebook. 'Let's also keep open Penelope killing Rachel. She comes home. Finds Rachel there. Rachel tells her about the affair, Penelope goes mad and kills her. Sometimes things are exactly what they seem.'

'That's not how it seemed.' Jack split open the crisp packets. 'Don't forget she's on CCTV. It *seems* that Christopher killed her. He had motive and means. Like you said, our job is to undermine the verdict if we can. From her comments I'm wondering if Danielle was with Maxine in London that afternoon. Or could that be Maxine on the CCTV covering for her sister? Mrs Cater said that Rachel expected Christopher to leave Danielle. Did Rachel force his hand so he killed her?' Jack snagged a crisp and popped it in his mouth. 'And there's a fourth possibility.'

'Which is?'

'A stranger murder. A random motiveless killer with no previous connection to the victim. The detective's nightmare.'

'Let's keep it simple. I know Dad threw the net wide in the hours after a murder and drew it in as evidence dictated. The police have done the legwork. We can start tight and work outwards. So for now, no wild card. Agree?'

'Agree.' Jack gave Stanley an illegal crisp.

They fell silent while a man brought their food.

'I should have given that charm to Penelope.' Stella nibbled a crisp. 'Or photographed it in situ and left it in Penelope's spare bedroom. If she misses it she'll link it to me.'

'It's good you took it.' Jack was tucking into his beef and ale pie. 'It might be relevant. Didn't Sarah Ferris have a charm bracelet?'

'Yes, but charm bracelets aren't rare.' Stella placed the charm on the table.

'If the Best Sister was Sarah's – it doesn't look new – then it proves Penny Philips is Danielle Hindle. How else would it be there?'

'We already know she is.'

'Yes, silly me! I meant that it links Danielle to Sarah Ferris.'

'We knew that too.' Stella was cross with herself. 'I should have confronted her with it.'

'Perhaps Rachel's killer dropped it. The house has been cleaned and redecorated since Hindle lived there.'

'The police would have found it. And if not, then we would have when we were cleaning.'

They contemplated the Best Sister charm, wondering if it told them anything new. Into the silence, Jack fed Stella a mouthful of his pie and mash.

If a previous partner had done that Stella would have dumped them for force-feeding. With Jack she loved him even more.

'Sarah Ferris lost her charm bracelet. Derek Parsley found it and put it on her wrist after she was dead. That was why Dad charged him with murder.' Stella trawled through her notes.

'Who has it now?'

'Presumably the police kept it as evidence.' Stella wiped tomato sauce off Jack's chin. Any previous partner she'd have passed them the napkin. Love was the weirdest thing.

'We could ask Kevin Hood. Or the Hindles.' Stella felt no more keen to see any of the suspects again than she did Penelope Philips. 'Theory two.'

'Mistaken identity. Hindle as intended victim.' Jack pronged a strip of chicken from Stella's Caesar salad and ate it.

'Cathy Ferris is in her seventies. Finish it.' Stella slid her plate across to Jack. This case had sapped her appetite. 'Cathy's slight, but it doesn't require strength to stab someone. She had the advantage of surprise. Rachel wasn't threatened by her killer, she turned her back on him or her.'

'Cathy and Alan have enough anger,' Jack agreed. 'But as for Maxine, wouldn't Cathy have recognized Danielle? Indeed, if any of the friends and relations had found out Danielle's new identity they could have found out what she looked like. I don't credit Cathy with thinking to frame Penelope. She's an honest soul.' He sprinkled vinegar over the garnish that came with his meal. For Stella vinegar was a cleaning agent.

'The killer wasn't cool. Besides, they'd likely anticipate that Penelope looked different,' Stella argued. 'There's only been one photo of her. With a prison officer on a street in Islington when she was rehearsing for release.' Hindle had gone unrecognized by passers-by. Except for a *Sun* photographer. *Lifer Luxury. Child-Killer on Shopping Spree.* Cathy Ferris had handed in a petition to Downing Street of a quarter of a million signatures demanding

Hindle never be released. Soon after, Danielle Hindle was out. Armed with a new identity she had melted into anonymity. Had someone found her out?

'In the twenties photographers made a living out of photographing pedestrians. There's one of my father's parents in Bond Street, my grandmother in her trademark fur coat, him in a top hat. Nowadays it's celebrities walking dogs or falling out of a nightclub into a cab with the latest date,' Jack said. 'And notorious prisoners trying on life outside for size.'

'Jason Hindle was specific that he'd stab Danielle. Cathy said Alan would stab her in the back. Just how Rachel Cater died.'

'A knife's an obvious weapon. Jason acts tough, but I doubt he's got a Glock in his bedside drawer. And I bet he still wets the bed. His mother, on the other hand, could head a drug-dealing gang no trouble.' Jack stacked their plates. He captured one of Stella's feet between his own. Their eyes locked.

'We have to work,' Stella said as if he'd suggested going to bed out loud. 'Maxine and Jason could have done it together.' She drew a dotted line between the names.

'True. The police found only one set of new prints, Rachel's. The others belonged to all of the Philips family.'

'Alan Ferris's dementia might be faked,' Stella said. 'He has a history of violence, the dent in their wall proves that. If not, he'd forget why he'd left the house as soon as he shut the front door. Joanne Marshall wanted to get far away from her husband's family. Why return to kill the woman who killed her husband's sister?'

'Revenge. Lee killed himself and Joanne Marshall blames Hindle. Not difficult to whiz back to the UK under a false name, commit the murder and be at Heathrow that evening,' Jack said.

'Quite difficult. Anyway according to one of these cuttings, Marshall was with a friend on the Manly ferry the day after the murder,' Stella said. 'Pretty hard to fake that. Cathy didn't like her, but I suspect that no woman would have been good enough for her boy. Don't forget that postcard too.'

'My mum would have been like that. Except she'd have loved you.' Jack corralled emptied condiment sachets onto his plate.

'OK, she goes on the list.' Stella moved swiftly on. She was sure that Jack's mother would not have approved of him being with a cleaner older than him. Despite this, Stella was sorry not to have met her.

'Let's go to yours now and Skype Joanne Marshall. It's morning in Australia.' Jack buttoned up his coat.

Now was the time to tell Jack about the letters. She pictured the envelopes, flat and smooth as if Terry had ironed them.

'I can't!'

'I thought you had the afternoon free?'

Stella felt shame that Terry had kept letters from a killer. *Why had he?*

'Let's split resources. I'll Skype Joanne Marshall, you find Nicola Walsh.'

'We're better together,' Jack said.

'From what I've gathered about Nicola she probably prefers men.'

'How did you gather that?'

'Danielle told us that Nicola liked Lee better than her.'

'I'm sure I'd have preferred Lee too. It's as likely Nicola would relate better to you.'

'Haven't you got Justin and Milly this afternoon?'

'Yes!' Jack cried. 'Bella will *kill* me.'

'Not if you leave now.' Stella shovelled the other bag of crisps into her rucksack. She had a long journey ahead.

Chapter Thirty

2019

Jack revelled in the squeals of laughter punctuated by furious instruction (Milly) and querulous protests (Justin), backed by Stanley's barks. All three creatures were in their element.

The box maze was at the children's nose height. Milly waving a stick that for the purposes of her complicated game was a witch's wand, tore along the paths bellowing when (again) she hit a dead end. Jack heard the clink of Stanley's dog tag as he cantered beside her. Justin had been made invisible, instructed to wait until he came 'back as a horse', a fate that had befallen Jack. Stamping and puffing by the back door, Jack did feel equine.

Although Robbie and Sarah's murders were decades ago, now that he knew about them Jack would never again take his children to the playground. Watching Milly, he fretted. Why had Stella split their tasks? She liked them to be a team. Had she found out that Bella had lifted the embargo on Stella seeing Justin and Milly and was hurt that Jack hadn't told her? Worse, was she reluctant to be a stepmother and was pulling back while she had the chance?

Milly sent up a spray of leaves with her wand. He *should* be there when Stella talked to Joanne Marshall. On a screen it would be hard to spot tics, impossible to glean clues from Marshall's home. He was better at reading personalities than Stella. Jack shoved his hands in his coat pockets to keep them warm even though he'd been told that horses don't have pockets. He was being unfair, Stella was observant. She would manage without him. Maybe that was the problem.

'Can I have water, Daddy? I can't get it cos you said not to climb up a chair for the tap,' Justin whispered from the doorway behind Jack.

'What? Of course, baby! Good for asking.' Jack shot a look at Milly hurtling about the maze. 'Does Milly know you've escaped?'

'She can't see me. I'm in-vis-a-bell.' Justin was confident in his sister's powers. 'I don't want to be a terror-ist. I'm thirsty.'

'Is that what you were?' Jack was aghast. He'd loved that his twins made up imaginative games. He saw himself at that age, crouched in the garden, his mother on a bench watching him build a city in the flowerbed. Emissaries of innocence, Justin and Milly hailed from a childhood world that for their father had been cut short. A world without terrorists. Bella would think it was his influence. *It was Harry!* He'd have words with Harry.

Jack's mobile phone rang as he handed Justin his giraffe beaker. He scrabbled for it amongst the debris of tea things (buttered bread and jam and milk like Jack used to have). The ringtone was Kate Bush's 'Running up that Hill'. It had been Bella's and his song. Jack only thought to change it when she called and then afterwards, Bella having got him in a flap, he forgot.

'Keep the children!' she bellowed like her daughter.

'What?' Jack's heart leapt. Bella was giving him custody. He'd never fight her on it, but to have his babies all the time was his dream. 'For ever?'

'Don't be absurd, Jack. Until tomorrow. I've got a rush job. Cactus Man is a friggin' mare. He tells me to do a longitudinal section and now wants a magni-bloody-fication of the developing ovules. The illustration is already crowded. I'll be up all night on a redraw.'

Bella was frequently infuriated by the botanists for whom she drew illustrations of plant elements. One – a world expert on cacti and succulents – often altered briefs as the job was nearing completion. Unavoidable if another plant specimen yielding new information was discovered. But Cactus Man was careless. A freelancer, Bella couldn't charge more than the cost of the brief. She'd get no payment for her extra work. Jack felt for her.

'What about Thingy?'

'His named is *Harry*. He's in the States closing a deal, he's very successful.' Bella was sibilant. 'And in case it slipped your mind, you're their father.'

'No need for Harry to have them *ever*.' Jack caught Justin scrutinizing him over his giraffe cup. Reaching down, he tipped the boy's soft curls from his face. For a toddler, Justin had the perspicacity of a wiser adult than Jack often felt. 'Always ask.'

The door crashed against the wall. Milly materialized by the dishwasher, her eyes smouldered. Stanley her familiar. *Mini Bella*. Milly levelled her wand at Jack and Justin.

'You are both naughty.' If Milly zapped him with her wand, Jack knew that his little girl would wipe him from the face of the earth.

'What the hell's going on?' Bella asked in his ear.

'The kids have a game going. In my maze.' Jack saw no need to upset Bella with terrorists.

He got Bella off the phone. 'You're staying the night!'

The children's shouts of joy were drowned out by the clatter of an underground train.

'Daddy, it's your telee-phone!' Milly whisked over. 'It says "work". She prodded at the screen with her wand. She pronounced it 'wauk.' Jack must remember that Milly had the reading age of a twenty-five-year-old.

'A train! That's *totally* cool!' Justin clapped his hands at the picture of the District line train on Jack's screen.

Totally cool? Harry the Deal Closer was a dead man. 'I'll have to answer. Then we'll make plans!' Jack promised the pairs of beady eyes.

'Jack, old son, we've had a one under and what with the norovirus, soon the punters will be driving themselves!' For the bearer of bad news, Marty Winton was upbeat. Jack knew what was coming. 'We need you for tonight.'

A one under. Every driver's dread. A member of the public had jumped onto the rails in the path of a train. Jack thought of Lee Marshall. A suicide had untold ramifications. The event – not always fatal – cast a pall over the team; some drivers gave up the job. When it happened to him, Jack had appreciated the support from drivers, trackside staff and the office where the suicidal 'passenger' had bought their ticket. 'I'm on my way.'

Pulling on his Transport for London jacket, Jack trawled his mind for someone to look after the children. He could only think of one.

Chapter Thirty-One

2019

'I've seen the letters that you sent my father.' Tearing the paper, Stella underlined the already underlined heading in her notebook: *Meeting with Penny Philips*. Without meaning to, she'd added Terry's phrase, *A murderer is capable of murder.*

Philips had shown her into the lounge of her safe house, actually a flat, in Broadway, a village twenty minutes from Winchcombe.

Decorated in safe beige and magnolia, the room contained two armchairs and a table and chair for eating. The radiator was off or broken. Afternoon sun streaming in through the window offered no warmth. Stella huddled in her Barbour.

'Terry believed me.' Penny had invited Stella to sit. She had remained by the door, blocking the exit. Perhaps she intended to make Stella ill at ease; Stella tried to hide that Hindle had succeeded.

'He arrested you for murder. He'd never have let an innocent child get life imprisonment.' Stella felt an icicle of doubt. She often heard Terry's advice worming in her ear. He'd said nothing about what to do if a murderer wrote to you. He'd never told her about Hindle's letters. After her teenaged vigils outside

Hammersmith Library when she'd seen that he was well enough to work, but not to see her, Stella had stopped asking Terry how to be a detective.

'I was nine, for God's sake. They stole my childhood!' Hindle was outraged.

Stella's memories of her childhood were isolated incidents with the equivalent of cliff-hangers. What happened after the man chased her at the river? Had Terry arrested him, or was that wishful thinking? The family dog ran away. Who found him? She did know that if she'd murdered a child – or two – it would be burnt into her brain. Prison wouldn't lessen her guilt. Stella repeated the question that had brought her there. 'Why did you write to Terry?'

'Terry listened. He said I was on his team. *Chrissakes*, they let me do all that studying and they wouldn't let me be a lawyer. They've spent taxpayers' money keeping me behind bars and educating me. I can't pay them back. How mad is that!'

'I suppose they're worried you might kill again.' Stella said it.

'I've brought up a child, they should have taken her away if they thought that. She's gone anyway.' Sitting in the other armchair, she tapped at her front tooth as if checking it was in place. 'Terry was pleased when I got pregnant, he'd be a grandfather.' Penelope sat in the other armchair. 'Him and me, we had a telepathic thing.'

Stella was stumbling in a fog. Her mum kept grumbling that Stella would never give her grandchildren. Had Terry felt that too? What did she mean, 'telepathic thing'?

The sun went behind a cloud. The room darkened. The flat was off the main street in Broadway, the window faced the back of an Indian restaurant. On a previous visit, Stella and Jack had bought a map from the bookshop. Although Stella had a satnav, she'd wanted tangibility so had used that map today.

'Terry didn't believe in that stuff.' Stella had a flash vision of being in Jack's arms, smelling him, soap, apple shampoo…

She should have asked him to come with her. He'd have put a stop to talk of telepathy.

'Is that right?' Hindle dabbed her lips with gloss.

'Your daughter is convinced you killed Rachel Cater.' Stella made herself focus on the case. 'Is that just based on your, um, your history?'

'I have an alibi. The camera never lies.' Hindle's expression was stone.

'Actually it does. That might not have been you in Dalgarno Gardens.' Stella was more forthright as the idea took hold. 'You told the police where you were that day and they found your image. Maxine was also out that afternoon. She left her hairdressing salon for half an hour. Not enough to get to Winchcombe so she was discounted as a suspect, but enough to wear your coat and hat and be seen on CCTV in the area where you...' she couldn't say murdered, 'near the playground.'

'Maxine doesn't know where I live.'

'She told us that you have a big house, a child and husband. She knew what car you drive.' Stella was pushing it. The woman had a history of cold-blooded violence. Was she reformed? She could think nothing of crushing Stella's neck as she had Sarah's.

'It was all over the media when Chris was arrested.' Hindle was scornful. 'And believe me, Maxine would never lie to the police to get me out of trouble.'

'The link between you as Penelope Philips and Danielle Hindle was never made. The police ensured of that. You look very different to the last public photo of your old self.'

'Maxine would expect me to have all those things. When we were kids, she went on that I always landed on my feet. She's the world's biggest victim. Don't get me wrong, Stella, I don't mind in the least that the Cater bitch is dead. She would have brought trouble to our family. But, contrary to the theory you are clearly trying to shore up, I had no motive. It hasn't worked out at all well for me that my husband is banged up for a murder that my daughter is trying to pin on me. I should be in your shoes.'

'What do you mean?' Stella knew what she meant.

'Terry said I'd make a good detective. He reckoned that I was treated unfairly about those kids.' Hindle chucked the tin of lip balm onto the table. It rolled toward the floor. She made no move to pick it up. 'Why are you here?'

Those kids.

'If my dad made a mistake he'd have owned up.'

A murderer is capable of murder.

Stella heard a car door slam. For a wild second she hoped it was Jack.

'And Terry said you had good manners.' Her eyes slid over Stella with undisguised disgust.

Terry had talked about her. No way. He would not have replied to Hindle. (Now Stella, like Jack, could not think of her as Penelope Philips.) *Hold the boundaries, fine to feel compassion, but don't forget you're a detective.*

Terry was always the detective. He had not replied to Hindle. Her mother complained that he cared more for victims than for her and Stella. Her fog thinned.

'The police triangulated the signal on your phone to London.' A punt. In her reading of the case Stella had not found this evidence.

'Triangulated? Lah-dee-dah! I'm not up on technology. I missed out on everything. I didn't go to a nightclub until I was twenty-five.'

Stella couldn't imagine spending her teenaged years in prison, becoming institutionalized and dependant on a routine. Actually, she could get the routine.

'If you were in London obviously you are not the killer despite what Carrie says. We're considering the possibility that Rachel's killer discovered your real identity, came to the house and lay in wait. You were the intended victim. If so, he or she will try again.'

'You're in above your pay grade, Stella. So I have enemies, whoop-de-doo! Tell me something I didn't know. I've moved on from all that. I suggest that you do too. My daughter will come to her senses and renege on your bill. When she does, I'll cover it. Now go off and clean something, there's a dear.'

Stella held her own: 'I think that you know who murdered Rachel Cater. You may not realize that you know. Please just think.'

'Ooh, nice one, Terry's daughter.' Philips tapped her front tooth again. 'When I told Chris about the past he lost it. I showed him photos of Danielle. The playground where they found Sarah and the slide which Robbie fell off. Chris went and told that woman. That meant I had to tell Carrie.'

'It's better to be honest.' She talked as if Danielle was someone else. Perhaps to her she was. It was uncanny.

'I've got a suspect for you.' Philips was jeering. 'There's this tabloid hack. She hung around Terry and found out he wrote to me. She'd love to put the knife in.' Philips retrieved the tin of gloss and replenished her lips.

Lucie May. Terry's erstwhile girlfriend. Suzanne's enemy. No wonder Lucie had been interested when she heard that Carrie Philips was coming to the office. Suddenly Stella knew Lucie was already on the case.

'Chris bit off more than he could chew with Cater. She was going to the papers about me. She planned for them to live on the cash. She had him in a vice.'

'Do you believe your husband did kill Rachel?' Had Hindle and Philips been in it together? Highly regarded in Winchcombe, they had a life to protect. Perhaps they'd decided that Christopher shoulder the guilt. With good behaviour and no previous history of violence, he might be out in ten years. Stella remembered Jack's suggestion. 'Did you pay someone to murder Rachel Cater?'

Terry advised against antagonizing a suspect without backup. Stella hadn't told anyone she was going to the Cotswolds. Not even Trudy. Stella had only once been in a fight. Aged eleven, Liz held her bag as she squared up to Kim Payne. Stella had expected it to be like in Westerns, each cowboy taking turns to punch. Kim had pummelled her to the pavement. Alone in her bedroom, Stella had cried.

'I should have got you to kill her. Cleaners mop up anything for a fee, don't they?' Hindle tapped her tooth. The sound set Stella's own teeth on edge. Jack might call it a sign of nerves. Stella reckoned that it was a scare tactic. It was working.

'Broadway is near Winchcombe. You should leave this area.'

Tap. Tap. 'Cashman ran checks, but we know that the police can be wrong. Still, if you say it, I should listen!'

Cold. Calculating. Manipulative.

'It could be a matter of time before the killer finds you.' Stella felt cruel saying it.

'Terry would be proud of you!' Hindle said. This time there was no Liz to hold Stella's bag. 'Is that a threat?'

'Jason said that he'd stab you if he found you. Your family are affected by the repercussions of the two murders.' It was easy, after all, to be blunt with a woman who had murdered two children.

Inflame the suspect to provoke them to spill information.

'Jason's a vicious little tyke, but he hasn't the guts to go for me. Maxine's a liar. She has no idea where I live. If she did then she and Jason would have sold me to the press by now. I'm worth more to them alive.' Danielle Hindle went to the window. 'Max wouldn't stand me having a bloke, a kid and a house while she's doing hairdressing like every girl in her class. Mum would kill me.'

'Did Terry write back to you?' Stella asked the question that had brought her to Broadway. 'There's nothing in your letters that suggest he replied.'

'Terry liked face to face.'

'What do you mean?' The mental fog was back. It had been the stupidest mistake to come without Jack. She was no match for a double murderer.

'I was the last person to see Terry alive.'

She was blindsided. Terry had seen no one on the day he died. Stella had painstakingly pieced together his last movements from parking tickets, shop receipts and the case notes. Terry had tailed a suspect to the south coast and done an overnight stakeout in his car. The next morning he'd bought pork pies and Coke from the Co-op in Seaford and as he left the shop he'd had a massive coronary. Jack had said that Hindle would be adept at mind games. Stella was out of her league. Jack should be here. All the same, as facts arranged themselves, she had to believe that Hindle was lying. She had not seen Terry.

'Here's a clue, Miss Detective. Who is keen to pin the blame on me?' Hindle was laughing at her.

'Carrie. You think Carrie killed Rachel Cater?'

'When I told her what happened to me when I was little, Carrie ran to Daddy. It wasn't me she wanted dead, it was that tart Cater. Carrie would not have coped with finding her father's mistress in her own home. Poor lamb.'

Stella picked her way through the scenario. Carrie Philips kills her father's lover meaning to frame her mother, but the plot pointed at Christopher. Carrie had asked Clean Slate to find evidence to pin the murder on Hindle and set her father free. Possible.

The trouble was that too many scenarios were possible.

Stella's rear-view mirror reflected darkness. Rush hour was over. The motorway was empty and on this stretch with no lamplight, it was like a tunnel, her headlights piercing the black. Rain spattered the windscreen. Her companion sounds were the creak of the wipers.

Stella wondered if this was what it was like for Jack driving a train. He'd said that apart from signals, there were no lights in the tunnels or in his cab. For the umpteenth time, Stella wished Jack was with her; even Stanley would be company.

After she'd left Broadway, Stella had gone for a walk along the high street. The trip to the Cotswolds had got her no further ahead. She still didn't know if Terry had replied to Hindle and was now tortured by the possibility that Hindle had actually met up with him. Why would he? Did he feel sorry for a girl starting again with a new identity? Terry believed that capital punishment was wrong. It was too big a gamble. No jury was infallible, innocent people had been executed. But why had he kept Hindle's letters?

At last Stella had returned to the van. The trip had thrown up more questions than answers. Her only comfort was for the miles she was putting between herself and Hindle. The woman spooked her.

The petrol gauge warning light was on. It signalled about twenty miles in the reserve. Stella blinked. How long had the light been on? It must be just now or she'd have noticed it. She'd make it to the garage. Except there wasn't a garage for twenty miles – she'd just passed a sign. Stella put the van into cruise at fifty, hoping to save fuel. It meant she was going slower.

The darkness and silence took Stella back to the night she'd driven home from Brighton after she had identified her father's body at the hospital. The experiences conflated so that it was as if Terry had only hours ago vacated the earth and left her.

Stella had considered booking a room in Winchcombe. She was tired and hungry (she'd forgotten about the crisps and now couldn't get to them). But she must see Jack. After looking after his children he was going to see Nicola Walsh. Like Stella, he never went to bed before one. She'd be home by ten. She'd suggest that she came over. She'd tell him about the letters and that she'd seen Danielle Hindle. Jack would hate that she'd put herself in jeopardy. He said her lack of fear wasn't a good thing. *Fear is a survival mechanism.* She'd point out that nothing had happened. Stella pressed the phone button on her steering wheel. She needed Jack's voice to break the silence. To fight off the encroaching night.

Name or number? the digital voice asked.

'Number— What!'

A man emerged from bushes metres ahead. He stepped out into the road and flagged her down. Stella swerved out to the middle lane. She pulled onto the hard shoulder and flicked on the interior light. A flicker in the offside mirror. The man, tinted red by her brake lights, was running towards the van. He held something in his hand.

'Don't bloody stop! Didn't Terry teach you the basics? He'll be targeting lone women. Those stupid enough to feel sorry for him. *Drive*,' the voice hissed.

Paralysed, Stella gripped the wheel like a learner driver. Her feet wouldn't move to the pedals. She heard the handbrake release.

'I. Said. Drive!'

A face was at the passenger window. A tap on the glass. He tried the handle. Something bashed against the window.

Without checking for oncoming traffic, Stella screeched the van out onto the motorway. She lost control of the van and the central reservation loomed. She yanked on the wheel and regained the lane.

Her system flooded with adrenalin. She looked in her rear-view mirror. In the insipid light of the interior lamp, she saw Danielle Hindle sitting in Stanley's jump seat.

Chapter Thirty-Two

2019

'Is she a nice woman?' Justin asked for the umpteenth time.

'Yes, Justy, she's very, very nice,' Jack said.

'Nicer than Mummy?' Justin sounded doubtful that this was likely.

'They're different.' Jack resisted saying, Yes, *much* nicer.

'I don't want to go.' Milly bobbed Mr Sssnake's head about like a ventriloquist's dummy. The woollen reptile, knitted for her as a baby by one of Bella's botanists, went with Milly on sleepovers. Justin had his bear which, for an unfathomable reason, he'd named Portus Teddy. Not that Jack could talk, his own bear had been called Walker and he had no idea why.

'You'll have a fantabulous time.' Jack pressed the doorbell. 'Stella can't wait to meet you.' Appalled by the untruth, he went on pressing until Justin, teetering on tiptoe, grabbed his sleeve. 'You should stop, Daddy.'

Jack snatched his hand away. He hadn't been able to reach Stella on the phone. She hadn't picked up his texts. As they waited, reality descended. Jack began to hope that Stella was out. Yet he had no backup. Jackie was in Manchester with her son. Suzie Darnell hated the unexpected. So did Stella. Lucie May…?

Picturing Lucie taking Milly and Justin on a doorstepping expedition, Jack jumped out of his skin when the door opened.

'What are you doing here?' Stella gaped at Jack as if he was a stranger come to mug her.

Despite his obsession with losing Stella, deep down Jack trusted her. She'd never two-time him. His suspicion rocketed. She had wanted him to interview Nicola Walsh on his own. She'd turned off her phone. She ignored his texts. She was with Cashman.

'Is this a bad time?' On the way Jack had constructed a scene of abject apology (him) and unalloyed joy (Stella) – at last she would be meeting his twins.

'It's half past ten,' she told him.

'I've got an emergency.' Insecurity made him belligerent. He grabbed a child's hand in each of his. 'But if you're busy…'

'What emergency?' Stella appeared oblivious of the children. *She hated children.*

'Mr Sssnake and Portus Teddy have nowhere to go.' Justin was straight out of Disney.

'No, Justin, that's not true—'

'Daddy said you were expecting us.' Milly was strict about facts.

Jack saw Stella's demeanour change. She snapped into gear.

'I *am* expecting you.' She stood aside. 'Would Mr, er, Sssnake and Teddy Portus… would they like to visit?'

'Yes!' Generally individual, the twins answered in unison. Jack had the eerie sensation that they knew exactly how to play the momentous encounter.

He hurried to his car – a fifteen-year-old BMW estate bought off a train driver colleague when Jack became a dad – and came staggering back with two holdalls. He felt duplicitous. A hitchhiker who, after thumbing a lift alone, is joined by a gaggle of companions.

Stella took one of the bags. She grimaced at the weight.

'Bella packs for every eventuality.' He babbled incoherently about emergencies, plasters, food for low blood sugar level, a million toys. He could not kid himself that Stella looked pleased to see them. From their dubious expressions he guessed that Justin and Milly had seen her reluctance.

'Mr Sssnake has to have a bed of his own,' Milly announced.

'No he doesn't!' Jack snapped. Then gently, 'He'll want to be with you.'

'Will Portus Teddy die?' Since the demise of his terrapin, Justin was concerned about the fate of all things.

'No, Justin,' Jack cried. 'None of us will.'

'That's actually not…' Stella ground to a halt.

He nodded at her. 'In your study, yeah, you've got that blow-up mattress. I'm sorry, but I haven't time to pump it up. I've been trying to get hold of you.' He sounded recriminatory.

'That's already… the case things are there.' Stella was sharp. 'In here.' She went into the living room.

Jack watched dumbfounded as, with lightning speed, Stella dismantled the sofa, stacking cushions by the window, unfolding the apparatus.

'I'll get bedding. *Stay*.' As Jack made to follow her, Stella put out the flat of a hand as if instructing Stanley. She *was* cross.

'Perhaps they could go up and clean their teeth?' Jack heard himself pleading when Stella returned and started stuffing pillows into cases, fiercely plumping them.

'They can do that in the kitchen. I'll get buckets for the loo.'

Jack was about to tell her that Milly and Justin were potty trained, but thought better of it. Instead he prattled a stream of reassuring bedtime words and kissing them both, fled to his car.

Driving away, the throaty roar of the BMW loud in the cul-de-sac, he merged today's 'one under' with Lee Marshall's suicide two years before. He was hot with irrational rage at Marshall for causing the mess. He'd fretted about whether Stella would welcome his kids. Her expression on the doorstep told him that she would not.

As he unlocked the door and boarded his train at Earl's Court, Jack reminded himself that he had left his children in the care of the woman who he loved most in the world. Hyper risk-averse, Stella was the safest pair of hands. Jack loved them all. What could go wrong?

Chapter Thirty-Three

2019

The bell had rung on and on. Stella had shooed Danielle up to her study (*Be totally silent!*). Then answered the door. From there things had gone from very bad to far worse. It was Jack. With his children. As she had taken this in, Stella's mind blanked with horror. A look Jack had mistaken for extreme reluctance to look after his children.

Once Stella was certain that the twins were asleep, she crept up and tapped on her own study door. Nothing. She peeped inside. No one. Hindle wasn't in the bathroom. Stella had locked her bedroom. She definitely wasn't downstairs.

She had gone. Stella sank onto her study chair. Now she could enjoy having Milly and Justin. Easing pain in her neck, she looked up. Light seeped around the loft hatch.

Pulse at top speed, Stella dragged down the ladder. Heedless of danger, her mini Maglite slippery with sweat, she climbed up.

Danielle Hindle lay under the eaves. A giant caterpillar in the sleeping bag that Stella had found for her. Beside her was a box from the Rokesmith investigation (the first case that Stella solved with Jack). She was reading.

'That's private!' Stella forgot to whisper.

'Terry was investigating this that last day.' Regarding Stella over her reading glasses, Danielle flipped over a page of the summary report. Prosaic, like a colleague at a meeting.

'You can't sleep up here.' Stella sounded feeble to herself

'Oh. What do you suggest? I join the wee bairns in your lounge?' Inexplicably speaking with a Scottish accent, Danielle shuffled to a sitting position against Stella's box of dolls. Back to her BBC voice: 'When Terry arranged to see me in the playground he said he had to go to catch a murderer. He wouldn't let me help. I was annoyed. I reminded him he'd retired. He was on the scrap heap. *Go home, do the garden.* He was panting and hot as if he'd done a marathon. I doubt he could have run for a bus. Of course he was dying.' She closed the report and snatched off her glasses. Seems the detective's daughter and her train driver solved Terry's case. He was telling the truth. He was about to go after a murderer. He should have asked me.' She gave Stella an icy glance.

'Dad always told the truth.' Stella had left her phone in her bedroom. 'You are not allowed to return to the area where you murdered those children. We're three miles from the playground. If the police knew you were here, they'd rearrest you.'

'How could they know?' Hindle cleaned her glasses on the edge of the sleeping bag. 'Going to snitch, are you? Coppers' nark! Terry said you were a goody two-shoes.' She slipped the report into the box. Stella resisted snatching it from her. Cleaning had made her strong and agile, but it would be beyond stupid to take on Hindle up here. Anywhere. Terry had taught her to be good. If he'd called her 'goody two-shoes' he'd meant that nicely.

'Be quiet until the children have gone. They're being fetched at seven. Then I'll decide what to do with you,' she told Hindle.

'You'll decide what to do with me?' The laugh was devoid of humour.

Stella knew that nothing was up to her. Her task – the challenge of her life – was to keep Jack's two children safe from a woman who had brutally murdered two children.

'Stella?' Hindle called softly.

'Yes?' Stella was closing the hatch.

'Thank you for letting me stay.'

'It's...' 'OK' stuck in her throat.

'I'm so happy to be in Terry's house.'

Stella did not sleep. She'd kept her door ajar although it exposed her to a ruthless killer. She'd sat on the bed, a triptych of agony reflected in the mirrored wardrobe doors, her senses sharp for sounds from the attic and from the living room. Once, when Hindle had gone to the bathroom, Stella grabbed her hairbrush and crept onto the landing. Hindle had pulled the chain and emerging she'd nodded to Stella (who supposed herself hidden) and returned to the attic. Her eyes screwed up in a grimace, Stella had dreaded that rushing water in the pipe would rouse the children. There was silence. Twice Stella sneaked out of her bedroom onto the landing to lock Hindle in then call the police. Twice she changed her mind. How would she even begin to explain?

Sometime towards dawn, Stella's head nodded and she slipped into sleep. She dreamed that she was cleaning an overflowing toilet at a crime scene. No matter what she did, the effluence rose, threatening to engulf her.

The bells of St Peter's church struck six. A breeze ruffled the blossom of cherry trees facing Rose Gardens North like an unseasonable snowfall. A middle-aged man wheeled a bike out of a house midway along the cul-de-sac. He ducked under the strap of his bag and cycled away along Black Lion Lane. Laser rays of sunlight banished vestiges of grey dawn, glancing off the white paintwork of Stella's Peugeot Partner van. They made jewels of quartz shards in the paving. The dawn chorus had competition. From Stella's house at the end of the terrace came the hum of a machine.

At five o clock Stella, her neck even stiffer than last night, her head aching, had heard noises in the kitchen. She found Milly feeding Stanley mounds of dog food. 'We got it from the fridge with a chair,' Justin assured her. Milly explained, 'Stanley says he hasn't eaten for a very long time.' Getting the hint, Stella offered them the Weetabix she kept in for their dad. Milly had informed Stella she only ate mooselli. Stella had informed Milly that there was only Weetabix. Observing Justin tucking into his, Milly had one biscuit and after experimentally nibbling at it with her spoon, wolfed down a bowlful and asked for seconds.

After breakfast, Milly announced it would be extra special to poo in the bucket. Stella would normally have been grateful at Justin's insistence that they use the toilet. She weighed up the lesser of two evils: that Justin's sense of propriety was offended; or that the children discovered Hindle. Despite her dream, the toilet won. She and Milly paced outside the bathroom while Justin pooed. When it was her turn, Milly demanded Stella come too and give her lavatory paper. Stella, alert for sounds in her study or above them which young and inquisitive ears would catch, doled out long strips from the roll before Milly was ready and got upbraided for 'not doing it like Mummy'.

Washed, dressed and fed, trailing their stuffed animals, Justin asked Stella what was happening next. Stella explained that Daddy was coming at seven. An hour and a quarter was a lifetime in which to divert two lively tots from a child-killer. Stella had settled on a walk with Stanley when Milly insisted that what she wanted most in all the world was to drive the big orange car. Stella had been puzzled. Only a nanosecond. She too was very keen to try out her new portable sanitizer. Bright orange and temporarily parked by the back door.

Milly quickly mastered the machine. She ignored Stella's weak attempt to supervise, and deep cleaned the kitchen.

Milly then steered the sanitizer into the living room where Justin, yellow Marigolds reaching to his armpits, was polishing the woodwork. He guided a beeswaxed cloth along the grain of the wood. He recited Stella's motto, 'a little cream goes a long way,' to the bear propped on the settee beside a giraffe beaker 'for when Portus Teddy got thirsty'.

'There are no clues left,' Milly declared.

'Germs,' Stella corrected her.

'Clues.' Milly was stern. 'We're detectives. Daddy says you have to find clues stain by stain!'

Hearing her own motto spouted with conviction from the mouth of a nearly three-year-old, Stella felt a flood of happiness. 'Maybe let me help?' She plugged in the sanitizer.

'I do it on my *self*!' On principle, Milly disagreed with everything that Stella said.

Justin was a reserved little boy. Like his father he made landscapes of minutiae: flower beds, a corner of the landing, his bit of their bedroom. Unlike Jack, he had a loud and boisterous twin sister. Justin appreciated that Milly carved a path for him. She followed his stories peopled with a huge cast of characters. Milly had taught her brother to ride a scooter (with four wheels) and work their clock radio after they were meant to be in the Land of Nod. Justin was a perfectionist like his mother. Like Stella. He must polish upstairs.

When they'd gone up to poo Stella had said a room by the lavatory was 'Out of Bounds'. If Milly hadn't been wanting to show Stella pooing she would have made them go in. Justin had never heard 'Out of Bounds'. He pictured Peter Rabbit. He knew about not touching things. They had to keep away from Mummy's desk with her drawing things. Justin supposed that beyond the door was a drawing board and sharp knives that they were especially not to touch. He could polish everything else. Couldn't he…

From the sitting room came the hum of the orange car. Milly was laughing. Justin felt pleased. Since Mummy's friend Harry had come, Milly didn't laugh much.

He planted Portus Teddy inside the neck of his jumper and turned the handle of 'Out of Bounds'.

'You're not allowed in here.' A lady swung around from the computer.

'I'm here to polish for Stella,' Justin faltered.

'Go away or you'll be in trouble. More to the point, so will I.'

As good at judging nuance as Jack, the boy gleaned that the lady shouldn't be in Out of Bounds either. Counterintuitively, this made him bold. 'Who are you?'

'No one!'

'You can't be no one.' Justin hesitated. Perhaps you could.

'Nose out!'

'Will I die?' Justin was solemn.

'We'll all die,' the woman snapped. 'Leave. *Now.*'

'Will you be all right all by yourself?' Justin bobbed Portus Teddy at her.

The woman smiled and Justin saw all her teeth.

'I'm always all right.'

Please can you take J and M into the office? I'll come there. Sorry! xxx

Stella was annoyed by Jack's text. They could have left the house earlier.

Minutes later, the house spick and span, she rounded up the twins. She struggled with the child seats which Jack had left with her (meaning that he'd known he wouldn't be back?), and mastering the clips, strapped them in. Stanley rode shotgun on Stella's cleaning equipment bag.

Milly struck up a song with Mr Sssnake. The verses were a jumble of words, but Stella got the chorus, 'Clean so deep, scrub-a-dub-dub.' As they sped along the Great West Road, she and Justin joined in.

The drama of the last hours ebbed. Stella made a plan. She'd leave the children with Trudy and return to the house. She'd drive Danielle back to the Cotswolds and then she would tell Jack that she couldn't work the case. Stella never ever wanted to see Hindle again.

'Clean so deep...' She'd got through the children's visit without them meeting one of the UK's most notorious child-killers. The danger was over.

'Clean so deep, scrub-a-dub-*dub*!'

Chapter Thirty-Four

2019

Barley Cottage was a large house on the river in Walton-on-Thames, it bore no resemblance to the little house in Braybrook Street where Nicola Walsh had grown up. Set behind railings, steps led to a faux Georgian porch. Verges were dotted with primroses and narcissi, bright yellow in the sunshine. Spring was in the air.

Jack was making it up to Stella. Instead of fetching the children from her house, he had arranged to meet Nicola, older sister of Robbie Walsh.

Beverly had emailed him a fact sheet. Nicola's husband was a commercial lawyer called Dominic. Nicola had one daughter and two grandsons. She didn't work. Her father, Robert, had died in 1998. Beverly hadn't tracked down Gillian. Jack hoped that the Walshes had found some peace in their later years.

Jack had been serious that Nicola might prefer seeing Stella. At nine in the morning, he was banking on Dominic being at work; he imagined the husband would send him packing.

Unlike Cathy Ferris, trauma hadn't marked Nicola, physically at least. Expensive make-up, facials and hair-dos plus, Jack guessed, shots of botox had kept the years at bay.

Forty-eight going on twenty-eight. In a crimson embroidered jacket glinting with gold threads and mustard-coloured trousers, Nicola looked smart for a chat with some bloke about the girl who'd murdered her brother. Maybe she always looked like that.

Jack flipped up the lanyard he used on cleaning shifts for Stella. *Clean Slate Operative*. The title could suggest a detective.

'Jack Harmon. As my colleague Beverly said on the phone yesterday, I'm investigating your brother's death.'

'Come in.' Ignoring his ID, Nicola floated down a carpeted hallway to the back of the house.

Jack's first impression was of clutter and discordant noise. Children's toys, dolls, an abacus, balls, bricks, a wooden tractor like the one Bella's mother had given Justin. Two boys struggled for possession of a battery-operated keyboard, the source of the clamour.

'Clear up this mess, Crispin,' Nicola told the older boy just as he got the keyboard off his brother who, bursting into tears, ran from the room. Nicola appeared not to notice. Crispin set about flinging toys into a travelling trunk like the one Jack's father had passed to him for boarding school. Jack's heart squeezed. Crispin could be Robbie Walsh.

'Tea, coffee. Something stronger?' Nicola led them to the end of the room and waved for Jack to join her on a sofa with the high sides and back roped together, a design Jack had never understood. It wasn't like you ever undid the ropes. French doors ahead and to his right were open onto a wraparound deck. Beyond, a lawn sloped to a private mooring on the Thames. It should have been idyllic, but it gave Jack the creeps.

Opting for nothing, Jack suspected that Nicola would have kept him company with the 'something stronger'.

'You want to know about Robbie.' Her dreamy smile revealed the work of a top-notch dentist.

Steeped in the fairy tales that he read to the twins on access nights, Jack saw Nicola was the princess in the tower. Her long tresses up in a French knot would come in handy were she minded to flee her waterside heaven for real life.

'Don't do that, Crispin,' Nicola said without looking.

With a sheepish grin, 'Robbie Reincarnated' stopped stripping the wheels off the tractor. His little brother was back. He sat, his expression disconsolate, beside a life-size Chinese woman who was bearing what looked like a sponge cake but must be a votive offering. Everything in the room was larger than life: a model dog, vast dining chairs that might have been carved straight out of a gnarled tree. Nicola and Dominic had flapped plastic in one of those emporiums selling items the size of a bus that, imported from faraway lands, gave a home an instant air of the exotic. There were three chess boards laid out on the table in the room. It reminded Jack of the clocks in the Dali jigsaw. The room could be an art installation that expressed how families never talk.

'I won't trouble you for long.' Nor would he. Jack felt rotten for troubling Nicola at all. This could be why Stella had baled out. She hated the undercover thing.

'It was a long time ago?' Nicola sounded unsure of this.

'Are you in touch with anyone from those days?'

'My mother is in a home. She asks if Robbie is coming. She's got dementia. Everyone does these days.' Nicola sighed as if dementia was an annoying fad.

'What about the kids you hung out with?'

'"Hung out with."' Nicola repeated the phrase as if trying it for size. 'Kevin Hood arranged our mortgage years ago. Not seen him since. We've paid it off. Dominic rated him.' As if this was the point of Jack's question.

'Anyone else?'

'No.' She gazed out at the river. A willow tree at the bottom of the garden added to the perfect scene. 'Lee and I met. On a train the Spring before last Spring. Said we'd keep in touch. We didn't.' She picked up a stray ball from the carpet and began kneading it.

Nicola had not pulled off a murder. She was having trouble forming sentences. Mentally, Jack deleted her from the suspect list. 'Lee Marshall killed himself soon after you saw him.' That was a bit mean, but he needed to wake her up and clicking his fingers was rude.

'The *shit*!' Nicola hurled the ball at the Osborn and Little wallpaper. It bounced away; putting up a hand, Crispin did a fielder's catch. Cool.

'Lee killed his sister and never had the guts to admit it!' Nicola shouted. Jack had woken her up.

'Wait! What? You're saying Lee killed Sarah?'

'He didn't look after her properly. Especially after… after.' She subsided into her chair.

'You told the police that when you ran away from Derek Parsley, the man from Abba, Lee was holding your hand?'

'There was a killer on the loose. Lee should have stayed,' she said.

'Why would you think there was a killer on the loose?' Jack probed. 'The police believed that your brother fell off the slide. It wasn't until Sarah was murdered that they investigated Robbie's death. I'm looking into whether Danielle Hindle pushed Robbie off the slide. Hindle's never admitted she killed Sarah Ferris, and certainly not your brother.'

'Danni hated that Lee loved me.' Nicola rubbed her palm as if at a stigmata. 'She was my best friend. She pushed Robbie off the slide and forced Sarah to keep it secret.'

'How do you know?' Jack tried to contain his excitement. 'There were no witnesses. Kevin Hood found Robbie. I think they suspected him for a while.'

'Sarah saw it happen.' Nicola went out onto the terrace.

'Did she tell you this?' Jack went after her. The garden was geometrically neat, beds of palm-like plants, their spiky leaves casting cut-out shadows on the lawn. A willow tree shaded a nook beside the river. 'Are you saying that Sarah witnessed Robbie's death?'

'Lee didn't believe her. If he had, Robbie and Sarah would be alive today.' Nicola's fingers dug at her palm.

Jack resisted pointing out that Robbie would still be dead. 'Lee told you this on the bus?'

'The top deck was empty. Some man goes and sits next to me. "All right, Nick?" I recognized Lee immediately. I could have died. Lee started going on about how I was the love of his life and we should have stayed together. I put a stop to that. Dominic would divorce me. That's when Lee told me about Sarah. I said to his wife he was in a state. Going on about how he should have believed Sarah and how the police sided with that bitch. I remembered Danni boasting she was sending them clues and working at the police station. She was a liar. I told his wife, Lee got like the whole world was against him.' Nicola glanced at an expensive watch. 'Is that the time?'

'Nine thirty. Yes.'

'I think I will have something. All this talk of Lee. Sure that you won't join me?'

'It's too early for me.' Jack regretted the judgemental response.

'For me too.' Deflated, Nicola sat down on one of the patio chairs and leaned over the balustrade. 'I'm sorry that Lee's dead.'

Jack pictured Lee and Nicola, shadows of the children they had been, raking the ashes of a poisoned past. Danielle Hindle's crimes had shattered their lives. Lee had jumped in front of a train. In front of his wife too. Nicola was likely dependant on drink, drugs too, going by the drifting manner.

'Did you tell the police what Lee said?' he asked.

'No.' Nicola rose from the chair and returned to the room. She picked up a toy car that Crispin had missed and handed it to the little boy by the Chinese figure. 'Play with that, darling.'

'Perhaps he expected you to tell them, but no reason why you should,' he hastened to reassure her.

'Danielle has already been found guilty of murder. She can't be tried twice, double identity or whatever.' She gave a sudden laugh. 'Freudian slip. She does have a double identity! What do I mean?'

'Double indemnity. But that's being tried for the same murder twice. Hindle was never charged with Robbie's death.' Jack wanted to snatch at the glimpses of Nicola as a happy humorous woman. He hoped that Dominic loved her.

'Lee made me promise not to say.' Nicola wandered restlessly around the room. Her grandsons watched her as they might a play they made no sense of. 'He gave me that bracelet. I couldn't say no.'

'Bracelet?'

'Lee reckoned it was bad luck. I was so relieved when she took it to charity. His wife didn't want it either or he'd have given it to her.'

'Do you mean Sarah's charm bracelet?' Jack wanted to halt her perambulations and demand she be absolutely clear.

'Lee made me have it.' She sounded aggrieved.

'Can I see it?' *Best Sister.*

'I said it's gone to charity and good riddance.'

'Were all the charms on it? Like, um, Best Sister?' So near and yet...

'Lee bought that for her. To please Alan as much as Sarah, I always thought. His stepdad still hated him.' She paused by the trunk and took out a doll. It was missing a head. Crispin's work. 'His poor family, his wife. It's Cathy I feel for. She didn't deserve that.'

Driving away, Jack felt for the broken woman who, medicated, nipped and tucked, meandered through each day. All the same, she'd fairly whacked that ball against the wall, so she had fight in her. He couldn't see her committing a frenzied killing. Even getting herself to Winchcombe. Then there was the Best Sister charm.

He only had Nicola's word for it that she'd taken the bracelet to charity. Had she worn it when she went to find Hindle? Perhaps to mock. *Look what Lee gave me.* In the struggle Rachel had ripped off a charm. Except Nicola had brought up the bracelet and had needlessly tied herself to a crime scene. If only they had access to the police files.

Nicola had recognized Lee after decades when she wasn't expecting to see him. She'd know Danielle Hindle too.

Nicola had probably imagined she'd seen the Best Sister Charm. She'd been keen to get shot of it. He'd suggest to Stella that they take her off the list.

When Jack arrived at the Clean Slate office he was surprised to find the children with Trudy in the reception office. They didn't greet him. Suzie, deep in her database, didn't look up. No sign of Stella.

Justin was cross-legged in Stanley's bed reading a book that Jack didn't recognize as one of Justin's stories. Stanley was on his lap. Milly was engrossed in a game on the spare computer. Bella didn't approve of them using computers. Jack generally argued that technology was integral to the world in which Milly and Justin were growing up. Today it annoyed him. 'Where is Stella? And Beverly?'

'Stella had to pop home for a file then she called in saying she'll be in later. Beverly's upstairs. She's trying to get you a prison visit with Christopher.' If Trudy took offence at the inadvertent inference she wasn't up to childminding, she didn't show it. She was all smiles. 'Would you like a drink of anything, Jack?'

'You're all right, thanks.' Right now he could fancy something stronger.

'I've done a sheet!' Milly jabbed at the screen. Jack saw the remains of an iced doughnut in the post tray. The kids weren't allowed sugary food. On that he and Bella agreed. He was about to say so when Milly's next comment mollified him. 'Stella made it change colour when you tap it. I can count my toys.' She was filling in an Excel spreadsheet. Now he'd seen it all. Jack examined the chequered grid. Nearly three years old. Milly was a genius!

'Stella did the cal-coo-lashon. She's going to put us in the cleaning man-you-well.' Seated on two reams of paper, Milly spun in the chair.

Jack realized that Justin's 'book' was a copy of the Clean Slate staff manual. *Bliss*.

'Justin and Milly have been helping Stella clean her house,' Trudy said. 'Milly has been deep cleaning. Justin polished. Isn't that fantastic?'

Jack could have punched the air. Stella had welcomed his children into her world. He loved her.

'I did went to Out of Bounds!' Justin gave a start as the words popped out by accident.

'Where is out of bounds?' Jack imagined a magical country full of light and beautiful music invented by Stella.

'You shouldn't have gone there!' Milly nosed the mouse at her brother. 'Stella said no. *I* didn't go.'

Jack had a bad feeling.

'Stella must have kept them out of one of her rooms,' Trudy said.

'The person was nasty,' Justin admitted. 'I did polish. For Stella's surprise.' He confided in Stanley, 'The person said go away.'

'What person?' Jack asked.

'What did we say earlier, Justin?' Trudy arched her eyebrows.

'We. Must. Not Tell. Lies!' Justin was obedient.

'Good boy!'

'He doesn't lie.' Jack defended his son.

'There was no person in the room was there, Justin?' Trudy smiled encouragingly at Justin.

'He makes persons up.' Milly did a 'what can you do?' face. 'They make a lot of talking at bedtime. Mummy says they must quiet down so we can sleep.'

Jack knew that Justin had countless imaginary friends. The main ones being the Bluebell Family who drank milkshakes and lived in a cave. Jack fretted that the Bluebells were Justin's perfect family. He and Bella fell far short. Did his little boy want his parents to live in the same house? Jackie had assured him that Justin was simply imaginative. Both his children were level-headed and secure. Jack wished that when he was little he'd invented friends. After his mother's murder, he'd been alone.

The door opened and Stella came in. She saw Jack and hesitated as if displeased. A fleeting impression. She pecked him on the cheek and went into her office. That bit was usual, Stella never showed affection at work. She reappeared with a sheaf of opened post that Trudy had left for her.

'What file did you forget?' Seeing another cloud pass across Stella's face, Jack was cross with himself. She didn't want to say what it was in front of everyone.

'Portus Teddy is in the van,' Stella told Justin who, Jack was troubled to see, also seemed shifty. Was he scared of Stella? 'I'll be back in a minute. Then I'm going to Skype Joanne Marshall.'

'I'll get it.' Before Stella could object, Trudy took Stella's keys and left the office.

'I'll go too.' Jack wanted to thank Trudy for looking after his children.

When he came out onto Shepherd's Bush Green, he couldn't see her. He went to the side road where Stella usually parked her van. It wasn't there. Then he recalled that Stella was renting hardstanding outside a house near Uxbridge Road.

Jack saw Trudy in the driver's seat. The engine was running. Trudy was going to drive off. Jack broke into a run. By the time he reached her, Trudy had switched off the ignition and was getting out.

'What's the matter, Jack?' she asked.

'Nothing!' he reassured her. 'I wanted to say you've been great with my two scraps. Way beyond the call of duty!'

'I don't call them a duty. Your children are delightful.'

'Oh... I'm glad you think so.' Jack was incoherent with happiness.

'You and your partner are doing a splendid job! Here, take Portus Teddy, I have a dentist appointment. Tell Stella it's in the diary.' Jack was charmed that Trudy had taken the trouble to learn the bear's name.

A slip of paper lay in the gutter. It had rained earlier, an April shower. The paper was dry, so it couldn't have been there long. 'Trudy, did you drop this?'

'What is it?'

Jack unfolded the paper. 'GL54... that's Penelope Philips' postcode. We don't need it now.' He shoved it in his pocket.

'Careless of me. It must have fallen from Stella's van as I got Mr Portus.'

They parted outside Clean Slate. Trudy asked Jack to tell Stella that she had another dentist appointment. With Stella not having been there, she had no chance to tell her. Jack felt like telling Trudy that she didn't need to justify herself, and certainly not to him. Stella wasn't a dragon, she expected her staff to have lives.

When he returned he found Stella leafing through the message book.

'Thanks for stepping in last night.' Jack was suddenly awkward.

'No problem.' Stella shut the book. 'Did you see Nicola Walsh?'

'Yes. I'll come round later for a debrief.'

'Let's take a rain check. I haven't got hold of Joanne Marshall. When I do we can trade info.'

'It should say, "Polish the wood so it is an apple!"' Justin told Stanley.

'That's a good idea.' Stella turned to him. 'Like a Cox's Orange Pippin with lines and specks?'

'Yes. Like that,' Justin agreed.

Jack should have felt joyful that Stella was treating Justin with respect and not warbling nonsense at him, like some did. But she had put Jack off again. Heavy-hearted, he bundled the children into coats and ushered them out. Justin with a copy of the cleaning manual, Milly parading a printout of her 'animals' spreadsheet.

He asked Stella casually, 'Justin mentioned seeing a person in your study. Who was that? An imaginary friend, Trudy thought.'

'Yes, probably.' *Too quick.*

Martin Cashman had stayed the night.

Chapter Thirty-Five

2019

Stella hauled down the loft ladder and, reckless of the murderer lurking there, clambered up. Terry's files were back on the shelves. No sign of Danielle Hindle. She hurtled down again. She flew into every room. She checked under her bed and even in the basement although the door was locked and she had hidden the key. Only the drifting scent of Molecule One in her study said that Danielle Hindle had ever been there. Rational though Stella was, she was ready to decide it had been a nightmare from which she had woken.

Once she was sure that Hindle had gone, Stella double-locked the door and slid across the chain. Her nerves jangled and despite her sweep of the house, Stella expected Danielle to walk in.

She sniffed the air in her study. Cutting through Hindle's perfume was the comforting tang of beeswax polish. The desk was shiny. Jack had asked her who Justin had seen in the study. Stella had told him there had been no one. A lie.

Justin had polished in here. His *person* was Danielle Hindle. Justin had been alone with a child-killer. As the truth sank in, Stella gulped for air. Stella had liked the twins. She'd seen Jack in them and strangely – ridiculously – herself. Distantly, she appreciated Justin's polishing, he'd made the wood gleam. Milly had got to grips with the sanitizer quicker than Stella. When she told Jack he'd side with Bella and stop her seeing his children again.

The computer sprang to life. It was a Skype notification. *Yes OK call. Jo.*

Joanne Marshall had returned her message. Stella had suggested they did the interviews separately because she'd wanted to tackle Danielle Hindle about the letters on her own. If she'd gone with Jack, Hindle couldn't have stowed away in her van. He was always ferreting behind doors and into dark corners, he'd have found her. Stella wouldn't have had to hide Hindle. She could have enjoyed having Milly and Justin to stay.

She'd decided to give up the case, but now that Joanne Marshall was in touch…

Stella texted Jack. *Can you come over? Please x*

The ping of another Skype. *Can speak now, bushed so heading for bed!*

Stella was stuck. If she put Joanne Marshall off, that could be that. Marshall's time constraints could spell reluctance to talk. Fair enough. The woman had migrated to Australia to escape a tragedy. Stella must strike while the iron was hot.

She pressed Marshall's icon – the Sydney Harbour Bridge – and chose the video button, hoping that Joanne Marshall would use her camera too. Stella had to see her. Belatedly she realized that the computer had been in sleep mode. It should have been off. Hindle had been looking at her files. How had she got the password? Involuntarily Stella glanced up at the ceiling. She'd scoured the attic. *Hindle was not up there.*

Stella had just decided that the line had dropped when a voice filled the room.

'Hello?'

'Hello! Hi! I'm Stella Darnell.' Trundling the chair up to the desk, Stella raked back her hair with a hand and prepared a smile.

A face appeared. Stella swept forward her notebook, keeping it out of shot. Marshall was partially in shadow, her background lit by a table lamp. Behind her was the picture of Sydney Harbour Bridge that she'd used for her Skype ID. In the blurred features Stella made out red plastic glasses matching red lipstick and a mass of red hair. Joanne Marshall looked like you didn't mess with her. She could have golloped up Cathy Ferris for breakfast. A television flickered, the sound, too distorted to distinguish words, conflicted with Marshall's voice. Stella could not ask her to mute it. A news programme showed the wreckage of a light aeroplane.

'Thank you for talking to me.' Stella's image was in the corner of the screen. She hadn't thought to plan a plausible impression. The window was a square of light. A morning dealing with a murderer had made Stella dishevelled. She pressed a button to delete it. There was a plunk like a pebble dropped into a pond. Her image remained.

'What are you doing?' Joanne Marshall leaned into focus.

'I was trying to delete myself. It's distracting,' Stella admitted.

Joanne Marshall gave her rapid instructions in a high voice. The sort that Lucie said would never do on radio. No gravitas.

'Thank you, Mrs Marshall, I'm not used to this.' The deletion revealed a photo in a gold frame next to the table lamp. Stella thought it looked like Lee Marshall. His wife still had a picture of him in her front room. Not the act of a wife who is determined to put the past behind her.

'Jo, please. Nor was I until I came here. It's great for catching up with folks overseas. Bar my delightful mother-in-law who's frightened of machines. She stopped at the Teasmade. We don't talk.' Joanne raised a glass of something, whisky maybe, to the camera. 'Cheers!'

Although she used Skype when her mum was visiting Dale in Australia, Stella was unsettled to be observed while you talked. Careful not to be seen, she consulted her notes from meeting Cathy Ferris. Cathy had claimed that Joanne wouldn't speak to her. Jo Marshall suggested the impasse was due to technology. Who was telling the truth?

'You don't get on with Mrs Marshall?'

'Cathy likes to keep busy, it drove Lee mad. She never sits still. I can lie on a sunbed from dawn to dusk.' Joanne Marshall swilled her drink in the glass. 'Cathy and Alan blamed Lee for Sarah's death. How cruel is that? I blame them. What are parents for?' Her expression darkened.

'What made you move to Sydney?' Stella indicated the picture behind Joanne Marshall then regretted the admission that she'd noticed it.

Marshall angled her screen to show the television. It cut out the picture of the Harbour Bridge. A woman was reporting beside a heap of mangled metal. A banner ticker-taped at the bottom of the screen. *Air Crash: Queensland landowner says, 'miracle no fatalities, no livestock killed, crew walked away.'*

'Why did you want to talk about Lee?'

Stella had wrestled with her story. Writing a book was a good one, but Jack had told Cathy Ferris that he was a friend of Lee. Jo Marshall didn't talk to Cathy. Stella took the plunge.

'I'm looking into the murders of Lee's sister and the boy Robert Walsh. Lee may have said that the detective leading the case was Terry Darnell? He was my dad. I'm writing his biography. I'm reading up on Dad's investigations and this was his hardest case because it involved a child who murdered children.' Stella had shut her eyes as she recited the story. Although she'd deleted the video of herself, she realized she was visible to Marshall. She opened them. If Skype was a lie detector test then she had failed.

'You're a cleaner. I Googled an interview about you following your father's footsteps. Can you write?'

'Yes.' Bristling at the inference that cleaners couldn't use a pen, Stella said the very thing that she had intended not to say. The truth. 'I also solve crimes.'

'Cleaning, detective, steering a mop and brush empire – hey, girl, I hope you've got a good PA! I asked because writing's hard.

Lee was offered six figures to spill the beans. He wouldn't make money out of Sarah. I wasn't precious. I had a go, but I couldn't string a sentence. When Lee had his breakdown and couldn't work, the cash would have been useful. He wouldn't hire a ghost writer either.' She fiddled with something off camera. 'Lee always threatened to top himself. I stopped listening. More fool me! Now I've got his ghost!' She didn't smile.

'I'm sorry for your loss.' Stella heard the cliché although she was sorry. She couldn't imagine what she'd do if Jack threw himself under a train before her eyes. Not that he ever would, he knew the pain it caused everyone at the scene. Except Jack said suicidal people could not be judged as selfish, it was unfair to treat them as stable. By definition they were not stable.

'Some days I can't imagine going on; others I get a glimmer of life beyond Lee. Then something happens to remind me and I'm back to square one.'

Time was meant to heal. Stella hadn't got used to her dad's death. As years passed, she grew less used to it.

'We can stop if you'd prefer.' Stella's instinct was still to drop the case.

'You're all right. Today was a good day. Your dad put away an evil monster. He deserves to go down in history. Where shall I start?'

'Where you like. Is it OK if I make notes?'

'Go for it. I make lists, or Christ knows where I'd be!'

If something ever happened to Jack, Stella vowed to handle it like Lee's widow. She too would go far away. A clean slate.

'On bad days, I'm so angry with Lee, I daren't leave the house or I'd commit murder!' Jo Marshall patted her hair. 'Lee never got over his sister's death. Whatever he looked like on the outside – job, marriage, mortgage, all that – he was a mess. His stepfather blamed him and although she never said, so did Cathy. And truth be told, Lee did play his part. If he hadn't been smitten with that snobby cow, Nicola Walsh, he might have remembered to take Sarah home. I said, "Darlin', at the end of the day there's no one to blame but that bitch who crushed Sarah with a brick." I blame the parents. They were responsible for Sarah, not a ten-year-old boy. Fancy letting kids that young play out after dark.'

'Have you met Nicola?' Stella was cross with herself. If she'd had gone with Jack to see Nicola then her questions could have taken into account what she'd learnt there.

'Once, yes. Miss Perfect led Lee on. She and the Hindle Witch had him under their thumbs. Lee was lovely. Not a bad bone in his body.'

'How did you meet?' Terry would start at the beginning. Although Stella knew they'd met in Germany she wanted to hear it from Jo Marshall.

'I was an army brat. He was a private. He left soon after that and we came to England. We moved to Bristol. I thought it was a good town to bring your children up in. More fool me! A good town to watch other people's kids growing up. When we'd see Lee's mum that tosser Ferris wouldn't have him at the house so we'd have tea out and go to Lee's dad's grave. Jolly! Cathy never visits where Sarah's buried, did she tell you that? Isn't that weird? Lee didn't think so. I think Cathy wanted to wipe out all the life that came after her first husband died.' She drained the tumbler.

'I met Cathy at Lee's grave.' Stella expected that if her child died, she'd never stop tending the grave. She did think it odd that Cathy Ferris didn't visit her daughter's grave. Wikipedia said it was the same churchyard. 'Did Cathy say why she doesn't go?'

'She clams up if you ask her. But the answer is it's where Alan the tosser was born. Newhaven down in Sussex. Too far for Cathy to visit with her hip. Lee and I went once. It was overgrown. Lee made us weed it. But we never went again so I daresay it's back to how it was now.' Jo Marshall adjusted her computer, briefly Stella saw a door with a handbag hanging off a hook before Marshall, as if she'd seen Stella notice, returned the screen to its original position. 'Alan Ferris should kill himself and do us all a favour.' Her face was expressionless. Possibly she was finding the call an ordeal. Stella had noted down the bit about Bristol being good for children. Lee and Jo Marshall had been childless. A term Stella disliked because it suggested a lacking. As Jackie had once said, why define someone by what they didn't have?

Jo Marshall's face was paralysed in a grimace, Stella looked away.

A message popped up: 'Weak Signal.' Stella realized that Jo's face wasn't immobile with grief. The screen had frozen.

'…if I'd known Lee was against kids, I'd have left. But I was young and stupid, I thought I'd make Lee change his mind. I secretly stopped taking the pill. After he killed himself, when I was going through his files, I found a letter confirming his appointment for a vasectomy. Lee always said he couldn't go through what happened with Sarah. It didn't matter when I said no child of ours would ever be left alone in a park at night. Behind my back Lee sneaked off and got the snip.'

Cathy Ferris had expressed anger that Lee's wife hadn't wanted children. The women's accounts did not match up.

The screen sprang to life. Stella was almost surprised to see Jo Marshall's face move when she talked.

'…Lee couldn't bear me to feel the pain his mum had. He even felt sorry for Alan. Sarah was the man's reason for living. When I said, how come Alan wasn't looking out for Sarah, Lee wouldn't listen. On the anniversary when Sarah would have been thirty-six, Cathy told the *News of the World* that Sarah would have had kids and a husband. Want to know what I think?'

'Yes.'

'Sarah would be dead by now. She'd have crashed a car, overdosed or got herself murdered. She was a right madam. To Lee she was a saint.'

Stella wondered how this fitted with Lee never returning to Sarah's grave. She was surprised that Lucie May hadn't covered it. Perhaps the neglected grave of a murdered child wasn't a good angle. Stella tuned back to Jo Marshall.

'…Lee was forty. On his nineteenth nervous breakdown, curled on the settee with a blanket over his head, crying like the kid he wouldn't have. I was sympathetic, course I was, but it was wearing thin. I had to support us both. I was a secretary, not earning a fortune. When he went under the train, guess what I thought?'

'What did you think?' Stella wouldn't risk a guess.

'You. Total. *Shit!*' Joanne Marshall grimaced. Again the screen froze.

The door drifted open. *Danielle Hindle.* Stella could believe that a child-killer was capable of walking through locked doors.

'That looks like one of those nineteen-fifties posters of horror films.'

Stella was too late to quell a shout.

'Stella? Are you OK?' The signal gained strength and her face moving, Jo Marshall was concerned. Stella's face appeared in the corner of the screen. She looked like she'd seen a ghost.

Jack was beside her, out of shot.

'I didn't hear my boyfriend come in.' Stella never called Jack her boyfriend. 'Jack is helping me write my book.' Stella enunciated clearly so that Jack took on the scenario.

'You didn't mention Jack.' Jo Marshall didn't look happy.

'Stella wasn't expecting me, Mrs Marshall. I can go away.' Craning into the frame, Jack was his most charming.

'*If* you're writing this book, best you're here.'

Stella didn't like the emphasis on 'if'. She'd hoped she'd convinced Jo. Jack said that a good liar believed their own lies. She could imagine writing a book about Terry. She caught Jack up with their discussion. 'Lee felt guilty for not minding his sister in the playground. Jo says he never got over it.'

'That would have been hard.' Jack perched on the edge of Stella's chair, his arm around her. This wasn't visible on the screen. 'Hard for both of you. Murderers don't think about collateral damage when they kill someone.'

Stella saw Jo Marshall relax. Jack had the knack of saying the right thing. For herself, she doubted many killers factored in damage limitation. No one had thought of Agnes Cater, left alone and definitely childless. A lack she would never make good.

'I gather that Lee was haunted by not listening to Sarah say that she'd seen Danielle Hindle push Robbie off the slide,' Jack said. 'I'd have been reluctant to repeat a murder accusation by a six-year-old. These days we credit small children with telling the truth – then, not so much.'

Stella remembered that Trudy assumed that the person Justin had said he saw in Stella's room was his imaginary friend. *Justin had told the truth*. But Trudy had no reason to think that Stella entertained murderers in her home.

'I'm not with you, Jack. What did Sarah say to Lee?' Even all the way from Australia, Stella sensed a drop in mood. She felt Jack's arm stiffen, he got it too.

Jack snatched Stella's pen and scrawled 'Help!' in the margin of the suspect list. He gabbled, 'Nicola Walsh said that you and her were the only two in whom Lee confided.'

Wrong.

The connection weakened. Jo Marshall's lips didn't move. 'Lee never told me Sarah was a witness to murder. They ruled that the boy's death was an accident. The Hindle girl never confessed. Lee never saw Nicola Walsh after he met me. I don't understand you.'

'No! That's right.' Jack nearly fell off the arm of the chair. 'Nicola said she hadn't seen Lee since they were kids.' He was dialling back. From what?

Jo Marshall's voice, suddenly grating, filled the room. 'When I said that Lee couldn't bear for me to have children, I should have been clearer. Lee wanted Nicola to have his kids. Nicky this, Nicky that. Hindle ruined our lives. Lee's blood is on her hands.

She robbed me of a family and of my husband. She's got both. Let's hope wherever she is she's rotting in hell.'

'Do you blame Nicola?' Jack asked.

Jo Marshall leaned back, her image almost lost in shadow. 'Watch out, Stella, your bloke's smitten. Men love hopeless women and poor old Nicky is a pharmacist's wet dream.'

Sensing that anything Jack said would make things worse, Stella dug him in the ribs. He tipped off the edge of the chair and vanished from the Skype picture. In a different situation it would have been comic.

'Nicola is on the same road as Lee. To nowhere.' Perhaps Jo hadn't realized that the television had come back on because, with evident irritation, she switched it off at the set.

'Do you know where Danielle Hindle is now?' Stella asked.

'Police protection at tax-payers' expense, life-long anonymity while the rest us are goldfish in a bowl of fools and knaves. I've got life-long animosity!' Jo gave a tight smile at what the pun.

'When did you move to Sydney?' Stella affected one of Jack's smiles.

'Been here a year. If Cathy's on at you to make me come back and fuss around Lee's grave with her you're filling a leaky bucket. I'm never leaving Sydney!'

The call ended. Stella was about to re-establish the connection when a message came through.

Think before you dig up other people's nightmares.

'That went well then!' She eased out of the chair and stood looking out of the window. The back gardens of houses in nearby St Peter's Square were lost in inky darkness.

'That was my fault,' Jack said from behind her. 'She was rattled by me coming in unexpectedly.'

'Jo Marshall had said all she was likely to say,' Stella said.

'She is angry with Hindle. She could have tried to get revenge.'

'She could have flown into Birmingham airport, stabbed Cater by mistake and left on the next plane. She has motive. Hindle ruined her life. But equally she's keen to escape her past. How easy is it to fly on a false ticket? And even if it is I doubt any deception would bear up to police scrutiny.' Stella returned to the desk. 'What was Nicola like?'

'Out with the drug fairies.' Jack yawned. 'She is another of Hindle's victims. If she was faking it, she's bloody good. She did imply she'd met Joanne Marshall. I didn't press her on that.'

'No. Jo didn't elaborate on Nicola except to say that men fell in love with her. Maybe she was jealous. She didn't look happy when you said Lee had met Nicola.' Stella went to close Skype. Jo Marshall's grimace stared out. *Marshall had heard every word.*

'Oh, brilliant you captured a still!' Jack reached for the keyboard and pressed print. 'Class act, Stella!'

'I didn't mean to.' Stella had forgotten that, in trying to erase her image on the screen, she'd pressed the wrong button. Instead she'd taken a picture.

'Marshall looks fit to murder! But if she was going to bump off anyone, Nicola would be as good a target. Lee never seemed to have got over her.' Jack gathered up the picture of Jo Marshall as it spooled off the printer. 'Marshall's left-handed. Didn't Cater's pathology report say the killer was a left-handed person?' He quoted from memory, *short-bladed, of a minimum of four inches. Gripped in the left hand.*

'How can you tell?' Stella examined the photograph.

'She's holding that mug with her left hand.'

'She used her right hand to use the TV remote,' Stella remembered. 'I use both hands.'

'Yeah, you do.' Jack smirked at her.

'Jo Marshall contradicted Cathy Ferris,' Stella said. 'Cathy said that Jo didn't want children. Jo told me that Lee was frightened of having a child in case it was murdered. Cathy never told us that.'

'She may not have known. She probably blamed her daughter-in-law for not having them. We saw that Lee could do no wrong,' Jack said.

'They both said that Alan Ferris told Lee it was his fault that Sarah died.'

'How cruel. Over time Lee would have absorbed that as the truth. Especially if Sarah told him that she'd seen Danielle murder Robbie.' Jack stretched his arms above his head. His shirt lifted from his waistband. Stella resisted placing a hand on his stomach, feeling the taut muscle. Either hand.

'Why not get Dale on to Joanne?' Jack yawned again.

'Dale isn't a detective.' Stella's brother was a celebrity chef in Sydney with no wish to follow their father's footsteps. 'You saw her text, Jo Marshall wants nothing more to do with us.'

'Exactly. Dale shouldn't let on that he's your brother. He has a different surname. He could drop a card through her door offering a two-for-one deal at his restaurant, free glass of bubbly, that sort of thing. I reckon she'd go for that. Once he's snared her over a plate of oysters, he can wheedle out illicit information from her.'

'I'm not involving Dale.' Stella was firm.

'Shall we cross Jo and Nicola off the suspect list?' Jack had brought up the spreadsheet. 'I vote Nicola goes.'

Stella wanted to cross herself off the case. It was usually Jack who intuited phantoms and bad vibes. All their cases involved murder. What was different about this one? It wasn't as if the murder they'd been asked to solve actually involved children. Rachel Cater had been in her thirties. If there was any doubt about who killed her, they should address it and give her justice. Stella couldn't let go.

'We'll exclude Nicola. Let's keep Jo Marshall. We're still considering Penelope Philips and her alibi is watertight too.' Stella had lost concentration. Only hours ago, Danielle Hindle had been there. If Jack knew, it would be the end.

Jack took Stella's face in his hands. 'Stell, when I came in I'd have sworn you looked scared. You're never scared. What was that about? Is the case getting to you?'

Stella exhaled. 'There's something I haven't told you.'

Chapter Thirty-Six

2019

Jack was oblivious to where he was going. Since leaving Stella's he'd walked for hours, heedless of cracks in the paving, bad luck was in his face.

He came to Little Wormwood Scrubs Park. The bandstand a shape in the sodium dark. Beyond was the playground where tonight's nightmare had begun.

When Stella told him that she'd been scared that the person creeping into her study while she was Skyping Jo Marshall was Danielle Hindle, he'd been upset. Hindle had entered Stella's nightmares too. Detective work was taking her into the netherworld of murder and untold emotions that had eventually consumed her father.

He'd reached for her as if, like Orpheus, he could bring her back to the light where she belonged.

'There's something I haven't told you.'

Stella had to tell him twice. His body comprehended before his brain. His limbs went to jelly, his head hurt as if his skull would shatter. Stella had allowed Milly and Justin to spend a night within feet of Danielle Hindle. He saw the ten-year-old's knowing smile. Old for her years. *Old enough to know the difference between right and wrong. Old enough to know better.*

Hindle had sneaked into Stella's van. A True Host, ruthless and smart, Hindle had beaten Jack. In the end they did.

'Why wasn't it locked?'

'It's a village in the Cotswolds, I didn't expect theft.' She said something about Hindle saving her from a mugger on the motorway. He had batted that away as an irrelevance.

In black, Jack was with the darkness. He entered the playground, his breath clouding like smoke. Clenching his cheeks between his teeth he tasted blood. Justin had said that he'd talked to a person in the 'Out of Bounds'. Why hadn't Jack pushed for detail? Because he'd believed that the 'person' was Cashman. Stella hadn't bargained for Justin – a perfectionist like herself – wanting to complete his polishing. Jack hadn't bargained for who the person really was. Jack groaned. His precious boy had been alone with Hindle. Jack couldn't protect his children every minute of the day.

'It takes three minutes to strangle a child! Justin would never imagine that someone would hurt him. With that bloody sanitizer on you wouldn't have heard him shout for help!'

'Yes I would.' She had lied. 'Psychiatric reports said Danielle Hindle was no longer a danger to the public. She was allowed to bring up Carrie.'

When Stella tried to defend herself Jack went over the edge.

'You let a child-killer near my children! Just because you don't care about them you exposed them to danger. That room is jam-packed with scalpels!'

'I do care about them.' Had she said that? he wondered now. As if sleepwalking, Jack swung up onto the jungle climbing frame and balanced at the top. The lights of Dalgarno Gardens twinkled beyond the park.

Stanley had trotted around their feet in agitation. Jack was a friend but he was behaving like an enemy.

'She slept in the attic.' Stella had pointed at the hatch.

'I know where the attic is!'

'When you arrived out of the blue, I couldn't think how to say no. She'd made me promise not to tell anyone. She was listening. I never expected you'd ask me to look after the twins. Bella said I wasn't allowed.'

'Don't make this my fault! Tell you what, it won't happen again. You made it clear you don't want kids. I hear it from your mother often enough. Pity you didn't say so before we got involved!'

Jack had thrust his fist at the wall, the idea obliquely borrowed from Alan Ferris when Terry told him that his daughter was dead.

Stella had tried to hold his hand. Was he all right, she'd been concerned. He had felt no pain although now his hand hurt like hell. He had shaken her off and walk out of the room.

Stella had pleaded with him. *We need to talk*. He'd barged past a neighbour wanting to check that Stella was all right.

'I'm fine...' he'd heard her say.

Nursing his hand, Jack jumped off the climbing frame and went over to the swings. Ghost swings in the ethereal light. He'd pushed Milly here. In another lifetime. He sat on one and set it going. Despite his coat, Jack shivered. Like Orpheus, he was condemned.

The roundabout appeared to be moving. Pushed by ghost children. Jack's anger receded. He loved Stella. Her expression when he'd brought the children was not reluctance to care for Justin and Milly, she'd been trapped. He hadn't given her a chance to refuse.

It was Stella who had made the first move six months ago. Jackie and Beverly had both had a go at him.

'Ask her out. Invite her for a meal,' Jackie had urged.

'She hates eating in restaurants.'

'Get a takeaway. Tell her you love her.' Bev all loved up herself said it was easy.

Jack was bedevilled by what he knew would be Stella's response.

'I see you as a friend. Almost a brother. I don't mix work with pleasure. We are a team, let's leave it there.'

'I still have feelings for Martin Cashman.'

Tortured by this exchange, it paralysed him. Months went by. Jack said nothing. Nor did Stella, which proved him right.

Until the day she had stopped him in the hall of a house in Chiswick they were cleaning for a sale. She had pulled him to her and kissed him. Long and more passionate than he could ever had dreamed of.

'I love you, Jack.'

As he remembered her words now, Jack was furious with himself. Tonight he had ruined everything. He had taken her love and trampled it to nothing.

Jack wasn't aware of leaving the playground. Stella had kept Danielle Hindle out of sight. She'd protected his children. More than that, she'd found a way to entertain, to delight them. Stella had given them something of herself. Justin disobeyed her about the study because he'd wanted to give Stella something back. Justin had understood that cleaning mattered to her. Justin's father was a bloody fool.

Jack flagged a taxi on the Ducane Road and gave the woman his destination. *Home*. The cab chugged past the hospital where Stella had been born. Stella didn't have scalpels in her office. That was Bella, the children's mother, who left them out, despite his insisting she lock them in a drawer.

Stella had lived amidst shouting and animosity when her parents' marriage was disintegrating. She still shrank from loud voices and confrontation. Tonight he'd shouted unforgivable things. Stella had done her best for his children and he had flayed her.

The taxi dropped Jack by the statue called *The Leaning Woman* beside the Great West Road. He passed the subway entrance. The mouth of a cave. He crept through the cherry trees to Stella's house and took up a position behind a bush. Light through her bedroom blind told him she was awake. Of course she was. Jack fought back tears. He was more than a fool. He was a shit.

A woman stepped into the lamplight yards from him. She went to Stella's door.

Two faint taps.

The door opened. Jack had no difficulty recognizing Stella's late-night caller. Stella checked the street before she ushered Danielle Hindle inside.

Jack smashed through the trees. At *The Leaning Woman*, he stopped.

There was only one place he could go.

Chapter Thirty-Seven

2019

Stella's van wasn't outside her house. Trudy knew that sometimes Stella parked at a distance to mislead unwanted callers. Beverly had let slip that once Stella had had an ex who stalked her. That, and the fact that when she wasn't deep cleaning she was hunting down murderers, made Stella careful.

Trudy knocked. There was no light, but that meant nothing. If Trudy didn't want people to know she was in she kept lights off at the front. She peeped through the letter box. She was met with a warm draught of air. A black cloth was draped over the aperture to prevent anyone looking through the flap. Sensible. And annoying. Trudy knocked again. Hastily she looked behind her for a neighbourhood-watching busybody. The trouble with those people was they missed anything that mattered.

Ever since Stella had found out who Penelope Philips really was, Trudy had known Stella was in danger. She let herself into Stella's hallway. The file of letters to be signed – given the late hour an absurd passport to entry – was under her arm. She'd needed an excuse. Stella hated to be fussed. Trudy couldn't tell her the real reason for her visit.

She called out. She had no wish to catch Stella unawares.

Dread mounted when Trudy found each room empty. She texted Stella. Already knowing she wouldn't get a reply.

It wasn't always a satisfaction to be right.

Chapter Thirty-Eight

2019

'Sit there. Don't move,' Lucie barked. 'I'm doing this for Stella. Any silly buggers and I'm calling the police. *Capiche*?'

Lounging on the settee in Lucie May's Murder Room, Danielle Hindle covered a yawn with her hand.

'Yes?' Lucie zoomed in on Hindle. 'As you know from the last time you and I had a chat, I'm onto you.'

Lucie had met Danielle Hindle. Stella should have known.

'She didn't tell you!' Hindle spotted Stella's surprise. 'Our trusty crime reporter kidnapped me in the playground when I was little. She put me all over the *News of the World*. She tried to convince Terry that I did it.'

'The promise of fame flushed you like a toilet. You boasted about the brick and the charm bracelet.' Lucie was a match for Danielle Hindle. You spilled your own beans.'

'I don't have to do what you say.' Hindle pouted.

'Actually, Madam Death, you do. You're breaking the terms of your licence. I've got a gigabyte-size file about you.' Lucie jerked a thumb at the iBook on her desk. 'I press "send" and the next episode in your toxic life will be syndicated around the world in the time it took you to murder an innocent child.'

Stella was sure that if Hindle were to try anything the police would be Lucie's last resort. Stella hoped that, smart though she was, Danielle Hindle wouldn't guess this.

'Is that a yes?' Hands on hips, carrot crudité between her lips like a Churchillian cigar, Lucie glared at Hindle.

'Yeah, yeah.' Hindle got out her lip balm.

'Why are you here?' In trademark black woolly jumper (a legacy – the only legacy, Lucie would grouse – of an ex-husband), cerise leggings and silver Converse high tops, Lucie didn't look scary, but Stella knew better. She hugged Stanley close.

'She made me.' Danielle nodded at Stella.

Stella's decision to bring a notorious child murderer to the house of a tabloid reporter had been counterintuitive. Lucie had loved Terry. Perhaps for that reason she'd helped Stella and Jack on past cases. Ruthless though Lucie was, Stella had learnt that she could rely on her. Now there was no one else. Stella had split up with Jack (he would never forgive her catastrophic mistake). Jackie was away. She'd considered Trudy, but it would be beyond unfair to ask her. And Trudy would insist that Stella call the police. She'd done that when she'd discovered a break-in at Stella's house soon after she'd started working for Clean Slate. The right thing to do, but then it had given Martin Cashman a reason to come round and do a security audit. Right now, the police – Cashman in particular – would be no help. In her situation Stella had decided that Terry would go to Lucie.

'Don't get clever, lady, why did you sneak into Stella's van?' Lucie crunched on the carrot. She hurled the sprout in the general direction of her waste bin and missed.

'She told me that my daughter wants to kill me.' Danielle applied her lip salve.

'That's not what I said.'

'Carrie thinks that Chris only had an affair because I told him about those dead kids.' She did a kiss and shut the tin. 'She is right. Chris wanted a shoulder to cry on and Cater saw her chance.'

'I didn't say it was Carrie,' Stella said. 'I warned you that Rachel Cater may have been killed by mistake and that very likely you were the intended target.'

'I don't have any enemies.' Hindle opened the lip salve tin again and repeated the application process. Stella hoped it was a sign of nerves. 'Who else would it be?'

'Are you serious?' Lucie took the tin off Hindle and tossed it at the bin. Bull's eye. 'Dude, the whole nation wants you six feet under.'

'Jack and I think that Rachel Cater's murder is linked to the playground murders in 1980. On the face of it the relatives and friends of Robbie and Sarah have alibis. Maxine said something that suggests she knows where her sister lives, but she was in her salon most of the afternoon. We don't think either Joy or Jason Hindle know. This is our list.' Stella passed Lucie her notebook.

'If Max had told them, Jason would have come asking for money. My mum would have slain me alive!' Hindle was gruff. 'It's unfair.'

'Unfair. Give me strength!' Lucie snapped. She looked at Stella. 'Where's Jacko?'

'He's... er... busy.'

'Busy-schmizzy,' Lucie snorted. 'He needs to get himself here pronto. What is he, a part time 'tec?'

'Poldark has dumped Stella because she had me for a sleepover.' Although she didn't have the salve, Danielle Hindle dabbed at her lips.

'What did I just say?' Lucie was concentrating on Stella's notes. 'Why have you crossed off Nicola Walsh? She's hot for it. That monster there wrecked her life. Have you talked to her?'

'She's on uppers and downers and enough voddy to sink a ship unless she's being wrung out at the Priory. Nicky couldn't harm a bluebottle, let alone some bitch like Cater,' Hindle said.

'How do you know?' Lucie demanded.

'I read the papers.' Hindle shrugged. '"The Fate of the Playground Kids Who Lived." Wasn't that you?'

'No,' Lucie snapped and Stella guessed Lucie thought it should have been her story.

'Jack talked to Nicola. He doubted her capable,' Stella said.

'Lor lummy! Nothing would stop me hacking my worst enemy into pocket-size pieces.' Lucie returned to Stella's notebook. 'Jason and Joy Hindle. My guess is you can dump them. They don't have her brain.' She curled her lip at Hindle. 'Kevin Hood. He's the only one with a circumstantial link to both cases. He was in the kiddy gang and he goes to Winchcombe to do odd-jobs for his mum-in-law. Bit of a wuss, I thought.'

'Have you met him?' Lucie seemed right on the case. Bleakly, Stella knew this was just as well. She no longer had Jack.

'Leave Kevin alone,' Hindle exploded. 'He's done *nothing*.'

'Touchy!' Lucie contemplated a new carrot. 'What does Kev know that you don't want us knowing? Does he come round and do odd-jobs for you too?'

'I haven't seen him since he was a boy. No way would he want to kill me.' Hindle subsided into sulky silence.

'Stell, why don't you and Jack have a crack at Hood? Pretend you're buying a house and want a loan.'

'We did that,' Stella said.

'Go again. Push him to admit that he and the Evil One here are still playmates.'

'Don't you listen? They've split up.' Hindle smirked. 'Ask me, she's better off without him. He's hunting out a babysitter for his kids. Stella has a life of her own.'

'I'm warning you!' Lucie waggled a finger. To Stella, 'I give Jackanory an hour before he's round at yours, sheepish and contrite.'

Stella's phone buzzed with a text. *Saved.* Trudy had a bug and wouldn't be in work tomorrow. Trudy had never been off sick. Stella's already low spirits went subterranean.

'There is always the unlikely and impossible.' Lucie cackled. 'That the police got it right and your hubby murdered his mistress. But life, and death, is a cliché. Believe me, I've seen blokes carted off from the courthouse for doing the bleedin' obvious.'

'Bev's applied to get a visit with Christopher Philips approved,' Stella comforted herself. She still had Bev.

'They turned *me* down!' Lucie flared.

'Don't you dare go there!' Danielle Hindle was on her feet.

'Stella can do what she likes. Sit down.' Lucie's tone could have cut through metal. When Hindle was back on the settee, Lucie began ripping strips off a reel of drafting tape and lining them along the edge of her desk. 'Here's how to play it, Stell.'

Usually Stella would be irritated at Lucie taking over, but not tonight. She watched as Lucie stuck newspaper photos on her Murder Wall. Danielle Hindle the girl. Chris Philips' arrest. The smiling faces of the murdered children. The Philipses' Winchcombe house.

'If Christopher Philips is protecting someone, smoke him out.'

'It ain't me.' Hindle had got the lip balm out of the bin.

'Carrie broke my photographer's camera when Mr Daddy was sent down. If you're gagging to replace it, don't be shy.' Lucie slapped up one of Carrie outside the Old Bailey addressing a cluster of microphones.

'Shame she stopped there.' Hindle glowered.

Stella fixed on a carpet stain. Without Jack, the only reason she wanted to go into a prison was to clean the cells.

'Eddie Hindle's dead, Alan Ferris is brain-dead.' Lucie dotted Stella's suspect list with her carrot. 'Lee Marshall's topped himself and his wife was in Sydney when the girl was stabbed. Suppose you've considered that Marshall came back from Oz on a false ID?'

'I've talked to her.' During the Skype chat, Jack had put his arm around her. 'Jo Marshall fled there to escape her past. She was angrier with Cathy Ferris for leaving Lee to mind Sarah that day than with Danielle, er… you.' Stella nodded at Hindle.

'My name is Penny Philips.' Hindle tapped her tooth.

'Child-Killer does it for me.' Getting up again, Lucie added the dead children's mothers Cathy Ferris and Gill Walsh to her gallery. Their faces were shadowed with grief. Lucie annotated the photos with Post-It notes on which were crosses and noughts, presumably denoting her own suspect list. 'I agree with Stella. This is not about Cater.' Lucie jabbed the girlhood picture of Hindle. 'It's about you, ducky. It always has been. Your husband restored antiques, that takes care. He's not the sort for a crazed attack.'

'You're really saying the killer thought I was Cater?' Hindle appeared intrigued.

'Someone mistook you for a thirty-year-old, good going. That hasn't happened to me since last week.' Lucie ran the top of her hand under her chin. 'Stella's on the nose, as per; you are in danger. Don't get me wrong. I'd leave you outside the house like an old armchair for collection. But you're more use to us alive than on a pathologist's slab.'

It was all Stella could do not to go, '*Ner!*'

'Stella keeps an open mind, like Terry. Mine's airtight. Here's what went down. When you told Carrie that you were the Devil Child you smashed her world. Carrie killed Daddy's mistress and she'll kill you.'

Hindle slow hand-clapped. 'Time to hang up your suspenders and retire, old woman. Carrie hates violence. A mother knows her daughter. I *know* that Carrie didn't murder Rachel Cater.'

'Who is this?' Lucie put up an enlarged image of the CCTV. Hindle in a scarf and winter coat on Dalgarno Gardens. 'Someone got all dressed in warm clothes for a Spring day. Or was it they didn't want to be spotted on candid camera?'

'It's me.' Danielle returned to her lip balm. 'Keep up, old woman. These two already established that.'

'How dare you be rude to Lucie?' Stella stormed. Her head filled with a rushing sound as if she was behind a waterfall.

Lucie put out a hand to steady Stella. 'See that spot of white? Now, in this image I've blown it up. *Voila*.'

Stella narrowed her eyes. 'It's a watch.'

'Take a look at Madam Death's watch,' Lucie said. 'My! What a fancy jewelled Swiss chronometer you're wearing, Red Riding Hood.'

'You can't tell what kind of watch it is from the picture,' Danielle Hindle snarled.

Stella spoke as she got it. 'But you can tell which wrist it's on. The watch is on the left. Yours is on the right.'

'Stella by name, Stellar by nature,' Lucie cried. 'Let's go again, Danielle. Who is that woman?'

'My name is Penelope.' Philips kissed the air. 'I swap my watch to the other wrist when I'm somewhere I shouldn't be. It fools the likes of her who hound me.'

'You didn't fool me.' Lucie's eyes gleamed. 'You're using your left hand to smear that stuff on yourself. I'd guess you're nifty with a knife in that hand too.'

'No comment.'

There was a knock on the door. Stanley bolted from the room. They heard the irregular thump-thump of his hind legs taking the stairs together after his front paws.

Stella found him launching himself at the letter box. His piteous mews signified a friend. She opened the door.

'What are you doing here?' Jack saw Stella.

'I've come to see Lucie.' Stella gripped the banister. 'About the case.' Jack would think Lucie the last person they should consult.

'You two kiss and make-up, we've got a job on.' Lucie glided out of her Murder Room.

'Why are you here?' Stella asked Jack as they reached the landing.

'Danielle Hindle's at your house.'

'No she's not.'

'Don't lie, Stella!' Jack's face contorted. 'I *saw* her.'

'She's here.' Stella pushed the door to the Murder Room wide.

'Hey, it's Ross Poldark.' Danielle Hindle waved her lip balm. 'Come and play Murder in the Dark.'

Chapter Thirty-Nine

2019

Clean Slate was like the old days. Trudy was apparently off sick so she wasn't in the office. Suzie was at her desk. Bev had gone to get biscuits. Only Jackie was missing.

Jack had hoped to talk to Stella after leaving Lucie's last night, but she'd driven off. At least they were speaking, albeit politely. Lucie was minding Danielle Hindle which, given Lucie's attitude to her, was on a par with prison.

'Trudy's done a summary of the case thus far.' Stella laid down a sheaf of stapled pages. 'She emailed it to me.'

'That's not her job!' Jack exploded. Trudy had assumed Justin had made up the person in Stella's office. She'd called it a lie. Jack was cross that he'd gone along with her. All because he'd presumed it was Martin Cashman. A knot in his stomach tightened.

'Good of her since she wasn't feeling well.' Stella squeezed a teabag into the 'I ♥ Cleaning' mug which Jack had found for her in the local hospice shop. 'Hope she's OK, she's never been ill before.'

'Time she was then.' Suzie jiggled her mouse on the desk. 'You slave-drive that woman, Stella.'

'Trudy drives herself.' Jack defended Stella.

Had Stella told her mum that he'd shouted at her? Jack was nervous. If need be, Suzie would fiercely defend her daughter. He doubted that mention of Hindle would tip the balance.

Bev burst into the office, she was talking into her mobile.

'...bring ID, copy that. No sharp implements, no drugs. Copy that. No mobiles. Copy that. They'll be there at fifteen hundred hours sharp. Roger.' She put a packet of digestive biscuits on Jackie's desk. 'Not sharp as in knives. I meant punctual. Cool! *Thank you.*' Beverly chucked her handset onto Trudy's desk. 'You guys are going to jail. Without passing go!'

'Nice one, Bev! How did you swing it?' Jack opened the biscuits.

'Trudy suggested we ask Carrie Philips to get her dad to agree and she did!' Beverly shrugged off her puffa jacket. 'You've got a visit this arvo. Wormwood Scrubs is down the road, what's not to like!' She did a twirl.

'We needn't be undercover,' Stella said. 'Christopher Philips knows why we're coming.'

'I don't get that Philips would protect his wife.' Bev drank from her mug.

'Because when Hindle—' Jack couldn't remember if they'd agreed to tell the team Penny Philips' real identity.

'It's not like she needs it. From Trudy's summary, Lady Penelope sounds a stroppy madam,' Beverly continued.

Stella went into her office. Jack felt bereft.

'I'm tempted to think Martin Cashman got the right man.' Keen on her new yoga classes, Bev was doing a tree by the filing cabinet. 'Rachel looks nice in the pictures. She couldn't help falling in love with a married man. I did that. With a woman. Not that Cheryl was married. And she was already splitting up.' The tree toppled. 'Maybe Christopher was a father figure, Rachel's actual dad died when she was ten.'

'Cashman wasn't working that case,' Jack reminded her.

'So why did he turn up at Stella's crime scene?'

Stella had told Beverly about that.

'Christopher probably saw that his marriage to Penelope Philips was a wrong turning.' Suzie would be thinking of her relationship with Terry, who Jack believed was the love of Suzie's life. Terry could never have met his wife's sky-high expectations of perfection. Had Jack failed to meet Stella's?

'It will be Penelope or Carrie that he's shielding. Fathers lose their heads over daughters. It doesn't make them better parents.' Suzie was creating a graph of that month's customer acquisitions.

'We should go.' Stella was back with her bag, Barbour over her arm.

'What if Carrie framed her mother?' With a croupier's ease, Beverly pushed a stack of biscuits towards Jack. He shovelled them into his coat. 'But her plan backfired and her dad got the blame. It's why Carrie's trying to free him. If my dad killed someone he could rot in jail. But if Carrie did it she knows he's innocent.'

'She could confess.' Ultimately, Suzie was as law-abiding as her daughter and Terry.

'If she planned to dob her mum in she's got to try again. Maybe she wants her dad to herself!' Beverly fixed her gaze at a far-off spot somewhere beyond Middle Earth and, palms meeting above her head, attained the perfect tree.

Jack watched Stella unpack and repack her rucksack. Notebook, pens, a book of sticky tabs, phone charger. She left out the poo bags, they weren't taking Stanley. Jack often felt a rush of love for Stella as they set off to interview a suspect or a witness. They were a team. Not now. Stella would never forgive him.

Have you forgiven Stella? He shut down the thought.

'There's something we haven't told you.' Stella zipped up her rucksack. She was looking at her mother.

'Go for it.' Beverly whipped out her notebook.

Stella was going to tell them what he'd said to her. Jack felt pure fear.

We've split up. Jack said terrible things, there's no way back. We'll continue to work on this case, but when it's over we're going our separate ways...

'Does the name Danielle Hindle mean anything?'

'She murdered those children.' Beverly was first.

'You're too young to know that, Bev!' Suzie was caught between admiration and annoyed to be pipped at the post.

'I'm not,' Beverly protested. 'Once, when I was little, I got lost in the park and Mum said, "Don't do that again or Danielle Hindle will get you!" The girl lived near us.'

'What about Hindle?' Suzie said.

Stella told them. She said that Hindle had been at her house last night and was now at Lucie's. She left nothing out. Including that Justin had met Hindle. Stella said that she was very sorry about that. She did not mention that Jack had shouted or what he'd said.

'They enjoyed themselves,' Jack said. 'They want to come again.'

Tracking the progress of a 228 bus outside the window, Stella hadn't heard. Was the bus number a sign? Jack turned the digits into letters on a telephone. CAT? BAT? ACT?

Suzie went and stood beside Stella. A mother sheep protecting her lamb. Jack wanted to drop through the floor.

'If Lucille Ball doesn't think the CCTV woman is Hindle, who does she think she is?' Suzie wouldn't be generous about Lucie.

'It could be that she happens to look like Danielle and it's a coincidence.' Stella sounded miserable. Jack hated himself.

'There's no such thing as a coincidence.' Bev quoted Jack. He felt mildly better. 'If it's not her, why hasn't who it is come forward?'

'The police didn't release the picture. Martin wanted to prevent the press identifying Hindle.' Stella turned from the window. 'Personally I think it is her.'

She had seen Cashman. 'That's a stretch!' Jack was consumed with jealousy. 'How would Cashman know what Hindle looks like now?'

'We should call her Philips in case we make a slip in front of people.' Beverly was stern.

'Martin was kept in the loop,' Stella said. 'I imagine for exactly this reason.'

Martin now.

'That makes sense.' Beverly sucked her pen. 'A woman is found murdered in the house of a double murderer. The Met had to muscle in. Probably annoying for the Gloucestershire detectives.'

'More likely Lucie May is wrong and the woman in the CCTV is Hindle. Sorry, Philips.' Suzie collected her stapled reports from the printer.

'For some reason Hindle wanted to leave us in doubt,' Stella mused. 'It's as if she wanted to put herself in the frame.'

'Maybe she's protecting someone too?' Beverly said.

'I have a question.' Suzie tossed her reports into Trudy's in-tray.

'What?' Stella looked exhausted, Jack longed to hold her.

'Have you two split up?'

Wormwood Scrubs prison fitted the Dickensian image of a high security jail. Forbidding flint-clad towers recalling the Tower of London had for a century incarcerated many of Britain's notorious murderers. A warning of what awaits the wicked, the edifice stood next to Hammersmith Hospital where many west Londoners – including Stella – were born.

Jack emptied his pockets (stones, a furred Werther's Original, loose change, phone), and stepped through the screening portal as if into a life where Stella and he had their mortgage and were living happily ever after in their new home.

Instead, they were visiting a lifer in D Wing. Notices in the visitors' centre warned that it was a criminal offence to bring phones or drugs into the prison. The list of prohibited clothing and accessories included no ponchos or hot pants. Jack thought that wearing hot pants with a poncho should be a criminal offence anywhere. *You must wear only one pair of trousers.* Good idea. He'd never have thought of that.

The visitors' centre was crowded. A boy of Justin's age in a TK Maxx tracksuit played listlessly at a Lego table. An older girl held a doll, both inanimate. The prevailing mood was of defeat. It matched Jack's. He and Stella hadn't 'kissed and made up'. Stella had not answered her mother's question. On the way to Wormwood Scrubs they'd planned the interview. They had both wanted to be 'bad cop'.

Two black men, father and son, Jack guessed, talked in hushed tones. Jack caught enough to gather that they were visiting the younger man's son. There were more women than men, more black people than white, and the average age was twenty something. He'd read that prisoner diversity didn't reflect the outside population. Here was proof. Christopher Philips, white, middle class and professional, would spike the data. If the man was protecting his wife or his daughter Jack wondered if being in prison had weakened his resolve.

'They know we're police,' Stella muttered. 'Dad always got spotted.'

'We're not police.'

Stella shrugged. 'We're on the same side.'

Jack decided that now was not the time to say 'speak for yourself'.

'Let's be nice.' Just as Jack was hoping that Stella was suggesting making up, she said, 'If we upset Philips he'll end the visit. Bottom line is to gauge if he murdered Rachel. You'll know.'

Stella still had some faith in him.

*

'I told Carrie this is a waste of time. Not mine, it's something to do.' Christopher Philips tugged at the sleeves of his prison shirt.

He was a shadow of the lean unremarkable-looking man in the photographs. Bald patches like alopecia showed through thinning hair. His shirt was too big, shoulder bones jutted. In his shambling gait to their table Jack had seen no trace of the high-flying auctioneer.

'Christopher, we know you didn't murder Rachel.' Jack leaned as close to him as he dared within the strictures of no touching or palming razor blades. 'Carrie thinks you're protecting your wife. That's credible. She told us Penelope's real identity.'

'Vermin!' Christopher raised his voice. A prison officer gave him a warning look. 'Carrie shouldn't have done that. I agreed to talk to make you stop. Tell Carrie her mother did nothing. It was me. I don't want her wasting money on you leeches. *Carrion.*' He polished his specs on the corner of the HMP shirt.

'So you still have standards.' Jack couldn't do 'nice'. Whatever else this man had thrown Rachel down a drain shaft.

'Rachel was going to tell the papers about Penny. I lost it. Have either of you got children?'

'I have,' Jack obliged.

'You'll know that your own life is nothing. All that matters is that they survive. I will not see my daughter suffer.'

'She is suffering. Carrie came to us because she got nowhere with the police. She believes that Danielle killed Rachel Cater. Perhaps you do too?'

'Carrie thinks that her mother should rot in jail. But she loves her really and it wouldn't help anyone if Penny were in prison instead of me. Penny's confession was a shock. I handled it badly. Instead of being there for my family, I blubbed to Rachel and made it worse. I never loved that… that girl.' Philips rubbed one lens so hard, it popped out.

Stella made to give it to him and stopped. *No touching.*

'Rachel wanted me to sell the story. It would fund a new start. Why should she care about Penny? I was stupid to kiss her.' Philips snapped the lens into the frame and crammed the specs back on. 'I said we had to end it. I loved Penny. Rachel and I could still be friends. She was the best secretary.' Perhaps hearing how ludicrous – worse than that – he sounded, Philips blinked. 'She went for me. I had to kill her.'

'Are you worried that murder is in the genes?' Stella asked pleasantly. 'That Carrie is a killer?' Stella was bad cop after all.

'What? No!' Philips went white.

'At primary school, Carrie hospitalized a friend for stealing her lunchbox.' Stella hadn't told Jack this. 'Carrie was the same age as Danielle Hindle had been when she killed Robbie and Sarah.'

'Carrie said sorry. The girls are still friends. Penny is not that child, she had nothing to do with that now.' Philips broke his glasses again.

'Do we change?' Jack still got jealous after all these years.

'Rachel had to be dead.'

'Had to be dead?' Jack repeated. *A summary execution.*

'She couldn't have survived.'

'Christopher, are you saying that when you put Rachel down that shaft she was still alive?' Stella was there before Jack.

'She must have been dead!' Philips spoke into a fist.

Jack recalled the phantom smell drifting up from the darkness.

A signal sounded. A voice called, 'Visiting's over!'

'Was she conscious?' Jack hissed. Philips had not said this in court.

Stella moved towards Philips as if she might fling him to the floor.

A prison officer was zigzagging through the tables towards them.

'Good girl, Rachel said.' Philips mumbled to Stella. Carrie is—'

His speech was indistinct. Jack wondered if he'd spoken at all.

'Return to your cell, Mr Philips.' The officer's neutral tone betrayed neither respect nor deepest disgust.

Chapter Forty

2019

'You can't barge in here!' Wrapped in a pink fluffy dressing gown, Nicola Giles' protest was feeble.

'Ready for bed, Nick? Or is this you getting up?' Lucie was already in the sitting room.

'I'm calling the police.' Nicola slumped onto the sofa, the threat apparently empty. 'I haven't got anything else to say. You still owe me for last time.'

'It's in the post!' Aiming vaguely for the semblance of a friendly smile, Lucie delved into her safari jacket and waved a newspaper cutting at Nicola.

'My daughter will be here soon.' Nicola didn't believe herself.

'Not since she caught you drunk in charge of her kids she won't.' Lucie smoothed out a black and white photo of a coffin being unloaded from a hearse. Mourners looked on. 'Remember this?'

'No.'

'Yeah, you do,' she snapped. 'That's you by the hearse. Couldn't resist a fond farewell to your old flame. My old ma always said vanity is our undoing!'

'I lost touch with Lee after Robbie and Sarah died.'

'That's not what you told my friend. C'mon, Nick, you said it for Jack, say it for me!' Lucie's eyes glittered.

'I met Lee on a bus. He gave me his bracelet.' Belatedly, Nicola heard what Lucie had said. 'Your friend? He never said he was a reporter.'

'Where is the charm bracelet?'

'I told him, it went to charity.' Nicola rubbed an eye. Lucie knew this was a sign that she was lying.

'Yeah. But we know that's rubbish. Where is it?'

'She took it.'

Lucie launched into a line from Charles Aznavour's 'She'. Her terrible singing was guaranteed to get the truth out of the best liar.

'That one.' Nicola indicated a woman in a black hat wearing dark glasses that took up half her face. 'She said she'd take it. That bracelet was bad luck.'

'Very charitable to share the bad luck.' Lucie watched a team of rowers pass by on the river below them. 'All the charms there? The Best Sister one that Lee bought for little Sarah, you didn't feel like holding onto that one?'

'She took it. Said it reminded her of him.' Nicola reached for the empty glass on the arm of sofa then thought better of it.

'Got on well, you two?' Lucie wheedled.

'All right.' Puzzled, Nicola contemplated the glass.

'Course you did, you had Lee in common.' Lucie took the glass and going to a huge drinks cupboard beside some Chinese statue thing holding a cake, she rustled up a good strong nippet for Nicola. 'So when did you last see the lovely Mrs Marshall?'

Chapter Forty-One

2019

Penelope Philips had been moved to a safe house. According to the postcode that Trudy had copied from Stella's satnav, it was one of a row of flats above a gift shop in Broadway. Trudy picked her way around wheelie bins and flattened cardboard boxes to a flight of steps.

The terrace was scattered with cheap garden ornaments, a plastic table and chairs. The outside of No 1 was bare paving. A come-down from the grand house in Winchcombe.

Trudy was doing detective work. She was sure that Penelope Philips was too smart to chuck away a very comfortable life by murdering her husband's mistress. If that woman had done it, Trudy was sure that police would still be looking for Cater's corpse.

Trudy had seen Justin's guilty expression yesterday and, from Jack's face, Trudy saw that he'd guessed his son's hasty admission that he'd been talking to his imaginary friend was a lie. Jack probably assumed that Justin had met that detective who'd had an affair with Stella. Jack was sick with jealousy of Cashman, it was written on his face. Trudy could be objective. Betrayal wasn't in Stella's vocabulary.

When they'd met by Stella's van she'd been tempted to warn him.

Don't squander the love of this special woman.

A PA's job was to get ahead of the danger. Jackie Makepeace had been there for Stella, but now, potty about her grandchildren, her eye was off the ball. Jack was wrapped up in his kids. Beverly was too busy learning to be a private eye and fussing with the joys of married life to watch out for Stella. Lucie May had been obsessed with Stella's dad, but out for a good story, she'd chuck Stella to the wolves. Trudy wished that Stella would stick to cleaning. She was swimming in treacherous waters and only Trudy could see it.

Yesterday, Stella had left the office to work from home. But Trudy didn't believe her. Nor from his twitchy behaviour did Jack. Last night Stella had been out when Trudy called by. By then Trudy had worked out where Stella had been the afternoon before and wondered why Stella hadn't entered her second – solo – visit to Gloucestershire in the Investigation Log. Trudy had found the destination address on Stella's satnav and she realized the identity of Justin's imaginary friend. Stella had gone to Gloucestershire the previous afternoon to see Penelope Philips. She had not come back alone.

Trudy hadn't spotted Jack until he was almost at the van. Jack didn't trust her any more than he did Stella. She'd turned off the engine and greeted him. Stupidly, she'd dropped the slip of paper on which she'd scribbled the postcode, but Jack was too preoccupied with Stella to notice the postcode was Broadway not Winchcombe. She was pretty sure that he had believed her story that the paper was from Stella's van. But you never knew with Jack, he'd been traumatized when he was about the same age as his kids. Jack didn't believe anyone.

Trudy checked that Stella's van wasn't on the street or in any of the car parks. The coast was clear. She knocked on the door.

'Can I help?' A man was coming up the steps behind her.

‘I was looking for Penelope.’ Talk about taking your eye off the ball.

‘Are you a reporter?’ The man looked familiar.

‘Are you a friend of Penny’s?’ She barred the front door as if on guard. Turn the tables, make him the threat. Any minute the woman herself could emerge.

‘Yes.’ He was curt. But she noticed he checked behind him as if he could be caught out.

Expensively suited, neat haircut. Mid-forties. Pilates and jogging might give Trudy an edge because although he was thickset, the red cheeks were not from healthy outdoor living. A dossier case under his arm precluded the police. God squad? Too aggressive. Trudy realized why she knew him. From the case files. ‘Kevin Hood!’

‘Do I know you?’ He went pale beneath the web of broken veins.

‘Seen your website.’ She did a smile. ‘Why are you here?’

‘Penelope Philips is my client.’ Kevin Hood was a bad liar.

‘She’s not in.’ Trudy stood back. Hood knocked and frowned when he too got no answer.

‘Is she expecting you?’

‘Why wouldn’t she be?’ Trudy saw she’d made a mistake. Hood’s face darkened. The terrace had one flight of steps. There was no other way out.

The police had chosen a property hidden in plain sight. The neighbours were holiday renters. No one would pay attention to the occupant of No 1. At the back of the main street there was nobody to pay attention if Hood carried a knife.

He was still at the top of the stairs. She had only to push him. In films that did the trick, but if Hood lived she’d have to finish him with her own penknife. She’d never killed a man.

As if reading her mind, Hood moved away from the steps. He unzipped his document case and began scribbling on a yellow legal pad.

Who’s fooling who?

'When you see Penny, say I called.' As Trudy went down the steps her neck tingled with the likelihood that Hood might do to her what she'd considered doing to him.

'Who shall I say called?' Hood was leaning over the balcony rail.

'A friend. From the old days.'

Trudy would have to tell Stella she'd been to Broadway and met a witness. Stella would think she had strayed into business that wasn't her own. She would change her mind if Trudy told her that she'd found Rachel Cater's killer.

Chapter Forty-Two

2019

The hallway was littered with unopened envelopes, junk mail and takeaway leaflets. Peeling off latex gloves, Cashman negotiated his way around the boxes of incontinence pads.

Stella was masked against the heady aroma of dried blood, stale faeces and urine. Laced with the stench of decomposition. *Cashman again.* 'I was told this was an undiscovered body? Is it a crime?'

'You offering to solve this death too?' Cashman harrumphed. 'Nothing to see here. This is due to self-neglect and disintegration. It's not unlawful intrusion. Like the job sheet says, clean up and go.'

Stella was dismayed. Cashman had been her dad's best friend. He'd never spoken to her like this. OK, so at the Philipses' house he'd been strict, but not unpleasant. She squeezed past the burly detective in the narrow passage. According to the job sheet, the deceased occupant had been found in the kitchen. She moved aside more cartons of incontinence products and a stack of Ensure – a supplement drink – encased in plastic.

Everywhere, there were emptied tins of food erupting with mould, sauce bottles and dirty plates. A canister of Mr Sheen was a poignant sign of intention overwhelmed. Supermarket bags spilled out of a cupboard. A tower of newspapers had toppled over. Stella trod on something. Under her plastic over-shoed boot was a splash of blood. *She'd killed something.* A grinning plastic Noddy in his red jacket, hand raised in a wave.

There was blood, a black encrusted stain. It had dripped from the table where more blood pooled around a cornflakes packet and a litre of full cream milk that was long past cheese or yoghurt.

'He died over his breakfast,' Cashman said. 'Cut himself. Bled to death. A neighbour reported the smell. After a month. No relatives, no friends. No one to miss him. Same story.'

Stella knew that, as young constables, Terry and Cashman were first-responders to such a scene. Lucie had said that if you lived alone, ten to one you died alone. Stella pictured the bowl and spoon draining by the sink in her dad's kitchen after his death. Terry had died in public outside a shop. Another way to die alone. Unlike Terry, the man who'd lived in this filthy chaotic flat had no daughter to clean up his life.

'...looks like the old guy was peeling an apple.' Cashman pointed at a rotted lump mired in blackened blood. 'Knife slipped. Hit a vein. Pathologist says death was from blood loss. No phone. Fainted. Couldn't call for help. Not that he'd have got any. We canvassed the flats, no one knew him. It's crammed with clutter.'

Cashman sounded unfeeling, but Stella knew that he talked like a telegram when he was upset. It wasn't clutter. Stella had met a declutterer on a previous case. And many times she'd cleaned homes that needed one. Hoarders saw parting with anything as akin to murder. Then there were the collectors who stuck to one line. Toy cars, antique cake decorations, porcelain nymphs. This man's home, stuffed with unused incontinent pads, junk mail and used food containers, was what happened when a person lost their grip on the daily round. It could happen to anyone.

While Stella relished doing the deepest of cleans – she could handle bodily excretions and decomposing matter – she wasn't used to the fact that no amount of sanitizing made a happy ending.

'Mr Clark's wife died five years ago. He'd get out to the pharmacy to pick up scrips. And the supermarket for a bit of shopping. No one noticed when that stopped.'

There were footsteps in the passage. The team had arrived.

The brief was for 'Remediation'. Deepest of deep cleans. Unseasonably warm Spring had accelerated decomposition. Clean Slate would dispose of the mattress, the box spring base. To prevent pathogens spreading they'd remove the sub-floor in the kitchen, chasing where blood had seeped. They would de-infest the flat of insects that had lived off the corpse.

After the prison visit, Jack had suggested a debrief back at hers, but unable to face him, she'd taken refuge in the crime scene job. Added to this, Stella was getting worried. She shouldn't have left Hindle with Lucie. Lucie was no longer young or as tough as she made out.

'I need a word, Stell.'

'Are you calling a delay?' Stella raised a staying hand to Donette who was hefting in the bag of tools.

'No.' Cashman stepped out of Donette's way and tipped his head to the front door.

Stella joined him on the street beside a brand new black Lexus. *Did he want her to admire his car?*

'You need to back off!'

'Pardon?'

'You're way out of your depth. Stick to what you do best!' He gestured at the Clean Slate van.

'I've got this scene under control.' She was icy. No one told her how to do her job.

'I'm talking about the Cater case. It's over. The right man is doing time. Listen, Stell, take this the right way. I promised Terry

I'd watch out for you. That's what I'm doing! I'm ordering you off!'

Had Lucie broken the habit of a lifetime and called the police? How did he know about Hindle? Stella's mouth went dry, she was in serious trouble.

'...did you think you could drop in on a convicted felon without me knowing?'

He didn't know about Hindle. Inadvertently, Stella smiled.

'It's not funny!' Cashman sputtered. 'Philips had an affair. It spiralled out of control, he panicked. He had to get rid of Cater. He's a common or garden killer. He'll stay in jail until he's off the zimmer and feeding through a straw.'

Although Martin disliked that Stella was a private detective – wrongly, he considered cleaning safer – he did respect her solve rate. Once, during their affair, he'd shared details of a live investigation with her. Jack insisted that Stella had never seen the real Cashman. She was seeing him now. Brutish and dictatorial. Wounded, she sniped back.

'Chris Philips believes his daughter did it. Rachel told him.' From his face it was clear that Cashman didn't know what Philips had said to her in the prison. Cashman could have Stella for withholding information.

'He's winding you up.'

'Danielle Hindle thinks Carrie did it too.' If hung for a sheep...

'You've talked to Dan— Penelope Philips? *Jesus*, Stella!' Cashman leaned on the bonnet of the Lexus.

'We do whatever the client asks us if it's legal.'

'I'm begging you, Stella.' Cashman softened. 'Walk away. This is messed up, it's not for you. Family are the least reliable witnesses, you know that. And this family is toxic.'

'I'm keeping an open mind. Maybe Christopher Philips did do it. But if there's the slightest chance that he's protecting his daughter or his wife, or both, we have been paid to investigate.' Stella sweltered in her protective suit. 'Did you double check Danielle Hindle's alibi?'

'Don't call her Danielle Hindle! You're playing with an incendiary.' Fiddling with his car keys Cashman was locking and unlocking the vehicle. 'And yes we did check it. Penelope Philips admitted she was in London. All alibis check out. We were discreet. Maxine Hindle was at her salon. She grabbed half an hour for lunch, but had no time to get to Winchcombe and in the likelihood it occurred to you too, we have her on a camera the other side of the borough. It's definitely Hin—Philips in Dalgarno Gardens.' Unconsciously, Cashman had slipped into treating Stella like a CID partner. 'Jason was at home with Joy and their phones agree. Lee Marshall went under a train two years ago. His wife went back to Sydney where she'd grown up and yes, she was down under that afternoon. Local police spoke to her. Nicola Walsh was withdrawing dosh from an ATM outside a bank in Kew. But Nicola – and this goes for all the surviving parents too – struggles to manage her own life let alone stop someone else's. The point is, no one knows who Danielle Hindle is now. Christ, even Lucie May can't find her.'

'Maxine Hindle knows,' Stella said.

'How do you know?'

'She as good as told us. She's jealous of her sister. She reckons she's landed on her feet.'

'She could have read that in the papers. They know Hindle is married and has a daughter.'

'Alright so I could be wrong.' Stella felt for Martin, he'd lost Terry too. She made a decision. 'I found this at the house in Winchcombe. I was going to give it to you.'

She fumbled into the depths of the suit and found the charm in the pocket of her jeans.

'Best Sister.' Cashman held it up to the light. 'We never found that.'

'I thought Derek Parsley found the bracelet and put it back on Sarah's wrist. This was missing.'

'He did. That's why we suspected him. One of the reasons.

That Hindle girl had it all along. Terry said she did. She lied when he asked her.'

'Was the charm always missing?' This had never been made public.

'Yes. Where did you say you found it?' He looked at her sharply.

'In the house. When we went to see Penelope Philips. I shouldn't have taken it.'

'No, you shouldn't. But then if you'd left it, she'd have found it and hidden it. It's all too late now. She would have denied it was Sarah's. But how has she kept it all these years?'

'It might not be Sarah's. Christopher Philips was an antiques dealer – he could have found it.'

'She could have hidden it in the playground. She was caught on the CCTV.' Martin pushed off the bonnet, buffing the paintwork with his sleeve. 'Terry always said you'd make a skilled detective.' He dropped the charm into an evidence bag.

'He said that about you.' Stella hoped Martin's detective skills didn't run to realizing that Danielle Hindle was in Lucie May's spare room. She was grateful they were getting on. She needed Cashman on her side and, after all, he was a link to her dad. And – she felt bad for thinking it – he could give her an insider's view of the case.

'Christopher Philips is protecting someone. Meeting him, I don't think he killed Rachel Cater,' Stella mused.

'After one half-hour visit?' Cashman was angry that his being Mr Nice hadn't put her off. 'We do not need you and that Engine Driver stamping in with his size tens, compromising the safety of Penelope Philips or her daughter.' He opened the car and got in. 'Stella, I can't cut you any slack. You're on your own. If I have to, I'll revoke your PI licence like that!' He snapped his fingers. 'It's only what Terry would do.'

Pause. Stella and Cashman both knew that using Terry was a low ploy.

'Did Dad see Danielle Hindle after she got out?' Stella's head felt as if it was splitting. She needed to know and she really did not *want* to know if he had.

'That's against the rules. Listen, Stell. That girl was evil. A natural born killer. Terry wouldn't have met her. You know that. Like Terry said, you knew him better than all of us.' He fingered the car's black leather interior.

'Did Dad think she was innocent?' Penelope Philips had said Terry had thought so.

'None of us imagined her guilty. She seemed like an ordinary cheeky kid hanging about to get attention. She wanted to be a detective. It's what we dreamed of, Terry and me, our kids following in our footsteps.' Cashman looked wistful. Stella knew that his daughter was a maths teacher and the son ran a bike repair shop. 'All the same, this is police work, Stella. The right man is doing time for Rachel's murder.' He swiped on his seat belt. 'I trust you. But that bloke of yours is hand-in-glove with Lucie May. If Lucie got a whiff...'

'So, Terry never saw Philips when she was released?' Stella wanted to put her hands over her ears to block out the answer.

'No. He did not. If Hindle's told you different, it's to wind you up. The whole bloody family is playing you. That kid was a liar and believe me, she hasn't changed.' He'd forgotten about calling Hindle by her new name.

After Cashman had gone, Stella got out her phone thinking to tell Jack about the charm. Jabbing at keys she accidentally opened the Skype picture that she'd taken of Jo Marshall.

Stella took up Jack's suggestion and forwarded the photo to her brother, asking him to look up Joanne Marshall. There must be dozens of Joanne Marshalls in Sydney. It was a small needle in a very big haystack.

Christopher Philips believed his daughter had murdered Rachel. Why? Stella watched a fox slink across the road. She'd got a client who got paid to go out at night shooting foxes. Stella couldn't imagine killing anything. Her client said it was just a job. Was that what Danielle Hindle thought as she stood on her hands and crushed Sarah Ferris with a brick? The pathologist's report stated that 'The deep abrasions to the neck implied that the attacker applied force, the hyoid is crushed.' Stella knew that the hyoid was a bone shaped like a horse shoe in the neck. Hindle was a smart child. Smart enough to know that by throwing her whole weight onto Sarah she would crush the life out of her. Stella found she had stopped breathing as she pictured the murder. Hindle had done a handstand on Sarah. A twisted version of a child's game.

Rachel Cater's murder was just as brutal. Not the work of a paid assassin who'd now moved on to other jobs, other victims.

Carrie had been going to stay with her parents the evening that Cater was murdered. Perhaps she'd arrived early. Christopher had said that Carrie was good. If she'd killed Rachel Cater she was far from good.

Jack would call the fox a sign. When Stella returned to the deep clean, she was still trying to decipher it.

Chapter Forty-Three

2019

'Selective hearing,' Jack said when she told him.

They were in Stella's kitchen drinking tea and taking stock. Chewing the cud of a case was how their relationship had begun. Stella had rung last night after her scene clean and asked him over. As if nothing was wrong between them.

'Chris Philips thinks that Carrie did it, but as my mum said, fathers don't necessarily know their daughters.'

Had Terry known Stella? Did he know Milly?

'We're down to two possible motives for Rachel's murder.' Stella updated the suspect list. 'One, the killer was really after Danielle Hindle and two, Carrie, Christopher or Penelope intended Rachel as the victim.' She turned the laptop around so Jack could see the spreadsheet. She had added more columns and populated cells wth freshly discovered information.

'I think it's Danielle,' Jack said.

'Lucie thinks it's Carrie.'

'Let's hear it for open minds!' Jack didn't point out that Stella had spelled 'grieving' wrong.

'If we only count the three stars, we have four suspects, actually five with Kevin Hood.'

'I'd give him a one,' Jack said. 'The guy was on his knees, the only person he'd be likely to bump off is his bank manager.'

'Hood had reason to be in Winchcombe. He could have seen Hindle, discovered where she lived and gone there to kill her. Only he killed Cater.' Stella corrected 'grieving'. 'I think he was hiding something.'

'I didn't notice.' Jack had been dreaming of getting a mortgage with Stella. 'Lucie said he was creepy.'

'You're always saying Lucie's a worse judge of character than me,' Stella said peaceably.

'Am I?' Jack grabbed her hand. 'I'm so sorry, Stella. You're a good judge. You keep an open mind and stick to the facts. This list proves it. It's only that I worry that you trust too easily, that's all.' He paused. 'Stella, I'm sorry altogether. You were great with the kids.'

'I'm sorry too.' Stella went red.

'The murderer didn't kill Rachel on the spur of the moment. He or she brought the murder weapon with them. However frenzied that attack was, it was planned. Afterwards they took it away.'

'I keep an emergency cleaning kit in my bag, it doesn't mean I intend to clean.' Stella could be obscure. 'Hood was nice about Danielle even though she killed his friends. That rang strange to me.'

'It could have been misdirection. We would definitely suspect Hood if he'd been horrible about Hindle.'

'If you kill someone you don't like, it doesn't achieve anything,' Stella said.

Jack had a long list of who he'd like dead. Starting with Danielle Hindle and featuring Martin Cashman and Harry.

Stanley was hovering at his feet. Jack patted for him to jump up. Mistake. Stanley resisted neediness. In many ways, Stella and Stanley were similar.

'OK, I'll take off a star,' Stella said. 'Are you OK with the rest?'

'Joanne Marshall looked fit to kill anyone in her way.'

Name	Role	Age 1980	Age 2019
Robert Walsh	Victim One	6	-
Sarah Ferris	Victim Two	6	-
Nicola Walsh	Sister of V1	10	49
Robert Walsh Snr	Father of V1	?	?
Gill Walsh	Mother of V1	?	?
Lee Ferris	Brother of V2	10	49
Cathy Ferris (Marshall)	Mother of V2	?	?
Alan Ferris	Father of V2	?	?
Penelope Philips (Hindle)	Killer: V1 and V2	10	49
Christopher Philips	Husband: Killer (V1 &V2)	N/A	55
Carrie Philips	Daughter: Killer (V1 &V2)		26
Joy Hindle	Mother: Killer (V1 & V2)	?	?
Eddie Hindle	Father: Killer (V1 & V2)	?	?
Maxine Hindle	Older sister: Killer (V1 & V2)	13	52
Jason Hindle	Younger Bro: Killer (V1 & V2)	6	45
Kevin Hood	Childhood friend: (V1 & V2)	4	43
Joanne Marshall	Married to Lee	N/A	44

Dead / Alive	Status	High *** Med ** Low *	Rule Out
D	Pushed off slide (?)		
D	Stabbed and neck crushed.		
?	On prescription drugs & drinks. Not capable.		*
D	Died 1998.		*
A	In nursing home. Dementia.		*
D	Dead at time of murder – 2017.		*
A	Grieving, visits son's grave. Not strong.		*
A	Dementia.		*
A	Capable & killed before.	***	
A	In prison. Could be guilty.	***	
A	Brought case, thinks was her mother. In CCTV?	***	
A	Capable of murder, but does not know daughter's location.	*	*
D	Fatal RTI 1994. Under bus.		*
A	Capable. If she knows DH is PP. At hairdressers. CCTV elsewhere.	*	
A	Capable but unlikely knows where PP is.	*	
A	Creepy. Hiding something.	**/***	
A	In Australia. Angry with Lee and Cathy.	**	

'But we've got no evidence that she was in the UK. Shall I add another star to her?'

'No, you're right. Two is enough.'

'Hey, I forgot! I took your advice. I asked Dale to find Marshall. If we get eyes on her we'll be better placed to decide.' Stella turned to him.

'That's great!' Jack bit his lip to hide a silly grin. Now would Stella take more of his advice and airbrush Cashman from her life?

'Martin says Hindle is innocent. He's angry that we know her new identity.'

Or maybe not.

'When did you see him?' Jack caught himself tapping his front tooth like Hindle.

'He came to yesterday's scene.'

'I thought a man died alone in his flat. Was it a crime?'

'A crime of sorts but no. Martin came to warn me off.' Stella looked briefly upset.

'Hindle was the one who told us who she is. He should take it out on her.' Jack's good feeling evaporated. 'And leave you alone.'

'I didn't tell him what Christopher Philips said to me about Carrie. Her being a good girl.' Stella was staring at her screen. For a moment Jack wondered if she was telling the truth. Then he hated himself for doubting her. Again.

'We need to decide what to do,' Stella said. 'We should tell the police, if not Martin. Except you didn't spot Carrie was a True Host when she came to the office.'

'Christopher could have misheard. A True Host is a psychopath not a woman who kills her father's lover in a frenzy.' Jack felt pleased. Stella rarely referred to his True Hosts as a thing.

'Or I misheard. It's just why would he say Rachel told him Carrie was a good girl if he wasn't worried that she was far from good?' said Stella.

'Let's ask Carrie.'

'Yes.' Stella leapt from her seat, just missing Stanley. 'You'll know if she's lying.'

He'd been joking.

When they first began working on murders Stella would have shrunk from asking a witness a question that might be considered rude or aggressive. Now she was all for going in guns blazing.

'If a dying person told me the name of the person who attacked them, I'd believe them.' Stella was riffling through her Filofax. 'If Carrie is innocent, she'll be upset that her dad believes her capable of murder.'

Jack nearly said that nothing would convince him that Stella could murder. But he didn't want to hear the false ring in Stella's response when she said the same about him.

'We've got a good solve record. Carrie could expect us to solve this one. She was taking a chance hiring us,' Stella said.

'Maybe, subconsciously, she's hoping we'll hand her in.'

'Simpler to confess.' Stella didn't do 'subconscious'.

'Or as we considered, maybe Hindle's also protecting Carrie,' Jack said.

'How would that work? The CCTV gave Hindle an alibi, not her daughter. Although at Lucie's Hindle let us think it might not be her. Martin said the whole family is winding us up.'

Stella kept calling Cashman Martin. What did that mean? 'I think you and I are both able to distinguish fact from fiction.' Jack was haughty. 'As it happens I don't see Hindle protecting anyone but herself.'

'Let's see Carrie and test her reaction.' Stella began an email. 'Where shall I suggest we meet? The office?'

'What about the playground?' The Martin thing was getting on his nerves.

'Perfect.' Stella began to type.

Stella never failed to surprise him. Jack was still getting over his astonishment when he realized that Stella was looking at him. 'Sorry, what did you say?'

'There's something that I haven't told you.'

Chapter Forty-Four

2019

'Clean Slate Cleaning Services, Trudy speaking, how can I help?'

'It's me, Trudy.'

Stella hadn't appeared for their meeting. It was Trudy's favourite time of the day, early, before the others arrived when she had Stella to herself. This meeting would be special.

'Where are you?' Trudy fought disappointment that Stella was on the end of the phone instead of in her office.

'I'm going to work from home. With Jack.'

'Oh!' Trudy chucked her pen onto the desk.

'Are you OK?'

'What? Yes!'

'After yesterday, with your bug.'

'I'm fine. Thank you.'

'Best leave early. Give yourself time to recover.' If Stella asked Trudy what was wrong, it would be an opener to what Trudy had really been doing yesterday. If she told her, Stella would come in. But Trudy wanted to see Stella's face when she told her. Jack's too.

'Please look over the leisure centre contract. Cancel those

estimate meetings and rearrange for next week.' So Stella planned to be out all day.

'I need to talk to you about yesterday.' Trudy was glowing. Stella needed her every step of the way.

'Don't explain. Just get better. Actually, please could you block out tomorrow too? I'm going to concentrate on the case. We're nearly there.'

After Stella ended the call, Trudy sat without moving.

We're nearly there.

Well, that had to be wrong.

Chapter Forty-Five

2019

'Terry did meet Hindle.' Jack laid down the last letter.

'She was lying,' Stella snapped. 'Martin said Terry never would have met.'

'How would Cashman know?'

'They worked together. They were best friends.'

'Do you tell your best friend everything?'

'Yes.' Stella thought of Jackie.

'Men are different.' Jack ran his fingers through his hair. 'If Terry did meet Hindle, and I mean *if*, he would implicate Cashman by telling him. I imagine he would have wanted to avoid that.' Jack nodded at the letters. 'Did Cashman know that Hindle wrote these?'

'No, or he'd have said.' Stella had wanted Jack to be sure that Terry hadn't seen Hindle.

'How come you never found the letters before? You said they weren't hidden.'

'There's stuff up there I haven't looked at.' Stella had never told Jack about the last of Terry's unsolved cases.

'How did she smuggle letters out of prison?' Jack wondered.

'She could have given them to a visitor.'

'Not easy. As we discovered.' Jack said. 'But we're prison-visiting novices. Bet it's easy for a hardened criminal.'

'Hindle was a hardened criminal,' Stella said.

'She was born one and she's stayed one.' Jack still had Hindle as the prime suspect. Stella wanted to see Kevin Hood again. She didn't really think it was Carrie.

'I wrote Terry letters.' Stella was taken aback when the words slipped out.

'I guess living away from him, and when the phone was expensive, it was a good way to connect. Where are your letters?' Jack looked about the kitchen as if expecting to see a folder labelled 'Stella's Letters'.

'I never sent them to him.'

'Oh. Goodness, Stell!' Jack shuffled his chair close and took hold of her hands. 'When I was at boarding school there was time after tea when we had to write letters home. Mine were to my mother. I handed them in to the teacher. My mum was dead, so they couldn't have sent them. I still wonder what they did do with them. If Dad was given them he never said. What did you do with yours?'

Stella knew that Jack was chatting on to save her face.

'Threw them away.' She looked at their clasped hands.

They listened to the digital tick of the clock. At last Jack spoke.

'Listen, darling, Terry kept Hindle's letters as evidence. If you'd sent him letters, he'd have kept them. Not in the attic. In pride of place, maybe by the bed where he would have reread them.' He kissed her fingers. 'Like I do with the kids' notes.'

'It doesn't matter.' Stella squeezed his hands and got up. She began whisking about the kitchen tidying. 'I'd hoped that the letters would give a clue to Danielle's thinking.'

'They have. She comes across as manipulative and evil.' Jack leafed through the letters. 'This one about meeting Terry in the playground gives me the creeps. I know it's hard to contemplate, but could she be telling the truth?'

'Martin said not.' Stella slammed the milk carton in the fridge. 'Terry never broke the law.'

'No, well, it could be a fantasy. Return to the scene of your crimes with the detective who caught you.' Jack was leafing through the papers. 'To be honest, Stella, I'm thinking these letters are authentic.'

'I'm not saying they're forgeries.' Belatedly remembering the milk carton was finished, Stella took it out of the fridge and put it in the bin. *Why had Terry kept them?*

'There's one letter missing.'

'What? How do you know?' Stella stayed by the bin. Her innate rationality had deserted her. The letters had become Hindle herself and Stella wanted them out of the house.

'She says, "I've given you my new address, please write and tell me what's going on."' Jack looked at her. 'There's no address on any of the letters, not even on the headers. So either Hindle told Terry where she'd moved in person, or she put it in a letter. In the last year of Terry's life, Hindle wrote to him every month.' He held up the sheets of paper. 'Between these two there's a gap of two months and then…'

'He died.' Stella finished Jack's sentence. 'Dad did *not* meet her.'

'Then there's one missing.' Jack stacked the letters. 'Who's been here?'

'Not Martin.' Stella's head ached.

'Of course not.' Jack examined his hands.

'Justin and Milly.'

'There's no way my kids steal,' Jack exclaimed. Stanley shot out of his bed, ears alert.

'You asked me who's been here.' Stella felt her head might explode.

There was silence. The rapprochement was still shaky.

'Danielle Hindle,' they said together.

'Except that makes no sense,' Stella said. 'I hid the letters under my mattress. Hindle never went in there.'

'She'd been in prison, checking under a mattress is first base,' Jack said. 'Stella, I know it's always me going on about rehabilitation. But I've found my limit. I don't buy that Hindle's childhood crimes were an aberration. She reeks of True Host. She was alone here when you took the twins to the office. Plenty of time to do the place over.'

'The bedroom door was locked.'

'I thought Justin polished the whole house? Didn't he do there?' Jack sounded disappointed to hear that his son had missed a room.

'No.' Stella had read the experts' reports stating that, no longer a danger to the public, Danielle Hindle could be released. Experts could be wrong. 'Danielle never left the study. That's where Justin found her.' She saw Jack's expression harden at the mention of Justin meeting Hindle.

'A shame you didn't make copies.'

'My memory. I did copy them.' Stella smote her forehead. 'I took the letters to work the morning after I found them.' She went to the hall, Stanley trotting behind.

The photocopied sheets were tucked in the laptop compartment of her rucksack. 'Danielle couldn't have found them. I kept this in my bedroom and obviously I took it into work the next morning.' Stella flicked through the pages. 'It's not here.'

'That exonerates Hindle. And the twins.' *Terry had met Hindle. She had given him her address face to face.*

'She must have met Terry. It's the only thing that makes sense.' Too often Jack read her mind.

'Let's go to bed,' Stella got in before Jack said that he was leaving. If Jack went now their relationship was over.

They trooped upstairs. For the first time in bed they faced different ways. Stella buried her face in the mattress. Jack counted and recounted bars of light slanting through the blinds as if they were Hindle's letters, until he fell into a fitful sleep. Downstairs in his nook by the fridge only Stanley snoring in his bed slumbered peacefully.

*

Stella awoke from a dream that she hadn't had for months. She'd been searching in vain for a WC with a lockable door and a toilet not overflowing with shit. She flung on her dad's dressing gown and went to the bathroom. Her own lavatory was intact. She peed and washed her hands, regarding her reflection in the mirror. Dog walking and cleaning gave her a year-round healthy glow, all the same she looked terrible. Drawn and every one of her fifty-three years. With no chance of sleep, Stella padded into her office and turned on the computer.

Dale had Skyped a message back to her. She was ludicrously pleased. She didn't know Dale well. Their childhoods had been separated by history and hemispheres.

Dale had done more than pop a half price voucher for his restaurant through Jo Marshall's door. He'd knocked.

> The bloke who answered had never heard of Joanne Marshall. He'd lived there for thirty years. Are you sure it's the right place?

Stella guessed not. Five thirty a.m. was afternoon in Sydney. She Skyped Jo Marshall. It rang out. She tried again.

'Hello?' The screen stayed blank.

'Hello? Jo?'

'How can I help you?' Jo Marshall sounded official. Had she forgotten who Stella was?

'It's Stella. Stella Darnell? I'm investig—' In the nick of time, Stella remembered her story. 'I'm writing about the murd— the Hindle murders, for my dad's autobiography?'

'Biography. Yes?' Jo sounded cold. Stella should have texted first. She'd ambushed Marshall. Stupid. She too was unprepared. She couldn't say that she'd sent her brother round and he'd discovered Marshall didn't live where she said she did.

Jack advised that, if lost for words open your mouth and see what comes out. Advice that had landed Stella – and Jack – in hot water. Still…

'I need to confirm your address so that I can send you the book before it's printed to check for facts. But you must be happy about it because if—'

'I trust you.' Jo Marshall cut off Stella's incontinent flow.

'You shouldn't. I mean…' Stella's dressing gown fell open, exposing her breasts. She yanked it shut and hoped that she was on audio only.

'I texted my address already.' Now Jo sounded annoyed.

Stella's brain went into overdrive. She'd run out of nonsense. Had Dale got it wrong? 'It's just—'

A bell rang. The sound shrill and reedy over the line.

'It's not a practice,' Jo shouted at Stella.

'A practice?' What did she mean? *Life isn't a rehearsal.*

'It's a real fire!' The line went dead.

Stella stared at the screen. A fire alarm. Jo Marshall had had to evacuate her flat. Of all the times. If it had happened. Stella scrolled down her Skype contacts.

'Hey, sis.' Dale's face was bathed in Australian sunshine.

Chapter Forty-Six

1980

'We're did a compatshon and Kevin won. He can't beat you. He's a wanker for saying it!' Jason was beside himself.

'Don't swear.' Danielle spun her chewing gum around her finger. She'd come to the playground looking for Lee because when she'd called for him his mum said he was out. But her brother and Kevin were alone. 'Seen Nicky?'

'She's down the cemetery with her mum,' Kevin said. 'I saw them go. With flowers. They didn't see me,' he said as if it was mission accomplished.

Cheered by the definite absence of Nicola and still hoping that Lee might turn up, Danielle bothered with the boys. 'What competition?'

'Staring,' Kevin mumbled. The boast had been in a moment of elation. He'd never beaten Jason at anything. The playground had returned to normal proportions.

'That's stupid.' Danielle launched herself upward on a swing and scoured the park for Lee.

'I said you'd win,' Jason said.

Danielle scrabbled the swing to a stop. When Jason was born Maxine had adopted their baby brother as hers. In fights and squabbles, the two rarely rooted for their middle sibling.

'Go on then.' World-weary.

'I'm referee!' Jason was mutinous as if there was anyone else there to claim the role.

'It's a stupid game.' Kevin shuffled on the asphalt.

'Which you thought I would lose?' Danielle was icy.

'Sort of.' Kevin rubbed at his nose.

'Loser has to stamp on three snails.' Jason surprised himself with the brilliant idea.

Kevin's expression was unreadable.

'Go!' Jason yelled.

All the children went still. Danielle and Kevin met each other's gaze. Jason watched them.

Danielle would not lose. Despite this conviction, she began to feel strange. Kevin's eyes were an impassive blue. Like Maxine's dolls. Like the dead cat. Kevin stared into her brain. Her eyes began to smart. Danielle fought the urge to look away. *She would not lose.*

Kevin stared at Danielle.

Danielle thought he was smiling. She blinked.

'You've got to murder the snails now.' Jason looked on the edge of tears. His sister knew that he'd never forgive her, she had let him down.

'That's easy.' Danielle Hindle didn't have to lie. Murder was easy.

Neither of the Hindles noticed that Kevin was still staring at Danielle.

Chapter Forty-Seven

2019

'That's her.' Stella pointed at a figure passing the bandstand.

'She came.' Jack didn't know if he was relieved or not. In her email, Carrie Philips had complained about meeting at the playground and hadn't actually agreed. Oddly for him, who on his night-walks sought out murderers, Jack felt dread. Stella appeared calm. Intending to record the exchange, she'd placed her phone on the bench. She would tell Carrie.

Seated beside her on Robbie Walsh's bench, Jack reiterated their plan. 'You do the talking. I'll chip in. I'll block her if she tries to attack you.' He liked the notion of protecting Stella.

'She won't,' Stella said. 'If Carrie murdered Rachel, she'll tough it out. If she didn't, she'll be upset that her dad thinks she did. Either way she won't go for me. She's a lawyer.'

'Lawyers break the law.' Despite Stella's confidence, Jack slid closer to her on the bench.

'Move away. She'll think we're together.'

We are. Aren't we?

Carrie was upon them before he could speak.

'Why are we meeting here?' she demanded. Aquascutum- and

Hermès-upped, she gripped a bulging Mulberry briefcase. Every inch the busy successful barrister.

'Do sit.' Jack offered his seat. 'I never sit this close to Stella.' *Idiot.*

Carrie Philips remained standing.

'Like I said in my email, this playground is the key.' Stella's hand took in the primary-coloured equipment. 'The solution to the murder of Rachel Cater lies in the events that happened here in 1980.'

Poirot incarnate.

'Predictable!' Carrie put down her bag. If she went for Stella, the case was in Jack's way. 'I deliberately didn't tell you my mother's identity because I knew you'd be sidetracked. It's too bloody obvious. No one killed Cater by mistake for my mother. The murderer *is* my mother. That evil bitch found Cater in our house and dealt with her.' Carrie Philips shot her coat sleeves. Jack circled her. But still, like a checkmating chess piece, the bag was in the way. 'Anyone with half a brain can see that Dad's protecting her. Not that he was ever going to tell you. He's too damn loyal for his own good.'

'Sit down.' Stella dispensed with good manners.

Jack was amazed when Carrie sat down. She fixed on the yellow chute which had replaced the tower slide. From which her mother had pushed Robbie Walsh to his death.

'Christopher is protecting someone. It's not your mother.' Stella talked to the chute.

Carrie's face was expressionless. The tiniest movement of her right boot told Jack she was listening.

'Your father is protecting you.' Stella turned to her.

Carrie didn't move. Stella had read her right. She was playing it cool. *Not guilty.*

'You were due that evening. Did you arrive early and find Rachel and—'

'No.' Carrie picked Stella's phone off the bench and hurled it at the jungle frame. Falling short, it skittered across the ground.

'Daddy knows that if I'd seen Cater I'd have gone nuts, but I would not have hurt her. Why would I be trying to save him if it was me? I'd say so.'

'Why would Rachel's dying words be that it was you?' Stella might be chatting in a teashop. Philips hadn't actually said that, but Jack wouldn't correct her in front of Carrie. If it was a shock tactic, it was a good one.

'He couldn't have.' Carrie retrieved Stella's phone. 'Shock and awe might have been your old man's crappy technique, but I'm a prosecution lawyer. Your tricks are water off a duck's back.' She spoke into the phone. 'For the benefit of the tape, you're sacked.'

They watched Carrie Philips speed-walk towards Dalgarno Gardens.

Stella sniffed as if she was getting a cold. She examined her phone. 'Lucky this playground is rubberized.'

Still sniffing, Stella was like Stanley on a scent.

'How her father could say Carrie was a good girl beats me.' Jack was still unnerved. 'She must always have been a handful.'

'I don't think he said that.' Nose to the air, Stella gathered up her rucksack. 'I know her perfume.'

'Oh, right.' Jack had hoped Stella was going to crack the case.

'Someone I know wears it. These days my memory's rubbish. I can't think who it is.'

'It's nice.' Jack was endlessly impressed that Stella could name a smell at fifty paces. If she did remember, perhaps he'd get it for her birthday.

'Good Girl.' Stella swung open the playground gate.

'Who is?'

'It's the brand of Carrie Philips' perfume.'

Chapter Forty-Eight

2019

'Clean Slate for a fresh start, Trudy speaking, how—'

'—and the rest! Lucie May speaking and I'm way beyond a fresh start. Listen, Trudes, patch me through to the boss, would you?'

The reporter. It had been hate at first sight. Lucie May was one of those women who only lit up when a man was there. She was a troublemaker. Although, Trudy grudgingly had to admit, she was good at what she did. Trudy knew that it was May, not Stella's father, who pointed the finger at the Hindle girl.

'Stella isn't here. Can I pass on a message?' She would not tell Lucie May where Stella was. In fact Trudy was annoyed, Stella hadn't told her what she was doing this morning. That was becoming a habit.

'I'll call her mobile.'

'Stella doesn't want to be disturbed. She and Jack are incommunicado. Her phone is on divert. To me,' Trudy lied.

'In flagrante delicto, do we think?' May cackled. Then, extra slow as if speaking to a child, 'Tell. Stella. We're going to the ground zero.'

'You can tell me.' Pen poised. 'It'll be easier for Stella.'

'She'll know what I mean. *Grazie. Ciao!*'

As Trudy slapped a note on Stella's desk, she too knew what May had meant. *We're* going…? Frowning, Trudy returned to her desk.

'Where's Stella?' A woman in voluminous black, a long skirt and blouse, scarf trailing, stood in the middle of the room, her hands on her hips.

'How did you get in?' Trudy kept her nerve.

'I've started coming in through doors, windows are so unreliable.' If Trudy was meant to laugh, she didn't. 'Jack gave me a key. He's my ex.' She didn't meet Trudy's eyes.

'I doubt that.' One thing about Jack was he'd never give his ex the key to his present partner's work place.

'I have a copy. For emergencies. Like this one.' The woman pointed at Stella's office. 'Could Stella mind my two for an hour? Jack's not picking up. He wants to be a father, but where is he when he's needed? The kids asked for Stella. Sooo…' The woman's expression suggested that the notion was preposterous, but what could she do?

So, this was the infamous Bella who kept Jack on a tight rein. Trudy looked around. 'Where are they?'

'Boo!' Justin and Milly flew out from behind their mother's skirts.

'Oh my God!' Trudy did a shocked face. Then to Bella, 'Stella isn't here.'

'When will she be back?' Justin jammed the knuckle of his forefinger into his mouth.

'When will she be back *please*,' Trudy told him.

'*Please* can I have Stella?' Milly chirped.

Ground zero. Trudy knew who Lucie May was with and she knew where they were going.

'I have to go out.' Trudy snagged her coat from the stand by the photocopier.

'Take them with you. They need fresh air.' Bella sailed to the door.

'A good idea.' A *very* good idea.

'They're sharp. Put them down.' Trudy gestured at the pair of scissors peeping from Milly's fist. 'Come on, we'll go and play.'

Minutes later, as they were leaving, another woman appeared. Trudy tutted, Bella had left the door open. The woman wore a leather jacket, hair up in a French knot.

'I need to see Jack... *Oh*.'

She exclaimed, 'What are you doing here? Are they after you too?'

'Wait downstairs and don't go outside,' Trudy told the twins. 'Come with me.'

Trudy steered the woman into Stella's room. Passing her desk, she picked up the scissors with which Milly had been playing. The woman stopped on the threshold of Stella's office.

'Jack's not here.' The last words that Nicola Walsh would ever say.

Chapter Forty-Nine

2019

After Jack had left Stella cleared up the kitchen, sluicing their cereal bowls, drying and putting them away. Bella had called. She had left the children with Trudy at the office.

'I thought Bella didn't want them near me.' Stella had been astonished.

'She changed her mind, I was going to tell you. The children see Harry so Bella could hardly stop them seeing you. Now she's gone and landed them on you without warning.' Jack had looked sheepish. 'Like I did.'

'She hasn't left them with me.'

'She should *not* have landed them on Trudy. I'm really sorry, I'll have to get them. Justin at least will play quietly while we talk.' Jack had grabbed his coat and run from the house.

Good Girl.

Hearing was supposed to be a dying person's last sense. Stella suspected that hers would be her olfactory faculty. As she was dying, Rachel had perhaps managed to articulate the last thing she had smelled. The name of the perfume of her murderer.

Good Girl was the perfume that Stella had sniffed on Carrie Philips in the playground. She and Jack had agreed that Carrie's outrage was genuine. The perfume should have shored up their suspicion, a clinching piece of the jigsaw.

The email awaiting Stella was also genuine. Carrie requested they send a bill for expenses incurred. She ordered Clean Slate 'to cease and desist further investigation'. Stella told Jack that her agreement would be binding. They could hand their findings to Martin Cashman and leave it to him to pass on to the Gloucestershire Constabulary. Jack had looked mutinous, but he had agreed.

Yet a niggle lurked. Who else wore Good Girl perfume? Stella couldn't bring it to mind. (Lucie would call it the menopause.) Stella should have pinpointed the answer in seconds.

Jack hadn't wanted to leave Stella alone in the house. Carrie could be the murderer and even if she wasn't, she'd been blisteringly angry and there was always a first time to kill. Stella assured him her doors and windows were locked.

She snapped off the Marigolds and fitted them on the 'glove puppet' (one of her favourite objects). Upstairs, she switched on the computer. Dale had tried to Skype three times. She was startled by loud knocking.

Jack had been quick.

Leaving her phone on the desk, Stella ran down and opened the door.

It was Kevin Hood.

'Oh. Hi!' Her mind raced. Hood was near the top of her suspect list. *Mother-in-law in Winchcombe. Creepy.* He wasn't wearing perfume. Stella forced a smile.

'You played me.' Hood stepped into the hall and closed the door. 'You're not a cleaner, you're a detective.'

Chapter Fifty

2019

Jack slotted the BMW into a tight space behind Shepherd's Bush Green. All the way he'd cursed Bella for leaving their children with a virtual stranger.

He'd kept it to himself that he didn't believe that Carrie was the killer. It was too much of a stretch that Rachel had recognized the perfume and that Christopher knew it was the brand that his daughter wore. But Stella trusted him to know a killer when he saw one so he must trust her skills too. That was what made them a team.

His own prime suspect had not changed. Once a murderer always a murder. It was the return of Danielle Hindle to Stella's that worried him. Before he'd got in the car he'd checked the grove of cherry trees opposite her house, bashing at the bushes to rout her out if she was lurking there. She was not.

As he reached Clean Slate's front door, Jack's phone rang. He didn't recognize the number. 'Hello?'

'Jack, mate, Dale. How's it going?' The hearty voice boomed in his ear.

When he'd first met Stella's older brother, Jack had suspected he was a bounty hunter come to claim half her inheritance.

Adopted at birth, he'd not been named in Terry's will. Stella had never heard of him. As it turned out, Dale did get half of Terry's house, but only because Stella had persuaded him to accept it.

Dale had been the first to see that Jack's feelings for Stella were not brotherly. In fact, before Jack himself. Dale had been pleased that they were an item as he called it, but promised Jack that, 'if you hurt my little sister you're dead!'

Stella had told Dale that Jack had shouted at her. Jack dropped his car keys on the pavement. 'Right, ah... Dale. Hi!' He scrabbled for the keys. 'I'm sorry, Dale.'

'What for? Oh my God, is Stella OK? What's happened?' Dale shouted.

'No. She's fine.'

'Stella's PA said she was working from home. I tried her there and her mobile which took me back to the PA. I Skyped. *Nada*. It's about Joanne Marshall. The woman Stella asked me to check out?'

Stella hadn't complained about him to Dale. Jack fitted his key in the door. It didn't unlock. It was already open. Someone had left the snib down.

'...I'm keen to do my bit,' Dale said. 'Is Stella with you?'

'I'm about to see her,' Jack said.

'I headed over to Marshall's apartment. To see if there was a fire?' Dale had the Australian inflection of raising his tone at the end of sentences as if asking a question.

'I don't know about this.'

'Stella Skyped me last night when you were asleep.'

Maybe seeing Carrie Philips had pushed it from Stella's mind.

'She'd spoken to Marshall and the woman got antsy about her address. Then a fire bell went off and she vamoosed. Stella's hunch was bang on. I found nothing. No emergency services and not a whiff of smoke.'

'Meaning she gave us a false address.' Jack would have kissed Dale had they been on the same side of the world.

'Could be. I tried the neighbours in case I'd got the address wrong. An elderly woman offered to do the rounds with me to see if someone had left an appliance on. I felt bad. I'll stick a voucher for two through her door.'

'Thanks for trying.'

'I wasn't keen to leave it there.'

'No really—' It was good that Stella had involved Dale, but now he was doing that thing people did, digging a role for himself. He'd fulfilled his remit. Now they knew that Joanne Marshall had lied about where she lived. It was likely that she was keeping her past at bay. In that situation Jack too had lied.

'I've been looking at that snap that Stella sent through. The one of Joanne Marshall on Skype?'

'Yes.' Jack was in the passageway. Trudy could overhear. He must end the call.

'There's a date at the bottom of the screen?'

'It's when they talked.' And the evening when Stella had admitted that Danielle Hindle had slept under the same roof as Justin and Milly.

'Jack?'

'Go on.'

'…the date doesn't match her telly.'

'There's no date on the screen.' Jack recalled the image with a ticker-tape banner under the image of the wrecked plane. *Queensland landowner says, 'miracle no fatalities, no livestock killed, crew walked away.'*

'The Cessna came down by the ranch and missed the livestock. Insane! The farmer is one of our suppliers. Davey's wife and kids could have been wiped out.'

'Awful.' Now Jack understood Dale's concern. 'Is Davey OK?'

'As good as gold! He's grown a beard for charity, looks like a settler!'

'Amazing.' Jack had grown a beard last year to cover a rash. Lucie May had said he looked like Abraham Lincoln and not in a good way.

'You're not getting it, Jack. Going back to that chat Stella had with Mrs M. It was this week?'

'Three days ago.' It hadn't been a question and no, Jack wasn't getting it. *Why hadn't Stella answered Dale's call?*

'Davey's beard is three weeks old.'

'Well done him.' Jack made more effort.

'The crash was a couple of months back. Why was it on telly this week?'

'A rehash? Maybe the pilot was charged with careless driving. Flying.'

'That wrecked Cessna is old news, done and dusted. ABC is twenty-four hours, that's a live rolling banner on her screen. As if it just happened.'

'It's a recording!' Jack got there.

'Why would Joanne Marshall play a recording?' Dale was patient.

'Dale, you're a wonder-horse!' Jack punched the air. 'Marshall played a clip of Australian TV to make us think she was in Australia!'

'Is she a prime suspect for this murder?' Dale asked.

'She is now.'

'Stella, call when you get this!' Jack panted as he took the stairs to reception. 'Now!'

The door was locked. Through the wired glass pane he saw that the room was empty. Trudy had settled the children in Stella's room beyond. He had a text. *Stella*. No, it was Lucie.

Tell Detective Stella we're at the playground. I bet Monster PA didn't pass on the message. She hates me!

Jack was fumbling with his keys when Beverly came down the stairs.

'Bev, are the twins with you?' Beverly was great with the kids.

'No. Why should they be?' Beverly appeared puzzled.

'Fair enough.' Silly question. Trudy was minding them. That was fine, Jack told himself. The key was jammed in the ring.

'Here let me.' Beverly took the keys off him and deftly untangled it. She unlocked the door.

'Milly, Justin? It's me, Daddy.'

'They won't be here on their own.' Beverly was looking at him strangely.

'What do you mean?' Dread blossomed in his solar plexus.

'Trudy's out. The phone's on divert to me. Justin and Milly aren't here. She'd have said.'

Jack strode across the office and barged into Stella's room. He reeled backwards. The scene was crazy, he made no sense of it.

Beverly was on the floor at his feet. She was administering CPR. A woman lay on her back by Stella's desk. Blood glistened on Stella's new carpet. As the scene took shape Jack saw a deep gash across the woman's throat.

Jack forced himself to be objective. The amount of blood suggested that the attacker had severed the carotid artery. A paired scissors had been plunged into the woman's chest. Right where her heart was. When Beverly got up, Jack saw the woman's face.

'It's Nicola Walsh.' He hit the numbers on his phone. Nine. Nine. Nine.

Sitting back, Beverly gave up her revival efforts. 'What a terrible way to die.' She gave a deep sigh and got up. 'This is a crime scene. We're contaminating it.'

'Police. Ambulance. A woman's been hurt. She may be dead.' Gripping the receiver, Jack barely took in his own words. Next he rang Bella.

Bella's phone was off. Silently Jack cursed her. Typical of her to collect Justin and Milly and not tell anyone.

'I didn't hear Nicola arrive.' Good in an emergency, Beverly was containing her emotions. 'Trudy called my extension. She said she was going out to meet a client. She didn't mention Nicola or the twins.' The colour completely drained from her face. 'Maybe Trudy never left.'

'Where are my babies!' Jack shouted.

On the half landing, Beverly tipped open the toilet door with her fingertips. The two cubicles were empty.

Jack willed Justin and Milly to burst on them, 'Boo!' Panic engulfed him. Beverly sensed this. She whispered, 'If Trudy has them, she'll have taken them to the playground for a go on the swings or something. They'll be fine.'

If.

Jack went icy cold. *Trudy had killed Nicola.*

'Nicola could have arrived after Trudy left; you said the door was on the latch.'

They heard the door buzzer. Beverly ran downstairs.

'Where's the body?' Martin Cashman demanded. He was clad in plastic overshoes and gloves, his hair awry.

'Through there.' Never in his life had Jack been pleased to see him.

'Great, and you have tramped everywhere.' Cashman broke his stride. He looked at Jack, suddenly stricken.

'It's not Stella,' supplied Jack.

Cashman teared up with relief.

'It's Nicola Walsh.' Jack saw this sink in. Cashman had known Nicky as a child.

'I tried to resuscitate her,' Beverly said.

Cashman went into Stella's room.

Janet, another of Terry's protégés. The police must have flagged up Stella's address and sent in the big guns – indicated they sit. She took their names. 'Tell me what happened. Who found the body?'

Beverly told her that Trudy had left an hour ago. Possibly with Jack's children, that was unconfirmed.

'Why do you think Trudy Wates has your children, Jack?' 'Was Jack already here when you came downstairs, Beverly?' 'Who is the client – address?' 'How long has Trudy Wates worked here?' 'How old are your children?' 'Have you tried their mother?' 'Are you saying that you both discovered the body?'

'We're wasting time.' Jack smashed his fist down on Trudy's desk and knocked something onto the floor. A black stiletto shoe. Trudy wore flat shoes. 'Whose shoe is this?'

'Don't touch. Please.' Janet bagged it. 'It's not a shoe, it's a bottle of perfume.'

'It's Trudy's,' said Beverly. 'Good Girl. My sister wears it too. Apparently, Trudy's husband gave it to her before he died. Suddenly of cancer. Or in an accident. Whatevs.' She batted away the pointless perambulation.

'What is Trudy's husband's name?' Janet asked as if it was not pointless.

Beverly shook her head.

Nicola had met Lee's wife. Upset over the fallout with Stella, he hadn't asked Nicola when she'd seen Joanna Marshall.

'Lee reckoned it was bad luck. I was so relieved when she took it to charity. His wife didn't want it either or he'd have given it to her.'

'Her husband jumped in front of a train.' Mentally, as Penelope Philips had done, Jack snapped the jigsaw pieces into place. When Stella and he had debated who could have stolen the letter to Terry in which Hindle gave her address, they'd forgotten Stella's mystery break-in months ago. Trudy had discovered it and called the police. *Trudy had been in the house.*

'Like Lee Marshall,' exclaimed Beverly. 'Oh, you mean—'

'Yes! Trudy is Joanne Marshall. She found Hindle's address from...' Jack remembered that no one but himself and Stella knew about the letters to Terry.

'Good Girl, Rachel said... Carrie...' The words Christopher said Rachel had uttered on her last breath. Jack's mind raced as myriad clues slotted into meaning. *Agnes Cater told them her daughter had to buy Christopher's presents for his family. 'It must have been torture, but she never complained.' Rachel*

had known exactly what perfume Carrie Philips wore. She'd been trying to tell Christopher that she recognised her killer's perfume. It was same as Carrie's. And Trudy's.

'Are you saying Trudy killed Rachel?' Beverly was there with him. 'I get it. Trudy goes to Winchcombe intending to kill Hindle because she killed her husband's sister. Course she only knows her from childhood photos so when Rachel answers the door she flies into a frenzy and kills her. Then she makes a run for it.'

'Nicola Walsh met Lee's wife. When she came here she recognized Trudy as Joanne Marshall. Trudy – Joanna – hated Nicola because Lee loved her all his life.' Jack crashed open the door. 'Trudy has killed two women. She has taken my children. She will not hesitate to...' He couldn't finish his sentence.

'Hindle's in a safe house. How could Trudy know where that is?' Beverly was behind him on the stairs.

Jack got the answer as he stepped out onto the street. 'She checked Stella's satnav.'

Beverly grabbed his arm. 'Jack, why would Trudy harm the twins? Joanne Marshall told Stella she'd wanted children. It was Lee who didn't. Leave it to the police. We've no idea where to start looking.'

'You said,' As he recalled Lucie's text, Jack quoted Beverly. '"She'll have taken them to the playground for a go on the swings." Come *on*.'

Chapter Fifty-One

2019

'Do you know how much time and money you've cost me?'

Stella saw it was ridiculous to think Kevin Hood dangerous. Hunched on the settee beneath the lounge window, pinching at his nose as if trying to pull it off, he looked miserable.

'I'm sorry.'

Even the most sympathetic witness can be a good liar, Terry's voice reminded her. Stanley continued to sleep at the other end of the settee. So much for canine protection.

'We're investigating a murder.'

'My wife said to keep my chin up, one job leads to more. She said you coming was the start of things. Except it wasn't, was it!' Hood dashed at his eyes with his sleeve. The nose-pinching had been to stop himself weeping.

'Luck can turn on a sixpence.' Where had she got that from? Stella ripped a tissue from a box by her bluetooth speaker and gave it to him. If Hood was faking tears, he was a good actor.

'Danielle Hindle.' Hood blew his nose with a trumpeting snort. 'I saw her in Winchcombe. I recognized her immediately. I never forget a face.'

Stella nodded.

'I mean *never*. I'm what they call a super-recognizer. I have to stop myself greeting people – in a supermarket, on the street – as I don't actually know them. If a woman has sold me a train ticket or rung up my shopping they're seared into my memory. They'd think I was mad if I said hi when I saw them somewhere else. But when I saw Danielle, I couldn't stop myself. Penny as she is now, could have blanked me, but she said, "Hi, Kevin, it's lovely to see you." She even remembered my name. She invited me back to hers for tea.'

'She lives in the house where Rachel Cater was murdered.' Time to stop Friends Reunited.

'Oh. My. God. *That* murder!' Hood bunched up the tissue in a fist. 'You think Penny killed her husband's mistress? No way!'

Stanley raised his head and gave a low growl.

'You told the police you were with your mother-in-law on the day that Rachel Cater was killed. She vouched for you.' Keeping an open mind had let facts escape. Stella had entirely forgotten this. 'It would have been easy to slip out for a few minutes.'

'Penny can't remember what went on in the playground. It was long ago,' he said. 'I was with my mum-in-law until we returned to London. She was staying with us. Ask her? Ask my wife.' He checked himself. 'Please don't ask my wife. For heaven's sake, Penny didn't know her husband was playing away, how could I know?'

'Why are you seeing her now?'

'We're friends.'

'Is that all?' This was a permutation that they hadn't considered. Kevin and Danielle disposed of Rachel and then Christopher.

'Yes, that's all.' Stella had no idea why she believed he was telling the truth. Perhaps she could read people after all.

Kevin picked up a sheet of paper from under the coffee table. It was the Skype printout of Jo Marshall. Stella had put it down when she'd come to turn down the heating and forgotten it was there. In the meantime, presumably thinking it a good game,

Stanley had taken a bite of it. One of Jo's hands was missing. It occurred to her to ask. 'Do you know her?'

'Yes.' Hood pulled a face. 'She was outside Penny's flat. She pretended to be her friend. That got me suspicious.'

'You saw her here? In the UK! When?'

'Yesterday. I was in Winchcombe doing chores for my mum-in-law. I diverted to Broadway to see how Penny was dong. This lady was sniffing around. I sent her packing.' He examined the photo. 'That must be a wig. Her hair was a kind of blondish colour, highlights like my wife has. She wasn't wearing glasses.'

'Yet you're sure it was her?' Stella was suspicious. Was Hood trying to put her off the scent?

'I would know her anywhere.'

Stella's phone rang.

'Stella, it's Martin. I'm at your office. We need to find Jack Harmon. Is he with you?'

'Jack? No.' Stella looked at her watch. Jack should be back by now. 'What for?'

'Murder.'

Chapter Fifty-Two

2019

The towers of Wormwood Scrubs prison loomed tall above the rooftops. Crows soared overhead like paper cut-outs, stark against the sky. It was meteorologically Spring but a damp low grey cloud hung low over London.

In the playground, the jungle climbing frame and chute were deserted. The only people there were two middle-aged women. The younger of the pair sat on the swing, the other was taking her photograph.

'Clutch the chains,' Lucie instructed. 'Smi-ell.'

'I know what you're doing.' In sunglasses and scarf, Danielle Hindle glared, stony-faced. 'You're making it look like I'm happy those kids died here. That's not what we agreed.'

'We must show readers your softer side.' Lucie considered this a big ask. 'You think they'll get that from you looking fit to kill?'

'They need to think I'm sorry.' Hindle scowled. Lucie pressed the shutter.

'Are you?' Lucie lowered the camera.

'I told you and I told Terry. I'm a different person. Readers need to see that. They want Danielle Hindle dead. Well, she is.'

She folded her arms. 'This will show Carrie what it was like for me.'

Good luck with that. Lucie swiped through her photographs. They showed a grim woman with granite features, an unbending Tory Councillor or sadistic games mistress past her prime. Or a retired child-killer. *Perfecto.*

'Are we done?' Hindle snapped.

'Not quite.' Cackling, Lucie bent down and fiddled with the catch on a large box at her feet. The yellow of the lid was answered by the giant yellow chute a few metres from them.

Lucie had known that Hindle was too smart to spill for cash. But at their first encounter decades earlier, she'd rooted out Hindle's Achilles' heel. Danielle Hindle craved attention like a thirsty person in a desert. Since her release from prison over a quarter of a century ago, Lucie had looked for her. Out of the blue, Terry's daughter had handed Hindle to her. With triple A availability. In hours of (mind-numbing) monologue Hindle had said nothing new. '*...Danielle hated her family. She was top of the class at school. Terry shouldn't have arrested her. It wasn't fair what the papers said. Sarah Ferris was no angel...*' That didn't matter. Lucie had enough. A story that had begun with the horrific murders of two innocent children in a playground would end today. A born theatrical, she'd shoot the photo to end all photos.

For Lucie the Cater murder was a sideshow. Very sad, obviously. She had the scoop of the century.

Child-Killer Is Unrepentant.

If only Terry could read it.

'After this, Jack and Stella will post you back to Gloucestershire.' Lucie made no bones about her relief. Murderers weren't great company.

'Lucie!' Two childish voices rang out across the playground.

A woman holding two children by the hand was coming towards them.

'Did you arrange this?' Hindle continued to swing.

Lucie wished she had. Two kids playing in the background was genius. Except they were Jack's kids.

'Who's she?'

'Stella's PA. I'll get rid of her.'

'I saw you here before on that chair,' Milly told Hindle. She tried to point at Robbie Walsh's bench, but Trudy tugged her away. 'You were nasty.'

'You tried to steal someone's sweatshirt. That's wrong,' said Hindle.

'We're not meant to talk to strangers,' Justin reminded his sister.

'Shut up,' Trudy told the children.Then to Hindle. 'You are seriously talking about right and wrong? It was wrong to end the lives of those children.'

'Listen, Trudes, take them away, yeah?' Lucie knew that Stella had got her PA typing up case notes. The woman was working outside her remit. 'Don't be a vigilante. I've got this.'

'You go. There's no story here. It's nothing to do with you.'

'These kiddies are to do with me,' Lucie said sweetly. 'I'm friends with their daddy.'

'And with us,' Justin said.

'And you, yes,' Lucie melted. No one had ever called her their friend.

'You shouldn't have brought them,' Hindle said.

'You're hot on child safety now?' Trudy sneered. 'Shame you didn't think that when you had Robbie and Sarah at your mercy. *Danielle*.'

'The parole board ruled that Danielle was a substantially changed character. She did not pose a significant risk to the public.' Hindle sounded like a public announcement.

'It's not about what *you* might do. That's where they get it wrong. No amount of good behaviour can make up for what you did. Lee will never breathe free air, he'll never bring our kids to play on that swing,' Trudy said.

Something flashed in the failing light. Her arm across Milly, Trudy Wates held a knife in her left hand. She was Stella's PA. Why she was batting for the wrong side? Beware pissing off your typist.

Lucie recalled the pathologist's report for Rachel Cater. *A minimum of four inches. Gripped in the left hand.* She flipped through her mental Rolodex. And found the answer under M.

'Joanne Marshall. All the way from sunny Sydney.' Lucie was triumphant.

'Got there in the end, old lady.' Marshall dismissed Lucie with a glance.

'She's called Trudy,' Milly said. 'She's nice.'

'No, darling, she's not,' Lucie smiled at Milly. 'Milly, Justin, come here to me.'

'Quite the reporter, aren't you.' Joanne Marshall tilted the blade. 'Give me Hindle then the kids can go. Otherwise, there'll be two more benches in this playground.'

'That's blood on your shirt!' Lucie went cold. 'If you've hurt them—'

'The lady who came to see my daddy at Stella's job cutted herself with the very sharp sizz-ers.' Justin was helpful. 'Trudy did stop her.'

'Come and tell me about the lady,' Lucie crooned. But Justin couldn't get free of Marshall's grip. For the first time he appeared to realize that something was very wrong.

'Nicola Walsh was always in the wrong place at the wrong time,' Marshall gripped the knife.

'Most people are.' Hindle glared at her.

The prison towers were lost in cloud. It was getting dark.

'Let them go.' Lucie tried not to plead.

'No!' A man's voice.

In the descending gloom, Lucie saw Jack racing past the bandstand. *Shit.* Jack wouldn't be able to play it cool. Any other way of playing it would be fatal.

Hindle took advantage of the distraction and made for the yellow chute.

'Stop there.' A flash of blue steel.

In a macabre version of Grandmother's Footsteps, Hindle was brought up short. She was close to the bushes where she'd murdered Sarah Ferris.

'That was stupid.' Trudy held the flat of the blade to Milly's throat. It was only a frigging penknife but still she could decapitate her in seconds.

'Don't!' Jack clasped his hands as if he was praying.

'Jack knew all along, didn't you?'

'No heroics, Jack,' Lucie hissed at him.

'Lee never got you out of his head, he was wretched,' Joanne told Hindle. 'You wrecked our lives.'

Lucie mapped them out. Hindle, Joanne Marshall and herself were a triangle with Jack slightly to the side. Justin had only to go a few metres to get to his dad. But he'd have to pass Hindle and Lucie was sure the woman would think nothing of making him her pawn to balance out the hostage situation. However, if he made for Lucie…

Marshall had her eyes on Hindle. Lucie tipped her head, beckoning to Justin.

Justin might be nearly three, but he got the message. *Come on.* He flicked a look at Marshall's hand clamped on Milly's chest. He shifted. *Yes, that's my little soldier.*

Justin moved closer to Milly.

Three-year-old boy chooses to be hostage with twin sister.

'You think using kids as a human shield bothers me?' Chewing gum, Hindle sauntered around the chute. Lucie saw the cocky ten-year-old who'd fooled Terry.

'Stay back!' Joanne Marshall whirled around in time to stop Jack sneaking up on her.

Then Lucie spotted Beverly. Indistinct in the rain-induced dusk, she slipped past the climbing frame. Lucie felt nervous. This was the Keystone Cops. She trusted no one but herself.

'You murdered my husband. Now it's your turn.' Joanne Marshall was getting down to business.

'He did that all by himself. You weren't enough to keep him.' Hindle's laugh made Lucie go cold. 'You botched it up last time. Think you'll succeed second time around?'

'Lee couldn't bear me to go through the despair you inflicted on those mothers. Every Christmas, all those birthdays we missed. You murdered my children.' Marshall's voice was full of despair, Lee had saved her nothing. 'My husband died before my eyes.'

'Lee didn't want your kids. Believe me, if Nicky had come looking for him, he'd have had a whole brood with her. You were an also-ran.'

'Don't rile her.' Lucie kept her voice low. 'She will hurt those children.' Wretchedness had made Marshall oblivious to the value of life.

'Like I said, do I care?' Hindle was unadulterated evil.

'What about my article?' Lucie had to try. 'This is not the attention that you want. Carrie will care.'

'She can die here, in her killing field.' Joanne Marshall jerked Milly's head and exposed her neck. In the dimming light Lucie saw Jack flinch as if he'd been electrocuted. He too knew that with one sweep of the knife it would all be over.

Stella's lungs burnt, blood drummed in her ears. She pushed on through the grey mizzle. As she passed the bandstand she saw people. Insubstantial. Motionless. As she stared, they took form. Lucie was a couple of metres behind Jack. There was something at her feet. A box. Stella recognized the yellow lid. *It made no sense.* Trudy – Stella must think of her as Joanne Marshall – was hugging Jack's children. Stella had got it wrong. Joanne Marshall wasn't a killer. She was keeping Milly and Justin safe from Danielle Hindle who, by the yellow chute, was far too close to her.

Stella saw the knife. Joanne was not protecting Jack's children. She retreated from the gate and, keeping to the shadows, crept along the playground perimeter until she was behind Joanne.

A hand on the cold metal railing, Stella's nerve failed. She should wait for the police. She looked at Jack. She knew that expression. He was about to go for the knife. He wouldn't make it. The pounding in her temples was like a mallet smashing bone. Stella gripped the railings. She had no choice. She had one chance.

The railings were a metre high. If she made the slightest sound, Trudy would hear. It would be over. She heard Terry: *Don't overthink it. Smooth and steady.*

Five, four, three, two, one. Stella shucked off her jacket and hoisted herself over the fence. Jack saw her. He stared through her. Jack knew how to be invisible. *Make me invisible*, she silently implored him.

Not daring to breathe, Stella ran through her plan. Grab Joanne's hair, jerk her head back. The pain would divert. Go for the knife with the other hand. She would give Jack and Lucie valuable seconds to get the kids. It had to work or—

...hungry like the wolf...

The music came from behind her. It was her ringtone.

Stella forced her hand through the railings and scrabbled for her jacket, trying to shut it down. Knowing all the time that it was futile.

'Stella, nice of you to join us.' Joanne dragged Milly closer to Hindle. Milly struggled but Joanne was too strong for her. Jack started towards them. Joanne tilted the knife so the blade was a fraction from Milly's neck. A line of blood beaded on her skin.

'Please. Don't.'

Stella would never forget the anguish in Jack's plea for his children's lives.

'Drop the knife, Tru... Joanne.' Stella tried and failed to inject her voice with authority. 'It's over. The police are coming. This won't bring Lee back. It isn't what Lee would have wanted.' Stella traded on the relationship with her PA.

'I'm not on your payroll now, Stella,' Joanne said. 'Don't tell me what my husband wanted. You never knew him.' She readjusted the knife. 'Oh, and do tell the wonderful Jackie that getting you publicity for your detective agency not only led a murderer's daughter to your door, but me too. I read your interview in the *Guardian* last year. If Jackie intended to reach a different class of reader than the rags that bitch writes for it worked. But for that article I'd never have heard of you.'

'Stella, I think she's saying that but for you, Rachel Cater would be alive.' Hindle flashed a smile.

'No one's responsible for a murder except the murderer.' Lucie growled.

'We had lots of candidates for Jackie's old job. We might not have employed you,' said Stella.

'Yes you would. Lee always said I get whatever I want.' Marshall blinked as if she might cry. Stella saw that she wasn't a cold-blooded killer like Hindle. Anger and grief for what Hindle had done to the children and their families had driven Joanne to madness. But surely Lee had been wrong, Joanne had got very little of what she wanted.

'How did you know Hindle wrote to Terry?' said Lucie.

Stella went cold. Then hot. Lucie knew about the letters.

'Lee said that, before she was arrested, Hindle boasted about working with your dad. She told Lee she caught his sister's killer. She said she and your dad wrote letters. He cried in my arms, saying even the police were on her side.' She looked at Hindle.

'How did you know she went on writing and that Terry kept them. No one knew.' Lucie asked the question that Stella couldn't bear to voice.

'No one saw what she was like. Not even Lee. You made excuses, a bad home, father in prison, mother going with all sorts. She took you in. Except me.' Joanne hugged Milly. 'I know her kind. She would have gone on writing to Terry Darnell, he was all she had. I knew he'd have kept them. Your dad was holding out for redemption. She's not sorry and she never will be.'

'Of course Terry kept my letters.' Hindle looked happy. 'I kept his.'

'My dad never replied,' Stella yelled. It took every ounce of control not to launch herself at Hindle. *Did Terry write back?*

'Lee *hated* you.' Looking at Hindle, Marshall pressed the flat of the blade into Milly's neck.

'Daddy, I don't like this game,' Milly squeaked.

'No, darling. Soon we'll go home.' Jack turned to Joanne Marshall, 'Do what you like to Danielle Hindle. Let me take my kids.'

'No child is innocent.' Marshall might be imparting useful information. 'If Stella's so-called detective father had realized that she pushed Robbie Walsh off the slide, Lee's sister would have lived. Lee would be alive now.'

'My dad could never have known that.' Stella took the bait.

'You have disappointed me, Stella.' Marshall shook her head. 'You and me, we'd have been a team. Instead you protected a monster.' For a split-second Marshall forgot about Milly. She took the knife from her neck and jabbed it towards Stella.

'I'm not a monster. I'm a married woman. I have a daughter. My name is Penelope Philips.' Hindle sounded so reasonable, kindly even. It made Stella's skin crawl.

Joanne Marshall's voice cut the air.

'You can start a new life. You can change your name. You can be the perfect wife and mother. It means nothing. You will always be Danielle Hindle, the girl who murdered two children in cold blood.'

One moment was all it took.

Everything happened in the right order. If it had happened differently, Milly and Justin would have been dead.

Jack tore across the playground to his children.

Lucie flipped open the lid of the box and began chucking out the contents.

The jungle climbing frame appeared to buckle then it vanished. Stella was enveloped in billowing fog.

She heard a cry. A terrible animal sound. She blundered towards it but became disorientated. She trod on something and, losing her balance, fell onto all fours. Pain shot through her knees.

The penknife lay on the rubberized ground. There was blood on the blade.

Stella scrambled to her feet and pushed on. She smashed into a yellow wall. The chute.

Lucie was sitting in the mouth of the chute. She looked exhausted. Stella reminded herself that Lucie had to be older than she let anyone think.

'Did you hear that?' Stella shouted although Lucie was right next to her.

'They've got her.'

'Both of them.' Lucie's spiral reporter's pad was on her lap.

'It's not a bloody story!' Stella was inflamed. Lucie could at least pretend to care.

'Hindle the psycho and your killer PA. It's over.' Lucie gave her a weak smile. 'Actually, could I have one of your ciggies, darling?'

'I don't smoke, Lucie. I never have,' Stella said. 'How did you get that dry ice?'

'Borrowed your account number. It was meant to be the photo to end all photos. The scoop of the century.' Lucie stared at her pad. It was blank. 'I meant to take a piccy of Hindle in curdles of cloud. The devil in the playground. Shame about that.' She turned over a page. 'Pay you back. I'll put it on expenses.'

Lucie had been at the office the day they'd delivered the dry ice. She must have hatched the plan there and then. Nothing passed her by.

Lucie took Stella's hand. Her fingers were icy cold. Stella expected her to want help getting out of the chute, but she didn't move. 'Proud of you, Clean-Up! Pure gold, like your dad.'

Stella quelled fury with Lucie for dipping out of the situation to capture her story. The nice words would soon be balanced with sarcasm.

'Stella?' Through wreaths of dry ice, she saw Martin Cashman opening the playground gate.

'Coming?' Stella tugged Lucie's hand.

'You're on it, Stell.' Lucie let go and returned to her pad.

'Jack didn't murder anyone.' Stella vented her frustration on Cashman.

'I know.' Cashman splayed his palms in apology. 'Joanne Marshall has confessed. It means nothing, she wasn't under oath. But it's a start.'

Police officers, their hi-vis jackets bulked out by Kevlar vests, were fanning across the lawn towards the playground.

'She also put her hand up for Rachel Cater. Said she wished she'd got Hindle. She managed to stab her, but it's a scratch. Lucie stopped her. Our roving reporter, who knew!' Martin lowered his voice. 'There'll be many who will wish Marshall had got Hindle.'

Stella felt bad for being cross with Lucie. She had taken part, after all. She glanced back. Lucie was bent over her pad. She deserved her story.

'I need to find Jack and his children.'

'She saved his kids too. Troupers, the pair of them.' Martin gestured across the playground.

Jack was carrying Justin on his shoulders. Riding high and proud, the little boy clasped Jack under the chin. Milly skipped beside them. As they passed the climbing frame she made a grab and swung from the lowest bar. Jack paused and when she landed they went on to the gate. Stella saw someone break through the line of officers. Bella swept Milly into her arms and hugged her.

A family reunited.

'Job done,' Cashman murmured. Stella followed his gaze.

Janet – Terry had said she was one of Hammersmith's best detectives – was escorting Danielle Hindle towards the strobing lights of police vehicles on Dalgarno Gardens. Stupidly, Stella looked for Terry.

'Can I drive you home?' Cashman said.

'Thanks.' Stella looked for Jack but he'd gone. She went to the railings for her Barbour. The missed call was Cashman. He'd texted. *We're coming*. The inopportune call had saved her life. She'd never have got the knife off Joanne Marshall. The woman was desperate, she didn't care who she hurt to get to Hindle. Stella looked around the playground. Despite the cheery play equipment, it would never be a place of innocence.

Something was bundled in the chute. Not something. Someone.

'*Lucie*.'

Chapter Fifty-Three

2019

The fog had thrown her. Not fog, Penelope realized. Tear gas. Except she wasn't crying. She never cried. Then she realized what Lucie May had in her box. If she'd taken the picture with the ice, it would have been a character assassination.

The crazed wife of Lee didn't notice. Penelope was about to say that it was pointless to keep the kids. They were innocent. The girl had the makings of a bitch but her brother was sweet, he reminded Penelope of Kevin. She'd always had a soft spot for him.

Once all hell let loose she'd moved quickly. But suddenly Joanne Marshall was there. Penelope tried to dodge the blade. She backed into something. That damned chute.

Marshall came at her. Penelope had cried out. A howl of frustration and fury. She'd seen the knife go in but felt nothing. Not at first. It hurt now.

Ages ago she'd pushed Robbie off the slide. Or so they said. She was a different person now. It was water under the bridge now. Then Sarah threatened to tell tales. Because they were dead they didn't get any blame. People forgot what they were really like. It wasn't fair. None of it was.

'Get up.' Lucie was rubbing her head. 'Stop hiding down there, you abject coward. Marshall's in handcuffs. Soon you will be too.'

'Will you still be doing the profile?' Penelope had asked.

'Of course. It's my job.' Lucie sank onto the edge of the chute and got out her pad.

She had been taken away in a police car. No Terry this time. Penelope found herself looking for him. He'd been kind. Not like this lot, chuffed with themselves for catching a mad woman. Like kids playing a game.

In her hospital bed Penelope began to map it out. New name. New life. Christopher and Carrie would come round, she'd make sure of that. Then they could get back to normal.

Chapter Fifty-Four

2019

Five to ten. The blinds in the CID office were drawn up. Dust motes danced in sunlight streaming into the room. The floor space filled with desks, a table, filing cabinets, two plug-in radiators and cupboards. One piled with miscellaneous redundant objects, a half-drunk bottle of mineral water, a tin of Coffee Mate, several redundant landline phones, their receivers bound in place by the cables.

It was two days since the two murderers were arrested in the Wormwood Scrubs playground. For Stella, it might have been months or minutes because, shocked by the course of events, time had no meaning.

Danielle Hindle and Joanne Marshall were in custody. Hindle had broken the conditions of her licence and would return to prison for two years. Her identity had been blown. Joanne Marshall had wasted no time telling other prisoners on remand. Marshall had been charged with murder and attempted murder. She had withdrawn her confession and, like Danielle Hindle, expressed no remorse for brutally depriving Rachel Cater of her life and Agnes Cater of her daughter. If she was found guilty, Cashman had told Stella that her sentence would be harsh.

Stella had come to Hammersmith police station to give a witness statement. Janet, Terry's one-time colleague, was taking it. Not generally the job of a chief inspector, but Stella was special. They were alone in the CID office. The other detectives were, Stella presumed, out solving crimes.

'You're a great witness, Stella. This account is clear. It fits with Jack Harmon's although, with his children being involved, naturally he was more subjective.'

Stella had made herself relive the day. Starting with Carrie Philips in the playground, Kevin Hood turning up at her house, the confounding moment when she understood that Trudy was Lee Marshall's widow. Finishing with the playground.

A framed commendation certificate was propped carelessly on its side beside a transistor radio. As if the officer's 'dedication, professionalism and leadership in the case of a kidnapping and assault' was all in a day's work. The radio was scrawled with the owner's initials. Stella knew that, however honest and true the occupants, items in offices walked.

'...I understand that the dry ice that Lucie May used was ordered in your company's name. Do you have a licence?' Janet gave an 'I have to ask' shrug.

'It's not for public use.' Stella had expected this. Lucie had purloined Clean Slate's supplier number and ordered a box of pellets to be sent to her home. Technically a crime.

'It's like Lucie expected trouble.'

'I think she planned a photograph of Hindle emerging from dry ice in the playground. For an article.' Stella recalled Lucie's comment when she was sitting in the chute. *'The scoop of the century.'* 'We use it for cryogenic cleaning. It's an effective decontaminant, sometimes more appropriate than applying chemicals.'

A whiteboard was marked with days of the week. The grid headed 'Who Is Doing What???...' The question marks and dots suggested disagreement over task allocation. Stella noted that two p.m. the previous day had been scheduled to restore Mr

Henson's property – a Rolex watch – to him. Trudy couldn't have put up with the groaning filing trays.

Trudy didn't exist.

'Lucie May did use the ice in a public space.' Janet pulled a face. 'Did you know about the order?'

'No,' Stella said. 'If Lucie hadn't created a smoke – *dry ice* – screen Marshall would have killed the children.' *Dedication, professionalism and leadership.* 'Lucie saved Milly and Justin's lives.' Lucie had saved Danielle Hindle.

'She was brave,' Janet agreed. 'I doubt we'll press charges. Gloucestershire police suspect that Penelope Philips left the safe accommodation the night *before* she turned up at Lucie May's. Philips denies it. Did Lucie mention anything to you?'

'No.' Lucie hadn't mentioned anything.

'It's an offence to harbour an ex-prisoner out on licence within the environs of their crime. Philips was forbidden to go within ten miles of the area.' Janet tapped the pages of Stella's statement straight on her desk.

'Hind— Philips might have held Lucie hostage.' Stella's heart missed a beat. She was going to be arrested. That was what Janet had meant by 'special'.

'We can't ask Lucie.'

A pause as both women digested this.

She climbed into the ambulance after Lucie's stretcher. When the paramedic asked her about Lucie it was hard to hear over the blare of the siren.

What is Lucie's date of birth? I don't know. Was Lucie on medication? Apart from Hendrick's gin, Stella had no idea. She did know Lucie's next of kin. A sister and a nephew in Kew. They lived near Jack. She couldn't recall the sister's address.

Although she'd known Lucie most of her life, Stella discovered that she knew few facts about her. She gave Lucie's British Grove address and her occupation. 'She's a fine journalist. Brave.' Facts of a sort.

Lucie's eyes were shut. The paramedic was saying she might have hit her head. The stab wound in her stomach was shallow. She should not be unconscious.

Then the woman stopped talking and was fiddling with tubes. The ambulance picked up speed.

'One more thing,' Janet asked.

One more thing. That old trick. Stella quelled the urge to bolt from the room.

'Penelope Philips says that she saw Terry on the day he died. Did she tell you?'

'She's lying. Terry didn't see Hindle after the trial.'

'Thought so,' Janet agreed. She shook her head. 'Joanne Marshall fooled the Aussie cops. A friend of Marshall's is facing a prison sentence for riding that ferry across the bay and giving Marshall her alibi. People do these things without thinking of repercussions. Some of us grow up knowing it's wrong to lie.' Janet slid the statement across the desk, indicating paragraph breaks with a finger. 'OK, Stella, you know the drill, if you're happy with each point, initial and sign.'

This statement (consisting of: 3 pages each signed by me) is true to the best of my knowledge and belief and I make it knowing that, if it is tendered in evidence, I shall be liable to prosecution if I have wilfully stated in it anything which I know to be false or do not believe to be true...

Happy? Would she be happy again? Stella scribbled her signature on the line.

'What about that coffee?' Cashman caught up with her in the foyer.

'Actually, I—'

'Stella!' Justin and Milly clung limpet-tight to her legs.

'The twins wanted to clap eyes on you. See for themselves that you escaped from the Nasty Lady.' Jack looked deep into her eyes. '*Are* you OK, darling?'

'I am now.' Stella kissed Jack longer than she'd ever kissed anyone in public before.

'Let's get out of here,' he whispered.

Stella told Cashman, 'Another time.'

The twins each took a hand and, with Jack, they came out of the station. They were immediately assailed by cameras, shouts, flashes, microphones were thrust at them.

'Give them space.' Martin Cashman cut a swathe through the crowd.

A horn blared. Jack's creaky old BMW estate was parked at the kerb.

'Jackie's back from grandmother duties. We're due there for a slap-up tea.' Beverly was in the driving seat. 'And guess what, Carrie Philips has paid the bill. She said we did what she wanted. Got her dad out of prison and put her mother back there. It'll be a while till they play happy families. Hardly a happy ending.'

Tomorrow she and Jack were taking Cathy Ferris to Newhaven. They would all tend Sarah's grave. Stella had suggested it as a way of assuaging Cathy's grief. Stella knew she was also doing it for herself. If she cleaned the headstone it might keep Lucie alive. Bonkers thinking.

Jack leaned in and clipped on Stella's belt. 'Love you, Stella Darnell.'

'Love you back, Jackanory.' Stella never used Lucie's name for Jack. She saw him register this. 'After Jackie's I want to go to the hospital.'

'Yes.' Jack stopped smiling.

Bev pulled out into the traffic and made for the Broadway. A few reporters, some lugging TV cameras, gave chase. Above the furore Stella heard a cackle. She checked in the wing mirror.

'Have a nippet on me, Sherlock!' No Lucie.

Obviously not. As Janet had said.

Lucie May had forced herself between Marshall and Hindle. Marshall had stabbed Lucie and pushed her out of the way to go on to attack Hindle. She'd been too late – Hindle had got away. Lucie had fallen and hit her head on the chute. The first serious injury in the playground since it had been renovated fifteen years before.

Lucie's skull had been fractured in a childhood injury, her sister had told the doctors. The break was exactly where she sustained the second blow. An unlucky fluke. Lucie had sunk into unconsciousness moments after Stella had left her to speak to Cashman in the playground. Brain scans showed serious bleeding, but it would not be possible to assess the damage until Lucie woke up. *If* she woke up.

'Clean so deep, scrub-a-dub-dub…!' Milly struck up with her cleaning song. Stella joined in. Then Jack and Beverly. They sang at the top of their voices.

Today was the first of May. The sun was shining, daffodils in the park were in full bloom. Summer was here. Terry had said, *Smile and you feel like smiling.*

Jack was beginning to accept Harry in his children's lives. And Bella was letting her see them. Jack would be taking part in the interviews for Stella's new PA. They didn't need to play Happy Families. *It was real.* Her mood didn't lift. Bev was right, it was hardly a happy ending.

'Clean so deep, scrub-a-dub-dub,' Stella kept singing.

Epilogue

2011

Terry wiped a hand down his face. It came away damp. The air was cold, snow was due and yet he was in a flop sweat. Today was meant to be a good day. If only Stella would answer her phone. He wouldn't ring Clean Slate. Like him, Stella didn't mix work with pleasure. This was work, but with Stella on board it would be a great pleasure. Terry glanced at his phone again. Stella hadn't texted.

In her note Danielle Hindle had said that she had something to tell him. So Terry agreed to meet her. In the playground. Not superstitious nor bothered by astrology yet he dared believe that his stars were lining up. Today was the day.

Hindle would finally express remorse for Sarah Ferris's murder. She would admit she had pushed Robbie Walsh off the slide. Then he would never see Hindle again.

'…Carrie got a first at Cambridge. She's going to law school!'

'What?' His face was running with water.

'Were you even listening?'

'Carrie's going to law school,' he repeated before he remembered that he didn't have justify anything.

'That proves you weren't listening.'

'What did you want to tell me?' He mopped his face with his hankie.

'You all right?'

It wouldn't be concern. If he wasn't all right, he wouldn't listen to her. Lucie had always said that all Hindle wanted was attention. Cashman had spotted that at the off.

'Fine. You said you had something to tell me.'

'I just told you!' She slapped the arm of the bench. *Robbie's bench.*

'Was that it?' He got up. Feeling dizzy, he sat down again. 'What about the murders?'

'What murders?'

'The ones you did.' He pointed at a yellow chute. To where Sarah's body had been found.

'That's all done with. I've moved on. You should too, Terry.' So thoughtful.

'Aren't you sorry?'

'For what?' She looked genuinely curious.

Terry found himself wishing that, like last time, Lucie would turn up. He wouldn't mind if she succeeded where he'd failed. And got Hindle to say the words. *'I'm sorry.'* To let those children rest in peace.

'Come and see my house. We're having a party to celebrate Carrie,' Hindle said. 'Meet Chris. See my Carrie. Winchcombe's a lovely place.'

'You know I can't do that.' He'd been to Winchcombe for another case. He wasn't going to admit it. As it was, she crawled inside his head like some kind of rot. 'Sarah and Robbie, what made you kill them?' It wasn't how he would start an interview. A direct accusation tempted a 'no comment'.

'You've left the police. Let go! Play golf.' She was smiling but he knew that face. Hindle liked to get her own way.

'Did they upset you? Was Sarah going to tell on you?' He used the language of the ten-year-old he knew was still in there.

'You and Christopher have a lot in common.' She tugged his sleeve. Terry jumped as if she was electrified.

'This is the last time that we'll ever meet!' His breaths were fast and shallow. He'd promised himself to keep calm.

'...we wanted to add an extension. It's a listed building so we're hampered.' Hindle was dabbing on lip salve. Eucalyptus. Terry had used it at post-mortems to disguise the smell of decomposition.

'...there's five bedrooms, three with en-suites. A huge garage. If my family could see me.' She gave a dry laugh. 'The house is full of real antiques. Chris has a shop selling them, I put it in my letters. I've kept yours. I read them over and over.'

'I never wrote to you.' His chest tightened. Had he written back? Recently he couldn't trust his memory. She made things up. When he got home tomorrow, he'd chuck out her letters.

He'd tell Stella everything. The meetings, the letters. Stella would tell him he was stupid to have kept them. No, that was Suzie. Or Lucie. Stella never judged. In his mind, Terry was talking to Stella and was appalled to see Hindle on the bench. He got up and this time there was no dizziness.

'This new-fangled equipment is a joke! She looked at the chute. And this!' She stamped her boot on the rubberized ground. 'You'd bounce if you fell off that climbing frame. There should be the outline of a body like at a crime scene. Today's kids are wrapped in cotton wool.'

'We don't do that at crime scenes,' Terry couldn't help saying.

'Not "we". They. You're not police now. I was careful with Carrie. They were waiting to come down on me like a ton of bricks if she got a scratch!'

'Does your family know?' Her bright chatter drilled into him. Terry smacked at perspiration on his cheek.

'What?'

'That you murdered two children here in this playground.' The judge had said Danielle Hindle knew the difference between right and wrong.

'Why would I tell them?'

'It's the truth. Otherwise your life is a sham.' Terry smelled decomposition now. She had gutted him.

Stella hadn't rung.

They should replace this old thing, it's rotten.' Danielle picked at a splinter on the bench.

Terry saw the playground of his youth and of Hindle's childhood. The lumbering roundabout. The tower slide from which Hindle pushed Robbie to his death. The rocking boat. The stain of blood seeping from under Sarah. Life *was* a sham. Only death was real.

'I have to go.' He felt he was pushing through water. 'I'm on a case.'

'Sure you are.'

'I'm meeting Stella.'

'Fancy your daughter being a cleaner! You were full of how she'd follow in your footsteps.' Her tone was flinty. 'She could clean for my Carrie.'

'I'm very proud of her.' He'd never discussed Stella. Had he?

'It must hurt her never visiting. Or writing. Not like I do.'

How did she know? The playground was a kind of hell. Horses on giant springs, swings on chains, a jungle climbing frame all primary-coloured instruments of torture.

'I wanted to be a detective. They won't let me.' She kept pace.

You'd never guess that the middle-aged woman in expensive coat and boots, Gucci bag on her shoulder, was the Playground Murderer. Terry would. His job had taught him to know evil.

'...that stuff they write in the papers. It's a stain on my character,' she whined.

'Enough.' Terry stopped, his hand up. 'Listen to me, Danielle...'

'My name's—'

'Do those families a favour. Admit what you did. Tell them about Robbie and Sarah's last moments. Tell them why you killed their children. Give Lee Marshall that angel charm, I know you've got it.'

'I have no idea what you're talking about. Why would I keep that charm?'

'Because you can kid yourself that Jason gave it to you. Except you're not his best sister. You're no one's best sister.' Terry clutched at his jacket, shutting it against a sudden sharp breeze that cut to his heart.

'I'm going to pretend you didn't say any of that.' Danielle put on sleek leather gloves, forking into the fingers to fit them on. 'Go home, do the garden.'

Terry strode away.

On Dalgarno Gardens he tried Stella again. She didn't answer.

The next day was a Tuesday, but for Terry, it was D-Day, his trip to Seaford had been a success. When he got home he'd go and see Stella at her office. She get why he'd come.

Terry followed signs and found a car park behind the Co-op. He paid for half an hour – the shortest period; at the outside he would be fifteen minutes – and displayed the ticket. Seaford was a retirement town. This early on a parky January morning there were few locals about. Too frigging quiet. Skirting around pedestrians progressing slowly with the aid of walking frames or wheelie shopping trolleys, Terry couldn't imagine growing old here. A dog lashed to a bench gave intermittent howls. It reminded him of Hector the dog Stella had chosen from a litter of spaniels when she was three.

A man stepped out of the chocolate shop opposite Seaford's Co-op holding a beribboned box. He shoved it in his pocket and headed off towards the car park.

Terry retreated into the heated supermarket where he snatched up a pork pie from the chiller cabinet, hesitated, then made it two; he'd missed supper. He grabbed a can of Coke. He broke into a sweat and, swaying, put out a staying hand. He needed to eat, that was all.

Terry Darnell faltered in the doorway of the Co-op. Darkness squeezed him from the sides. His carrier bag felt heavy. Darkness pushed from above. Then from below. He made for the street. Sunshine, a snatch of pavement. It seemed to Terry that his phone was ringing and that he answered it.

'Stella?'

'Dad, it's me. I'm coming.'

The woman who had queued behind Terry when he got his pork pies and can of Coke tutted when she ran into him. When he fell down, she shouted for someone to call an ambulance. She was a nurse, so when she tried to resuscitate him, Terry would have had the best chance. But before the paramedics arrived he was dead.

Acknowledgements

My thanks to Gary Haines, archivist at the Victoria and Albert's Museum of Childhood. I spent a happy day in the building's basement poring over papers. Gary pointed me to the archives of Donne Buck, a key innovator of adventure playgrounds in the nineteen sixties and seventies. As I read about playground equipment safety (the lack of) up until the eighties I felt relieved to have got through my own childhood with only a broken arm.

As ever I'm grateful to Stephen Cassidy, retired Detective Chief Superintendent with the Metropolitan Police, and to Frank Pacifico, Test Train Operator for the London Underground for being on call. Any errors around the police and trains are mine.

I continue to greatly appreciate the opinion of my treasured reader, Shirley Cassidy, The Detective's Mother.

Laura Palmer, my editor at Head of Zeus is a pure joy to work with. Lucky me. My thanks go to the wonderful HoZ team including Lauren Atherton, Blake Brooks, Jenni Edgecombe, Clare Gordon, Daniel Groenewald, Ian Macbeth, Victoria Reed, Chrissy Ryan, Suzanne Sangster, Jon Small and Nikky Ward. Liz Hatherell copy edited with kindness (she never put *idiot* in the margins when I got timings wrong). My thanks go to Jon Appleton, Christian Duck and Sophie Robinson on proofs.

Georgina Capel Associates always have my back. My agent George is simply fab.

I'd like give a big clap to actor Anna Bentinck who has read the audio for all of The Detective's Daughters bar one. (I've listened to ensure I'm not the least knowledgeable at book groups.) It's so moving to actually hear Jack and Stella's voices. Anna's done a great job.

I wrote most of *The Playground Murders* in the little town of Winchcombe, a setting in this story. Food Fanatics kept me in lattes, North's Bakery in sourdough bread, and John Keeling Newsagent's in a daily paper. The Emporium (not a bookshop) kindly stocks my novels and is a treasure trove. Cotswold artist Guy Warner lives two doors down, Guy and his partner Lizzie are a fab creative support.

Writers need reading outlets, not least because we're readers too. I visit many bookshops. They are magical spaces in which to browse and buy. Librarians too are creative and inspiring. For me public libraries, in particular Brighton, Chiswick, Hammersmith, Lewes and Winchcombe are vital sources for research.

Lastly, and top of the bill, thank you to Stella and Jack's readers. Your considered heart-warming messages inspire me on those tougher days in a writer's life when cleaning behind the bath panel seems a better option.

A letter from the publisher

We hope you enjoyed this book. We are an independent publisher dedicated to discovering brilliant books, new authors and great storytelling. If you want to hear more, why not join our community of book-lovers at:

www.headofzeus.com

We'll keep you up-to-date with our latest books, author blogs, tempting offers, chances to win signed editions, events across the UK and much more.

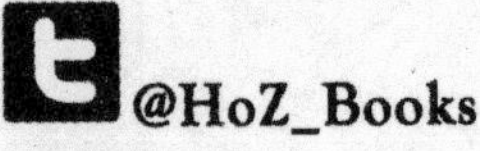

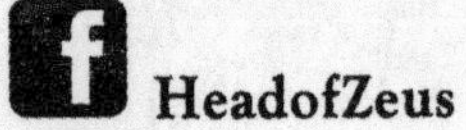

HEAD of ZEUS